Acclaim for *Haussmann, or the Distinction*

"LaFarge's novel offers various pleasures on almost every page. Like a fine French dinner, with many entrees and no exits, the book deserves to be slowly savored."
—*The News & Observer* (North Carolina)

"*Haussmann* effortlessly combines brains with soul, intelligence with emotion. In the end, it's not just a novel about remaking a city, but an inspired work about the love of creating literature."
—*The Commercial Appeal* (Memphis)

"[A] tremendous novel, which is every bit as grand, gracious, and sophisticated as Paris itself . . . An astonishing amount of research, a believable tone, and a captivating story all come together to make this work a stunning success."
—*Publishers Weekly* (starred review)

"*Haussmann, or the Distinction* is a stunning and wise historical novel. As deeply imagined as Dickens's London, Paul LaFarge's Paris is a cityscape of rubble and grandeur, of poverty and greed, and of the sweeping scene of a changing social order. The aims of this brilliant work go beyond the re-creation of history to the contemplation of what we make of history; why we are seduced by the new, yet yearn for the re-creation of a carnival past. The characters in this moving drama of love, betrayal, and exploitation are so beautifully drawn they call to mind what fiction should be."
—Maureen Howard

"LaFarge has a fine historical imagination coupled with considerable narrative gifts."
—*Chicago Tribune*

"Paul LaFarge is a grandly inventive, elegant writer, and his nineteenth-century Paris is far more than a fictional echo of history. It is a city full of vivid experience—love, death, ambition, failure, ghosts, cacophony, music, and unforgettable beauty."
—Joanna Scott

"Highly original . . . [with] all the underpinnings of a Dickensian yarn . . . observed with the humorous eye of an amused gossip . . . Delightful."
—*Booklist*

"Thanks to the author's unfailing enthusiasm and erudition, we are granted the privilege of a permanent appointment with the busiest of all prefects: a rendezvous with history. . . . Paris is a the~~~ ~~nd LaFarge knows his way backstage."
—~~rt~~ford Courant

"As a tale of love, longing, and obsession, *Haussmann* is both moving and vast. LaFarge creates and populates his own kind of Paris, a place that inhabits history but frequently flirts with, and is often seduced by, imagination. A kind of nostalgic fiction, *Haussmann* is a novel in the classic, sweeping style of Balzac or Hugo, yet it maintains its modernity. It is a vainglorious past as seen through the scrim of a pedestrian and not-too-cynical present. By turns hilarious and magical, *Haussmann* is, in the end, entirely enchanting."
                                                    —*The Missouri Review*

"[An] ambitious, fantastic novel, deliberately reminiscent of Borges, if not Balzac."
                                                    —*The Baltimore Sun*

"An original and engrossing novel . . . LaFarge's storytelling instincts are superb, and his novel captures precisely the shadowy, misty affectation of France in the Second Empire."   —*The Virginia Quarterly Review*

"Paul LaFarge's *Haussmann* is an extraordinary novel. I'm immensely impressed by his erudition, the authenticity of the historical 'pastiche,' and the wit and intelligence of the prose. . . . Fascinating."
                                    —Charles Palliser, author of
                                        The Quincunx and *The Unburied*

"[A] lavishly imagined and highly entertaining historical novel . . . informed and densely detailed. . . . The tensions among duty, artifice, and passion are thus vividly played out in a superbly realized period setting. There's a hint of Isak Dinesen in LaFarge's lush romantic images of sheltered lives seething with unacknowledged desires and complexities. An unusual, and unusually compelling, novel."
                                                    —*Kirkus Reviews*

ALSO BY PAUL LAFARGE

The Artist of the Missing

HAUSSMANN
OR THE DISTINCTION

A NOVEL BY PAUL LAFARGE

PICADOR USA
FARRAR, STRAUS AND GIROUX
NEW YORK

www.picadorusa.com

Picador ® is a U.S. registered trademark and is used by Farrar, Straus and Giroux under license from Pan Books Limited.

For information on Picador USA Reading Group Guides, as well as ordering, please contact the Trade Marketing department at St. Martin's Press.
Phone: 1-800-221-7945 extension 763
Fax: 212-677-7456
E-mail: trademarketing@stmartins.com

Grateful acknowledgment is made to the Bibliothèque nationale de France, Paris, for permission to reproduce the following images: "Our architecture will need a few people to bear it out . . . " (B89847); "Yvonne Ductronc, ca. 1872" (G55495); "Paul Poissel in 1880" (G55525).

Library of Congress Cataloging-in-Publication Data

LaFarge, Paul.
    Haussmann, or the distinction: a novel/Paul LaFarge.—1st Picador USA ed.
    p. cm.
    ISBN 0-312-42092-7 (pbk.)
    1. Haussmann, Georges Eugène, baron, 1809–1891—Fiction. 2. France History—Second Republic, 1848–1852—Fiction. 3. Paris (France)—History 1848–1870—Fiction. 4. Urban renewal—Fiction. 5. City planning—Fiction. I. Title: Haussmann. II. Title: Distinction. III. Title.

PS3562.A269 H38 2002
813'.54—dc21   2002066773

First published by Farrar, Straus and Giroux

First Picador USA Edition: October 2002

10 9 8 7 6 5 4 3 2 1

for Y.

Absolute power quickly tires of monologue, it likes a reply, it organizes a dialogue; that is its coquetry.

—JULES FERRY

NOTE TO THE ENGLISH EDITION

PAUL POISSEL IS NOT a well-known writer in France. His poetry is still read by people who study the literary ancestry of Lettrism and the Oulipo, but his novel, and indeed the fact that he wrote a novel at all, has largely been forgotten. When *Haussmann* appeared in 1922, few reviewers knew what to make of it—"this book," one of them wrote, "that lives in the past as though it were the present, and the present as though it were the past." The only person who had a definite opinion about the novel was Baron Haussmann's grandson Valentin Pernetty: "This infamy that masquerades as Art," he wrote in a letter to the *Revue des Deux Mondes*, "ought to be burned, and its author flogged in the public square," which was, sadly for him, an impossibility, Poissel having died two months before *Haussmann* was published. The book fell into obscurity, and there it might have remained if I had not been looking in the Bibliothèque Nationale for something entirely different, information about the May 1968 student revolt in Paris. I must have filled out one of the library's call slips wrong, because among the pocket editions of titles on anarchy, the New Theater, and the role of the Situationist International was a small volume bound in dull-green cloth: Poissel's novel. Of course I cannot claim that I discovered *Haussmann*. Others have found it before me: Walter Benjamin mentions it in a letter to Gershom Scholem, and Michel Leiris refers to the book in his *Roussel & Co.* With this English translation, however, I hope to free *Haussmann* from the purgatorial circles of nineteenth-century scholarship and to set it before a wider audience. I hope the reader will forgive me for undertaking such an obscure and unfashionable project, and will have the patience to read *Haussmann* through. The novel may be constructed in the old style, but it raises questions— How to build new things without demolishing old ones? How to preserve the past without living in it?—which are as worth asking today as they were a century ago. If there were no other reason than this to read *Haussmann*, it would still be worth reading; but there are other reasons, which I shall trust the reader to discover.

A note about the tone of the translation: Poissel's style was already archaic, and willfully so, when he wrote *Haussmann*. I have done little to modernize it, although in the places where the author uses a twentieth-century turn of phrase, I have done my best to find an English equivalent. I have left in French those few words which would lose all meaning in translation, and have generally not translated the characters' names, even when they are puns. Some of the characters and events Poissel describes are fictitious; others would have been obscure even to his contemporaries. As historical correctness does not seem to have been the essence of Poissel's project (see the Afterword), I have left these references mostly unannotated. The few footnotes are entirely my own.

P.L.

PAUL POISSEL

HAUSSMANN
OU LA DISTINCTION

❦ roman ❦

à Paris,
chez les Éditions du cire perdu
1922.

The title page of the first (and only) French edition of
Haussmann, or the Distinction.

PART I

MADELEINE

(1840)

1

THE BIÈVRE

THERE IS A STORY that Baron Haussmann, who rebuilt Paris in the middle of the last century, on his deathbed wished all his work undone. —Would that it died with me! he is supposed to have said, though as he died of a congestion of the lungs his last words may have been garbled. If the doctor who heard them and, astonished, wrote them down, made no mistake, then we're left with a riddle, for in life Haussmann seemed incapable of regret. Regret is a backward-turning emotion, and the Baron was famous for straightforwardness; he made the boulevards and razed the crooked lanes where tanners' sheds fronted cracked courtyards and sewer ditches spilled over into the bins of wire and paper petals of the artificial-flower makers for which the city, before his arrival on the scene, was famous. To Haussmann's German name and the sense of order which, we can only assume, came with it, we owe the sidewalk cafés with their six tiers of wicker chairs, the public urinals and Morris columns for theatrical advertisements, the insane asylum of Sainte-Anne and the park at Boulogne; to him we owe the rows of plane trees which in summer catch dust and sunlight in their leaves, and the pastime of strolling that caught on as the sidewalk widened into the twentieth century. Stop a moment on the avenue Foch, one afternoon, and thank Haussmann; stop again on the boulevard Raspail on your way home, weigh the oblong package of dates tucked under your arm, and wonder why the Baron, having made all this, wished it undone? Was it selfishness? Or as death approached did he see for the first time that the Emperor had been wrong, the speculators had been wrong, the engineers had been wrong, he had been wrong—did he see that, in all his work, there was something to regret?

To answer these questions we'll need the story of a girl. She was called Madeleine, after the church which on clear mornings sends its shadow almost as far as the rue de Surène: a minor axis compared to the great north-south sweep of the boulevard de Sébastopol and the boulevard Saint-Michel, but one which, in its daily growth and diminution, threatens to reveal the truth, that Paris is not made of axes but of sorties toward every compass point, which wind with the wind from forgotten tanneries and follow the tributaries to the Seine just as they did in Roman times. The story of a girl becomes the story of a road, of many roads; the roads lead us back to old buildings; and now, if we look inside the buildings, we find Madeleine, a tanner's daughter, born to dye and the evil smell of skin. But to get from Madeleine-church to Madeleine-girl we must cross from the Right Bank to the Left. We'll do so— why not? for our architecture will need a few people to bear it out—in the company of an old lamplighter, Jacob his given name, returning from his rounds on the Île de la Cité. He has been looking in convent windows. Though modest in his other tastes, Jacob has an appetite for three things, innocent enough singly, but which together constitute a vice: for lamps, for curtains, and for nuns. It's best, he thinks, bootnails clicking against the flagstones of the otherwise quiet bridge, if the light is behind the curtain. To see the shrouded form pass into the lit square of the windowpane, a walking sarcophagus one would say for all the drapery it's wrapped in—and then to stand, stick in one hand and matches in the other, as the woman kneels and the shadow-wimple is lifted from her invisible face... To watch the shadowy motions of a nun at her prayers behind a lit window is perhaps the greatest pleasure one can know in this life, as it combines religion, lust, and flame, the three forces which vie—so thinks Jacob—to consume the world. When the lamp within goes out, then it's time to raise the wick, strike the match, burn one's disappointment in rapeseed oil until dawn. If you know a lamplighter, then you know that streetlights are only so many monuments to failed voyeurism. Jacob wonders whether the new gaslights, far from extending the city's life into the night, won't blind Paris to itself; then, arguing with himself, he proposes that streetlights are simply a reversal of the normal nighttime order of seeing and being seen. The well-lit streets become blind, while the cloisters, under cover of darkness, open their eyes. Then Jacob has crossed the bridge. The thin streets behind the Quai Saint-Bernard urge him to hurry; the Ursulines are impatient for him to finish his rounds.

Let him go for a moment. Listen instead to the gurgle of the Bièvre stream, and smell the strange smells which rise from between its banks. Shit and tannin and the smell of rotten meat; faint beneath these the brackish smell of the water, which grows greener and thicker on its way through the city until it dilutes itself again in the Seine. Nothing lives in the Bièvre, although there is much in it that was once alive, and much which, silting the banks downstream, will give rise to life again. Nothing lives in the Bièvre, as a rule, although many people live by it, and in general find in this circumstance occasion for regret. Tanners mostly, who in their sheds and huddled factories prepare humans to wear the skins of beasts; and mercers, wine-market porters, and students little better than walking tuns of wine, who rest their heavy heads on their blotters and prepare with a groan for the coming of night. And families; and families with children; and lamplighters. Children in Paris in the year 1840 have more fates available to them than any other children in the world. Theirs a monarchy, a republic, a new empire, and theirs its fall; they have revolutions ahead of them, and the possibility of choosing sides again and again. They are at the head of the army of children who will overflow the city, swelling it like a belly. These swollen-bellied children will change the map not by revolution, but by numbers. They'll clamor for homes, factories, parks, shops, diversions; in 1871 they will cry briefly for brotherhood and for liberty; but by then their work will already be done. The city will have grown to fit them; for justice they will have blocks of apartments, and for liberty, parks. Before all that they will have to be apprenticed, and before that survive the difficult period between birth and work, when children are most susceptible to poverty, disease, beggary, blinding, suffocation, and abandonment.

Or, in Madeleine's case, to both of these last two at once: born to a tanner's dying wife, she was dropped in the Bièvre. There she was saved by pollution, for the river was already so laden with debris that nothing more could sink into it. She was spared, at least, for as long as it took a lamplighter to distinguish her gurgle from the gurgle of the water and pull her with his lighting pole to the bank.

Forget the interpretation of dreams; what we need is a good psychology of last wishes. Why would a dying woman wish not to be survived by her only child? Revenge on the killer who split her open, and was caught red-handed, covered in blood; or the opposite. A motherless child grows only halfway into the world: one part of it always remains undeveloped, red-fisted, wailing. Perhaps tenderness moved the tanner's wife, or a sense of responsibility carried too far: she wanted to take no action whose consequences she could not oversee. Or perhaps—but the tanner won't think it until much later, when he enters into conversation with a cat—perhaps she whispered some word which was not *Drown*, or said *Drown, drown it*, but meant something entirely different... Of all our wishes, it is the last ones that are most likely to be misunderstood. In any case she died. And Armand the tanner carried his daughter, nameless, to the river, and threw her headfirst into the evening-blue sewer. Later he would wonder whether even the streetlamps mourned the death of his wife, for they stayed dark all night.

Madeleine, a naturally buoyant child, rose quickly into Jacob's dusky world. She walked before she spoke, and long before she walked she learned to see. She stared out from her basket of swaddling at whatever was most distant, the grinning green ensign of the Benedictine Tavern if she happened to be facing the window, or the pot- and rag-filled recesses of Jacob's cupboard if her face had been set toward the room. The lamplighter lived in a cul-de-sac on the Left Bank, called by its tenants the cour Carence. The buildings there had been old a hundred years before Jacob moved in; their ill-built walls bellied outward, and were kept from collapsing only by wooden struts, so that, from a distance, in poor light, the *cour* looked a little like a buttressed cathedral; but if any deity had to take charge of the *cul* of that *sac*, it would not be the Gothic god of light and fire, but another, grimmer, a god of soot and leaks and things sinking earthward. No one entered the *cour* who did not live there; the dark stonework and half-hung shutters encouraged the eye to move on, and quickly. And yet the inhabitants of the cour Carence were not, by and large, displeased with their home. Yes, it was a shambles, but it had been run-down so long that no one knew what it had been run down *from*; and, as its condition

had been stable for as long as anyone could remember, the tenants wondered if it hadn't been this way all along. They balanced flowerpots on the windowsills and hung the low sky
with laundry, and if you had asked them whether they would
give the cour Carence up for the new buildings on the rue
Saint-Jacques, which was wide enough for two carriages to pass
side by side, they would have told you that there might be better buildings elsewhere but in a hundred years they'd be run-
down, Monsieur, whereas the *cour* would stand just as she was.
The street was its own town, one of thousands that bore the
name Paris lightly, the way distant provinces revere an emperor
whose face, whose envoys, even, they will never see.

Like any town it was the sort of place where everyone knew
everyone else a little too well, and so of course they knew
everything about Madeleine. The neighbors said she was a regular ape; before she had control of her bowels she had learned
perfectly to mimic Jacob's stare. When the first anniversary of
her discovery passed, and then the second, and she had not yet
spoken, the neighbors called her an ape indeed, and pointed to
the fine black hairs that poked from the wrists of her baby
clothes. She'll swing from trees, said the half-deaf Mme Arnaque, who kept a varnish shop on the ground floor; and crack
nuts with her teeth, said one-eyed Fauteuil the upholsterer. Jacob called their predictions resentment, because his child might
be a great noblewoman's daughter, whereas their brats were
common beyond doubt. As if to bear him out, a month before
her third birthday, Madeleine began to speak, and to speak! Jacob had never heard anyone talk so unless it was the bailiffs
who came periodically to seize Fauteuil's furniture. "Altogether
not to my liking," she trilled, and "nevertheless I insist," as
though some count or lawyer had been sneaking into his room
in the evenings to instruct her in the language of the court (or
the courts, which were, to Jacob, the same thing). It was so hard
for him to imagine the source of these words, which bubbled

through his adoptive daughter like a noble gas, resisting con-
junction with anything in her environment, that he paid a
friend to take over his lamplighting work for a week, hid himself in the pantry, and waited for Madeleine's secret tutor. No
one came. With slow wonder Jacob began to believe what he
had boasted of for nearly three years, namely, that Madeleine
was born of aristocrats. He invented details to impress Fauteuil,
who padded the story and passed it on to Mme Arnaque, who
added the gloss of her own imagination. Soon it was known
that the lamplighter's black-furred child had been found in a
wicker basket lined with eiderdown; pinned to the silk of her
baby clothes was a golden seal, engraved with a well-known
coat of arms.

When she was five, Madeleine shed most of her hair; in the
same year she forgot her aristocratic manners, and became, in
appearance at least, a normal child. But the parallel superstitions
of her infancy left her immune to intimidation of all kinds: she
knew that the hairiest criminal might have a magistrate's ear,
and the haughtiest aristocrat might, under his high collar, be
furred.

This was in January 1848, when the whole country seemed
to share her suspicion. When Jacob went out at dawn to extinguish the lamps along the Seine, he found the sides of the
buildings white with posters that said the King was a crook and
his ministers a gang of thieves; the republicans were hoodlums
and the bourgeoisie were out for what they could get; the rad-
icals were bloodthirsty demons from Italy or the Pit, and the
reformers cowards who ought to be bled white, not, the posters
intimated, that it would take much. Bring the lot of them to
Justice! the posters cried, which caused Madeleine to remark,
when Jacob told her about it, that Justice must be lonely if she
wanted so much company. It was as good an understanding of
the winter as any other.

Nothing was in order then: in the name of the people,

everyone wanted something different, except the people themselves, who wanted something that had no name, something that was named when two opposing crowds shouted one another down. Every day the sun hung later in the sky, but Jacob swore that the February nights were longer and darker than those of December. By the end of the month it was so dark he couldn't see what lay before him in the street. Was that an overturned carriage? Were those soldiers? What were they whispering about? The darkness has driven us all mad, he thought, and opened the glass that protected a streetlamp from the wind. Fortunately there were still lamplighters to put the world aright. Jacob struck flint to steel, lit the wick, and adjusted the flame. For a moment the whole scene appeared as clearly and as still as an engraving, and indeed when engravings of it appeared a few days later in the newspapers Jacob would look for himself, but he would not be there, because lamplighters are the catalysts of history, provoking events in which they themselves have no part. At one end of the street, soldiers on horseback raised their swords; at the other, men with rifles crouched behind a barricade made of cartwheels and cobblestones. Then someone shouted, — The lamp is lit! The lamp is lit! — After that, Jacob told Madeleine, I don't know what happened. Yes, the lamp was lit, but you couldn't see anything for all the smoke. — What did you do? — I ran away. If that's what they want light for then let them get it from someone else.

So the monarchy ended. When Jacob returned to work three nights later, his first act was to extinguish the streetlamps of the Second Republic, or at least the ones that had not already burned themselves out.

Nothing was in order then, and least of all children. They played at piracy under bridges and fenced with sticks in muddy fields, gouging and slashing their way from one war to the next. Madeleine was the conqueror of Russia, and of China choked

with reeds by the riverside; the river children paid her tribute
in mud and boots and birds, brass buttons plucked by the current from the coats of suicides and bottles which, when you
held their mouths to the wind, spoke in the sour mumbling of
drunks. While Jacob made his rounds, Madeleine crowed at her
courtiers' flattery: Jean Fauteuil brought her a velvet hood, and
Carrosse the wheelwright's son made her a scepter from a cart
spoke. Charogne the son of the butcher brought the greatest
gift of all, a third-best cleaver, notched and speckled with rust,
for Madeleine's sword. The river children, who had no great
gifts to offer, being the sons of fishermen, were content to carry
her through her new domain on their shoulders. Hooded, waving her cleaver about, Madeleine divided up the land and set
the others to governing it. Carrosse she made the Prefect of the
ditch, and Charogne of the knoll; she gave the river children
powers of life and death over muddy plots, and Jean, her favorite, was made Minister of the Interior and told to keep a
close eye on the rest.

When the toll collector's wife came out shouting, — Allay!
Allay! Time for you children t'eat, and shrieked at the executioner
who sat on her son's shoulders, Madeleine answered, — But
Madame! It's just an amateur theatrical. They're held all the
time in the houses of the rich. — When you're rich, said the
toll collector's wife, then do as you like! And until then don't
go about playing with knives. Madeleine looked down at the
woman with contempt. She knew without having been told
what Jacob thought of her: that a baby found in the Bièvre was
not bound by the rules of rich and poor, of what you were and
what you might become.

2

CURTAINS AND VEILS

NAPOLEON THE FIRST, who never conquered Russia, wanted the Madeleine to be his Chamber of Commerce. In this campaign, too, he was unsuccessful, as the church was in those days too far from the center of the city, the old courts and bankers' rooms of the Palais-Royal. If only Napoleon had been more patient! Russia might have yielded in time; and Paris grew to envelop the church which he left half-built. With enough patience you may have anything—but who has patience? Not Madeleine; by her tenth birthday she was tired of her riverside games and dreamed of playing on a larger stage. The cour Carence no longer seemed the whole world to her, nor even a very large part of it.

— Are we going to live here forever? she asked Jacob.

The lamplighter had no answer. — Do you want to leave?

— Yes.

— Why?

— To see something else.

— Ah, said Jacob, and from that day on he took Madeleine with him on his rounds.

— These are the houses of rich and noble men, he said,

pointing out the worn facades of the buildings on the Île Saint-Louis, which had grown tired after three hundred years of watching the same families make the same mistakes, over and over, and now yawned behind a blanket of dried-out ivy.

— It looks just like where we live, only perhaps a little bigger, said Madeleine.

— It's all like that, said Jacob. It's not what's outside that's different, but what's within. He tapped sagely at the corner of his eye.

Good advice, and if Madeleine had taken it she might have been happier than she was; but all she understood from Jacob was that one should live in a pretty decor. By that measure the cour Carence was as deficient as ever.

When they came to the convent Madeleine stopped. — Who are those people?

— Nuns, said Jacob reverently.

— What do they do, nuns?

— They hide indoors all day and never go out.

— Is it beautiful where they live?

— It must be.

— Very beautiful?

— Come on, said Jacob, let's go home.

Madeleine asked him all sorts of questions about nuns and their habits, but he would say no more. She must have understood what was behind that silence, though; for when they'd reached the cour Carence she declared, — I want to be a nun, then. She said it again and again in the days that followed. At first Jacob wouldn't hear of it, but as time passed and he thought of what he would do with this girl, how he would marry her and what would become of her if she was not married, his resolve weakened. Madeleine's did not. On the eve of her twelfth birthday Jacob led his foster daughter to the convent of Saint-Grimace, in the rue de la Licorne. There he presented Madeleine to a woman in a wimple, and explained how he had found her. If, in his explanation, he added a few aristocratic embellishments—that she was floating in a wicker basket lined with velvet; that from her neck depended a golden seal with a coat of arms, which he had, alas, pawned in a time of need—he must be forgiven, for these details had been part of Madeleine's story, in his imagination at least, for so long that he could not do without them.

Sister Geneviève, the doorkeeper, promised to explain the matter to the Reverend Mother, and closed the door on Jacob's hope of seeing a convent from the inside. When she opened again she announced that all had been arranged, and that the lamplighter need not come back. Jacob hobbled off, disappointed, to drink out the afternoon in a café and to dream of mullioned windows casting diamond-shaped shadows on the floors of cool and unimaginable rooms.

Madeleine, left alone with the nuns, began her education in an interrogative mode: — Why am I here? she asked Sister Geneviève, who smelled faintly of gin, and had agreed to be Madeleine's voice in the convent until she herself should learn to speak properly. — Because there is nowhere else for you, Sister Geneviève answered. Convinced less by Jacob's words than by his nervous manner, his admiring stares, and the complete lack of resemblance between man and girl, Geneviève would keep Madeleine for several years in the expectation of the day when her family would come to claim her, and reward the nuns by filling their coffers, and, incidentally, Geneviève's bottle. The day she learned the truth about Armand the tanner and the Bièvre would be Madeleine's last in the convent. But that day was a long way off; in the meanwhile Madeleine had to wonder what she meant about there being nowhere else. Nowhere?

And the reed field, and the courtyard where Charogne had showed her the joints of steers and horses? — Such stories! Sister Geneviève wondered at the strange career of illegitimate children. — Were you really... no, don't tell me. You'll find this a better place than the one you've left. Puffing juniper breath into Madeleine's face, Geneviève knelt to look at her child— her "find," as she would tell the other sisters that night—one last time, then led her to a small but comfortably furnished cell that contained the wherewithal for the arts, completely alien to Madeleine, of reading, writing, and prayer.

Saint-Grimace was the convent's unofficial name; it had another which doesn't concern us now. Expropriated by the Revolution from its original quarters in the faubourg Saint-Germain, it had settled in an old hotel on the rue de la Licorne, its back to a quarter of cutpurses and assassins and its unsuitably windowed facade craning toward the Sainte-Chapelle and the Palace of Justice. If Jacob had been braver or more curious, he might have learned that those windows belonged to the convent's guest rooms, and that the shadows he watched were not nuns but society ladies who had accidentally got themselves pregnant. They came to pray before the convent's single relic, a weatherworn but nonetheless frightful statue whom the nuns called Saint Grimace, for the miscarriage of their children. Their long hair cast wimple shadows on the curtain, and their clothes, in silhouette, hung at a modest distance from the curves of breast and belly. But Jacob never got past the convent door, from which we conclude that voyeurs, like speculators, are easily fooled, because, having seen something which not everyone sees, they stop looking.

Though it received mothers enough, Saint-Grimace was not in the business of educating children. Accordingly, Made-

leine got a great deal of attention, most of it kindly though little of it comprehending. In the morning Sister Aphorie instructed her in the lives of the Christian martyrs and the duties
of a religious order: how to walk slowly, to pray softly, and to
cast her eyes heavenward without raising her chin. At midday
Madeleine helped deaf Sister Eulalie with the cooking, and in
the afternoon she had writing lessons with Sister Geneviève,
more prayer, and then a stint in the kitchen garden with Sister
Nénuphar, who instructed her in the secrets of fennel and pars-
ley, and plucked onions from the earth with her long, deft fingers. It was a regime to banish homesickness quickly. Never
before had so many people, and respectable people at that,
treated her so deferentially, or with so much compassion. She
had her own room, her own rush-stuffed bed, her own bowl at
mealtimes and in between the company of a dozen women
who called her Little Sister, and told her, winking, that if she
stayed with them she would make an advantageous marriage.
Madeleine was horrified when she found out what they meant:
the nuns would wed her to an oil painting of a green-skinned
man, ill-fed and bleeding, who presided over their doings in the
chapel and the refectory. In secret she resolved that she would
never put on a costume she was oath-bound not to remove; in
the meanwhile she enjoyed the sisters' ministrations. Madeleine
settled into the calm of the convent's days, while outside in the
Brumaire dusk the President of the French Republic, Louis
Napoleon, nephew to his greater (and shorter) namesake, had
himself made Emperor and the nation shook at the prospect of
civil and foreign wars. There were no wars, and Brumaire
ripened into Fructidor which was called June; blossoms fell in
the courtyard and Sister Nénuphar snapped peas off between
her fingers and gave the sweet crescents to Madeleine to eat.

One afternoon Sister Geneviève showed her how to write a
letter, and taught her phrases she hadn't heard since she herself
uttered their like in Jacob's attic:

My dear Mother,

   I write this Letter so that you will not fear for the Safety of my Person, nor for that of my Character. I am being Educated in a most Charitable Convent, which is on the rue de la Licorne and receives Visitors on Saturdays if you would care to see it.

   Your most humble and respectful Daughter,

                                        MADELEINE

Having copied this message painfully onto a fresh piece of paper and folded it in thirds, Madeleine looked up.

— Now you must address it, my dear, said Sister Geneviève.

— To whom? asked Madeleine.

— Look into your heart, my sweet child, the nun replied. What street do you see there? The rue Saint-Dominique? or the rue de Grenelle? Where is your dear mother the Countess? Or, pardon me, sweet child, should I have said the Baroness? The Du... No, my dear, you must look into your heart and address it yourself.

— All right, said Madeleine, and wrote in bold, uncertain flourishes, "Maman / by the Seine," for she could think of nowhere she would rather see her mother than on the muddy riverbank, where she might be entreated to join in a game of kings and queens. — Have I done well? Madeleine asked, handing the paper to the nun.

— Very well, dear child, very well, groaned Sister Geneviève.

This might have gone on for a long time, for Sister Geneviève drank patience by the bottleful, and prayed nightly that her cup would be renewed—but then Madeleine met a real aristocrat, who with a snap of her stick-thin fingers ended the innocent dignity of those letter-writing days. Her name was Nasérie

Élise de Saint-Trouille, the daughter of the Marquis de Saint-Trouille, who was even then selling off his estates one by one to finance the stable of racehorses on which well-bred gamblers lost almost as much money as the Marquis did himself. Nasérie's pedigree was the only sound thing about her. Small and dark-complexioned, the girl had been consumptive practically since birth, and, as if to disprove the maxim that suffering makes saints of us all, she was capricious, secretive, jealous, and given to confabulation. She might have corrupted the entire convent if her weak lungs hadn't confined her to her cell, where a brazier heated the air day and night, summer and winter alike. The doctors told Nasérie that, if she kept to her room and drank all the potions they prepared for her, she might live long enough to go to balls, be married, and bear children—which prospect reassured her so little that she slipped from her cell practically every night and wandered the damp, chilly corridors of the convent from vespers to matins. Contrary to the doctors' expectations, she did not die, and found besides that Saint-Grimace was a more agreeable place when she had to share it with no one but the cats who haunted the courtyard. A nurse told Nasérie about the girl who'd been brought to Saint-Grimace by a lamplighter (who loiters shamelessly in the street after his work's done, they clucked, so keep your curtains drawn!). The rumor was that Madeleine was a duchess's natural daughter, and the lamplighter a ducal footman in disguise, sent to protect the girl from the Duke's implacable wrath. Nasérie decided that she must meet the little noblewoman whose story might serve as a romantic subplot in the grand, dark sweep of her own decline.

It's hard to say who was more surprised, Madeleine or Nasérie, when, late one night, the marquise visited Madeleine's cell. Nasérie found her bent nearly double over a copybook, atoning for the violence she'd done to the alphabet. She thought: Well! she doesn't *look* like a duchess's daughter: pale and pudgy, yet somehow gangly as well, her hands dotted with ink, Madeleine might have been a clerk's brat gone wild among her father's pots and pens. Madeleine, for her part, thought she'd been visited by a ghost. There, in the doorway, stood a girl in a robe that covered her from neck to toe, a girl who—but it was the robe which, first and foremost, held Madeleine's attention.

Its base was of muslin that had yellowed a little with time, so that the designs that nearly covered its surface seemed carved in ivory. The robe had not been embroidered all at once. When Nasérie's great-grandmother had it made, it was decorated only with a pattern of fruit and vines interwoven around the cuffs, at the hem and neck. In 1818 Nasérie's grandmother, a modestly adventurous woman, left the family estate for Paris, where she became a patroness of the arts. Twice a week she sat embroidering, just as her mother had, while around her the wags of the Restoration pricked one another with their needlelike wits. Her salon made no recorded contribution to the letters or the science of the time. Its only tangible product was the robe that Nasérie's grandmother embellished with scenes from her favorite myth, the transformation of Daphne into a laurel tree, which, as she used to say, represented all that was most virtuous in woman: immobility and a slow but regular blossoming of wit. Nasérie's mother had the good sense to be bored by the salon's raconteurs. Though constant of heart, she was quick of spirit, and liked to think of all things—the blossoms that fell from the trees, the clouds, and the wheels of carriages—as eddies in a great, invisible current, which might at any moment carry her to the farthest parts of the globe. To fill the time until that moment she taught herself to sew. Nature was never so closely interconnected as in the scenes Nasérie's mother added to the family robe: golden ducks floated on a border of blue water; below the surface swam blue-green fish; the fish had eyes the color of the ducks, and the ducks eyes the color of the fish, and the blue thread that composed the water below, above stitched out the family coat of arms.

The handiwork was admirable, and the hands that worked it more so; in no time they caught the attention of a superstitious young gambler named Jean Henri-Ange de Saint-Trouille, whom we shall hereafter call the Marquis. He and Nasérie's mother had two things in common: both believed that all phenomena were connected in a way that would someday prove profitable, and each mistook the other for a harbinger of their expected rewards. Nasérie's mother wanted to leave at once for Africa, so the Marquis ran off to bet her money on a black-nosed horse named Aethiop; it lost; they postponed their departure for a while; and in a year Nasérie was born. The Marquise fell into a funk, and changed her opinions of the world. The invisible current, she decided, pushed her backward rather than pulling her along; she was not surprised when, succumbing to it, she was returned first to her mother's house, then to an infirmity like childhood, and at last to a state very much like the one she must have enjoyed before her birth, only more enduring. By then only the bodice of the robe remained unembroidered. As this was the area where Nasérie was most susceptible to cold, a heavy design of her choosing was promptly added. It comprised grapes, tongues of flame, horses, and tiny ships, and Nasérie insisted that it told a story, though what the story was she would not say. In short, it was a robe as noble as any you'll find in France, and could, in its convolutions, its crests and faded borders, take the place of many books of genealogy— which were often counterfeited at the beginning of the Second Empire, when titles were issued as eagerly as promissory notes.

Nasérie was thin as a ghost. Her wrists were no thicker than kindling sticks, and her neck supported her head the way a fruit seller holds a large melon in the palm of his hand, balancing the

unsteady oblong with an expert twitch of his arm. Her face
might politely have been called medieval, if by medieval you
meant greenish and flat. Only her eyes had life: they were large,
and so dark that you could hardly tell the iris from the pupil.
When they moved, which was often, you had the sense that
they drank the light; when they were still, they were like the
ponds you read about in fairy tales, where the candles of those
who've drowned there shine faintly from far below the surface.

— What are you doing? she asked.

— I'm writing a letter.

— To who?

— To my mother. Madeleine covered the ink-spotted paper
with her arms.

— The duchess?

Yes, and why not a duchess? It was a good response to fling
back at the girl who stood, uninvited, in her doorway. — That's
right.

— Which one? Nasérie asked.

— What?

— Which duchess?

Madeleine blushed. Until that moment she'd thought that
duchesses were like kings or emperors: it was unimaginable that
there could be more than one of them at a time. — Are there
many?

— Seventy-five not counting the new ones. There's the
Duchess of Uzès, the Duchess of Elbeuf who's also the Princess
of Lambesc, the...

— I don't know which one she is, Madeleine admitted. She
gave me up when I was very small. Madeleine gave an account
of her adoption which differed from Jacob's story only in that it
included, in addition to the velvet blanket and the golden seal,
a mysterious letter, the contents of which Jacob had sworn not
to reveal to her until she was of age.

As if she'd forgotten her illness for the duration of the story and only remembered it afterward, the marquise coughed. — It's cold in here, isn't it?

— Why aren't you in bed, then?

— I have permission to go wherever I want. It's because I'm going to die soon.

— You are? Of what?

— Of medicine. I take seven different kinds every day. My father pays three doctors to choose them, and they cost thirty francs each.

— The doctors?

— The medicine. The doctors cost much more than that. Two of them belong to the Academy of Medicine, and the other is from London. Then there's Nurse Chairedepoule who keeps me company at night, and Nurses Venine and Ventousse who keep me company by day, and the pharmacist...

— Who are you? Madeleine asked.

— Nasérie Élise de Saint-Trouille, said Nasérie. When my father dies I'll be a marquise, with a house of my own and a horse that wins races. She coughed energetically. — Oh! I feel dizzy. You don't mind, do you?

Nasérie lay on Madeleine's bed, arranged Madeleine's pillow under her head, and wrapped herself in Madeleine's blankets. She rested the back of one hand on her forehead, as if in the last stages of collapse. A moment later she wriggled and sat up.

— Your mattress pricks.

— It's straw. Isn't yours?

— Hardly! Nasérie described the feather bed which her father, the Marquis, had ordered for her, and how it was too wide to fit through the door and had to be hoisted in pieces through the window of her room, and assembled there by an old carpenter with a mouthful of nails. On top of the bed was an eiderdown in a duvet of Nankeen silk, and on top of that another covering, and so many pillows that one might make a wall of

them which reached, if Nasérie could be believed, all the way
to the ceiling, and made of the bed a sort of fortification. — I
would have thought your mother would do as much for you.

— Oh, she's waiting to see how I, to see how I do on my
own.

Nasérie considered this possibility, and evidently found it
romantic enough to be plausible. — I'm freezing. Come here.

Madeleine sat on the edge of the bed.

— The doctors say I won't live through the winter. Don't
you have any more blankets?

Afraid that Nasérie would die on the spot if she didn't do
something, Madeleine crawled into the bed and put her arm
around the marquise's shoulder. — Is that better?

Nasérie propped her chin on the heel of her hand. — You're
not *too* plain. Blow out the candle, or one of the sisters will
come in.

Even in the darkness, Madeleine thought she could make
out Nasérie's eyes, dancing about like the candle's afterimage.

You've probably heard awful things about convents and nuns
and their pensioners, about the little societies that get by on a
surfeit of fabric and a dearth of male company, about the love
which dare not, as they say, speak its name, although other people are quick to call it whatever they like. So, if I tell you that it
was from Nasérie Élise de Saint-Trouille (you'll forgive me if I
repeat her name more than is necessary, but the names of aristocrats are like snuff; one splutters through them with a tingling, embarrassed pleasure, which would probably be better
hid behind a handkerchief) that Madeleine learned to take
pleasure from the body which, until then, had served her
chiefly as a way of getting about, and occasionally as a badge of
her curious origins, you'll probably draw all the wrong conclu-

sions. You'll blame Sister Geneviève for it, and the other nuns, Sister Eulalie and Sister Nénuphar and Sister Aphorie, who sang the most beautiful orisons, and go away thinking that these old Parisian nuns were just as bad an influence on their pupils as any nuns anywhere. So that you don't misunderstand me, I'll tell you just what happened that night, when Nasérie feigned the symptoms of an illness which was all too real, and Madeleine, ignorant of the dangers of contagion, put her arms around an aristocratic nightdress and held the coughing girl, who, she found, was no thicker than a bundle of reeds.

It was a night of storytelling. Nasérie was confined to bed for sixteen hours out of every twenty-four, and with that time she imagined whatever she liked. She had already devised the entire story of Madeleine's life up until her arrival at the convent. And though selfish in other ways, Nasérie could not keep a story, any story, to herself. So, as the stars appeared over the courtyard and the market carts clattered down the rue de la Licorne, Nasérie whispered to Madeleine how her mother was the daughter of the Duke of Noailles. A slip of a girl who looked, in Nasérie's imagination at least, much like Nasérie herself, she had fallen in love with a lieutenant of cavalry, possessed of little more than a splendid moustache and an equally fine black horse. The Duke of Noailles, who in this account was just like the Marquis de Saint-Trouille, only much richer, forbade his daughter to love a man whose title was written on his upper lip, and who could leap effortlessly atop his whole inheritance. But his prohibition, as such prohibitions often do, had just the opposite effect, which was that the young duchess slipped from her room at night (this part of the story Nasérie told in vivid detail, lingering especially on the ruses by which the girl escaped the servants who watched her), and joined her cavalier in the courtyard, where he hoisted her into the saddle and took her to Aix-en-Provence, a city famous for its warm climate and almond candies. In Aix the young couple were married by a one-eyed priest; then Madeleine was born, and the duchess, whose hips were really too narrow for that sort of work, died (here Nasérie's imagination failed her altogether, though she was never closer to the truth). The cavalier was killed in a duel not a week later, defending the honor of his horse, which some sharp-shooting rake had called a nag.

The innkeeper was left with the orphaned Madeleine, and would have sold the girl to the beggars of Aix, who intended to put out her eyes and cut off her leg and send her to beg for the rest of her life. But just then the Duke arrived on the scene, having tracked the young couple all the way from Paris with his hounds. He snatched the infant from the innkeeper's arms, smote the beggars roundly with his silver-chased stick, and for good measure skewered the rake whose aim was better than his eye for horseflesh. The Duke couldn't raise the girl himself, nor did propriety allow him to acknowledge her as his descendant (the one-eyed priest, it turned out, had been defrocked long before); so with great regret he set Madeleine adrift on the Bièvre in a basket lined with red velvet, with a letter hung about her neck. He took the fine black horse home to his stable as a consolation. Of course Jacob was the Duke's former servant, discharged long ago after a misunderstanding with a chambermaid; he remained loyal to the House of Noailles and plucked the basket from the river before it could come to harm, and if he had kept quiet about his former service to the Duke it was because he did not want the incident with the chambermaid, which was painful even in memory, to come to light. And now, Nasérie concluded, all that remains is for the Duke to die, and for a handsome young lawyer from Aix to discover that your parents were married not by the one-eyed priest but by his brother, a most pious and binocular curate, and then you'll be the heiress to the Duchy of Noailles, which I hear is very large, and comprises three castles or more.

Three castles or more! Madeleine held Nasérie tighter, until the embroidered robe pressed through the fabric of her own gown and engraved its pattern on her skin. — Ow! said Nasérie, don't crush me so. But she did not roll away. — If you were a great lady, said Nasérie, you'd give me a kiss, for that's what they do amongst each other. Madeleine kissed her. — And you'd kiss me again, but ah! not so hard, that's better, there. So, under the paling stars, which had already crossed innumerable love affairs and would cross countless more before they were retired in favor of the psyche's simpler constellations, Madeleine discovered what it was to court, or to be courted, she didn't know which. An affair of the lips, mostly, which left one tasting faintly of soap and more faintly still of salt.

After a minute Nasérie turned on her side, tucked the crown of her head under Madeleine's chin, and went to sleep. Madeleine slept in turn. She dreamed of a stone which stood in the middle of a field; in her dream she asked it questions. — Is it true that I'll be a duchess? — The same thing comes to everyone, the stone replied. — And have three castles? — To everyone the same thing comes. — And will Sister Eulalie be kinder to me then? — To everyone, to everyone, the stone replied; that seemed to be the limit of its vocabulary.

When Madeleine woke up, before dawn, Nasérie was coughing quietly but violently into her fist. — Are you all right? — Yes, Nasérie gasped, but I must go back to my room before Nurse Chairedepoule wakes up. She rose from the bed, and, shaking in her nightdress, unlatched the door and disappeared into the darkness of the hall, from which the sound of her failing lungs returned only faintly. Madeleine loved her then, and let no one say that this love was improper, for we are all bound to fall in love with anyone who can forget their own dying for long enough to tell a beautiful story about someone else.

3

SAINT GRIMACE

MADELEINE WOULD HAVE FOLLOWED her anywhere. If Nasérie had told her to leave the convent she would have done it; if she had told her to climb onto the rooftop and pluck the old bronze weathercock from its gable Madeleine would have climbed; but Nasérie had other kinds of mischief in mind.

— Why do you want to be a nun? she asked.

— Well, but Jacob... Madeleine stammered.

— *Ja-cob*, Nasérie taunted, Jacob, can he read or write? Does he keep a horse?

— No, admitted Madeleine.

— Then he's no better than an animal, said Nasérie, and though Madeleine stopped shy of that in her own estimation, she admitted that the lamplighter might know less about the world than her friend, whose room was cluttered with newspapers and illustrated novels. — You must learn to be a lady, Madeleine. Watch me. Nasérie drew herself up straight and walked slowly across the room, casting glances left and right as though to subjects who knelt beside her path. — Do you see? When you walk it is a procession. And when you smile it is an audience. Do you see? Look, this is how you would curtsey to the Emperor...

With this and other instructions Nasérie taught Madeleine
to live up to her imagined station. Mainly it seemed a matter of
moving slowly, smiling often and being pleasant to no one. Day
by day she mastered the difficult arts of haughtiness, grace,
and dissimulation, which she practiced on the nuns for lack
of a better audience. — Is something the matter, child? Sister
Aphorie asked, and Sister Eulalie bellowed that she didn't know
what had gotten into the girl, but that it was a rotten sort of
novice indeed who would not peel a potato. To Sister Geneviève alone Madeleine was more polite than ever. One day, at
Nasérie's urging, she gave Geneviève an address for her letter: Her Grace the Duchess of Noailles. Geneviève embraced
Madeleine tearfully, and went out holding the letter as carefully
as if it were a glass of spirits. She ran off in search of wax and
the convent's seal, which depicted a V of long-necked doves
over the motto ORDO PLACET ANIMI.

Christophe, the convent's porter, had to bear the brunt of
Madeleine's fancy. He returned from the faubourg Saint-
Honoré an hour later, sans letter but half-covered in mud, with
the news that the Duchess of Noailles was seventy-two years
old and the youngest of her sisters fifty-six; he noted too that
the Duchess's butler was of ill humor and unusual size.
Geneviève, bitterly disappointed, locked herself away for an
hour with a bottle of gin. Perhaps it had been a mistake to take
Madeleine in... But ORDO PLACET ANIMI was the convent's
motto, and the sisters had abided by it since before the Revolution. The calm spirit of the order soothed Geneviève, and the
bottled spirit did its part, and in the end Geneviève decided
that Madeleine must have made an honest mistake; perhaps she
meant another name or perhaps her mother was a friend of the
Duchess; yes, that must be it, and now that they had taken the
first step together toward recollection the real name would
come to her soon enough. Rather than confound Madeleine's

memory with any more letter writing, Geneviève had the girl copy passages out of the lives of the saints. — If you think noble thoughts, child, then you'll end up thinking of your noble mother—but don't hurry! She will come to you in time, in time.

Who *was* Madeleine's mother? She was buried in the Montparnasse cemetery on top of a dozen half-rotted paupers; her body joined the overflow of bodies that send miasmas into the neighboring streets on warm, still nights. Even her name has been forgotten; as for the circumstances of her life, you might as well ask what the color of Sister Geneviève's eyes was (blue), or what became of Charogne when Madeleine was not there to lead him around (his right leg had got caught under a cartwheel). But her name was Anne; she met Armand when she was a little past seventeen; the tanner used to wait for her in the courtyard where her mother was a laundress. She would come to him wrapped in someone else's sheet, and fold him in its stiff needlework. Anne said that she believed in a balanced world, where each misdeed corresponded to an equal amount of good done elsewhere, and each murder to a birth; her last wish was either the collapse of this belief, or its fulfillment.

— Harrumph! said Nasérie when she heard the news, — Of course she *would* deny it. But don't worry, when the Duchess sees you she'll repent. Of course by then you may already be married to a duke. And won't she be proud of you, when she sees you then?

Madeleine passed the winter in an ecstasy of appearance. She seemed to grow taller each day, and each day more languid in her movements; she dreamed of drawling nothings to titled

suitors in rooms resplendent with banners and religious artifacts. She had always suspected herself of aristocracy, but under
Nasérie's tutelage she began to understand all that a title might
comprehend: the privilege of living as one did in stories, always
at the center of the action. Some days she chafed to leave the
convent, and to begin her grand career across Paris's stage; but
Nasérie laughed, — And where will you sleep? Don't be a fool.
First you must be courted, and then established; then you'll wed
and then your adventures will begin. By day Madeleine prepared herself to be wooed by a gentleman; at night she gave all
her chrysalidal beauty to Nasérie, who accepted it, coughing,
and repaid her in warmest kind. A single story held them both
in thrall: Nasérie spun it all through the winter, and it promised, whatever turns it might take along the way, to lead them
to the bright heart of life, where what you imagine is nothing
different from what you are.

If only she hadn't been so impatient to meet her mother,
Madeleine thought much later, she would not have lost Nasérie
and everything might have turned out all right. But everyone
had encouraged her to be impatient: Nasérie with her stories,
Sister Geneviève who urged her to pray to Saint Rita of Cas-
cia, the patron saint of blind luck, and to Saint Gaetan of Auch,
patron saint of unreconciled children. Sisters Aphorie and
Nénuphar hinted that Madeleine's mother ought really to be
coming soon, even the deaf Sister Eulalie grunted that it was
about time for her to show up, and in short everyone led
Madeleine to hope that her mother would come any day, next
month, certainly before winter's end. So Madeleine, like her
foster father, became a devotee of windows, though for quite
different reasons. She expected that any of the convent's mul-
lions, its casements, any pane of glass into which she happened

to look might, without warning, be turned into a magic mirror in which she'd see her older and better-dressed self, her
mother, arriving in a carriage to deliver her into the life her
birth deserved.

It was only natural, then, that Madeleine took a special interest in the convent's visitors, who were all women, all noble
or at least well off, and, many of them, old enough that it would
be no embarrassment for them to call Madeleine daughter.
These lovely (to Madeleine they *were* lovely, though much later,
when she met some of them again, she'd find in them the ordinary irregular features, bodies sagging or otherwise awry like
arches built by a half-hearted mason) ladies came to the convent as regularly as the moon, and with the same inscrutability
of purpose. When one of them was in residence—never for
more than a day at a time—the whole convent became quiet, as
though it suffered from the desire to say too much, got tongue-
tied, and finished by saying nothing at all. What do they come
for? Madeleine asked Sister Geneviève, who glared at her as
though she were a bird sprung unexpectedly from the bowels
of a clock. — Don't ask questions about things which don't
concern you, the nun said. When pressed, however, she admitted: — To speak to the Saint, that's why, and don't ask me anything more.

The thought that one of these noble women might be her
mother amused Madeleine at first; but as time passed and no
other mother turned up, as Nasérie whispered stories of doñas
and gräfins and British ladies (after the debacle with the
Duchess of Noailles, her imagination protected itself by going
abroad), Madeleine was annoyed, then unsettled, and at last
convinced that one of the carriages which rattled up to the
convent gate was *her* carriage, that one of the ladies was *her*
lady, come to take her home. She watched them from a window overlooking the courtyard. Each time a carriage came in,

Madeleine said, *there she is*; even when she found out that it was only "a friend of Saint Grimace's," or "a poor pilgrim," as Nénuphar called them, Madeleine could not give up the idea that the visitor was hers, somehow, if only by the general right by which orphans, exiles, and madmen lay claim to the world in general because they have no particular place in it. By this right Madeleine climbed up to an empty storeroom high above the courtyard, from where she could spy on the ladies as they spoke, so to speak, with the Saint.

She didn't understand their ritual, but she told Nasérie all about it. — It's got something to do with a chair, and with praying, and with touching the statue, *here*. Madeleine poked Nasérie just above the navel.

— Goose! You didn't hear what they said?

— Mother Superior read it from a book. I don't think any-one else said anything at all.

— You mean she touched the statue's tummy?

— The statue touched hers, with its finger, or, I mean, she made it touch hers.

— There?

— Here.

— Mm, said Nasérie, and did it make her happy?

— I don't think so. She fell off the chair and Sister Nénuphar had to catch her in her arms and hold her up. And she was crying, I think. Afterward she kissed Nénu and the Mother Superior, and Nénu held her, so.

— Was she very beautiful?

— She was.

— More than me?

Madeleine said nothing. But after that it was only a matter of time—two nights, or three—before Nasérie announced that it was time for Madeleine to learn the ways of married women.

— Let's go outside, she said. They did not dare bring a candle to light the way; in darkness they shuffled, hand in hand, to the end of the corridor, down a flight of winding stairs, fearing at every turn to bump into Sister Geneviève or one of the other nuns. But Geneviève had drunk herself to sleep hours ago and the convent was silent. It was cold in the courtyard; their breath hung in the air behind them like a trail of mist. The night was clear, and the moon had just risen on the other side of the rue de la Licorne. — Over here, Nasérie whispered. She led Madeleine toward the fence that separated the courtyard at large from the little enclosure which belonged to the statue of Saint Grimace. — Oh no, Madeleine said. But it was too late; Nasérie had already lifted the latch and swung open the gate behind which the statue kept watch on the ascendant night.

Saint Grimace was a saint in conjecture only. His statue was found in the courtyard of the convent's new quarters, providentially, said the old sisters who had spent Republic, Consulate, and Empire pauperized in the Ardèche. The nuns were the first to see the features of a saint in the rain-etched stone. They hinted at it to their confessor, who joked with his friends about the magical properties such a statue might have, especially on women carrying unborn babes. The joke got out and on the way it somehow ceased to be a joke; soon the embryonic bastards of the Restoration were brought en masse to the garden where a stone man, saint or no, pointed a menacing finger at the horizon. The statue's origin was much disputed. The nuns told their guests that it was the last trace of a Carolingian chapel; the finger in this account was raised toward Montmartre, where Saint Denis had been handed his head and told to carry it north a mile or two. Skeptics said that the statue had been commissioned by an innkeeper to frighten the drunks who might otherwise have spent the night in his stables. Classicists and geologists held that the statue was much older, from the time of the emperors Constantius Chlorus and Julian the Apostate. They chipped flakes from its side to prove it could not be a saint—then sold the flakes to pious collectors, and thus secured both their finances and their reputations.

About the present statue, however, everyone agreed: it was desperately ugly. Half-hidden by creepers, it stooped at the back of the garden; its chest had been hollowed by rain and the geologists' depredations, and its arm was barely able to support the weight of the hand which did, undeniably, point a long index finger toward the northwest. Legs: buckled; shoulders: round; it had a full inventory of mis-carved or malformed extremities; but its face outdid them all. Saint Grimace stared through the vines like a martyr to ivy and winter; his features gathered in petrified agony around his nose, which, like his finger, pointed accusingly, but, unlike the finger, was aimed at the sky. His rolling eyes were crossed; his mouth a hole which, had it been deeper, would have been able to swallow hand and nose at once; his cheekbones protruded almost as far as his protruding ears. Eyes, nose, mouth, and cheeks together gave the Saint an air of surprise, as though he had, in the middle of his agony, seen something not at all to his liking. Or, as the skeptics would have it, as though he had *not* seen something. Candles burned around the basin at the Saint's feet, and a chair was set before him so that the visitor could present her belly to be blessed by his forgiving hand. There were ancillary rites to be observed: certain prayers were read aloud, and certain hymns intoned; but the essence of the ritual was the presentation of flesh to stone, their momentary union, ripe, eroded, ephemeral, and enduring.

Nasérie, whose coughing had worsened as the season declined, must have wanted to feel what the great ladies, the countesses and baronesses, the bankers' wives and merchants' daughters felt—they who, like her, had a great deal of money, but who, unlike her, were free to enjoy it where they would. Perhaps she thought the Saint would cure her as he had cured the others, though she had only the faintest notion of the real causes and symptoms of their disease, being more or less preoccupied by her own. Or perhaps she knew what horizon the statue really pointed toward, and was ready to travel in that direction without hope of return, to end her own life before it had really begun. In any case it was a way out. One touch and she could quit the stuffy bustle of her sickroom; either her disease would take flight or she would do so herself. Having been ill all her life, she might have been ready to accept any means which would allow her, at last, to leave her bed. Some lives are like that: nothing but last wishes from the get-go. Though such people may feast at every meal, it does them no good, for, to them, it's nothing but the last banquet before the scaffold. Nor should we do anything to restrain them—how, having reached their ultimate desires early on, are we to tell them that they must forget what they have learned, and return to some earlier, penultimate craving?

Nasérie pulled open the gate and stepped into the Saint's enclosure. — Come on, she whispered. Madeleine followed. — Hold the chair! The wood was cold in her grip. With a little difficulty and a suppressed cough, Nasérie climbed onto the chair. At thirteen, she was a little smaller than the ladies who habitually scaled to that height, so that, instead of pointing at her stomach, Saint Grimace's finger caught her squarely in the chest. The stars looked on as though nothing had happened.

— Go on, Nasérie said. You try it.

Madeleine hesitated.

— I'll hold the chair for you, go on!

But Madeleine would not climb up. — What was it like?

— Ssh! It was like... it was like going down into a cave, and
then coming up again. Isn't it bright? Nasérie pointed at the
moon, which, as far as Madeleine could tell, had not changed
its hue, but had only risen and grown, to the eye at least, a little
more distant. — It was like being rubbed with oil... Like being
covered in soil... Nasérie sighed and rubbed her eyes. — See for
yourself.

But Madeleine did not climb up that night, nor did she ever
touch with belly or breast the Saint's worn finger. It seemed to
her in that moment that the world traveled in two directions:
forward, the direction she was going, toward riches and chandeliers, balls and lovers and children; and backward, the direction of Saint Grimace's finger, toward an unknowable but
potent beginning. To touch the Saint's finger would be to reach
toward what she had forgotten, and that Madeleine—who had
only just discovered how bright the future was, and how many
unheard-of things it promised her—would not do. She gave
Nasérie all sorts of other reasons: she was afraid the nuns would
find out, she wasn't really curious; she didn't want to make
Nasérie steady the heavy chair; she was cold and shouldn't they
go inside?

— How will you marry a duke if you don't have the
courage to stand on a chair?

Madeleine took Nasérie in her arms. — My goodness,
you're going to freeze, she said, and it was true; where the marquise usually was warmer than your average citizen, now she
was as cold as yesterday's roast, and nearly as clammy. — Let's go
back, she said, and led Nasérie, in whom revelation was too
fresh for her to protest, indoors to the safety of her cell and her
scratchy, narrow bed.

4

THE MIRACLE

—————

THE BELLS OF SAINT-LUC rang the last reasonable hour when Nasérie might get back to her cell undiscovered, and still she slept, immobile, breathing slowly, her hands folded on her chest like the effigy of a Crusader carved on the lid of his stone casket. — Nasérie! The sky was bone-gray and it came down almost to the tops of the streetlamps. — Wake up! Then the corridor was full of footsteps; someone knocked on the door and Sister Geneviève was calling, — Madeleine? Before she could answer, the door opened and a torrent of nuns and nurses came in. First Geneviève, then a pair of old ladies as alike as two walking sticks—the nurses Venine and Ventousse, Madeleine guessed—then Nénu and a frightened, red-faced woman tugging at her bonnet and explaining that she didn't know *what* had come over her. They formed a loose semicircle around the bed, their faces frozen in a sort of ceremonial horror.

— What, said Nurse Venine (or Ventousse), is *this*?

Nurse Ventousse (or Venine) said, — What are they *doing*?

And Sister Geneviève, leaning forward as though to make sure that she wasn't seeing double, asked, — Madeleine?

— I...

The two nurses leaned closer; one prodded Madeleine's arm
and the other tugged at her hair. — What has *she* done with
our marquise? — Who is she? they asked.

— Ladies, please don't worry, said Nénu. I'm sure it's nothing...

The nurses interrupted: — Is that window open? — Has
she been sleeping on the *ground*?

Madeleine felt the way she imagined an animal feels before
it is butchered: cold, though its heart is still beating, already dis-
sected in the imagination of a half-dozen hungry customers.
She began to cry. — It's not my fault, she said, when she could
speak, really it isn't. I told Nasérie not to touch the statue. I *told*
her...

—The statue?

—What's she talking about?

—Madeleine? Sister Geneviève had turned pale; so had
Nénu. Only the bonneted nurse, Chairedepoule, it must have
been, blinked and shook her head and insisted that *Nothing* like
this has *never* happened to me before!

A number of things must have happened very quickly then,
because Madeleine felt dizzy, and the room, though it didn't
move, was turning slowly; it was light and then dark and Madeleine was entirely alone. Days passed; nuns came and went
without speaking, though they must have spoken, for Madeleine remembered, afterward, that she had learned all about
God, and about Hell. Until then Madeleine had got her notions
of divinity from the lamplighter, who believed in an all-seeing
but distant Creator whose spirit moved through the world like
the gas in the pipes laid under Paris's streets, a dangerous and
intoxicating invisibility that cast its light here and there, generally in the richer parts of town. But here was Sister Geneviève
sitting by her bed, informing her that God was like the empti-

ness at the bottom of a glass: impalpable and invisible and yet right there, waiting to tell her that the fun was over. Even if this most puissant God wouldn't take an interest in her until she'd drained her cup, Geneviève said, it was certain that a very personal Devil had found her already and that unless she gave up her evil ways—but what was she talking about? Everything was so vague; only the light that sank through the upper portion of Madeleine's window, the winter light that dispatched nighttime as grudgingly as a post-office clerk, was real—the Devil would become such fast friends with Madeleine that she would never afterward be able to send him away. And so Geneviève embarked on a description of the manifold tortures of Hell—

For which we'll require only the brief observation that Geneviève, not long after she'd sworn herself into a habit and a new name, decided that spiritual purity ought to have physical sobriety as a substrate, and swore off drink. No need to describe everything she went through in the three weeks when she was tried as surely as any saint, though with a less majestic result. I'll only say that the description of Hell which she advanced for Madeleine's benefit was richly and imaginatively populated by spiders. In Hell, said Geneviève, everything that was pleasant on earth is torture: you'll always be thirsty, but no sooner do you lift a cup to your lips than you see, just below the brim, the green eyes of a great, fat spider staring up at you; you throw the cup down but too late, the spider crawls into your mouth... Or was that Madeleine, dreaming? She dreamed so many things: that she was at home with Jacob again, that she was alone in a dim palace full of rooms without doors, or windows, or stairs; that Nasérie had come to see her, but would not speak. Then she knew that she was dreaming and when she woke up Sister Geneviève was waking her up.

— Child? The nun looked at Madeleine with the helpless

suspicion that people feel when they are caught up in something they do not understand.

— Sister?

— Come on, hurry up. Eulalie needs your help in the
kitchen.

Something had changed in the convent. Pale and incredulous
nuns whispered to one another and seemed to pay the statue of
Saint Grimace a little more attention than usual. French and
English doctors were seen in the refectory or walking toward
the Mother Superior's office, as were the convent's confessor
Father Surcis and a succession of priests, who despite the solemnity of the occasion were in good spirits; they laughed and
wagged their fingers at Saint Grimace, shook their heads and
called him a sly devil to have tricked them for so long. No
one spoke to Madeleine except to direct her to do her ordinary work. By day she tended the garden, and sang, and
read how Saint Sebastian was stuck through with arrows;
at night she lay awake wondering what had happened to
Nasérie. Madeleine felt her absence as if it were the presence
of an annoying visitor, a mutual acquaintance who insisted
on talking about Nasérie, and passing on the most unlikely
rumors about the marquise's health and whereabouts. The
Absence of Nasérie rubbed its hands together as if it enjoyed very much all the terrible things it was saying; and no
amount of cold-shouldering or even tearful entreaty could
make it go away. Madeleine sat up in bed, unable to sleep,
listening to the Absence as it told her for heaven's sake not
to *worry*! After all, it was such a disgraceful thing for them to
have been in love at all that, if the marquise were gravely ill
or even dead, it was really for the best! Don't give it another thought, the Absence said. Nasérie's eyes closing, for the

last time, without having seen you; her poor body almost doubled up by coughing, and blood probably spotting the walls, oh, but there's nothing you can do about it, and even if you could, you'd do well to remember what Geneviève said about the Devil and evil little girls! The Absence was quiet for a moment, smiling to itself at the beauty of its tableaux, and at their variety.

Someone turned the handle of Madeleine's door: the Absence looked up and vanished.

The grapes on Nasérie's robe had ripened; the ships tossed; the horses reared and the ducks swam across a slightly more uneven sea. Her head sat more firmly atop her neck, and her shoulders did not hunch forward as they had before, so that her posture was almost graceful. Her cheeks wore a fine color, and her eyes had grown clear and untroubled. She carried a wooden box under her arm and she was smiling. When Madeleine tried to embrace her, however, Nasérie held out the box instead. It had a picture of China painted on it in lacquer. The people in the picture looked smaller than Madeleine would have thought, and older somehow.

— Do you like it?

— It's beautiful.

— Keep it, then.

— But Nasérie, what's happened to you?

— Haven't you heard? the marquise asked. It's a miracle.

She told Madeleine what had happened: how something had shifted about in her lungs which gave the French doctors cause for hope. They redoubled the doses of all her medicines, and ordered her to drink broth spiced with pungent herbs twice a day, and they expected that if things kept improving at their current rate Nasérie would be well before winter. Only the British doctor sighed and shook his head; he made such dire proclamations about false recoveries that the French doc-

tors on the spot bet him a bottle of wine that the girl would
not so much as cough by the Toussaint.

It was a miracle; all the nuns said so and the Marquis de Saint-
Trouille was inclined to agree. Hadn't his horses won two races
in a row that season? And didn't good fortune always come in
threes? The Marquis gave half his winnings to the convent as a
sort of bet on Nasérie's recovery; the other half he bet on his
horses, which lost, but this left him convinced that, in accordance with the rule of threes, his daughter would soon be well.
He began to speak of her as already cured; as he moved in good
society the word of her miraculous recovery soon spread. Infirm heiresses turned up at the gate of Saint-Grimace. In the
span of a month the convent took in a girl who could neither
move nor feel her legs, a deaf-mute who ate with her fingers,
and a girl whose only sign of illness was her refusal to take off
her large and malodorous velvet hat. Between them, they
brought in enough money to put meat on the sisters' table
every night. The Mother Superior spoke of refurbishing the
chapel or even of building a new one; Nénuphar expanded the
garden with an eye to selling its miraculous produce, and Sister
Geneviève went to sleep every night with her hand closed on
the stem of a drinking glass of leaded crystal.
     Flushed with the anticipation of the convent's success, the
Mother Superior wrote to Rome with the story of what had
happened, and requested that Saint Grimace be officially canonized. A few weeks later a letter came from the Curia, announcing the visit to their convent of Monsignor Ipatio
Ottonase, papal investigator extraordinary. The nuns, as one, fell
into a panic of preparation. The convent had never been so
clean as it was that summer, nor had the stained-glass windows
ever admitted so much light. The candlesticks on the altar

shone and the soups bubbled with inventiveness. Sister Aphorie
strained her voice for hours each morning, and Nénuphar
tended ruddy peppers which, according to her calculations,
ought to ripen just in time for the Monsignor's visit. A nearly
festive air infected the convent; the nuns slept better, ate more,
prayed louder, and, on clear nights, walked arm in arm around
the courtyard, whispering ecclesiastical jokes at the expense of
Father Surcis. Even the statue of Saint Grimace, they thought,
gaped at them with more amused anguish than usual.

Madeleine had known Nasérie for only a short time, but already she could not imagine how she had lived without the
marquise, who knew intimately the family of her imagination,
and disdained to know any detail of the real life which she had
endured in the cour Carence. Nasérie hadn't even promised
that she would come back to visit Madeleine when she was
better and went about a full-fledged rather than a sickly marquise! Perhaps she doesn't mean to come back, Madeleine
thought. When she's well she'll have the whole world to amuse
her and why would anyone who had the whole world to
choose from choose to come back to Saint-Grimace, to visit a
girl who doesn't even know who her own mother is? That was
the Absence talking. Somehow it had returned; it whispered to
her even when Nasérie was in the room, holding her, terrible
things. Night by night Madeleine found herself talking less to
Nasérie, and more to the Absence, which would not leave her
alone. The marquise was generous about it as she was about
everything, now. Even her stories had changed: there weren't
any dukes or duchesses in them, only simple and virtuous children who lived in Paris and experienced various mishaps and
overcame them, somehow, and got married to handsome soldiers in the end.

But Madeleine couldn't stand not knowing. At last, to make the Absence for once be quiet! she asked sweetly, — You *will* come back and visit, won't you, when you're better? As Nasérie said nothing she asked, a little less sweetly, — You won't just *leave* me?

Bent over Madeleine's snuffling face, Nasérie whispered, — I'm going to run away.

— What?

— Otherwise they'll never let me go.

— Of course they will, said Madeleine. Isn't your father going to take you back, when you're better?

— But where will he take me?

— To parties...

— Parties! Nasérie made a moue. I don't care about them anymore. She whispered: — The important thing, Madeleine, the important thing is to be free.

— Free! And do you think you'll be free, if you run away?

— O yes. I've read all about it. The children of Paris run wherever they want to, and steal everything they need.

Nasérie described the life she would lead as an urchin. First she would take shelter in a gardener's shed, and she'd bring blankets with her so she could be as cozy as you please; then she'd meet the kindly Beggar King who would take her in charge, and show her to his underground domain, where merry cripples cackle by the fire, and fist-sized diamonds, in pure crystalline ignorance of the laws of economics, grow from the walls. Burglars would bring her perfume and well-meaning bruisers would fight for the honor of kissing her hand. And she would live among them, not wanting for anything, but always perfectly free, until the day when a soldier of the Emperor's guard would catch sight of her: a beautiful waif singing in an empty, sunlit alley... Then the usual course of elopement, pursuit, and perhaps a duel to round things off at the end.

Madeleine, dismayed, tried to tell Nasérie that it was not like that, that the marquise was better off being a marquise, that if there was indeed a wonderful story leading her anywhere it led in the other direction, away from the poor, virtuous or no, and their endless wants.

— Silly Madeleine! You only say that because you don't know how to *live*, really. Oh, Nasérie sighed, I'll have to come back for you, without me you're as helpless as... as a newt.

Which amphibian reminded Madeleine of the Bièvre, and gave her misgivings fresh fuel. They argued all night, Madeleine advancing warning after warning, and the marquise, perfectly untroubled, giving answers which, though intended to soothe, in general had the opposite effect.

At last Madeleine seemed to swallow something within herself, some hope. — When are you leaving?

— When I'm ready.

— I'll go with you.

— *You?* I wouldn't dream of taking you. Who ever heard of the beggar-king befriending two urchins at once? *You* wouldn't even climb up on a chair, Nasérie said, something of the old fire in her eyes.

The Monsignor Ottonase was expected any day, and Sister Geneviève, who had decided that Madeleine's value as a witness to the miracle outweighed the spiritual benefits the girl reaped by being punished, coached Madeleine in what she should tell him.

— The marquise came to your cell with unearthly assurance, said Geneviève.

Madeleine repeated: — The marquise...

— She spoke softly, and smiled with so much tenderness... And when you said, Oh, Nasérie, you must not climb up on that chair! You know the nuns will be angry! she replied, No, the nuns will not mind, for it is the Saint's own will. And when you think of how grateful you are to Saint Grimace you must remember to cry.

— I will cry, Madeleine agreed.

— And promise me you won't, under any circumstances, say anything about...?

Nasérie came to Madeleine's room to leave off a few things which she wouldn't be needing any longer: a translation of the *Thousand Nights and a Night*, a wooden flute, a bar of scented soap. — I'm almost ready, Nasérie said. When she was gone, Madeleine lifted her skirt. Only that morning there had been blood between her legs, to compensate, Madeleine thought, for the blood that Nasérie did not cough up. Perhaps it was her punishment for not touching the statue. If only she had listened to Nasérie! With entirely unfeigned contrition, she knelt at her writing desk and prayed to Saint Grimace: *Please don't let Nasérie get better yet.* Madeleine regretted the words as soon as she had spoken them, even though no one could possibly have heard.

The next night a mist settled over the city, so thick that you couldn't see a lit window from the other side of the street. It was composed of river fog and dung smoke, of stoves warming themselves up for the crackling winter, of meat grilled over coals by the hawkers who touted Grilled Leg! Fresh off the Bone!, of snuff and sandalwood and rose water daubed behind the ears of aristocrats, of burning brushwood and the exhalations that rise from the graves of the newly dead. The mist bound all the smells of Paris together, and wrapped them in a

cloak of damp white, covering the city as though protecting it
from the clear October sky. It wended its way down the rue de
la Licorne, and turned the lamps there to will-o'-the-wisps,
leading voyeurs and travelers astray, so that those who sought
the brothel found the convent and vice versa. Jacob, who
sought neither, did his work quickly and left the street. The
mist stopped in at the Benedictine Tavern and made the whores
cough passionately, and curse their basement rooms, their low
fires and thin blankets. It found the gate of Saint-Grimace, the
courtyard, hid the statue and quieted the birds, climbed the
stairs, and met Sister Geneviève in the kitchen between one
drink and the next. *Ugh*, she thought, and remembered when
she'd been a pretty girl with a different name, and how Ma-
thieu the cabinetmaker had taken her into the back of his shop,
to give her some polish, he said, only if that was polish she was
much deceived, she was much deceived. He laughed at her after, and said she was too knotty a plank to make anything with;
she fled his laughter and, eventually, everything else, for a life of
hardening and setting and a bottle of liquor that smelled raw as
turpentine.

The mist touched the cheeks of the sleeping nuns, Eulalie
and Aphorie and Nénuphar, their red faces rising up out of a
mass of brown blankets like lilies in a pond, and each sneezed,
once, in turn, without waking. Madeleine was at the washbasin
when the mist came in. She fought its reek with the scented
soap Nasérie had given her, and scrubbed so vigorously that at
last she was armored in vetiver, lemon, and black pepper, armored she thought for all time against these smells that reminded her of the cour Carence. She went to bed and waited
for Nasérie to come.

But Nasérie had one last potion to drink, the foulest of the
lot. It must have been made from tar and brine, for it stung her
nose, caught in her throat, and kept stinging, and each time she

drank it she thought she might drown. The British doctor waited to see her drain it off, else she would have poured the whole bottle out into the fireplace, where most of her medicaments had gone until the charwoman found them there, a fortune of powders and pills ruined by ash. So the doctor beams and looks at his watch, and Nasérie tilts the bottle toward her lower lip, and thinks, *I'd die on the spot if only I could see you blamed for it.* The mist finds her then, and tickles something at the fork of her lungs; the doctor drops his watch; the bottle breaks on the hearth; the potion ends up mostly in the fireplace, and Nasérie doubles over as though this were the best joke of all, the little clots of blood she coughs onto her hand and nightdress. — There, Nasérie, there, my child. The doctor takes her hand; he smells like a horse, this long-necked fop; like a horse he flaps his lips and tosses his head. Nasérie is put to bed, but cannot lie still; the mist has found some funny bone deep in her chest and so she must laugh, and laugh, and embroider her nightdress anew. At least she has the satisfaction of dousing a doctor or two with their own hot preparations. Then she sinks back onto the cushions, the roses of her skin leafed over with green, and the doctors wipe broth from their frock coats, and they won't try to make her drink anything again, no, they'll never try to make her drink their medicine again.

Nasérie was always in the lead, so it was only fitting that she be the one to discover the greatest trick of all, the disappearance into pillows and blankets, into a cloud of black-coated doctors and nuns. Madeleine would have followed her anywhere, but how could she follow when the doctors would not allow her into Nasérie's bedroom? She stood in the doorway and tried to make out what was going on between their backs. There was no sign of Nasérie, or rather there were only signs of her: the enormous bed and the tables littered with phials and powders in twists of paper. And Father Surcis's red face turned

toward the red light of sunset, his eyes half-closed, his lips moving silently but with great precision, like an army on maneu-
vers. They would not let her in. — Get this girl out of here! the
doctors cried, and Nurse Chairedepoule was charged with seeing it done; she led Madeleine a little way down the corridor
and wiped the corners of her face roughly with a handkerchief
that smelled of snuff. — There, there, child, you'll soon have
your friend back, now run along!

But Nasérie was too clever for them all. She slipped past the
doctors one by one; they came out of her bedroom wiping
their foreheads on their sleeves. The London doctor was the last
to leave; he sighed and blew his nose, said something in English, then turned to his colleagues and announced, — Gentlemen, you've won your bet. But it was Nasérie who had won.
That night, when Madeleine sneaked into her room—the doctors had gone home, and Nurse Chairedepoule was resting—
and pulled back the covers to see her friend again, the bed was
empty. Madeleine opened the window and looked up and
down the street: a lamplighter leaned against one of the posts in
his charge; a pair of drunks stumbled riverward. Nasérie had
gone.

The next day they brought a box for her. The Marquis himself carried it downstairs, sighing like a gambler who spots his
horse only as it emerges at the rear of the pack. The box vanished into a carriage; the carriage rolled off at the head of a
procession of mourners, paid and otherwise, from which the
creaking of wheels returned like wooden laughter.

— Where are they going? Madeleine asked Sister Geneviève.

— To the cemetery, child.

— Why?

— To bury her by her mother, where the poor girl may at
last have some peace.

Only Madeleine knew what had really happened: how Nasérie had descended a rope to the street, just as she'd said she would, and run off, her bare feet silent on the cobblestones, her robe fanned out behind her like a peacock's tail, running toward the Pont au Change and a freedom beyond stories. And Madeleine, who remained, wept that Nasérie oughtn't to have left without her, that she would have followed, if only she'd known.

Sister Geneviève only sighed, and rested her heavy hand on Madeleine's head. Inwardly she worried that this meant the other paying guests would soon be leaving, too.

5

GHOSTS

_____

THE MONSIGNOR OTTONASE arrived the next day in a shining carriage, attended by three footmen in red livery. — Where is the miracle girl? he asked, and, on being informed of her present whereabouts, sighed and picked at his teeth with a polished fingernail. — It is too bad, he said. He declined all the nuns' invitations. He would not hear Sister Aphorie sing, nor taste Sister Eulalie's soup; he did not want to see the chapel. After a glance at the statue of Saint Grimace, he repeated his first judgment, — It is too bad, and drove off to sup with the Archbishop. The convent never saw nor heard from him again. Their letters to the Curia went unanswered from that time until the day, many years later, when the sisterhood disbanded and the convent was torn down to make room for a street. By then most of the nuns had lost faith in Saint Grimace anyway. Their spirits were worn out by hoping, and though they tended the statue as zealously as before—more zealously, in some cases, for despair is a better goad to action even than hope—they no longer expected anything from Grimace but the shriveling up of unborn promises. The Monsignor had spoken: it was too bad; and from that moment until the demolition of the convent

the stones of the courtyard and the cobwebs in the chapel
seemed to whisper, too bad, it is too bad, as though the words
had lodged there and no amount of cleaning could shake them
free.

Geneviève was right: the paralytic, the deaf girl, and the girl in
the velvet hat were called for by their parents; and Saint-
Grimace was quiet again. The convent had never seemed so
empty to Madeleine as it did that fall, when even the Absence
of Nasérie would not keep her company; nor had her straw
pallet ever been so uncomfortable as it was when she had it all
to herself, and could not find the place on it where she had
slept before. She stayed mostly in her cell. In three weeks
Madeleine read through the years of Scheherazade's captivity
(why didn't *she* run away, Madeleine wondered) and blew
mournful tunes on the flute. She cried and washed her face,
thought of Nasérie and cried again. When the soap Nasérie
gave her had been used up, and even the memory of it had
faded a little among the crisp winter smells of twig and charcoal, Madeleine came out of her seclusion. The nuns remarked
on how much she had changed. She'd given up her haughty
bearing in public and her sullen manner in private; the new
Madeleine was obedient, serious, pious, and quiet. If she was
also taciturn and smiled strangely when chastened, at least it
was an improvement over how she'd been before. The nuns,
happy to see some good come out of so much misfortune,
didn't ask her too many questions; which was just as well, for
her answers would certainly have given them cause for further
unease.

Madeleine had decided to become a saint. Every day between breakfast and dinnertime she retreated to the convent's
library, an attic which in the building's first life had served as a
storeroom for dry goods, and kept a little of their spicy smell,

softened by the thin must of old paper. There, curled like a question mark in the library's unique armchair, which she moved to follow the swath of diffuse winter sunshine, she read from the convent's collection of hagiographies. She didn't know what sort of saint she would become, a hermit or a martyr, a nurse in a hospital for victims of a pustulous disease, a mother by proxy to half a thousand hungry children, or the inhabitant of a *reclusoir*, one of the little towers built in the center of Paris for women with solitary inclinations but little desire to leave the capital. And this decision, she thought, she could put off for a little while yet. After all she had hardly recovered from the shock of losing Nasérie, and she did not want to settle on a sainthood before having read something on every saint, and there were so many of them!

There was even a life of Saint Grimace, written by one of the charlatans who'd visited the convent in the early days of its fame, and claimed to have found the saint's acts written on a scroll buried in the courtyard. Saint Grimace, in this account, had been a gentle man in life, a rich farmer moved by the fear of dying to the greatest acts of kindness and charity. His disposition was so morbid that, even as a young man, he seemed not only to have one foot in the grave, but to have planted both feet there, and to be pulling earth down around him with his hands. The most charming detail of this history, and the one that had convinced the nuns of its veracity, was the description of the Saint's house:

> Grimace lived in a sort of hut made all of straw, no larger than seven paces across; in winter the wind blew through the walls, and when it rained water dripped in from every part of the roof. What was more, despite the flammable nature of the house and the absence of a chimney, Grimace insisted on keeping a fire lit there in all seasons, so that his room was always stuffy and full of smoke.

When he was asked why, as he had so much money, and was besides so afraid of death, he chose to live in a house which was both flimsy and dangerous, Grimace said only that this form of habitation allowed him to live with a minimum of illusions.

Whether his fear of death had been an illusion, too, no one could say; but it was certain that, on his deathbed, the Saint's features were convulsed first by fear and then by wonder; to the family gathered in his smoky, dripping home he described the City of Heaven in such detail that he must certainly have seen it with his own eyes. He spoke of the breadth of the doors, the unusual form of the door knockers, the width of the streets and the gutters, the roofs of the palaces of the blessed, and of the palaces of the angels, which were roomier and had round windows in all the dormers. Unfortunately his family, having no vocabulary for architecture, could not communicate his vision in any but the most general terms, and so, despite the entreaties of a great number of people who had known the living Grimace, he was never canonized. The author of the supposed history went on to describe the Saint's statue, which, he said, citing several entirely fictitious authorities, had a "face so terrible that it could still children in the womb." Madeleine paled. She put down the book without having read the author's last observation: that terrible ugliness might, by homeopathic action, dispel ugliness and so give rise to beauty—and the reader was therefore advised to buy a cream made with powdered stone from the statue, available from the author for a reasonable price.

By the time spring came to lure Madeleine from the library, she had taken the first step toward sainthood: she resigned herself to

giving up great changes for small variations. In place of the neap
and flood of the Seine, she watched the rain fill the Saint's basin;
in place of her riverside games she read stories from the lives of
those blessed ones, who, if they had not conquered Russia, at
least had laid siege to something within themselves, starving out
complaisance, hunger, and the fear of being alone. Madeleine
felt something very like what she imagined the saints had felt as
she skipped meals to hide in a chair by the library window,
which overlooked the garden. From there she could see the
statue and the high wall behind it; beyond the wall other buildings rose, roof after slate roof, like waves under an overcast
sky. She was seated there one day with her legs folded and her
head bowed, in order not to be seen by the nuns, who in any
case preferred to ignore her, when she felt a space opening
within her chest, a sort of window through which she saw the
world not as it was but as it ought to be. This, too, was a small
rather than a great transformation: houses and trees receded a
little, as though to make room for more traffic. Madeleine closed
her eyes; she could see the crowd, the carriages, the plumed
horses and fine silhouettes behind panes of frosted glass. The
dead. That was who it must be, the dead on their way to heaven.
Hadn't Jacob told her that you could see the faces of the saints
through drawn blinds? She opened her eyes; it was midafternoon; more dizzy than beatified, Madeleine went downstairs to see if something might not be left over from the
noonday meal.

The courtyard was full of sun and the stuttering of agitated
birds. A three-legged cat had got in among them and caught a
sparrow in its jaws. Not quite dead, the bird joined the nuns in
shrieking and flapping fruitlessly. The cat could not have come
at a worse time. There was a countess in the courtyard who had
already begun the ritual by which Saint Grimace was thought
to work his powers: atop the ebony chair, hands raised in the

direction indicated by the statue's nose, she arched her back so that her belly almost touched the Saint's accusatory finger. The countess swayed in place while, around her, nuns reached for spades, rakes, and brooms; they struck the basin and hacked shrubs and vines in their impatience to be rid of the cat before the countess could take the intrusion as an omen, leave, and withhold the donation which the order had spent in advance. Madeleine caught a laugh in her palm; she remembered that she had just had a vision, and decided that she was not yet ready to concern herself with worldly matters, even if they involved a cat. This was an animal which, in these last lonely months, Madeleine had come to love. Cats are free, she thought, to walk wherever they like, anywhere in Paris they want to go. They hunt rats by the river and pigeons on the rooftops, whereas I stay here and wait and wait. (Of course, it takes no courage to love a cat: the certainty of feline indifference is a sort of carte blanche for us to be indifferent to ourselves. A friendly cat is like a meteorological phenomenon, a break in the clouds, which echoes a happiness we may or may not actually feel. Either the cat acts out of self-interest, in which case our feelings for it are irrelevant; or it recognizes in us a worth that has nothing to do with our behavior, in which case again it doesn't matter what we feel, or think we feel. The cat, most essentialist of animals, reassures us of the futility of self-examination.) And Madeleine loved most of all that which was catlike in herself, in other words, that which achieved freedom without struggle and independence without loneliness, and for all that never had to go long without food. This was a part of her which, since Nasérie left the convent, she felt had been very much neglected.

She was preparing to stroll indifferently across the garden when a deep voice cursed the gatekeeper and shouted: — Ai... ac! Then the speaker flung himself into the courtyard: a bearded

man in an apron and a low, round hat of the sort so rarely seen
in the convent that many of the nuns had forgotten altogether
that such hats were still manufactured, worn, and patched; they
stared at the intruder as though he were an apparition from
their pre-Revolutionary past. The man, for his part, pushed
past the sisters as though they were so many stumps or bales of
cloth. He shouted the same gargly phrase which, a moment
earlier, had been lost in the echoes of the porte cochere; for a
moment it seemed as though he were going to accost the
countess. — Ravaillac!★ one of the nuns cried, and swung her
broom so that it struck the stranger on the back of the legs just
above the knees. At this he turned so that the nuns saw his face;
two or three of them chose to leave then rather than risk looking at it again. Above the globular beard which covered his face
to the cheekbones, pits and sores pressed together so closely
that his eyes might have been two abscesses and his nose a red,
aquiferous boil. In contrast to the face of Saint Grimace—a
contrast which the nuns would make often in the following
weeks, although only in the privacy of their dreams and di-
aries—this living, shouting face seemed incapable of disappointment; it grinned, leered, stretched, opened its mouth as if
to bite. It was a face which expressed nothing but an endless
and undifferentiated appetite. In short, it was the face of a mad-
man. — My cat! it called. My cat Jacques! The stranger knelt
and plucked the cat from its spot at the basin's edge. Madeleine
forgot her saintly aloofness; she took a step forward, and another, to get a better look at the cat-loving lunatic, when
he turned to her, blinked, and roared: — O! O! Anne! Hey!
Anne!

He dropped the cat, which took advantage of the general
astonishment to escape into the city, the sparrow still dying in

★The mad monk who assassinated King Henry IV.

its mouth. Unnoticed by the nuns or by anyone else, the other cats followed.

What Armand saw: a ghost playing at being a ghost. A woman in a sheet—two sheets, perhaps, one black and the other white—walking toward him; a round, familiar face, smiling with curiosity. Armand, who, fifteen years ago, had settled a swaddled girl on the Bièvre's scummy surface, had endured many losses since then, the greatest of which perhaps was the loss of his sadness, and, with it, his reason. There had been Anne to put in the ground the day after her daughter was put in the water; then his workshop caught fire, and the firemen's pumps could pull no water from the river to put it out, as though the Bièvre, having saved Madeleine, would do him no more favors. Too drunk to learn another trade, he signed on as a beater of hides in the factory of his rival; nighttime often found him in an empty shed, swinging his stick at a calfskin already soft enough for ladies' gloves. So he persisted, getting thicker in the wrists and thinner everywhere else, until the cholera of 1849. It killed his rival outright and incapacitated all the chief assistants; the journeymen died in hospital, and such apprentices as remained after a month were carted off by anxious parents to the countryside. Only Armand was immune. He could have had the tannery then, if he wanted it; certainly no one would have had the courage to pluck the stick from his hands.

After Anne died, Armand, like his daughter, and for much the same reasons, discovered the love of cats. He began by feeding them and speaking in whispers to the street toms and piebald calicos who brushed his legs; then, wanting to engage in something more like conversation, he sat tailor-style on the floor and listened as best he could to what the cats were saying. He found that, like so many other things, understanding cats was mainly a matter of trust. Once they had accustomed themselves to seeing more of the tanner than his leather-aproned legs, the cats began to speak, at first among themselves and then, when they saw how carefully he copied the attitude of their listening heads, to Armand as well. They told him that they lived in a city of their own, coextensive with but not identical to the city of humans. The city of the cats was old in the way that only imaginary cities can be old; as there was nothing to it but myth it seemed to reach back to the farthest antiquity, when temples to Isis and Bast the cat goddess had been raised on the Île de la Cité. The cats told Armand that mice were, for all practical purposes, immortal; they hunted the same rodents that their ancestors had named and killed, and warned their offspring of the mice to be mistrusted and the rats to be hunted only by day. Armand took Jacques begging with him, and found that strangers were more likely to give a coin for the mouser's three legs than for his own carbuncled face. Were the cats immortal? Not exactly, Jacques said, although not quite mortal either. Were they their own ancestors, reborn? No, but their lives weren't exactly their own. Then whose? Ah, Jacques hissed, you should know, for this is where the city of the cats joins your city... Armand was informed that Paris's human dead returned as cats. Which meant that Anne? In some alley or courtyard of the night? Certainly, Jacques said; you have only to look. Nor should it surprise anyone that a cat said this: for cats, the indifferent mirrors of our wishes, are capable of the greatest lies. This was when Armand can be said truly to have lost his mind; to listen to cats is one thing, but to believe them is another. Full of hope, he followed his limping mouser about, dreaming of the day when he would again caress his wife.

What Sister Geneviève saw: a bearded Hun. Of course her name predisposed her to see every uninvited visitor as a barbarian. According to the *Vita Genofevæ*, it was Saint Geneviève, her namesake, who "convoked the young women, and engaged them in fasting, prayer, and vigils, in order that they could, like Judith and Esther, escape disaster," and so turned Attila and his army back from the gates of Paris. Such is the power of names. They are the blueprints from which the edifice of personality is built, and, like blueprints, names contain at least two views, plan and elevation: the name-as-word and the history of all previous namesakes. It might have been her name that drove Geneviève to gin* (although, given that she was born Josephine, and began drinking before she entered the convent, it's equally possible that gin drove her to Geneviève); it is certain that, when she saw Armand, there crossed her mind memories—were they her memories?—of offerings made at the city walls, great courage, the indomitable desire to repel. Yet history, given a theme, is prone more to improvisation than to repetition: for the fasting women we will have to make do with Madeleine, who had missed lunch; for vigils and prayer the countess and her attendant nuns will serve. And for the miracle of Attila's rout: Sister Geneviève, armed with a broom, beating the confused Armand until, staring all the while at Madeleine, he agreed to leave the courtyard.

Now we must give Armand some credit: before he turned to go, he had understood that the woman in the sheet must be not his wife but his daughter. Anne and not Anne, cat and not cat (Madeleine's cat love had given her, as it gives so many others, a slight squint, a wrinkled nose, and a mincing walk, the human expressions of felinity; and she had been born with fur! perhaps some trace of it remained on her, even then), his and not his.

All these things occurred to Armand at once, and he called out, pointing a finger no less magical in its effects than

*Or a pun on it: "juniper" in French is *genièvre*.

the Saint's, — I know that one! I knew her when she was a baby!

At which Sister Geneviève forgot her historical pretensions, and, twisting Armand's ear, replied, — Hardly!

But the tanner insisted: — My wife bore her! With my own arms I dropped her in the river! Jacques! Explain me this! I dropped her in the river and...

But Geneviève interrupted, and in any case the cat had already gone. — Hush! the nun said. And then: — Your wife?

Sister Geneviève was in conference with the Mother Superior all afternoon; then she went out and the other nuns were called in. Late at night the door to the Mother's office opened. A lozenge of light fell across the kitchen garden and Sister Nénuphar called Madeleine in. Armand stood in the corner of the office, rolling his eyes like a sheepish gargoyle. He had been pleased to find the world of convents even more marvelous than the world of cats, as the former involved something other than mice to eat, and wine to wash it down with too. He felt so complacent that he'd allowed the nuns to shave and scrub him until his face shone like a partly melted waxwork. With this face he grinned at Madeleine as the nun led her into the office. — Eh! my little girl! Sister Geneviève hissed at him to be still. Red-faced and listing as she walked, Geneviève had abandoned her historical role that afternoon for her second, punning namesake, gin. She ordered Madeleine to stand beside Armand, who smelt as strongly of soap now as he had before of sweat and piss.

— Stand still! Don't speak! enjoined Sister Geneviève. The Mother Superior rose from behind her desk. Apart from her role in the statue's ritual, Madeleine knew little about her. She gave occasional speeches to the sisters of Saint-Grimace on the subject of gnawing insects, but Madeleine had never listened for long enough to determine whether she meant the literal lice that infested the bedding periodically, or the figurative gnawing of vice whose cure was considerably more pleasant, involving as it did no stinging soap, no cold water nor hard brushes. The Mother must be terrified of vice and nits, Madeleine had thought with the superiority of a girl who, in her furred childhood, had seen plenty of both. Now the old woman poled herself across the room on an ebony cane, and reached up one gray hand to touch Armand's face. Her fingers did not shrink from the sores and pustules that covered the tanner's cheeks and brow, but took in the shape of each bump and bulge and ridge. Armand, the fool, closed his eyes and set his lips silently aquiver, praying probably, as though the Mother's touch were a blessing. And then—horror!—with the same hand that had touched the stranger's face, the Mother cupped Madeleine's chin. Her fingers, rough as stone and nearly as cold, found out the contours of the girl's face. Madeleine thought she could feel the gesture leaving slug tracks of oil on her clean, if not yet saintly, skin.

— Cheekbones, the Mother announced. A distinct resemblance. See for yourselves. First Nénuphar and then Geneviève repeated the ritual, touching Armand's face and then Madeleine's. Their warm fingers must have been less sure than the Mother's cold ones, for they each had to repeat their examination and then, as though to resolve a few little discrepancies, repeat it again. Madeleine, through all this, stood with her eyes shut and her nose disengaged as much as possible from her breathing. She did not want to smell the soaped-over sweat, wine, and cat smell the old man gave off more and more as time undid the nuns' ministrations. She endured the touching as a saint might have endured arrows, flames, prods, the iron tips of the screw, the pear, the cat, calling her to recant. Worse than their fingers, though, were their whispers. — A likeness, yes. —A family resemblance, Nénu said. — What? said Sister Eulalie.

— A family resemblance! You have only to feel their cheek-bones.

Even a saint might have faltered then. Madeleine was not a saint; she discovered in that moment that she had wanted nothing more than a respite from human affection and human sorrow. To be reminded, under such humiliating circumstances, that she could no more escape the one than the other, was more than she could bear. If she had wept, or argued—a family resemblance? How can you say that? Don't you know my mother is a duchess?—things might have gone differently. Saints are allowed to reason with their tormentors, and even cowardice has its place in the hagiographies, if only as something to be overcome. But Madeleine was mute, her face still, her eyes dry though very wide open.

No number of days in the library window could have prepared her for what happened next; it had so little to do with the stories she had read that she would never entirely trust stories again. First she grew hot all along the side where her father stood, then the heat became a prickling in her right armpit and a suspicious coolness of the crest of her forehead. Drops of sweat collected in her eyebrows and at the corners of her mouth; they slid down the side of her ribcage and followed the groove of her spine. At first Geneviève mistook the water for tears, and blinked at Madeleine kindly, but foreheads don't cry, nor do ears. Geneviève wiped her fingers on the sleeve of Madeleine's robe and gave the girl a look that made her sweat still more. Spots darkened her novice's gown. And still they kept talking about family resemblances and strange coincidences, and Armand mumbled, — Even more lovely than her mother! O my Anne, my poor poor Anne, if only she could see, so lovely!

Madeleine wanted him to stop; she wanted to be left alone, to collect herself, to be far away from this mouth that let her see how few teeth her father had, and how rotten they were. She wanted air more than anything.

— Hey! Girl! Armand called after her, and — Madeleine! cried Sister Geneviève. Even Nénuphar gave a surprised squeak. But Madeleine was free; she sprinted on cat feet down the stairs past the statue, through the convent gate. Ignoring all of them she raced into a bank of river fog and breathlessly welcomed the cool, criminal indifference of the street.

PART II

THE UNIVERSAL EXHIBITION

(1855)

6

HAUSSMANN'S WATCH

IT WAS AT THAT TIME that the boulevard Magenta cut cross-wise toward the Gare de Lyon, and the Bois de Vincennes joined the city by means of the rue Daumesnil; the boulevards Malesherbes, Barbès, Ornano, and la Villette spread like the fingers of a grasping hand into the northern suburbs. The thumb, the avenue de l'Impératrice (now the avenue Foch) was modestly conceived by the architect Hittorff. Haussmann scoffed: — Do you think, Monsieur, that His Majesty will be satisfied with your forty-meter boulevard? We need twice, three times that. Yes, I tell you three times: one hundred and twenty meters! And it was done. For in Paris at that time all gestures were exaggerated, as though the entire city were engaged in an amateur theatrical, doling out imaginary wealth to a succession of fakers and pretenders. For whose benefit was the show put on? Why, for the public, for the workingman and his statutory brother the bourgeois, for their wives and the little blond heads tousled by affectionate fatherly hands, for their mistresses and bastards and publicans and creditors and priests. For the public, the hubbub-breeding crowd, this parade of streets was mounted, to keep them happy while the Second Empire's censors censored,

while its spies spied. It was a command performance. Louis
Napoleon, the Emperor, wanted no more revolutions nor coups
d'état: he had lived through five regimes already and did not
relish the thought of a sixth. He had come to power on the
strength of a name which he inhabited like a gnome in a cathedral; he made every gesture large for fear it would not be seen
otherwise. He would have liked a war to lend the show some
glory, but the Empire depended on its banks, and the banks demanded peace.

Napoleon acquiesced, and with military precision attacked
the problem of Paris's inadequate streets and weed-choked
parks. He made Haussmann his field marshal in this campaign,
and the Baron obeyed him so thoughtfully that in many cases
the execution preceded the command. The Baron was not an
architect, nor a city planner, nor an engineer, nor a surveyor,
nor did he conceive utopias with his pen. Late in life, when
he'd been ousted from the prefecture for financial misdeeds,
Haussmann became the author of *An Administrative Campaign in
the Pyrénées*, a book of poems. It concludes with this moral:

> *All in all I wanted to show gaily*
> *That pleasure's not enough for man, but daily*
> *He must have at least the semblance of*
> *Undying love.*

About Haussmann's taste and imagination we need say no
more. In fact he seems to have had little to his credit but ambition, zeal, and the ability to go indefinitely without sleep. It
sufficed. Never had Paris seen a servant so devoted to public
works, or one so intent on getting them built. In addition to
the new boulevards, he drew up plans for three hundred and
twenty miles of sewers, which, if you consider that he built
only forty miles of streets, means that Paris was Haussmannized

eight times as much belowground as above. This was Haussmann's one truly original contribution to the city's well-being.
Where others saw the sewers as one ditch and another, he conceived of a network flowing from every storm drain, privy, and
urinal in Paris to a single Great Collector which would channel
the city's shit eight miles downstream to Achères, where no one
had enough influence to send it away. Then there were the wa-
terworks, and the plans for a new cemetery... They said that if
you passed the Hôtel de Ville at any hour of the night you'd
find one window still lit yellow: Haussmann's. Even when he
was in favor they said he was always plotting something. Indeed, when in 1855 Queen Victoria paid a visit to the Universal Exhibition, Haussmann put on a show so magnificent it
would have justified a lifetime of insomnia.

Tonight Baron Haussmann is giving the party of the year, the
party of the decade if the newspapers are to be believed. Everyone is here: the seven thousand most important people in Paris
and London and their various hangers-on, lackeys, manservants,
astrologers, secretaries, mistresses, corset tighteners and bearers
of smelling salts, not to mention gate crashers, wine stewards,
spies, and the correspondent from the *Illustrated Girls' Gazette*,
who's here to keep tabs on the fashions of the great. Invitations
litter the red carpet of the foyer, where a velvet pavilion bears
the twined insignia of England and France. All wars have been
forgotten for the event, that of 1812 as that of 1756–63; even
the War of Jenkins' Ear has been forgotten, and veterans on
both sides of the Channel have polished their ivory prosthetics
to make a good show of the peace. Ten thousand guests and half
of them in crinoline: if the fabric from the ladies' gowns were
sewn together into a single tent, it would cover the entire city
of Paris and the muddy fields of the suburbs from Neuilly to

Vincennes. The men, of course, wear black; in their dusky ranks
shine the sashes of ambassadors, the gold of military decorations
and the silver of civic insignia. The light from torches, gas jets,
chandeliers, sconces, and candles is reflected from nearly three
thousand bald pates, half again as many lorgnettes, not a few
glass eyes and of course the gold and silver noses of syphilitics,
as well as a single pair of ruby spectacles... But we're not ready
to meet those eyes yet. Not until we've heard the gossip: how
the Count de Morny is in on a scheme to buy up the back
streets of what will become the Trocadéro and sell them to the
city at a profit, and what handicaps are given for Sunday's race
at Longchamp. They say Queen Victoria is enjoying herself
tonight and finds Paris quite *feënhaft*, yes, she's German don't
you know? You can't trust a name to tell you much these days;
for instance Haussmann is no more German than you or I, and
the Count de Morny's no count at all, but the bastard son of
old Queen Hortense. Anyway the aristocracy's all rot; if you
want real nobility, look no farther than the gold chamber pot
being borne through the crowd. It belongs to the Baron James
de Rothschild, yes, he brings it with him everywhere, it's a
foible of his never to shit on base metal. We all have our peculiarities! Now the Emperor's weakness is for cigarettes; he keeps
them, loose, in the pockets of his coat and fishes them out one
by one as though each were to be his last, and after it the scaffold. No one can fathom the Emperor. Some say he's a socialist
and others that he's a tyrant; even his closest friends feel one
way about him when they wake up and another when they go
to bed. He keeps quiet in public, but perhaps that's because he's
been to prison, yes, as a youth, for conspiring to overthrow the
government, locked away in the Fort of Ham—which wasn't
easy for an ambitious young man to swallow. If you look carefully you can see the bars still in his eyes. Rothschild stands
behind him, and behind Rothschild stands Pereire, another

banker. That's de Morny behind Pereire—doesn't he look like the Emperor, a bit? Of course they're half-brothers, yes, Queen Hortense is mother to both. Scandalous! But we can't complain; if it weren't for scandal we'd have nothing to talk about. Who's the tall fellow behind de Morny, who looks as glum as a Jansenist at the ballet? Why, that's Haussmann. It's his show.

Imagine again the tent of ruffled crinoline in half a hundred shades of blue, rose, and gold. Call it a circus tent; the city's a circus with three circles corresponding to the three rings of fortifications built by long-dead kings to keep the barbarians at bay (for kings, unlike nuns, can't count on miracles): the Picturesque Poor of the suburbs; the Bourgeois Spectacle of the new boulevards, the banks and offices; and the inmost circle, the Aristocratic Entertainment of the Louvre, the Tuileries, the Palais-Royal. At the center of the circus you'd find Haussmann. Haussmann the Magnificent, the papers call him. He is the largest official of the Second Empire: well over six feet tall and broad as a wrestler; his thick neck and wide shoulders look as though they could bear the weight of the tentpole from which the whole show depends. In fact they support a head of medium size, nearly bald on top but ringed below by a fringe of dark hair like a helmet strap, the moustacheless beard which he grew to conceal his youth, and now, at the age of forty-six, maintains to conceal its passing. The rest of his features belong neither to youth nor to age (his photograph at twenty-two hardly differs from his photograph at eighty), but to a willful changelessness found most often in doctors, priests, and civil servants, who become old as soon as they accept their duties, and spend the rest of their lives waiting for the world to catch up.

The science of physiognomy has identified the chief components of the Baron's character as follows. Reserve as indicated by the backward straining of the neck and the lobeless ears; nobility betokened by the straight nose and high, though not protruding forehead. Sagacity can be seen in the size of the eyes and their distance from one another, which is slightly greater than average though not so great as to suggest a double or disjoint vision of the world. The even set of the mouth belies a scorn of obstacles. More could be learned if decorum didn't prohibit touching the Baron's head. From the bumps of his skull a phrenologist could tell you that his temples are crowned with patience, and circumspection is discreetly present in the orbits of his eyes; a slight overdevelopment of the back of the skull suggests a sensitivity, perhaps unconscious, to smell, memory, and regret.

Regret? Yes, Haussmann has lost his watch. This is the source of all his unhappiness; it's why he shifts uneasily from one foot to the other, shaking his wide shoulders like a wrestler who's just freed himself of the mat. It's why he can hardly exchange a single bon mot with the notoriously witty de Morny, who has been remarking on the similarity between certain women of Victoria's entourage and certain horses who will be racing the next day at Longchamp. Pereire whispers to him the details of a scheme for selling houses twice: once to a dummy Housing Fund and then to their eventual tenants, with the City of Paris collecting a small percentage on each transaction (don't be shocked! schemes like this were the order of the day, and Pereire wasn't the worst of the lot: I could tell you about the contractor who put his arsonist on the municipal payroll, or of the surveyors who cluttered the city with imaginary buildings, itemized in every particular, on whose demolition they collected a very real fee—to say nothing of the man whose red spectacles turn even now toward the platform where Haussmann stands...).

To Pereire's offer Haussmann replies in circumspect monosyllables, giving the banker to understand that the pockets of

Paris are deep enough without his fictitious fund. — Haussmann the incorruptible, Pereire laughs, when will you line your own pockets? When? The Baron pats his fob. He could have sworn that the watch was with him when he came downstairs to receive the first guests, that he'd had it in his pocket during the long and, if he could say so without fear of being misunderstood, the excessive dinner he'd given the Queen. — When I can't afford to pay my tailor, Monsieur, Haussmann replies. Pereire smiles at the Baron's wit as though it were a bug which he, again and again, was compelled to swallow.

In a minute the Emperor concludes his speech about Anglo-French harmony with a remark that his engineers are drawing up plans for a drawbridge over the Pas de Calais. The English, horrified, clap politely; Victoria curtsies and declines to respond. The little knot of schemers breaks free of the platform and disperses, rejoining the crowd. De Morny takes his place among the touts, and Pereire, distracted, nearly collides with Rothschild's chamber pot. Haussmann shoulders his way among his ten thousand guests, smiling no more than he must, his mind on the absent watch.

Under any other circumstances he would shrug and buy himself a gold repeater or silver-chased self-winder with diamonds scattered like stars across the face, not because Haussmann the private citizen would like such a watch but because it seems to him that the Prefect of Paris should pull nothing less from his vest to end an audience with *gravitas*, a quality more valuable than gold or diamonds to a civic administrator. Because the watch would belong to his Prefectoral self he could bill it to the city. He'd leave it to the city, of course, when he retired, a part of what he already imagines as the Haussmann Collection, housed in the glass cases of the Louvre museum or at least cataloged in the National Archives. This particular watch would be a showpiece of the collection. It was a gift from the

English Queen, to thank Haussmann for the avenue Victoria, christened just the day before. — You'll find it less diligent than yourself, my dear Baron, the Queen said, for I'm told that it loses a minute or two every year. She pressed the heavy gold disk into his hand and brushed his wrist with her spatulate fingers—a troll, the Queen, if the truth be told, but a queen nonetheless and a lady with whom—where's a clock?—Haussmann will, in a few minutes, have to dance. To appear before her without the watch would seem forgetful, or, worse, ungrateful. He must take it from his coat and say: Your Highness, they say your quadrille is as beautiful as clockwork. That's his line, the one he wrote for himself. When his aide-de-camp hears it, the orchestra will receive the signal and the quadrille will begin. Even if, as they said, the Queen dances as her soldiers fight, with a one! two! and have-at-you! the ball will continue as planned, as Haussmann has planned.

So the Baron wanders the halls of the Hôtel de Ville like a distracted automaton, poor devil. We won't follow him. Turn your attention instead to the scaffold he commissioned for the courtyard, an edifying piece of showmanship.

It rises from a basin of clearest water: not the Seine's muddy effluence, nor the chalky water pumped from local artesian wells—corpse water, some call it, as the rain filters through Paris's graveyards on its way to the water table, collecting a pale color and a faint sulfurous reek. You would think that only the poor and ignorant would drink this murky stuff, but you would only be half right. Eau de Montmartre, Eau de Montparnasse, Eau Père-Lachaise, the runoff from Paris's cemeteries was bottled and sold to the general public as a cure-all, a tonic enriched by the soluble parts of the virtuous dead. Benighted holy water! Pestiferous placebo! protested the Academy of Medicine, but to no avail. Parisians bought the murky stuff by the magnum, drank it down, and filled their children's cups with the overflow. In the long-gone year of 1855, *requiescat in pacem,* Parisians still needed to be close to the dead, to drink the dead.

Haussmann has plans to change all that. He will draw water from far off by means of an aqueduct which would have made the Romans proud, and let the dead flow where they will, onward, out of sight. In the meantime he makes do with water carted by the barrel from the Somme-Soude springs in Champagne, where corpse drinking is not the custom. Above the basin (from which, in the end, no one drank, although one of de Morny's nephews will attempt late in the evening to swim across it, and nearly drown, proving to the crowd the natural affinity of water for corpses) rises a double staircase, a replica of the one at Fontainebleau; its arms reach out as if to embrace visitors both insular and Continental. Atop the staircase, statues of France and England wave benediction to their assembled citizens; at the two nations' feet recline the nymphs Seine and Thames, bearing urns of the same clear water. They pour it into the basin; it is commixed, mingles, recirculates so that Thames flows from Seine's mouth and vice versa. *Feënhaft,* simply *feënhaft,* Victoria clucks to her entourage: as in a fairy-tale Paris and London are united (and better a fairy-tale, the entourage clucks back, than a drawbridge!). Haussmann's decor smacks to the public of Allegory; to those who know the Baron's passion for sanitation, however, it speaks of Public Works.

Outside the Hôtel de Ville, the Angles and the Franks mingle not in symbol but in liquor. What a spectacle! Paris teeming with Englishmen, come to see what the French have been up to since Eleanor of Aquitaine. For the first time the drinking classes cross the Channel to revel in the hot theaters and dank hotels which for the first time bear handwritten placards an-

nouncing that *here English speaks*. The first tourist hotels have
opened their already mildewed rooms to the petty bourgeoisie;
the sharps and shills make hay of such green visitors, and the
prostitutes carry phrasebooks to help them chat with English
and American gentlemen. *Je vous aime* means I like you, *vingt
francs* means Twenty francs and *quarante francs* means More than
that; when in doubt *Que dites-vous* means What is that meant to
mean? *Bonjour, monsieur. La nuit? Une heure?* Would you like to
come for a walk? *Quoi?*

But leave the prostitutes for a moment, and walk with me
through the Exhibition Hall, a palace of glass and iron on the
Champs-Élysées. Here you'll see whirring motors and rubber
wheels; in a pavilion all its own you'll find a magnificent example of the dark box, the camera that conjures the world into a
piece of paper. You'll find portraits of your charming French
youth standing riverside with a paddle—or is it a fan?—and
one leg in a skiff of the sort you'd heard still troll the Seine for
eels. You'll notice the girl whose ghostly photograph peers at
you from the inside of a locket, like the Shroud of Turin but
with tits; it might be another of the relics you've heard the pa-
pists carry around (aren't the teeth of saints trafficked in a secret
market in the basement of the Bourse?). There are pictures here
for the whole family: castles for the little ones and landscapes
for the sighing wife who's always wanted to go on a sketching
tour, well, Pardi! as they say here, let her sketch from photographs! You wish you were rid of the wife, for you've heard it's
jolly after sunset, when there's a Life Show in the Bal Mabille,
and girls come round asking if you wouldn't like to join in the
chorus, if you know what I mean.

At sundown you've had enough of the Exhibition Hall—
what's vulcanized rubber to a man with love on his mind?—so
you breach the gas-lit dark of the Champs-Élysées. Here's
theater! Half the city strolling arm in arm with the other half,

and not a few Englishmen among them. They shout to you that
they fell on their backs at Offenbach's; you must see the show!
These Parisians make fun of themselves almost as well as the
English do, and to music. The street pulls you straight along to
the cheap restaurants of the Palais-Royal, where you don't have
to think about what to order because everyone gets the same
thing, now *there's* a republican invention! and when you've had
your thigh—or was it breast—of well-spiced beast, you send
the wife back to the hotel and with new friends decide to
make a night of it at the Bal Mabille, for the girl in the locket
has printed her image in the camera obscura of your heart.
There's metaphor! Now you're thinking like a modern gentleman, like a citizen of the world.

The clock in the courtyard prepares a new hour. Haussmann
has been everywhere, from the banquet room where servants
disencumber the long tables of tureens and the carcasses of
birds, to the salons where all Paris is sacking his cellar, fortified
against the occasion with tuns of Bordeaux. He has begun to
suspect conspiracy in the disappearance of the watch. Someone
might have guessed his intention and stolen his prop, his line,
his part. For Haussmann there are no failures of design; there
is only one design superimposed upon another, replacing the
parts it covers, lines obscuring and obscured by other lines.
Who might have taken the watch? The Baron has enemies
enough: Rothschild doesn't trust him, and Pereire would like to
replace him with a less honest Prefect; but this isn't their sort of
mischief. Unreasonably—her little hands have been nowhere in
the vicinity of his vest—the Baron thinks of the new Empress,
Eugénie. It is easy to think the worst of her. Born Eugénia de
Montijo, a Spanish noblewoman, the Empress's rude, foreign-
inflected French and haughty manners recall, unpleasantly,

Marie-Antoinette, and make the Parisians pine for the guillotine. Even Haussmann, devoted to the Emperor, does not see
eye to eye with her; for that the diminutive Eugénie would
need a platform scarcely less high than the one Haussmann
commissioned for the courtyard. For the Baron, on the other
hand, to be on an equal footing with the Empress, presumed
mother of a presumed dynasty, Haussmann would have to step
onto the imperial dais where Louis Napoleon and Eugénie
stand arm in arm: this is precisely what the Baron is unable to
do, as all the portraits of the three of them attest. The Baron
must stand, his knee bent, inclining from the waist, while Louis
Napoleon extends a charitable hand to receive some document
from his favorite Prefect. The Empress, meanwhile, stares down
at Haussmann, extending her fan as if to ward him off. Strange
that such heights should separate them, for they shared a godfather: the old Prince Eugène, Napoleon's uncle, was guarantor of
Georges-Eugène and Eugénie's good breeding. But names do
not give us everything; they supply us at most with a disposition to nobility, drink, the repelling of barbarians. If names are
the plans, then we are the contractors, building mysterious edi-
fices with the materials at hand.

(In any case there is a good explanation for Eugénie's elevation: as a girl she was friends with writers. Stendhal bounced
her on his knee; Mérimée took her on secret missions to the
pastry shops of the rue du Bac. Haussmann, on the other hand,
could count only one literary mind among his acquaintances:
the poet de Musset, a classmate whom he had scorned even as
a child. If only he had known the secret key to imperial favor:
befriend writers! Then he might have lived his life differently.
He might have joined a salon, dandled poetesses, got drunk in
that other Paris which his boulevards at once engendered and
replaced: a crawling agglomeration of cutthroat cafés, flop-
houses, whorehouses, cold beds, lice, prison, crutch-hopping
beggars, lethal water, absinthe, and so on. But he did not know;

and so he resented Eugénie for having the Emperor's ear—and Eugénie resented him as well, because he was overbearing, tall, and Protestant.)

At last Haussmann, certain that a plot has been mounted against him, hurries to the upstairs bedroom where his wife is reading. Octavie, the next-to-oldest daughter of a rich Bordeaux merchant, was never beautiful, but age has thickened her body so that there's hardly a curve left in it: square-chinned and wide-waisted even in a corset, she looks mannish and uncomfortable, as though she were the prisoner of her brown dress. Octavie doesn't have much use for fashion. She's accustomed to quiet, the smell of horses, and the conversation of a family whose assets are all material. Paris, with its wild crowds of speculators staking other people's fortunes on the mortgages of hypothetical buildings, leaves her with the giddy disappointment of having won a prize at a carnival, which, when collected, turns out to be only a roll of scrip thick enough to strand her all night among the torches and clowns.

— On the lam, Father? Keeping Octavie company tonight is his younger daughter Fanny-Valentine, Valentine for short. Although she looks a little like her mother, and a little more like her father, Valentine is beautiful, as though everything ugly and superfluous in her parents had been polished away, revealing in their child a beauty latent in each of them. Her character has an unexpected charm, too: she's stubborn, unkindly witty or wittily unkind, depending on her mood, and quick to anger, but quick also to understand, and, Haussmann thinks, to forgive. She is his accomplice in the great scheme that is Paris, and she is dearer to him than watches or words.

— From all but you, Valentine. He kisses her cheek. Then, to Octavie, — Have you seen my watch, my love? He speaks quickly in order to forestall what he regards as her conversational excesses.

—Your what?

— My watch, the one I was given by the English Queen.

Octavie smiles. If only he could hear how he said those words, English Queen, as though so many queens gave him watches that he would have to wear a half-dozen vests to accommodate them all. And if he had six watches he'd do it, she thinks. — Isn't it in its box? In Octavie's carnival, Haussmann is a sort of juggler in reverse, constantly putting objects down and not finding them again.

It is in its box. — Thank you, my love. Haussmann always treats his wife civilly. For a civil servant it pays to be civil, ha! and especially to women, he thinks, and so, civilly, he bows, blows a kiss to Valentine and leaves. Octavie smiles at the sound of his heavy feet racing downstairs just as the bells of Saint-Gervais strike the hour into place.

At the bottom of the stairs the Baron is arrested by a cripple in red spectacles. His upper body is thick as a bricklayer's; his dusty coat harbors arms that look capable of plucking the knobs from balustrades the way a child pulls fruit from a tree. His legs, in contrast, are thin and infirm, as though he were a paralytic recently healed by faith; wide trousers spotted with road dust cannot conceal the gnarl of his knees, nor his glossy boots the burl of a deformed foot. His ruddy face is dry as stone. A man worth at most twenty thousand francs, thinks Haussmann, and half of that tied up in some miserable provincial estate. He must be one of those who bought their invitation to the ball, and considered it a wise investment, too, hoping for a return in gossip and influence. Haussmann, however, has no time to dispense. Five strokes of the hour's ten have already sounded; he must be on his way to the waiting Queen. He tries to step around the cripple, but the man will not be passed; he bows to the Baron and holds out his large hand, on which some small gold object lies. — Monsieur, he murmurs, you've forgotten your watch chain.

So he has, in his hurry, and a pity it is, too, for the Baron still wears the cheap fob chain he bought when he was secretary-general of the Vienne, his first administrative post. Though the rest of the Baron's wardrobe has been altered by his circumstances, on the subject of the chain he remains inflexible. Secretly he imagines the tag it will bear when the Haussmann Collection is displayed: "Ordinary Chain. This curious, rather cheaply made watch chain was the sign of Haussmann's honesty: though great sums of money passed through the Baron's purview, in his heart he retained the incorruptibility of a poor man." Well, but it's too late to go back upstairs and retrieve his own chain from the carping Octavie. He plucks the links from the other's dry palm, nods a thank you, and hurries as the clock strikes to attend to the business of dancing with the trollish Queen.

Only the correspondent from the *Illustrated Girls' Gazette*, who has kept out of sight all evening for fear that someone will discover he wasn't invited, witnesses this meeting, and he doesn't know what to make of it. Fortunately his beat is fashion, not politics. His article tomorrow will be on the Empire of the Crinoline, and he will content himself with the observation that there are many things in a modern lady's dress that, on the face of them, are difficult to understand.

7

THE DEMOLITION ARTIST

HOW EASY IT IS to misjudge character! Everything leads us to it, and first of all ourselves. We are so often misjudged, our grace mistaken for reserve and our fear for ambition, that we think other people must be as simple as they think we are. Haussmann had been in the public eye since the age of twenty-two, when he charmed all the daughters in the Vienne and outraged their fathers by building roads through their land. No wonder, then, that he saw nothing but pretension and mediocre means in the man whose watch chain he wore. In fact the eyes that followed the Baron and Queen as they stomped carefully through the quadrille belonged to the great demolition man, de Fonce.

Fonce was his birth name; he picked up the noble *de* on his way out of the Auvergne along with a thorough knowledge of every kind of hunger. What he had been before that is not important. Call him a blacksmith, for it would explain the reach of his arms, the girth of his wrists, and the fact that no muggy river breeze nor blasting noonday sun could make him perspire. He was one of those who, arriving in Paris with a grimy, tattered past dragging behind him like an old scarf, decided to get rid of it altogether and replace it with something more im-

pressive. Later, when he had built his fortune (or, more properly: when he had torn it down), stories would straggle in from
the provinces like poor relatives, demanding a share of the
spoils. It was said that Fonce had been a barber-surgeon's child,
and learned early the twin arts of coiffure and bloodletting. His
talent might have spent itself in the Auvergne, where a blood-
less population of shaved, trimmed, waxed, and curled heads
would have attested to its prodigiousness, but for a happy misfortune. When Fonce was ten the cholera visited his home in
the form of a contagious aristocrat, who stumbled from the box
of his carriage into the surgeon's parlor, where he lived long
enough to drink from a bowl, vomit onto the floor, and complain about the weather. Then he succumbed to the common-
est of diseases, and, *noblesse oblige,* passed it on to Fonce's
parents. After a course of self-administered leeching, they threw
in the towel and left the boy to his godfather in Clermont-
Ferrand, an insomniac blacksmith who escaped cholera as he
had revolution, republic, and empire, by never leaving the confines of his forge.

  Apprenticed for nine years, Fonce learned to hunger for the
light. His master, who had studied the Greek and Norse legends extensively, held that the business of smithery was best
conducted in darkness. Not once in the course of his apprenticeship was young Fonce allowed out into the town. By day he
slept and at dusk his master woke him with stern stories of
Jotunheim, land of the trolls. Whether the stories drove him to
it or whether it was the darkness was disputed by the gossips.
They agreed, however, that after nine years the apprentice
Fonce put his master to rest with a hammer, and escaped to the
main square of Clermont-Ferrand, to wait for the sunrise. But
nine years of forge light had weakened his eyes; the journeyman smith found that he could see only through the red lenses
which made of the sun another forge.

  He was spotted in Saint-Étienne, playing tambourine in

front of the church—and the girls of Saint-Étienne, they said, danced for Fonce without knowing it; for already he had learned the trick of putting himself at the center of things. Hunger for position soon gave way to other appetites: mothers in the cottages by the Rhône still tell the story of the red-spectacled tinker who lured half the riparian girls into his cart of pots and pans; there must have been a saint looking out for the girls, though, for none bore him children. In Lyons, where the hunger for money is so old and so long unsatisfied that it has hardened into the stones of the place Bellecour and the accentless French which is the Lyonnais nobleman's last currency, they say he played a blind palmist. He must have specialized in the prediction of disaster, for when he left Lyons (hounded out, some say, by agents of the Archbishop), so many door knockers were muffled in black crêpe that a doctor, passing through the city, would have diagnosed an epidemic. Heir de facto to a dozen aristocratic suicides, Fonce became de Fonce and came to Paris.

He might have been a thief of ruins, for they flourished in Paris at that time: men in drab frock coats who scoured the city at night for plaster, timber, and rubble. Many from the Auvergne took up that trade, for in their impoverished province everything had a value; they got rich on what others mistook for debris. In carts with oiled wheels they plied Paris's streets at night, collecting Baroque masonry and Renaissance timber to sell to the builders of the Second Empire, or, failing that, as wood and coal. The ambitious among the Auvergnats soon did their work by daylight; they won the contracts to dispose of entire buildings, and the contracts to tear them down. In drab frock coats still (your Auvergnat is a notorious miser), they bullied their workers, who with mattocks, spikes, and chisels prised apart the stonework of the last century and the century before that.

Not a few of these demolition men got rich, as there was no
shortage of tearing down to be done in Paris; for each street
Haussmann drew onto the map there were a half-dozen alleys
to be erased. The canniest of the lot, however, saw that connoisseurship would bring them still greater gains. To recognize
which fittings had value and which were best sold as scrap; to
distinguish the patina of age from a wash of cheap chemicals:
on this knowledge a profit could be turned. Better still to have
the sort of imagination that can dislocate objects from their
surroundings at will. If you see that the nest of drawers built
into a butler's pantry could be set to advantage in a boudoir, or
that the empty rooms of a flophouse are watched by a Renaissance cherub, then demolition is only the beginning of your
work: it is salvage that brings in the great rewards. For cities,
like people, prize most what they have just lost. The demolition
men became antiquarians, scavengers, and thieves who waved
their permits about as though they had been given a unique
license to the past. The stories of their ruses would fill an
account longer than this one. There is the one about the contractor Thome, who, in order to expropriate a recalcitrant tenant from his suburban home, had an exact replica of the house
built a few miles off in Neuilly, and under cover of darkness
transplanted the man's prize magnolias from the one garden to
the other; the man, a gardener by avocation, had no choice but
to follow his plants. Then there is the story of the enterprising
Guillaumot, who, by means of a sheaf of false deeds, convinced
a young couple that everything in their house had been expropriated, from the slate tiles of the roof to the slippers in the
bride's trousseau—and, some said, including the bride as well; it
was announced as a certainty that the young couple's marriage
lasted no longer than the house in which it was consummated.

Of all the city's demolition men, however, none was more
feared than de Fonce. His eyes, half-hidden by the tint of his

glasses, were uncannily sharp: show him a lock, his allies boasted, and de Fonce would draw you the key. He distinguished a Louis XV from a Louis XVI with no more difficulty than you or I tell the difference between red and green. In a soot-black square of canvas he could make out the portrait of a girl—and sell the portrait, too, black as it was, for he could tell you just how she held her head, to one side as though she'd seen something just behind your shoulder, and how she smiled as if to welcome it and at the same time held up her hand palm outward as if to ward it off. In the end you saw it, too.

On the strength of his eyes the demolition man grew rich. He sold so many smoke-black portraits and half-finished statues that his taste began to constitute a sort of style. If, in the foyer of some banker or newly moneyed civil servant, you saw a rough-edged slab of marble carved with what might have been the bas-relief of a hand; or if at the top of the stairs you found a tapestry of dusty, featureless wool in which your host pointed out hunting scenes and unicorns, then you would nod and say to yourself, de Fonce. And if you were like most rich Parisians of the time you would apply the next morning to the bureau where the demolition man received his clients: a dark, almost dingy room, entirely without ornament—because, de Fonce would explain, his honorable clients demanded so much that he could keep nothing for himself. De Fonce himself would usher you in; he wasn't proud. He would ask you to sit and explain to you in a rough voice (the relic, it's rumored, of his days in the forge) that within the city you inhabit there is another, of inestimable beauty: the city, Monsieur, of the overlooked. To this city de Fonce would offer himself as your guide. You would leave him poorer than you came, but in possession of something—a cornice, a balustrade, or a weather-eaten wooden figurine—which neither you nor anyone else had ever seen.

De Fonce knew his clients; he saw the same thing within

each of them: a ruin and a purse. For the secret of the demolition man's business was this, that people appeared no differently to him than did buildings. Each presented one face to the world and another to its tenant, without one view being for all that more real than the other. Each accommodated a number of appetites with varying success: in some it was the salon which was best-appointed; in others the kitchen, and in others the boudoir. Each had its secret places: not only, or even particularly, the attics and closets, but the view from the corner of a room, the spaces that reveal themselves when you stand where no one was meant to stand, the perspectives that hide where everyone can see them, but no one does. And the fittings! Their variety was almost without end. How could the four grades of oak compare with the sixteen classes of regret (for de Fonce, scorning the work of contemporary psychologists, had devised his own system for classifying the furniture of the mind): the mellow revisiting of tragic circumstances; the rich longing for voyages not made when one was young and the short-lived bitterness of a retort not spoken in time, which we, intuiting perhaps de Fonce's way of seeing things, call *esprit de l'escalier.* Just as a building becomes rich in artifacts right before it is demolished, so de Fonce found that he was best able to exploit his connoisseurship of human character by imagining those he met as near their ends. The demolition man addressed himself to a banker as he would to a dying patriarch, and to a civil servant as to a soldier polishing his boots the night before a battle with the Turk; he coddled artists as though they were already coughing their last lung blood onto ladies' handkerchiefs, and to physicians he sold pier glasses with the solemnity of an orderly counting out drops of morphine. He was, in fact, a perfect psychologist of last wishes, such as there had never been and may never be again.

What did the demolition man see in Haussmann's hurried

frown, his stride, his changeless face? It is not known. But in
the weeks that followed, de Fonce—or, more often, de Fonce's
friends—could be overheard asking questions about the Prefect. They learned that Haussmann could not be bought, that
he was unhappy with Octavie, that he had two daughters and
no sons; that the Prefect liked the opera and that he entertained
himself now and then by watching the demonstrations of turning tables, knocking spirits, mystical writers, and clairvoyants
which were all the rage in those days. When his friends told de
Fonce these things, they found him no more surprised than if
he'd rubbed the tarnish from an old goblet and found underneath the glint of gold.

A month passed and Paris, nearly sleepless in the long summer
light, swelled with visitors to the Exhibition. Contracts were
entered into for the purchase of cameras and telegraphs; archi-
tects returned to their drafting tables and with vague prescience
began to see what might be done with iron; the Bal Mabille
was consumed by fire after some guest—an Englishman, the
proprietor told the police; but the English papers made it out
to be a Prussian—bet a man that he could balance a kerosene
lamp on his nose and lost. The demolition men put on a sort of
exhibition of their own, tearing down half of three buildings
on what would become the boulevard Magenta, so that, like di-
agrams, their interiors stood exposed. The guts of buildings! In
them we see how Paris lived at the time: family crowded upon
family and a shop on the ground floor. Above the shop, wealth
and altitude were inversely proportional, as though the poor,
fulfilling nearly two millennia of virtuous expectation, had at
last become only lightly attached to the earth, and bobbed
against the cracked roofs of their garrets like aerostats, held
down only by skylights and children. Below the maids, painters,

plasterers, sculptors, letter writers, and one-room families of the garret were the modest apartments of the petite bourgeoisie, who measured soap in beakers that two centuries ago would have been the envy of every alchemist in the world. Here mothers listened enviously to the thin carpet which shook with piano notes rising from the apartments where frocked children took lessons in measures, scales, notes, and keys, the counting-houses of culture. The rich children listened in turn for the up-stairs children's feet pattering in petit bourgeois games and dances; the dancers whispered about the ladies who came to visit the sculptor in his chalky hidey-hole; the sculptor admired the half-clean faces of the children and remembered the limit-less mistakes it was possible to make with a piano. In short, this is Paris as it was before Haussmann: everything and everyone together. The sentiment of unity is strongest just before it disap-pears, for no one can stand unity too long: loneliness too is an appetite, and so we tear ourselves away even from bliss for the dumb pleasure of inspecting our own ragged edges. De Fonce, schooled in every appetite, could have told Haussmann as much; so could Madeleine.

Even Haussmann must have had some intimation that things were about to change when, one evening at the end of June 1855, an unliveried carriage rolled into the courtyard of the Hôtel de Ville, and the occupant (whom the sentries would afterward describe as soldierly, the footmen as aristocratic, and the housemaids as gallant, although to the unprejudiced eye he was nothing more than a broad-shouldered cripple, neither shabbily nor modishly dressed) sent word that he had come to reclaim his watch chain.

Ha! thought Haussmann, the fellow probably needs it to se-cure a loan. —Well, send him in, send him in, he told the foot-man, and at once regretted it: what if the man asked him for money?

But de Fonce did nothing of the sort. Indeed, he rather looked as though he would be happy to help Haussmann out with a gold napoleon or two if the Baron should ever have need of it. He apologized profoundly for having to take the watch chain back, but it was a gift from a lady, and under the circumstances...Was the Baron a romantic? The question caught Haussmann off-guard. — That is to say, sir, do you believe in the supremacy of Nature in the individual soul?

Well, Haussmann would allow that Nature had her place there, but in modern man it was less a forest than a park.

— Very like your Bois de Boulogne, eh?

— Well, laughed the Baron, if you like; indeed, in some courtiers he found that Nature took up no more room than a flowerpot on a windowsill.

— Ah! de Fonce laughed, the Nature within may be a flower indeed, but then she is a heliotrope, always turning toward the greater Nature without.

Their conversation, though it settled on no topic in particular, opened vast and crowded prospects within each subject it touched upon, like a colonial mail boat which lights here and there on the barely settled edges of an unfamiliar continent. It was well after midnight when de Fonce begged his leave of Haussmann, having come to the end of his own poor stock of ideas, and being unwilling to indebt himself any farther to the Baron's vastly greater hoard. They agreed to meet again as soon as it was convenient (the following week, as it proved), and again, and, still without having agreed on anything, Haussmann found himself possessed of a commodity scarcer than watch chains: he had a friend. Evening joined evening like pearls on a string; their pleasant and natural arrangement suggested to Haussmann that he and de Fonce had something important in common, though he couldn't say exactly what it was. Perhaps it was no more than a high estimation of the value of watch chains, or perhaps what drew the Baron and de Fonce together was the knowledge of incipient loss: one man with his eye on the city's future, and the other with a regard for the past.

But whose eye was whose? Or were the mismatched acquaintances, the one tall as an athlete, the other stooped as a buttress, like those mythical sisters who share a single eye, and, passing it from hand to hand, see wonders which none—having no idea that sight persists even after the eye has left their skulls—can describe? Among the topics of their conversation were: the sky (in which de Fonce, Haussmann noted with satisfaction, was as prone to see patterns as he was himself: horsetails of cloud mean changing weather; a fine day in November means trouble ahead), the state of the city (about which each said little, being afraid to say too much), the dancers at the Opéra, and the twentieth century. Later, the Baron could not remember how they came to the subject. Indeed, he found himself so closely in accord with de Fonce that he could never remember who had begun a given conversation. Ideas simply came into being between them, the way a spark appears between glass rod and silk scarf. That, the Baron thought, had been de Fonce's metaphor for it.

The demolition man was indeed possessed of a remarkable eye for the future; it was only natural that, as the Baron had his own sense of what was to come (take note, reader, that in his letters to Napoleon III he seems to predict the fall of the Second Empire and the loss of the Franco-Prussian War), they end up discussing not only their century but the one after. In this way certain differences emerged between them. De Fonce argued science, progress, and order: he predicted the rise of a global railway, transatlantic aerostats, a universal language like a second Latin that would be spoken in every continent by the operators of the telegraph. Georges-Eugène, whether for argument's sake or because de Fonce drew out his hidden convictions, took a metaphysical view of things. He told de Fonce about the fluid said to flow through sleepwalkers' brains, and wondered if some device might be found to channel it, a general collector for dreams; he spoke of the knocking language in which the spirits speak to the living, and predicted a day when men might as easily exchange messages with Aristotle as with an uncle in Bordeaux. — My dear de Fonce, he said (or was it the other way around?), every day we draw closer to the dead.

Wait, this is impossible. Haussmann, virtuoso of the straight-edge, champion of sanitation, a mystic? Nonsense. We would have heard of it from the biographers, if it had been so. Well. Call it a mistake if you will; after all the Baron and the demolition man spoke so much, and often late at night, that perhaps everything did get turned around. Haussmann the real rationalist, de Fonce the mystic, if you like. But let me ask you this: What is the business of stories, if not to present the other side of things?

8

A PICTURE OF VIRTUE

ON A SUMMER EVENING three years later, when the leaves on the saplings Haussmann had planted along his new boulevards (did you think that those trees were always majestic? But everything begins frail; eternity is nothing but a forgetting of origins) were the shape of girls' faces, and shone goldly in the eight-o'clock dusk, the Baron went to de Fonce's house on the boulevard de Courcelles, to speak with the demolition man about the troubling question of multiple personalities. He had just read in an illustrated newspaper the story of the worried German Sörgel, a shepherd sent to the forest to gather wood. Meeting a stranger in the forest, Sörgel killed him, cut off his feet and drank his blood; he returned home, described what he had done, and fell into a deep sleep. When he awoke he had forgotten all about it. Georges-Eugène thought: what if we are all thus divided? What if, in each of us, there are two divergent currents—for all the world like a sewer system run in reverse, drowning us in? Well, and then the question (which, as he formulated it, gave him the pleasure of knowing that his own mind still functioned analytically), the question, yes, of what Sörgel was, really? A shepherd? Or a foot chopper? Which is the main current and which the tributary? The Baron set down the paper and called for his carriage to be made ready. What would de Fonce think? Would the next century bring a science that could answer such questions, a sort of hydraulics of the mind?

De Fonce had just finished supper when he arrived, although it was close to midnight: the demolition man ate late when he was at home, a habit left over, if the rumors were to be believed, from his days as an apprentice. Haussmann was shown into the upstairs parlor, a tall room in rose and gilt. On the domed ceiling de Fonce had commissioned a fresco of the seven virtues instructing artisans in their work. Patience, it was often noted, held the arm of the smith. Almost supine in an armchair under Justice, de Fonce was smoking. And behind him, looking out the window at the gates of the Monceau park, locked for the night: — Why, the Baron said, it looks as though one of your allegories has fallen to earth.

She was not beautiful in the ordinary way. Her waist was too thick, and her bosom too small; her nose was straight enough but a little flat, as though it were pressed against an invisible window. Her complexion was fashionably pale, and her hair a very passable chestnut; de Fonce dressed her in elegant clothes and she wore them well, but there was something hesitant about her; she was like a foreigner who, although fluent in a language, now and then misses a word and pauses, grasping with her hands for something immaterial and hopelessly absent. Even so, there was something—even de Morny agreed there was *something*—about her which held the eye. The wits who frequented de Fonce's dinners tried to explain it: one said it was her eyes, which were, admittedly, large and dark; another that it was her lips, which seemed always about to smile and never did. A young abbot said her beauty wasn't in her features at all, but in her sobriety, which was singular in this frivolous age; an old diplomat countered that her charm lay in her ability to lis-

ten to anyone—the abbot, for example—for hours without appearing to be bored. Sentimental observers called her childlike;
more astute men said the opposite: that her spirit must be much
older than her body, to take everything with such equal grace.
Whether they could put words to it or not, what each of them
had seen was her ability to resist their influence absolutely. She
would never pick up a single habit from any of them; she
would not repeat their phrases, or adopt their views, or acquire
their tastes. They called her resistance beauty; it was a challenge;
it excited their interest. Only a very few of de Fonce's guests
saw something else in it, a ferocity which wasn't at all playful,
and which it would cost much to overcome. These few told de
Fonce he had a daughter to be proud of, and looked away.

Haussmann was not among them. To his mind she looked
every bit like that waif who sings so beautifully in Meyerbeer's
La Perdue—what was her name? Isola, he thought, remembering how he had approached the actress backstage and what em-
barrassing consequences there had been then.

— My dear Baron, said de Fonce, my adoptive daughter
Madeleine. Madeleine (he said, turning), you see before you the
man who built the park you like so much.

— Enchanted, Madeleine said, and held out her hand to be
kissed.

— Which one would you say she is, de Fonce? By her noble brow I'd call her Justice, and by the coolness of her hand
Chastity; although perhaps her patience with the ramblings of
an old man gives her away as Charity. What do you say?

De Fonce smiled an impenetrable smile.

— In any case, Mademoiselle, it is a rare pleasure. I knew
your father was a collector of treasures, but he never told me
that the most beautiful of them walks about on two legs.

— Hardly, Monsieur. My father has many more beautiful
pieces in his collection.

— Modesty! Ah, de Fonce, you rogue.

— Please, said de Fonce, won't you sit?

Haussmann found himself between the demolition man and Madeleine, who arranged herself on a low divan facing the Baron. How old is she? Haussmann wondered idly. — I hope I'm not interrupting...

— Nonsense! We were just talking about you.

—Yes, said Madeleine, my father has told me all about you.

— Ah? Then I'm afraid you have the advantage of me, for he hasn't told me about *you* at all. Eh, de Fonce? Haussmann laughed. She couldn't be more than sixteen years old. And yet what breasts! Small limestone-white breasts.

— Oh, I'm sure he didn't want to waste your time.

— Not at all, my dear. I was saving you as a surprise for the Baron.

— A pleasant surprise...

— Talk to Monsieur Haussmann, my dear, said de Fonce. Tell him about your music lessons.

— Oh! Madeleine blushed. They're nothing to boast of.

— Then you needn't boast, said Haussmann. The truth will be charming enough.

Madeleine looked at de Fonce. — Well, Uccellini, my teacher, you see, says that I might be adequate if only I sang with more *heart*. She pressed her hands not to that organ but to the white skin just above the top of her gown. — Signorina you haive the lovely voisse, she said in a passable Italian accent, but you spend too much time in this a-room! Madeleine laughed without embarrassment.

— You would have heard her if you'd come yesterday, said de Fonce. We were lucky enough to have a song out of her after supper.

— I regret it sincerely, said Haussmann.

—You'll have to come back and... to come back again, said Madeleine, and blushed.

Haussmann bowed. As he looked up he caught Madeleine's eye. She was looking at him curiously. When she saw that he was looking back she turned her head and laughed. — You must tell me all about yourself, Mademoiselle, he said, trying to find her eyes with his eyes.

So Haussmann never asked de Fonce his question. If he had, the demolition man might have told him about certain advances being made at that time by the psychologists of the Nancy School: they had succeeded in regressing not only hysterics but men of sound morals and character to any point in their youths. A thirty-year-old broker broke into the stutter he'd had as a ten-year-old boy, and admitted to being at once terrified of and consumed with curiosity about frogs, their knobby backs and the delicate articulation of their hind feet. And even that was nothing! For they could make a four-year-old of him as easily, and hear him speak of the days of the week as colors, and the months as musical notes. And then, and then, Baron, they regressed him ten years more and the banker became an eighty-year-old woman complaining of grippe and children drowned in the heavy rains of 1766! Many people inhabit us in the course of a single life, and still more if you count the lives we have had before this one; they spring one from the next like branches, or streets. Why, Baron, it would surprise me if you were the last to inhabit that great frame of yours; who knows if your successor will be a foot chopper indeed!

But Haussmann had forgotten all about the reason for his visit. He sat with de Fonce and Madeleine until well after midnight, when the demolition man offered him a cigar and withdrew, pleading ophthalgia, to a velvet-draped bedroom which was, rumor had it, heated by a coal stove every night of the year.

Georges-Eugène and Madeleine. Who knows what they did when they were left together in a room full of rose-colored virtues by a man to whom the virtues were invisible (de Fonce, you will recall, wore rose-colored glasses)? If the virtues could speak, they might tell us much: with what patience Madeleine and the Baron approached one another, first sitting a modest distance apart, then standing by the window to inspect some unusual feature of the night, then sitting again, this time closer together, and by means of surreptitious adjustments to the costume of one or the other approaching until at last their hips almost touched. How modestly Haussmann spoke of his own work, and how prudently Madeleine approved of it; with what justice she praised his renovation of the park beneath their window, and with what charity Haussmann inwardly fleshed out Madeleine's bony architecture, the plans and elevations of which he tried to discern through her dress. As they spoke, each heard in the other the echo of a quiet inner voice, the opposite of the conscience, which reminded them not of what they had done wrong, but of the uncanny correctness of all their mistakes, so that their lives, for a moment, seemed to have been guided by a benevolent fortune that smiled most broadly on their most senseless acts. Chastity separated their elbows by the breadth of a hair, and even honesty smiled when, at two o'clock, a servant came in just in time to see Haussmann pull his hand away from Madeleine's cheek.

— Excuse me, Monsieur, but Monsieur's coachman wonders whether he ought to wait? Or should he return in the morning?

— Will you walk me downstairs? Haussmann asked Madeleine. She led him through the marble corridors, which at that hour of the night were as quiet as though they had been altogether depopulated. Madeleine's throat was tight from the strain of speaking so much. She must have been flushed, too, for when she took Haussmann's hand he recoiled as though he'd touched a still-warm pair of tongs.

At the foot of the stairs Madeleine said, — And here I'll leave you. She did not leave at once, however, but stood on the bottom step, still holding Haussmann's hand. He looked at her as though by staring he could see her as she really was. A girl, the daughter of his friend. Come, this is ridiculous, he thought, and drew himself up to bow and wish her good night. He leaned forward, and somehow his feet managed to arch themselves so that he bent toward her more than he had intended (an involuntary action, doubtless, Baron, but you've missed your chance at understanding that!) and Madeleine, somehow misunderstanding his intent at precisely the same moment, reached up on tiptoes and kissed Haussmann on the lips. Uncomfortable as it was—Haussmann was a good foot taller than the girl—they held that posture for some time. Madeleine's mouth was small but deftly active; she pulled his tongue into it and held it there while her breath puffed warmly against his upper lip. Her neck smelled faintly of perfume and more faintly still of earth, as though she'd been mucking around outside. After a moment her head trembled and her hands tugged at the sides of his coat. Erotic transport? No, she was struggling to keep her balance. All at once the absurdity of the situation—the indignity of the situation—offended him; as gently as he could he took hold of both her hands and stood up straight. Madeleine breathed quickly, her eyes fixed on his. They looked at each other like that for a moment, Prefect and prodigy; then Madeleine hurried upstairs, disappearing a moment later between two of de Fonce's monumental urns.

De Fonce was in the garden, inspecting a piece of statuary. He had put on his professional demeanor, which was monastic, as

though he had forsaken sex and property in the service of antiques. — Have you ever seen anything like this statue? Haussmann admired the stonework, tired though he was and sick to
his stomach. The way the demolition man followed him around
with those glasses of his convinced Haussmann that de Fonce
knew everything. A stone face grimaced with the agony of one
burning at the stake; a stone finger pointed as though to accuse
the inquisitor. It was the ugliest bit of masonry the Baron had
ever seen.

    — Beautiful, he said, afraid that de Fonce would force him
to buy it.

    The demolition man smiled instead and began to speak
about the sky, which foretold rain.

    It reminded Haussmann of something. — There was a ques-
tion, sir, that I wanted to ask you...

    But de Fonce waved it away. — Come back any evening
and we'll take it up. Now you must rest, and I have work to do.

    Haussmann climbed into his carriage, nursing the suspicion
that he had played a part, unwittingly, in someone else's design.

9

MADELEINE'S EDUCATION

FOR A TIME, it might as easily have been months as days, she
lived in condemned streets: the Street of the Old Lantern, the
Street of the Cold Coat, the Street of Bad Words. It was only
practical. The houses waiting to be torn down asked her no
questions; the rotten roofs kept off the rain and the boarded
windows bore the brunt of the wind. She slept in a stone-
flagged kitchen, in the cobwebbed darkness under creaky stairs,
in a garret where the walls were dotted with something that
might have been blood or coffee or paint. No one saw her, no
one took her in charge. The city no longer noticed her; it was
as though she had passed through the hole in her chest into the
world that had opened up for her one afternoon in the library
of Saint-Grimace.

While Madeleine studied to be a saint, cartographers had
built wooden towers all over Paris, and from their tops surveyed
the city and recorded all that was visible on a great map. It was
the first time anyone had done so. Every street, every building,
every depression and elevation of the ground was measured and
rendered to scale. Even the trees in the parks had their place on
this map, and the graves in the graveyards: on the map they look

like plus marks, for the sign of the dead is addition, one plus one plus one, year after year. Much later, when Haussmann's work was done, people would look back and wonder when the old city had died. It was when they tore down the cloister of the Barnabites, some would say, and others, that it was the mutilation of the church of Saint-Leu-Saint-Gilles, the flaying of the rue de la Tannerie, the evisceration of the Old Calf Market. The truth is that the old city had vanished long before, before the first workman's pick pocked the first medieval facade. It died with the map: when all that was visible had been charted, the invisible, of necessity, disappeared. There was no longer any room in Paris for ghosts or river-born children, for talking cats or magic statues, nor for those who believed in them. Paris ignored Madeleine energetically; it had business to get on with.

History abandoned Madeleine, but time, against which history is nothing, continued to do its work. Having learned from Saint-Grimace to mistrust her body, she observed its increasing peculiarities with concern: the kink in her neck that came from sleeping pillowless or with her head propped against a beam; the tangle that stopped her fingers an inch from her skull when she tried to make sense of her hair; the incrustations of callus and dirt about her heels, which made her think of Hector, a beggar who had sung in the courtyard below Jacob's window. *Would I were sure of being immortal, ageless all my days,* he sang, and was found one morning broken-backed where a runaway horse had stepped on him in the night. Grime and snarl were like a motif embellishing the real changes. Like Napoleon in Russia, Madeleine grew breasts; unlike the Emperor she grew taller as well. If only she had something to eat! Madeleine could not walk as far as she had at first, when she scavenged the markets for whatever produce had been thrown away during the day; now she made do with what she found nearby, a scrap of bread, a vegetable no longer of any recognizable variety.

No one took her in charge, but Madeleine was not alone. Jacques the mouser came to pay his compliments and to apologize if he had done her any harm. Armand followed, his face downcast; he told Madeleine that he should never have let her go. What a family we would have made, you and I! he lamented, We would have tanned the hides of anyone who tried to part us. Sister Geneviève chased Armand away. She begged Madeleine to return to the convent, where there were beds and plates and food to eat, and heat, and what did it matter if Madeleine would never be a noblewoman? She would, at least, be warm. But Madeleine would not go back. There was no part for her to play at Saint-Grimace; she could be only what she was, a tanner's daughter, a beggar, a dependent, a starveling's bride. Better to be nothing at all, to listen to the wind, and to sleep. The light came and went; she lay still, dreaming of Jacob and Geneviève and Nasérie, always Nasérie, who held her close and told her stories about the Beggar King and the other, undiscovered urchins who always somehow had enough to eat. Once when she awoke she found the marquise sitting beside her.

— You know, Nasérie said, this is really all your fault.

— Nasérie?

— Who else would visit a poor pitiable creature like you?

— Where did you go?

— Where do you think I went?

— You ran away.

— Goose! In my nightgown, do you really think? Nasérie coughed. — Poor Madeleine.

After a long silence Madeleine asked, — Well, are you going to stay?

She lay beside Madeleine, and held her in arms that had grown no cooler since they last embraced. — Ow! You're skinny, Nasérie said.

— You're one to talk.

— I *am* one to talk, the marquise agreed.

— Will you tell me a story?

— Not tonight.

— Just one story.

— Well...you have to promise not to tell anyone I told you. Do you promise?

—Yes.

— Really?

— I promise.

— All right. Listen: You're no more noble than my nurse.

— I *know*. Madeleine sighed. — My father...

— Don't interrupt! You're no more noble than my nurse, but you'll live like a great lady, Madeleine, and you'll see everything. You'll find out, though, Nasérie said with an air of great superiority, that I was right. You should have touched Saint Grimace. You're going to wish you had, but it will be too late. Much too late! I just hope you remember that I told you so, when the moment comes.

— What moment?

—You'll see.

Madeleine thought about this. — That's not much of a story, she said.

— It's not a story at all, said Nasérie. It's like a story, though. I mean, it isn't, but it is, sort of.

— I don't understand.

—You don't have to.

Nasérie put her arms around Madeleine's waist; Madeleine closed her eyes. When she opened them again the marquise was kneeling before her. The sky was a shade bluer than black, and the dimmest stars had gone out.

— I'm going, Nasérie said.

— Wait! I'll go with you.

—You? You can't.

— I want to.

— Do you? She laughed and kissed Madeleine's forehead.
— Go back to sleep, my darling.

When Madeleine woke again the sun filled the squares of
the glassless window. Nasérie was gone; farther up the street,
men were hoisting stones into a wagon. After that she woke
only when she had to, and walked only until she could fall
asleep again. She did not dream of Nasérie, nor of Jacob, but
only of the river Bièvre pulling her into a greater, stiller current, and who knows where her dreams would have ended if a
hand hadn't touched her shoulder, and a voice hadn't murmured, — Well, but what's *this*?

It was de Fonce, of course, who found her sleeping in the
kitchen of an abandoned house in the faubourg le Roule,
curled up next to a mantel that might have brought him a
thousand francs. — What do we have here, he said, brushing
her hair away from her face. — Let's see, let's see. He licked a
corner of his handkerchief and rubbed the soot from Madeleine's cheek. What he saw must have pleased him, because he
picked the girl up as carefully as if she had been an old vase, set
her down in his carriage, and drove away without saying a word
about the mantel, which his foreman, astonished but grateful,
dismantled and sold on his own behalf. De Fonce brought
Madeleine to the house opposite the Parc Monceau, which he
had just purchased from a bankrupt admiral and refurnished according to his own somber taste. He carried her to a bedroom
upstairs and tucked her in; when she woke up, a maid was
pouring broth into a silver bowl and she wondered whether it
wasn't possible to live in stories after all.

From de Fonce Madeleine learned all the arts to which her
childhood vocabulary entitled her: to sing and to accompany

herself on the harp; to eat long meals, play whist, and dance list-lessly, as was the fashion among French ladies at the time. A lady is like a statue, de Fonce told Madeleine: her art lies in her still-ness. Men will enchant you, if they think that it will bring you to life! Madeleine listened, enraptured. The aspirations of her girlhood danced before her, but all that was rough and tender about them had become smooth and unyielding. She could make herself a lady, if she chose; it would be no miracle, but a work of calculation and of art. Sit in the light, my child, de Fonce whispered; your colors benefit from steady illumination. And never fold your hands too close to your chest! You needn't look as though you have secrets; it will be understood. When your hand is kissed, remember: it has no weight. You are an im-material statue, my child, a bubble. Venus was born of foam and hope! For Vulcan knows the weight of metal, and its worth; you won't trick him unless you're light. Be light! She obeyed. In de Fonce she had found the father of her inmost self: the father of smooth, clean flesh, free from carbuncles and the oily smell of cats; she touched the back of his dry hand and thought that, given time, she might learn his immunity from sweat.

De Fonce taught Madeleine the craft of being fashionable. If he did not know something himself he hired someone else to teach it to Madeleine, and so Uccellini the singing master was engaged, along with half a dozen professionals of the needle, the harp, and the dance floor. If Madeleine had any question about the purpose of all this education, it was settled when de Fonce introduced her to the Widow Couvrefeu, a faintly dis-reputable woman with rust-colored hair and fearsome eye-brows. La Couvrefeu, he called her; she called herself the Widow. She had attached herself to de Fonce according to the unfathomable law by which intelligence of a certain sort finds its way to money; as her wit, though dry, was entertaining enough, the demolition man loaned her the sums she asked for

and invited her often to dinner. In return, La Couvrefeu took
Madeleine on long walks and told her what to expect from
marriage and married men. Do not expect your husband to
love you any more than you expect your harp to knit, she said;
he is an instrument which must be used to the right purpose.
That purpose in La Couvrefeu's view was to serve as a sort of
poker in the hearth of womanhood, to stir the fire of adulter-
ous passion and to add fresh fuel when necessary. Madeleine
was dismayed—marriage, then, was to be nothing like what
she'd learned from Nasérie, or with her—but she took it coolly.
There was, the Widow Couvrefeu assured her, no other way.

In three years—don't be shocked, for we are speaking of a different time, even if it was pregnant with our century as we are
pregnant with last wishes, last regrets—the child had ceased to
be a child, and the father to be only a father as well. It happened suddenly, just after Madeleine's fifteenth birthday. De
Fonce gave a large dinner, and everyone drank as they usually
did; they toasted de Fonce and the health of his adoptive
daughter, and wished them both the best of luck in everything
they should undertake. Afterward Madeleine sat up late in the
salon, smiling at her fan while around her thick-stomached
artists and gaunt aristocrats played cards and japed at the ceiling
fresco like hounds admiring the moon. If anything, she felt a
little cooler than usual, though it was summer; her hands lay
crossed in the lap of her dress like ivory hunting horns. De
Fonce was in his office with a particular friend, drawing lines
on a map; he crossed the salon only once, and looked at her, the
briefest flash of eye over lens-tops. The next morning, leaving
his bed, Madeleine thought her feet had turned to ice; she
walked through the dawn-gold house without any sensation of
the ground.

De Fonce had certain peculiarities as a lover. In the first place he refused to touch her, even in the ordinary way that a father touches a child, when there were guests anywhere in the house. She understood that the demolition man could not in public give up the illusion that she was his adopted daughter (though for nearly four years the libertine imagination of great ladies and petty officials had entertained the story that de Fonce was fond of children, that he kept a little boy locked in an attic room and when he was tired of fondling boy or girl, would take his pleasure from the two of them together). She understood too, that de Fonce would not be hers forever, or she de Fonce's.

— Marry you? he laughed, on the single occasion when Madeleine—still a girl in some respects—mentioned the subject. — My dear child, I'd as soon put a hobble through your ankles. She cried then; de Fonce reassured her, resting his hand on the wing of her shoulder. — I'll marry you to a great man, he said, as great as you like! Only expect nothing from me, for I can give you nothing. It was true: though Madeleine hoped for the demolition man's child the way schoolchildren hope in secret to fall ill, her body refused to perform the simple trick it had played—if the crowd at Saint-Grimace were any indication—on half Paris's fashionable wives. This was the demolition man's second peculiarity. Though his flesh was hot enough, and his hands limber as a dancer's legs, from the point of view of posterity he might have been a statue indeed, coupling with a woman of stone. De Fonce's third peculiarity Madeleine learned when guests filled the house and she spun among them like a bobbin, filling the air with invisible threads of interest, disdain, surprise. It was this: the demolition man was impervious to jealousy. — Remember that you're free, my child, he said as she wrapped herself in a shawl and went downstairs to greet the greatest testamentary lawyer of the Second Empire. — Remember always that you're free.

Free she was, to call a carriage and ride in it where she would; free to visit the milliner's and have a hat of softest pelt fitted to the odd contours of her skull (never seen a lady with such a large head! the milliner mumbled around pins), and free to wear it where she would, in the Bois de Boulogne on a Sunday afternoon, when coaches rattled one after the other along the lanes, or to the theater, where de Fonce sometimes accompanied her. They had a box at the Opéra across from the Count de Morny; the spectacle in *his* box was more entertaining than the melodious, pathetic operas Meyerbeer wrote with the persistence of a spring-wound pugilist. In de Morny's box shadows tangled with shadows, and white fans rustled like pigeons in rut; innuendoes fluttered over the diminuendos and then sank again to pigeonlike cooing. Madeleine watched servants arrive with buckets and silver trays and the visiting cards of handsome guests, some of whom she recognized from de Fonce's dinners. It seemed a very small world that she had been given the run of, then, and at times Madeleine wondered whether this was really what she had dreamed of at Saint-Grimace. Hadn't her dream been larger? And more populous? And it had had a stately quality, too, hadn't it? Although perhaps that was because no one spoke. Watching the lawyers and colonels, the touts and tarts and baronesses buzz past, she felt a slight, inestimable disappointment. She consoled herself, however, with the thought that it must be more exciting, really, to be *in* the other box! She was sure that it would be more interesting than her own. De Fonce, though ardent in the stuffy heat of his own bedroom, was as chaste in public as a clerical uncle, and as sober. He sat through the performance without once looking up at the audience, a degree of concentration which was unheard of in those days when nothing significant could happen in the first or fifth act because no one showed up before the second or stayed in their seats past the fourth. Nothing held Madeleine back, least of all de Fonce; she might stand up, walk along the circular corridor, and tap her fan against the other door. But she stayed in her seat. Madeleine called herself a coward, and cursed her father for the coolness with which he let her make her own mistakes.

To the day he died, de Fonce boasted that his eye had never been so infallible as when it discovered Madeleine. He was so evidently proud of her that Madeleine never told him that he was wrong: he was not the one who saw her first. There had been a night, in the summer of the Exhibition... Somehow in her wandering from one ruin to the next she got lost, and came to the Champs-Élysées; the trees blazed with gaslight. It must not have been that late; the street was full, and in the alleys by the roadside couples linked arms and walked back and forth, unhurried, expecting nothing more than what the night had already offered them. Across the avenue, the bulk of one building shone more brightly than the rest. In style it might as easily have been a confection or a lampshade: a dome of light supported on walls of light, the whole held together by lace-thin lattices of iron. Madeleine closed her eyes and imagined her face becoming the color of the lamps. She thought she must positively glow. If Jacob could see her now! she told herself, and wondered what had become of the lamplighter.

A cool voice brought her from her reverie. — Is Mademoiselle going to the Exhibition tonight? The speaker, a young man with an extraordinarily long neck, stood so close that Madeleine could smell his breath, like the used-up vegetables at the bottom of a soup pot. He wore a precarious top hat and gloves so tight the seam over the little finger had split, revealing a tiny half-moon of whitish skin. Seeing that he'd got Madeleine's attention, he bowed. — May I have the honor of accompanying you? He spoke gravely and sweetly; he took

Madeleine's wrist and pulled her into the crowd. At the entrance to the Exhibition Hall her guide winked and waved at
the attendants; bowing again, he pushed Madeleine before him,
into a room that reeked of cigar, sweat, metal, wine, confinement, and hair oil. She would have liked to go slower, but her
guide tugged her along, calling, — Follow me, Mademoiselle!
Hey! You louts, make room for the lady! This way! On either
side booths and placards announced the Seven Wonders of the
Modern World, which soon multiplied, became fourteen and
twenty-eight, as though seven wonders, which might have been
good enough for a smaller time, would no longer do in Paris in
the middle of the glorious nineteenth century. A Railway Engine, an Electrical Tonic Machine, a New System for Raising
Chicks, a Pneumatic Hypnorotomachia like a bellows attached
to a sunflower, a Woodless Furnace of glistening pipe, a model
of the Battle of Alma in tin, an Improved Bridle and Rubber
Wheel, and inventions that would not end. They put to shame
the small marvels of the old city, for what was a lichened statue
or a child with fur compared to an Undersea Telegraph or a
System for Guiding Balloons? It seemed to Madeleine that her
entire life had been a sideshow to divert the crowd while the
real spectacle was prepared elsewhere.

— Here we are, Mademoiselle, the crown jewel of the Exhibition. Look! She saw only a black box on spider legs, with a
brass ring set in it like a surprised mouth. Beside the box—was
this the jewel?—stood a corpulent gentleman with a tufted
wart growing off his lower lip; he, too, bowed to Madeleine.
— Eh Marcel, the guide called to the other, I've found you a
great lady! We'll set her in gold, shall we?

— Gold indeed, Escamote, the other called back, and gold
only because we've nothing better. Now Madame, if you'll
come over to this chair... Marcel, smiling all the while, directed
Madeleine to a stool and arranged her on it. Somehow in the

course of adjusting her shawl the top button of her robe came undone; Madeleine raised her hand to set it right but Marcel stopped the gesture. — You're perfect as you are, Madame, only perhaps... his hand brushed the collar of her dress, pulling the unbuttoned sides a little farther apart. Madeleine blushed.

— Charming! Escamote called, I've never seen such a lady-like ladyship. He smiled at Madeleine with such sincerity—the smile lifted every feature on his narrow face; even his ears twitched with it—that Madeleine had to smile back. If only we could leave his warty friend, she thought, and her imagination wandered in the direction of the cafés outside where she'd seen dancing...

— Perfect! Madame, you've the exact face we want. Hold still, I beg you, Madame, hold perfectly still. Marcel vanished behind the black box; like a pudgy centaur he stooped with his torso, and, fortunately, his face, hidden under the drape. — Look at me? his muffled voice requested. Madeleine stared at the brass ring. There was a puff of light; the ring hung before her eyes no matter where she turned her head, a blue ghost.

— All right, Escamote said. I think we're through. Thank you, girl. He prodded her kindly off the stool. — That's all; you can go.

Madeleine stepped toward him. — But...

— No no, you were perfect, thank you. Well? Oh. Escamote reached into his vest and extracted a one-franc coin, which he dropped into Madeleine's hand. She closed her fingers around it. The Exhibition Hall had emptied out; a few couples turned slowly to the creak and bellow of the Self-Playing Organ.

It wasn't until she took the coin that she understood what had happened; then she fled the Hall and regained the darkness where, she told herself angrily, she ought to have remained all along. She didn't make much of it at the time, but much later, when she looked back and tried to figure out what had become of the old Madeleine who ran away from Saint-Grimace, she would identify this as the moment when a part of her which had hitherto been vital ceased to live, at least in the way people lived. It was as though the camera had arrested her within as it had without, and what she thought of when she thought of herself was not a person but a portrait, a cameo in a locket hanging close to her heart.

Madeleine would not have put it in those words; indeed, if you had asked her in the summer of 1858 whether she was happy, she would have replied lightly, — Of course. It did not occur to her to ask the question of herself. She was not un-happy; at most she was dissatisfied, sometimes, because she did so little with what de Fonce had given her. Madeleine wished for someone who would force her to use her freedom, some-one who would compel her the way rails compel a locomotive, guiding her toward a distant country where everything was warm, new, and moving.

10

THE FOLLIES IN THE PARK

KISSES PROMISE SPEECHLESSLY, and so we understand from them more than they were ever intended to say. To Madeleine, Haussmann's kiss promised the beginning of something magnificent. The day after his visit, she dragged the Widow to the Parc Monceau. Once it had been the private possession of the House of Orléans, but on the Emperor's ascendancy to the throne it was seized for the public good. Since then Baron Haussmann had, in his usual manner, been making improvements. Paths were cleared and lawns cut to stubble; landscapers pruned the trees which, like the House of Orléans, had too many minor branches for their own good. Walking from knoll to pond, Madeleine chattered to the Widow about marriage and lovers. She questioned Couvrefeu about her late husband, a purveyor of flannel uniforms to the July Monarchy, which, on account of its estival name, had little need of them.

— A man worth his weight in wool, the Widow said.

— Why did you choose him, then?

— Youth is always a mystery to age.

— Then why do you think that I'll follow your advice?

— Because M. de Fonce tells me to think so, the Widow said flatly.

Madeleine changed her approach to the subject. — But what a beautiful day it is! I think the summer must make every-thing look more beautiful. It's a pity that each season doesn't improve on the work of the last, but that they must always undo one another. Don't you think so, Madame?

Couvrefeu, to whom this train of thought was as yet unde-cipherable, nodded vaguely.

— If only Nature made the world more beautiful each year! But for that, I suppose, we must rely on the works of men. What a lovely little dog! Madeleine exclaimed, as a mouse-colored terrier emerged from the bushes with a rat in its mouth. — Do you like animals, Madame? I think they must be very happy here. Isn't this path picturesque? I think that the Prefect... you know, Haussmann... that he's done wonders. He's a remarkable man, isn't he?

— It's some sort of mutt, the Widow said.

Madeleine approached the subject of Haussmann several times more, but each time the Widow's replies, like a path that seems to lead to a distant gazebo but never quite reaches it, kept the Baron at a distance.

She must, however, have reported the conversation to de Fonce. One night when Madeleine and her adoptive father were alone in the salon, watching carriages pass, the demolition man waved his cigar at the lightless trees across the way. — That park is good for nothing but thieves and whores, he said. It should be torn down along with everything that is dark, for darkness is loved by criminals alone. And the Bois de Boulogne is ten times worse! It should be sold for firewood. No more darkness, no more crime!

Madeleine knew little of the Bois de Boulogne, but she had a vague (though accurate) impression that it had been refur-bished by Haussmann; so she defended it, and in a minute found herself defending darkness, too, for its importance to lovers.

At which de Fonce exploded as though he were a forge indeed, and she had just trodden on his bellows: — Then you do
love him!

— Hardly! Madeleine replied. The word had never occurred
to her before in connection with Haussmann, or, indeed, in
connection with anyone but Nasérie, and what she had enjoyed
with *her* was so singular a pleasure that, now that the marquise
was dead, she could not imagine ever having such a feeling
again. But so much, as de Fonce knew, depends on association!
When one word such as "love" becomes attached to the idea
of a person, it matters little whether other words like "never"
or "no" follow suit. The first word does its work; it clears
the ground for the hazy vision and inner warmth that, when
caused by another person, are called love. Love and Haussmann,
joined, formed their curious little edifice in Madeleine's mind;
when she discovered it and found it empty, she set out to fill it
as best she could.

To say that Madeleine's love was artificial is to say nothing
about it at all. Artifice, in love, takes care of what chance might
arrange but has failed to: a second meeting, a displaced curl of
hair, your favorite flowers swimming in an unfamiliar bowl.
Everything else, though it may seem haphazard—or even, if
you are nervous, artificial—happens necessarily or does not
happen at all. If de Fonce had not spoken, it might have taken
Madeleine a little longer to admit the word into the everyday
vocabulary of her thought; but it would have come there
sooner or later. Madeleine was predisposed to love Haussmann,
because she loved her own imagination, and Haussmann, in
Paris, in 1858, was the author of all that could be imagined.
When de Fonce's guests, full of the disdainful *sprezzatura* of
men who can make ten thousand francs in a morning and
spend it all on lunch, mocked the Prefect's self-importance and
the earnestness with which he undertook every public im-

provement, Madeleine contradicted them hotly: — I think
Monsieur Haussmann must be very intelligent, she said, and I
don't think his work is ugly at all. When the guests asked her
politely what evidence she'd had of his intelligence Madeleine
chose to keep quiet. — Nevertheless, she said, I insist.

A secret warmth held her in place; it anchored her to the
chair on which she sat, the table where she rested her hand, the
oil on the skin of the guest opposite, and the valet's lace cravat;
it sent out tentacles into the floor, the walls, the street, the park's
invisible trees. Everything lived; everything moved; she balanced atop a spinning ball and, with Galilean poise, took stock
of all that turned in her orbit. In the first place, she decided, she
must have a new shawl, and in the second a glass of wine, a
breath of air, another look at the neoclassical folly Haussmann
had commissioned for the park. If she had fallen in love with a
carter, Madeleine would have taken an interest in horses; but
what ecstasy to fall in love with a city planner, who surrounded
her, day and night, with signs of himself! Madeleine had never
felt so grand, or so dizzy. She had to go out; there was nothing
for it but to go out again; she called for the carriage and had
the coachman drive her to the Seine, to the Opéra and back
again, until at last she fell asleep in the warm enclosure, rocked
to sleep by the insistent benevolence of a city which pro-
nounced itself hers (creak!) hers (creak!) hers.

As the summer sputtered out in a string of ugly days, when the
sky gathered darkness each morning as though to storm, and
each afternoon suffered a failure of nerve, letting its clouds dis-
perse into haze, heat, and shadow, Madeleine wondered when,
or whether, the Prefect would ever return. She wondered lan-
guidly at first, stretched on a couch before the open window;
then restlessly, pacing the corridors of de Fonce's house; at last

she wondered furiously, and as the first droplets of rain wiped the dust from the windows she flung herself down into an armchair and with tears demonstrated her adolescent belief in the pathetic fallacy. The weather cleared; Madeleine brooded. In the music room Uccellini wrung his hands: after weeks of progress Madeleine's voice had faltered again, indeed it had become worse than it was before. — If you asalk then I will asalk atoo, said the Italian, and he refused to come back to the house until his pupil apologized for making an amockery of his teaching. Madeleine did not mind. She had given up hope that Haussmann would come, was glad, in fact, that he had not come, for his arrival would have threatened the coolness of which she was again the perfect mistress. She wandered the corridors of de Fonce's museumlike home, and felt kinship to the girls who stood on distant hilltops in pastoral paintings: remote, immobile, and preternaturally clear. De Fonce, who for days had been occupied with the details of an important contract, emerged from his study at last and found her motionless in an armchair with her back to the window. — I'm afraid you've been neglected terribly, he laughed. A girl your age shouldn't spend so much time alone! We must find you some company. Shall I invite La Couvrefeu to dinner?

— If you like.

— Or the Prefect?

— No! Madeleine thought she had taught herself not to blush, but evidently she hadn't learned the trick as well as she'd thought.

De Fonce laughed. — It's decided. We shall have Haussmann for dinner! He tickled her cheek, which vexed Madeleine beyond words.

Haussmann had not avoided the house opposite the Parc Monceau because of any particular feeling about Madeleine, one way or another—indeed no; he was the Prefect of Paris and it might be understood that he was too busy to make regular social calls on anyone except perhaps the Emperor and a few of his principal ministers; in any case too busy to visit friends to discuss topics in which he had only an intellectual interest. He had a great deal to do that summer. There was the vexing matter of his election to the Senate, which, although it had the Emperor's blessing, nonetheless his enemies sought to block; and then there was the business of the boulevard Voltaire. The old skeptic would have had convulsions of spite if he could have seen what a fuss his still-unenlightened countrymen made over the demolition of a church or two—didn't they see that the path of reason is straight, leads straight from one great mind to another; it cuts a gleaming roadway through time, thereby proving that the few ideas of any value in this world exist in direct relation to one another, unmediated by the dross of common thought.

The Baron sometimes believed, looking at the map of his works, that the civic order he created—the improved circulation of carriages, the sewers and the clean drinking water—was a benefit attendant on a greater, spiritual transformation, and it was this transformation which was his true work, to be carried out in the greatest secrecy and with the certainty that it would be misunderstood. In such moments, when he felt full, bright, sufficient to himself, Haussmann fancied himself as ministering not to the city's health but to its soul, the secret and unimaginably great consciousness which few men could discern and fewer still address. He would save the city not from congestion but from unreason, the gathering dark of a thousand years of thoughtless acts; he would sacrifice its stone confusion, to the last house, in order to save the few gestures of any true clarity (the Champs-Élysées, the Louvre, the Madeleine) which had been written as if by accident in the tangled and mediocre pages of the city's history. Not Haussmann Salvator, for he was only an instrument serving those grand designs, but Haussmann Redactor, who with his canceling pen would separate the light from the dark, preserving one forever and forever condemning one to be forgotten.

In these moments he felt the greatest humility: he was nothing in the face of the task which had chosen him. Of course, what he served was so great that no individual could hope to measure up to it; the contrast absolved him of all his personal insignificance. Whenever he returned from one of these reveries, he noted with pleasure that it was easier than ever to deal with his enemies on an equal footing, and even, throwing back his head a little, to assume the air of slight superiority which served him so well in business negotiations.

When, at the end of a trying month, he received an invitation to dine at de Fonce's, Haussmann was inclined to accept, if only because he had so often found that by taking his mind off the serious business before him he came more quickly to the solution of it. With his mind still full of the complex negotiations attendant on his appointment to the Senate, he scribbled a reply to de Fonce's note. In the confusion of the week that followed he forgot all about it, so that he ended up being even more surprised than Madeleine when, at eight o'clock exactly on the appointed day, he found that his carriage had stopped on the boulevard de Courcelles, and de Fonce's smiling footmen were waiting to assist him to the ground.

When it was much too late and everything had already been settled, the Baron saw how crudely he had been pushed about that evening, and how gamely he had run toward each sign offered him, like an old bull that charges the flag just to bring an end to a contest from which he has had nothing but frustration and stinging pain. Of course at the time there had been no pain, and the dinner, simple though it was, charmed him completely. In fact Haussmann enjoyed himself tremendously at de Fonce's. He enjoyed himself the way a man in the flush of power and health enjoys everything: as though it were appointed that all things would come to him sooner or later, and every pleasure he had not enjoyed in the present was only reserved for a still more delectable future. First he spent a few minutes alone with the demolition man in his office. They talked about business and then, inevitably, about the ideas which were the currency of their conversation, then it was time to eat.

Madeleine sat across from the Baron and the Widow Couvrefeu by his side. Excited by those opposite poles of womanhood—one old and one young, one fair and one dark, one top-heavy with expectation and the other, so to speak, bottom-heavy with cynicism—the Baron's wit nearly drew sparks from the silverware. Madeleine looked even more lovely than when they met for the first time (although in retrospect he wondered whether that wasn't because he had the Widow to compare her to). When he was being clever, the Baron drank a little more than usual; all the same he should have noticed that his glass was refilled more often than the others, so that, by the end of the evening, he'd had enough to be less than drunk but more, somehow, than sober.

So it was no wonder that, when dinner was over, he asked whether Madeleine might sing an air or two. She looked at de Fonce querulously. — Why, my dear, he said, if you think your voice... — There's nothing wrong with my voice! Madeleine retorted, and to prove it she stalked to the middle of the room, turned so quickly her dress lifted off the floor, and began to sing. Madeleine was right. There was nothing wrong with her voice; it suffered not so much from a discernible flaw as from the lack of any distinguishing beauty. An accomplished voice,

Haussmann thought at the time. (How different it seemed
in retrospect! Now Haussmann would characterize her voice
as homuncular, as though a little soprano had lodged itself
in Madeleine's chest and sang plaintively from within that
hollow enclosure in the hope that it would be released.)
After the third number Haussmann stopped her to inquire
whether by chance she might have learned any of the airs from
La Perdue? And would she sing one for him? It did not matter
that it wasn't recently rehearsed; it would give Haussmann great
pleasure just to hear the words, to hear Madeleine sing the
words.

Here we ought to say something about Haussmann and the
opera. Biographers note that when he was still a subprefect in
Poitiers, Haussmann distinguished himself by going to see
Auber's *La Muette de Portici* thirty-two nights in a row. So well
did he learn it that when, on one occasion, a soloist missed his
cue, the action on stage was momentarily accompanied by an
unearthly piping, as though spirits in the balcony were covering
for the fallible musicians below. The orchestra paused; the piping went on—then the whole audience blushed as one by one
they understood that it was only their subprefect whistling, perfectly oblivious to the absence of music anywhere else in the
house. So it was with Haussmann and music: he liked to listen
until he had taken the whole piece inside himself, and he could
play the principal parts singly or together. Then he felt as
though his head had grown to the size of an opera house; he
was his own audience, his own performance. The world quite
melted away, and all the problems which seemed pressing before were revealed as manifestations of an imaginary inade-
quacy, like a man worrying about where he will find crutches
when he has two perfectly good legs.

Of all the operas he had heard and heard again, few moved
him more than Meyerbeer's great *La Perdue*. These days, I'm
afraid, it won't seem like much: the story of a girl, Isola, in
Moorish Spain, who has a vision of the Heavenly City and decides that Islam's not the thing for her any longer. With the
help of a disguised itinerant friar she converts to Christianity;
afraid that her father, a magistrate, will disown her, she runs
away from home and joins the secret community of blind Cor-
dovan beggars. The beggars dance a ballet and then settle down
to hear Isola's vision. Convinced by the beauty of her voice,
they agree that, though they may be blind, they can see the
truth when it appears before them; one after another they lay
their admiring immortal souls at Isola's feet. Then comes the
pitched battle between the beggars and the Sultan's men, which
begins in a thunderstorm and ends in the palace harem, where
the beggars are slain and Isola taken prisoner. She's tried by her
father the magistrate, of course, and reprises her first aria, the
vision, which this time descends from the ceiling, an enormous
construction of canvas and blue paint. Who could deny the reality of such a Heaven? The magistrate converts on the spot,
and all that's left is their daring escape. In the fifth act (which
no one was expected to watch) the Sultan's son decides that
he's in love with Isola, too, and sets off across the desert to find
her; he saves her at the last moment from a poisonous serpent
that creeps out of a well.

Haussmann alone watched all five acts with rapt attention.
Perhaps it was because he had fallen in love with the actress
who played Isola, a trouper of nineteen or twenty named La Gavrotte. He loved her as soon as she opened her mouth to sing
her first aria: O the towers / rose and gold! / more beautiful
than azure to behold! Haussmann thrilled to the words, and, us-
ing his size to advantage, pushed his way through the backstage
crowd to her dressing-room door. La Gavrotte had just re-

moved her costume; she received him wrapped in a gold
robe, and, shifting from one foot to the other in an impatient
dance, daubed at her makeup while the Baron spoke. He
praised her voice, her grace, the tint of her face (rose and
gold indeed!), and the purity of her spirit as expressed in song.
He declared his willingness to take her anywhere in Paris,
and alluded to the penultimate act of *La Perdue,* in which Isola
converts the Moorish magistrate, her long-lost father. But
La Gavrotte would have none of it: her mother had been
evicted only the week before to make room for a round-
about which was, in her view, entirely unnecessary. She wiped
the last of the rose paint from her forehead and told Haussmann of a vision which involved him, the Prefect, inhabiting
the pipes beneath one of his public toilets. Another suitor
might have forgotten his passion then, but Haussmann, whose
emotions were as fixed as constellations—that is, they drifted
slowly across his spirit with the change of season and the hour
of the night, but could neither be controlled, dispelled, nor prevented from returning—held fast to his love for Isola, and simply subsumed his memory of the actress in his admiration for
the role.

All that pent-up admiration came tumbling out of him as
soon as Madeleine began to sing. It did not matter if her voice
was a little frail for the part, or even if she stumbled here and
there on Meyerbeer's ornate phrasing; those defects the Baron
corrected without noticing them; or if he noticed them they
gave him pleasure, reminding him of the perfect arias in the
opera house of his memory. Watching Madeleine sing, Haussmann had the impression that she was growing: first she was
Isola and then La Gavrotte and then she was herself again, but
not only herself; she was adorned with the warm memory of
other actresses and other parts. Why had he thought she was
too young? She was as old as the music, and as large; she filled

the room and refracted from every corner of it. Even when she had done singing and collapsed politely onto a divan, the music continued, within Haussmann it continued.

Something was wrong: Madeleine gave signs that she was not feeling well. She lay on the divan, fanning herself but apparently unable to speak.

— Exhausted, I'm afraid, said de Fonce. I'll send her to bed. He smiled sadly at Haussmann as though to say, Well, you haven't seen her at her best.

If only I had another hour with her! the Baron thought, bitterly disappointed, even though an hour earlier he had promised himself that he would go straight home after dinner, pay his conjugal respects to Octavie, and rest.

He resolved to do so after all and was about to take his leave when the Widow Couvrefeu piped up: — Bed indeed! The girl needs some air. Open the window!

De Fonce obliged. The night was cool but not unpleasantly so, and the breeze seemed to revive Madeleine a little. As she still appeared listless the Widow suggested that de Fonce take Madeleine out in the carriage. — The Baron and I can keep each other company for a little while, she assured him, and arched her fierce eyebrows playfully at Haussmann.

The promise of an unwanted flirtation following so closely on the heels of the disappointment of a promising one was too much for the Baron to bear. Turning to the Widow he said: — There's no need to disturb our host, Madame. As I will soon be going home myself—he stressed that so as to make things clear between himself and Couvrefeu—it will be no trouble for me to take Mademoiselle around the park and bring her back to you. Turning to Madeleine he said: — What do you say? Would you like to ride in the Prefect's carriage? Madeleine looked again at de Fonce, who shrugged as if to say, Do as you will.

In the carriage it was too dark to see whether she was really beautiful or not. Haussmann reached out with an explorer's caution until his hand touched something warm: her leg, he thought. — Do you feel any better? — A little, Madeleine said softly. She had been genuinely unwell after singing; if she exaggerated at all it was in drawing out her recovery so that they had circled the Parc Monceau not once but three times before she admitted to feeling herself again. Round and round they went, past the iron gate, the domed folly which looked like a Roman observatory, if only the Romans had built such things. Each time they passed a streetlight Haussmann said to himself: *She's very young*, and resolved not to touch her again. Each time the streetlight fell behind he reached out for her hand, her waist, her shoulder, the top of her breast. He kissed her mouth in darkness and this time she was neither young nor small; or rather he too had grown younger and smaller, he was contracting around the circle of her mouth and his mouth. He could not stop himself now. With careful mechanicking he undid the laces which held her dress together in the back, and so uncovered another centimeter of white breast. Had women always come in so many layers? Her corset had more eyes than the secret police, more hooks than all the anglers on the Seine. At last, with characteristic patience, he freed her nipple and enclosed it in his mouth. Madeleine's skirts, hitherto impassable, began to reveal themselves in the familiar character of a piece of demolition waiting to be done. Skirts and skirts and skirts later, her stockings glistened in the lamplight, which had allied itself at last with Haussmann's designs.

The Baron unbuttoned his coat and rid himself of his deco-

rations: the ribbon of the Great Officer of the Legion of
Honor, the Red Eagle of Prussia, the Order of Saints Maurice
and Lazarus of Sardinia, the Order of Francis the First of the
Two Sicilies, the Order of Notre-Dame of the Conception of
Villa Vicoza of Portugal, the Orders of Wasa, of Sweden, of
Norway, of Parma, of Baden, the Cross of a Knight of the First
Class of the Imperial Order of Saint Stanislas (Russia), and the
Commander of the Order of the Crown (Bavaria). His lower
garments followed with no regard for precedence. He lowered
his head until her thighs formed a study in classical perspective,
with the spandrel of her sex at the vanishing point. He tugged
at the tops of her stockings with his teeth, licked and bit the
flesh below. Madeleine was transported, or at least she sounded
so. There was the awkwardness again. But it was smaller now,
and the part of him which felt it was as distant as something
observed through the wrong end of a telescope. Haussmann
clambered atop the girl as best he could within the confines of
the carriage and given the chaos of her skirts, a decade of fashion spread out and crushed out of shape under his belly. The
rest was plumbing. It ought to have been a difficult moment—
he'd think, later—and in retrospect it seemed as though she'd
cried out; certainly she made enough noise, biting at his ears
and neck and chin like one of those women in Greek drama
whose role is to get drunk and disfigure all the men in the
vicinity. He might have cried out, too, although, given the
creaking of the carriage and the uncertainty of memory, it was
difficult for him afterward to tell.

— Shall I drive home, Monsieur? the coachman asked discreetly, and from the rear of the carriage came the mumbled
imperative: — Keep circling.

Round and round the carriage went; de Fonce and the
Widow Couvrefeu watched it from the window. De Fonce
started to laugh, and then, thinking the better of it, yawned.

— Well, the young lovers are off to a flying start, he remarked, and returned to his armchair. The Widow stood with her back to the room, no longer looking at anything in particular. She remembered the park as it had been twenty years ago. The Roman observatory was the last remnant of the Prince of Orléans' follies: before the Revolution, when aristocrats could still write their whims on the body of the world, he'd filled the park with pavilions and wonders of every sort. It had been a dreamland, a permanent festival of architectural excess, nostalgia, and high spirits. There was a Chinese Gate, Blue and Yellow Pavilions, and a Pavilion of Transparence such as can no longer be imagined; there was a greenhouse, a ruined Italian castle in miniature, a waterfall, a naumachia where boats butted bows in mock battle, a Temple of Venus, a Temple of Mars and even a Tent of Tartarus, a Mound of Diana with a view of the River Lethe; not to mention the Pyramid, the Blue and Yellow Gardens, the Pagodas, and a structure called the Temple of Marble because the Prince's stock of classical allusions had all been used up. When, in the heat of his passion, Couvrefeu's husband the wool merchant accused her (wrongly) of adultery and (rightly) of thinking him a boor, the Widow had gone there to cool off. Alone she walked between the blue-gold creations of a dethroned Prince, and thought that it was the way youth would look if it had been designed by an old man.

When the third Napoleon was crowned, and the park became the property of the state, it was decided that it would be more pleasing without so much fantastic clutter. The Widow had heard curious stories about the ensuing demolition. Apparently the Blue Pavilion offered more resistance than the Yellow; and in general it seemed that those follies which celebrated the darker elements of human nature were harder to destroy. The Temple of Venus was pulled down in a trice, but the Temple of Mars fought the hammers and chisels to the last; harder still to

demolish was the Tent of Tartarus, the poles of which seemed
to have been planted deep in the earth. In the end all that remained were the Roman observatory and the naumachia,
which was impossible to tear down by ordinary means; eventually someone had the idea of dumping the remains of the other
pavilions into it. This had the side benefit of silting the River
Lethe until it was a mere brook, which the park's new planners
deemed inoffensive to the bourgeois sensibility and so allowed
to remain.

Haussmann's carriage was still circling when the Widow
turned from the window. Rather like a vulture, she thought.
Feeling her age, she sat down beside de Fonce and enjoyed
with him a moment of the silence that sometimes joins the
conversation of two old friends like a third party, a mutual acquaintance who used to keep in the background but who will
have his say more and more as time goes on.

11

CAT AND MOUSE

AN ARTICLE APPEARED the next day in the *Lanterne*, one of the few opposition papers which Louis Napoleon hadn't closed down yet. "The Trick up M. Haussmann's Sleeve? A Pair of Spectacles," opined a scrivener with the unlikely name Viollet Fillier. Doubtless one of those snooping members of the press who show up at dinner parties in someone else's cravat, and take notes with miniature pencils on the insides of their cuffs. All the same, Fillier had managed to get a certain number of things right. He noted that the prefectoral carriage had stopped more than once outside de Fonce's house, noted, too that the demolition man had recently got involved in real estate speculation. Fillier could of course produce no evidence of actual wrongdoing, but he was not inclined to give Haussmann the benefit of the doubt.

> If proof of their collusion is wanting, it can only be because their minds are of such subtlety that their operations can scarcely be understood by the mortals who stand below their Financial Firmament; nonetheless, the course of History suggests that few secrets remain for-

ever hidden from Man. Inevitably a fiscal *Galileo* will discern their hidden movements, and their stars, like those
of every tyrant, will fall.

Haussmann threw the paper down. — As if I weren't
hounded enough! Did I tell you, my dear, that the Council
voted against my Water Memorandum of three July... The
speech that followed might have been better saved for the
Council. Its only hearer, Octavie, rocked silently in her chair,
her book politely lowered, although, as her husband thundered
on, she couldn't help but glance at the page, where a Swiss as-
cetic opined, *One hour of suffering in the mind is worth ten in the*
flesh.

When he was done she said: — I told you he wasn't a
proper acquaintance.

— Proper be damned! He's got a mind as good as a dozen
of your mystics.

— O, Octavie replied, I don't make any claim for their
minds, provided their hearts are good enough. She closed the
book on her finger, keeping her place. — Your demolition
man's got a bad heart.

— You've never met him.

— But I've heard you talk about him, and heard others, too.

— Others?

— All he sees is his own advantage, with glasses or without.
The little gargoyle! Just wait and see if he doesn't ask to marry
Valentine.

— My dear, that's absurd... Haussmann began, but Octavie,
having stated her case as violently as her manners would allow,
returned to her reading and would not look up again.

Haussmann reread Fillier's article unhappily and threw the
paper into the fireplace, where it smoked like a departing genie.
He kissed Octavie's forehead and went downstairs to his private

office, to draft a Second Memorandum on Aquifers and Aqueous Distribution which would leave the Municipal Council's
head municipally spinning.

The reporter for the *Illustrated Girls' Gazette* was walking home
by way of the Parc Monceau one evening, still fuming because
his editor would not print a review he'd written of Baudelaire's
translations of Poe—unfit for girls? but how would girls know
what to be careful of, if they were raised on sugared words and
paper dolls?—when an unliveried carriage stopped across the
street. An enormous nose stuck itself out the window, turned
from side to side, and, having smelled nothing that displeased it,
descended from the carriage, followed immediately by a large
man in a cloak. This figure knocked on a door which belonged,
as every fashion writer in Paris knew, to the demolition man
de Fonce. A servant opened, and the big-nosed stranger mumbled something and pushed his way inside. Mysterious, the reporter thought; but de Fonce was a murky character. Even at
his parties, which were the best-lit in Paris, there was something dim and hard to make out, as if the air around the demolition man were a lens that pulled everything slightly out of
focus. Money was the name of that lens. Really it was a scandal,
thought the reporter: you could write as much as you wanted
about de Fonce, but not a word about Baudelaire, or Poe.
Didn't anyone know what evil was any more? Resolved to re-
submit his review with a strident new preface to the same editor, the correspondent hurried on.

Inside the demolition man's parlor, Haussmann struggled
free of his cloak.

— Why Baron, de Fonce said, what a surprise! On your way
to a costume ball?

Haussmann took off the nose. — They're playing cat and
mouse with us, he explained. Haven't you read the papers?

If the demolition man found anything incongruous in the
idea of the Prefect as a two-meter-high mouse with a bald head
and twitching brown whiskers tied kerchieflike under his
snout, he kept it to himself. — Let me take your cloak, he said,
bowing low.

— How's your daughter?

— I'm sure she'll be happy to tell you that herself.

De Fonce sent for Madeleine, and excused himself almost
immediately: his real estate ventures required constant attention.

Madeleine and Haussmann faced each other across the
length of the room.

— Are you well? Haussmann asked, and stepped forward.

— Not too ill.

Haussmann picked up a small brass dog which happened to
be sitting on a table nearby. It wore a fierce expression, the sort of
statuette meant to sit at the feet of a dead Pharaoh and to
frighten evil spirits away. — You've recovered from your indispo-
sition? He stepped forward again, as though to show her the dog.

Madeleine retreated, covering a smile with her hand. — I
feel another attack coming on.

So a second game of cat and mouse began. In this one
Haussmann was the fierce tom, stalking mouse-Madeleine until
he caught her in a corner of the parlor, kissed her lips, and nuz-
zled her neck.

— That's better, Mouse, Haussmann whispered. — I won't
hurt you. How good you taste, my mouse, my morsel. Where
are you going? There's no hole where you can hide from your
housecat, your Hausscat, ha! Mouse, you inspire me. My
mouse-muse, that's what you are, ha! ha! Still laughing, Haussmann bit Madeleine's ear. A minute later footsteps passed on
the stairs and Haussmann let her go.

— You mustn't overtax your voice, he said loudly; and,
softly: — My darling mouse.

Outside, wearing the nose again, while he waited for his carriage to be brought round, Haussmann picked a flower from the beds in de Fonce's courtyard. He thought of putting it in his buttonhole, but decided that it would be indiscreet. With careless and wholly irrational secretiveness he tucked the flower under the seat of his carriage, and enjoyed its softly blossoming smell.

On September 2, 1858, Haussmann delivered his Second Memorandum on Aquifers and Aqueous Distribution to the Municipal Council. The document passed almost immediately into civic legend: a thirty-seven-page disquisition on springs and reservoirs, wells and drains, which did not once use the word "water." — I believe you'll find the question of the Aqueduct quite completely settled, he told the assembled Councilmen, who sat, as one, open-mouthed. — Are there any questions? There were none. With the restraint of an occupying army, Haussmann left the Council to its deliberations. Why bother with the disguise? he thought, on the way to de Fonce's. He was magnificent, and magnificence, if properly handled, conferred certain immunities on its bearer.

Madeleine was waiting in the parlor. — My father's at Batignolles, looking at rubble. He won't be back until this evening... if you came to see him?

— It can wait. Haussmann advanced tigerishly.

— What's happened to you, my friend?

— I'll tell you the whole story. The tone of his voice left no fear that he would omit a single detail. — But first... He gripped her waist. — Mouse, are you ready to be devoured?

— Wholly, said Madeleine.

Did you know that Haussmann was schoolmates with Berlioz? Yes, it's true. They studied music together under the great

Cherubini. Haussmann was a methodical and not untalented composer, who liked things to wrap themselves up neatly at the end. Berlioz let everything get away at the end in such a wildly singular manner that he was universally hated. Even Cherubini hated him. Once, in class, he asked Berlioz what a certain pause was doing in the middle of his composition?

— Sir, Berlioz replied, I wanted the silence to produce an effect.

— Ah, you think a little silence will please the audience?

— I do.

— Then make the whole thing silence, and please them better still!

Which of course Berlioz refused to do; he became noisier and noisier as he went on, until the orchestras mustered for his symphonies were the size of small armies, and might, if they had been trained in fighting rather than in art, have changed the course of the Franco-Prussian War. Haussmann boasted afterward, and truthfully, that he had got a better mark in music than Berlioz himself. It was years and years later—not until this moment, really, in the parlor, holding this beating girl like a part of his body which has only recently come out from under the covering of his skin—that he understood what Berlioz knew all along, the ineradicable truth to which he laid siege with his orchestral armies: the heart of passion is silence.

— B-Baron.

— Yes?

— I think...

— What is it, Mouse?

— You ought to... She trembled. — To...

Haussmann turned.

Caught up in his twin games of cat and mouse, it hadn't occurred to Haussmann that he might have a role in a third game, as real as the others, in which the cat lets the mouse flee from one place to another until the mouse has cornered itself at last. So skillfully had this game been conducted that, even as he saw de Fonce in the doorway, hand on his hip, tapping a misshapen foot, he couldn't comprehend that he'd been caught.

— Leave us, de Fonce told Madeleine. She fled the room, not daring to look at either of them.

Haussmann stood very still and waited for de Fonce to challenge him to a duel. He had never fought a duel, though he'd come close, when, long ago, he'd insulted a lawyer in the provinces. They fumbled with pistols in the foggy morning, and, finding the powder too wet to fire, called it off. After that they'd become friends. But Georges-Eugène would never forget the feeling that a hole was to be dug in his chest, and his reservoir of blood spilled, as though he was a patch of marshland to be drained. That was death: you became a sort of public work, an edifice for the enjoyment of the ages.

The demolition man was laughing. — Ah, my dear Prefect! If only you could see youself! You look like a schoolboy waiting to have your hand slapped.

—Your humor is out of place, sir, Haussmann said, still waiting for the slap.

— Why, isn't this funny? Don't be angry—I couldn't help watching for a moment—only you mustn't think that you can keep secrets from a friend like me!

— I won't have any in the future. You will not see me again; my trespasses with your daughter are at an end.

De Fonce chortled. — Trespasses! Trespasses are for poachers, whereas you seem rather in the way of stocking the woods with game!

Haussmann found the conceit in bad taste and did not reply.

— As for leaving, you must not think of it. But come, Baron, you look perplexed! Is what I propose really so complicated? You want to love my daughter; I have no objection. Why would I object?

— We've already been in the papers. Fillier...

— Is that what you're going to remember when you're old? de Fonce asked softly. Fillier?

— Of course not.

— You will, won't you? And when you're an old man you'll look at your old wife and say, Thank goodness that journalist never caught me! And your old wife—Octavie, isn't it?—will scratch under her nightcap and say, Yes, dear, you were always very cautious.

— I'm thinking of your reputation too.

The demolition man shrugged. — Live as fits your desire, Baron. Otherwise you are nothing, and no trace of you will remain on this earth when you are gone from it.

— But Madeleine?

— Unless I miss my mark, she loves you. Would it suit her if you never saw her again? I think it would not suit her. And I prize her happiness, Baron, above everything. Therefore I do not order you to leave; in fact I enjoin you to stay. If you don't, after I've spoken thus, I'll take it as an affront to my daughter, which is as good as an affront to myself. Do you want that?

Haussmann said nothing.

— Then sit down, and stop being afraid.

De Fonce bowed and left the room.

Georges-Eugène didn't know what to think. Madeleine was to be his, and all was well; there would be no scandal. Nevertheless he wondered whether he wouldn't have preferred, really, to address de Fonce at ten paces in the language for which there is only one answer.

· · ·

(We pass over in silence the fourth game, in which the Baron was the unwitting cat, Madeleine and de Fonce the clever mice, arranging *their* embraces so cleverly that the Baron never saw them. For mice, in order to win this game, must learn the knack of appearing not to play at all.)

12

M. ANONYME

WITH THE DEMOLITION MAN'S support, the affair flourished in more comfortable clandestinity. De Fonce, in the
course of his real estate speculations, had purchased an apartment on the rue Le Regrattier, in an old-fashioned neighbor-
hood on the Île Saint-Louis. — It's nothing grand, he told
Haussmann, but the street's quiet, and the concierge is discreet.
The lease on the apartment, which he obliged the Baron to
sign in the spirit of fun, was made out to M. Anonyme. This
was a gentleman from a large family. The Anonyme clan had
branches practically everywhere in the country, but the majority of them lived in Paris, or kept apartments there. It counted
among its number magistrates and ministers, men of letters and
polar explorers, bankers, generals, and, in short, members of all
those professions by which men set out to make a name for
themselves. Some nights, at the Opéra, there were so many
Anonymes in the house that you might think the family was
having a reunion, but nothing of the sort. The Anonymes did
not seek one another out; when they met during the intermission, they spoke warmly but did not call one another by name.
Another peculiarity of this clan was the fact of their all being

men, and all of them unmarried, although rarely alone. Lovely
demoiselles went everywhere with them, and showed them so
much affection that you'd think one of them, now and then,
might have become a Mme Anonyme. This never happened,
which must have been a great disappointment to the demoiselles. When they married, if they married, they got only men
with names, and had to quit the Anonyme family (although
they might receive visits from its gentlemen sometimes).

— Not that there's any question of marriage, of course, de
Fonce said.

Haussmann smiled weakly. — Not Baron Anonyme?

— I thought love undid all distinctions.

— Love is one thing. Leases are another.

It was strange to sign a different name. Haussmann had to
feel out the shape of it, the upsweep of the *A* and the *y*'s downward hook, the tendency of the *e* to fly off at the end.
Anonyme: it was a light name, a name to live upward to.

Certainly he seemed lighthearted when he came to de
Fonce's that night. — I've told everyone I'm meeting with
the Minister of Health, he said. But really there's no need! I
couldn't feel better. Are you ready, my mouse?

Madeleine, who had been expecting him an hour earlier,
clasped his hands in hers. How long she had been waiting for
this moment! Now she would find out what was happening in
the other box at the theater; she would live among dukes and
duchesses, real, sound of body and fully grown. She whispered *I
love you* in Haussmann's ear, then ran to de Fonce and whispered *Thank you*. She kissed his cheek, then ran back to the
Baron and asked, — Where are we going? Haussmann put his
finger to her lips.

A curtained carriage took them south and east, toward
the center of the city. Were they going to the Café Anglais?
Madeleine had heard all about it from de Fonce's friends, about

the scandalous things public figures did in private rooms to the
accompaniment of food that was anything but English. Or were
they going to the theater? It was late for the theater, but perhaps there were special performances for the city's most distinguished men, private shows where you sat in the exact middle
of the otherwise empty orchestra and at the end the actors
pelted *you* with flowers. Or were they going to the Tuileries?
Haussmann was intimate with the Emperor and Empress. Perhaps they were receiving guests—not many guests, half a hundred, say. Madeleine pictured a yellow-gold room, with a fire in
the hearth for coziness and harp music to fill in for the conversation which she couldn't imagine. My dear Emperor, she
would say, only that wasn't how you greeted the Emperor. Sire?
Your Majesty? Your Highness? Your Imperial Majestic Royalty?
Why hadn't de Fonce, who was such a good teacher in other
respects, prepared her for this? — My dear? she murmured
to her dear. How do you call the Emperor? — What? — How
do you call him? — What a strange question, Haussmann said.
He pressed his teeth to her ear, and sent his tongue spiraling
into her head as if it were a thick, pink word he wanted her to
learn.

Not the Tuileries then. They crossed the river and rattled
onto the Île Saint-Louis, past the ivied houses she had admired
with Jacob long ago. Aristocrats lived there, Jacob had said; that
must be where they were going. To see an old duke (must he
always be a duke? some wiser, if quieter part of Madeleine's
imagination asked itself), in retirement since the glory days
when French boots pressed down the world's mud and French
coats kept off the world's weather. A frail man in a reddish
dressing gown who would offer Haussmann a wine as old and
subtle as himself. He would be unable to rise—a war wound—
so Madeleine would kneel on the stone floor and she would
kiss his white, vein-furrowed hand and look into his vein-

colored eyes, and the old Duke would smile as though he had
found a daughter... So the imagination, like a city dweller out
for a walk, if left to its own devices, will wander from any start-
ing point to the same destination. Madeleine had established
herself in the Duke's household, and had, we must admit it, almost forgotten the fleshly Baron when the carriage stopped.
Haussmann pulled the curtains back a finger's width and announced, — We're here.

He helped Madeleine into the rue Le Regrattier, a narrow
and practically lightless street. On the corner, in a niche, stood a
statue of a woman whose head had been broken off. The in-
scription under the statue read, THE PERFECT WIFE.

— How strange! Madeleine said. Do you think they called
her that before she lost her head, or after?

Haussmann thought of his own wife, who complained
of pains in her midsection that neither doctors nor priests
could relieve. He had promised to write to a specialist in London—promised Valentine, that is; Octavie herself asked for
nothing. — Before, doubtless. I don't think the statues in Paris
have much of a sense of humor.

— Are you sure?

— Certain. Now come inside.

Haussmann followed Madeleine into the smell of long-
polished wood and moldering carpet that plagues every old stair-
well in Paris. At the first landing the Baron fumbled in his
pockets and came up with an unfamiliar key, with which he
opened the door to an apartment in which, as far as Madeleine
could tell, no duke had ever lived, or would ever dream of living.

— Well, Mouse, what do you think of our hidey-hole?

— It's dark.

As a favor to the young couple—de Fonce's phrase—the
demolition man had opened his warehouses and let their treasure pour forth into the apartment: a mahogany armoire borne

on the backs of griffins; candelabra that had been carried by
maidens through the drafty Norman castles which the spirits of
those selfsame maidens now doubtless haunted; a sofa in deep
brown velvet fringed in gold; and brown velvet drapes which
had suffered a little in the decades of their sabbatical. On the
mantel in the front parlor, the brass Egyptian dog which Haussmann had once admired kept watch, as though the place really
were a tomb. The windows of the front parlor let in murky
streetlight; beyond that all was dark or dim. Candles rather than
gaslight. And the smell! As though the teeth of the wood were
rotting in its mouth. But a room is a room, Madeleine told herself; what matters is who's in it. And she had Haussmann, who
turned about in the small parlor like a seagoing vessel trying to
moor itself to a riverbank.

— It'll be better when I light some candles, Haussmann
said.

— No.

— No?

— Dark is better. She took his hand. Where's the bed?

— It's over here. My mouse.

— My baron.

— Your nobody, my dear. Your no one.

In her room high up in the Hôtel de Ville, Octavie finished the
last volume of her Swiss mystic and began a letter to her
brother in Bordeaux. Dear Jean, she wrote,

We have had a spell of cool weather at last, and everyone
went to the Bois. How I wish you were here with me, to
take me riding! M. Haussmann is very busy with his wa-
terworks; Marie and Valentine are at an age when their
mother must be less important to them than their beaux.

And of course, one does not go riding here: one is driven. So it is better that you stay where you are, and watch over Mother and Father. I like to think of you there, your feet on the fire rail, and your eyes, Jean, your eyes looking ahead to tomorrow morning's mist, and the path between the old trees. Please do not think of me too much; or if you do, think of me as though I were there. For I *am* there, when I write to you, my feet warming next to yours, and when you wake tomorrow, remember that I accompany you. Your affectionate sister, etc.

Octavie puts her pen down. It is twelve o'clock. Her husband is not home, nor does she wonder where he is, for this is Paris, and these are the alien ways of that place, which she never expected to comprehend.

One night became a dozen, became a score of nights stolen from the world of names. By day Georges-Eugène Haussmann, Prefect of Paris, by night no one at all: a pair of hands touching Madeleine's thighs in the dark; a mouth pressed to her breast; a tongue on her lips, her ears, the convexities and concavities of her belly. The next morning, before dawn, a carriage bearing the arms of the Anonyme family (i.e., none at all) carried him home to Haussmann again. But now a secret life had been added to his own. He wore it hidden on the reverse of his coat, like a tailor's mark. Beneath his public costume he wore another, invisible, and so long as he wore it the world was a play. By day he spoke his lines; night took him, again and again, to the apartment on Headless Woman Street, to Madeleine. One night multiplied, divided, carried over; Haussmann and Madeleine came and went, undressed and dressed again, and the night went on and on, and on. In this way seven years passed.

Seven years. In all that time Haussmann never stopped wondering at the child he had found (memory was still kind to him
then, and allowed him to forget that, properly speaking, she had
been found for him), at her beauty and strength and at how little she changed. At twenty-four she looked little different than
she had at seventeen; her face was as fresh, her eyes as clear, her
movements as gently awkward as they had always been. Her
heart, too (if we sophisticates of the mind can speak of such
things), was unchanged: still yearning for experience, Madeleine
seemed to have taken no note of the fact that she'd spent seven
years in the company of the Prefect, who was, some would say,
the source of all experience in Paris. She still wished in her
quiet way that she could see what the city was *really* like, as
though it was really any different from what she saw: the procession of speculators and aristocrats who tromped through the
corridors of the theaters, sniffing out scandal and champagne.
What an innocent she was! Haussmann wondered sometimes
how she could go on like that. Yet she did go on, and did not
change; nor could he change her. She listened eagerly to everything he said, but it was like throwing stones into deep water; in
a second not a trace of his words remained. Haussmann spoke
of Octavie and how he regretted not having waited longer before he asked her for her hand, for a woman can be one thing
in Bordeaux and in Paris quite another; he spoke of leaving the
city some day with Madeleine, and living with her in the country somewhere; he said with some truth that he was tired of ad-
ministration, terribly tired, and that he would be pleased to
leave his job to a younger man as soon as he was sure that his
projects would be carried out. Yes yes, Haussmann said, they
would leave Paris together some day but not yet.

In the meanwhile, the apartment on Headless Woman Street
became a province of its own. To cheer the place up a little,
Haussmann filled it with objects from distant countries, from
Prussia and China and from Turkey, where he had friends and

powerful connections. In 1855 the Ottoman Emperor had sent
his viceroy Ismaïl Pasha to Paris, and Haussmann had made him
feel not a stranger in this, the strangest of cities. He had come,
he said, to learn; the Sultan was dissatisfied with Constantinople
and was thinking of making some improvements. They drove
around all night in an open carriage, and Ismaïl Pasha rubbed
his hands together with delight. — So magnificent! So magnificent! Is it real? Haussmann assured him that it was real. — It is
almost like magic, said Ismaïl Pasha, but really it is you who are
the magician. The Viceroy has been sending presents ever since.
A sword, a brass mask, boxes inlaid with ivory which smelled
richly of another world. A tusk arrived in the mail one day; a
month later the sender arrived in Paris with its mate. In addition to the tusk, he brought a mechanical bird which hopped
from one leg to the other and sang for as long as you kept
winding it. He sent invitations, too, begging Haussmann to see
him in Constantinople—though it is very poor and not full of
wonders like your Paris! Madeleine, enchanted by the bird, did
not believe him. Haussmann promised to take her there some
day to see for herself. In the meanwhile she had the bird to
keep her company, to sing of lands where everything was magic
which here was real, and vice versa; and she had the Baron.

In seven years Paris grew like a greenhouse plant, secured
with the stakes and wires of Haussmann's designs. Sewers there
were, and roads, and the foundation of a new opera house. The
streets were made so wide that no rabble could hope to barricade them, and Haussmann reassured the Emperor that he need
not fear revolution. The five regimes Louis Napoleon had lived
through were the only ones he would ever see, and the fifth,
the last and most glorious, the Second Empire, would last as
long, Your Majesty, as stone lasts, as long as parallel lines do not
meet. Some have called this Haussmann's great achievement,
for good or ill: he made Paris revolution-proof. This argument,

however, overlooks two important facts. The first is the year 1871, when the Commune and the Republic fought as bloody a war as was ever fought in Paris. The number of casualties on both sides attest to the failure of the boulevards to secure the city from anything, or for anyone, for long.

The second fact, frequently overlooked, is that Haussmann achieved something far greater, or at least more demonstrably successful: the Aqueduct. It was finished in 1865, and there was a grand opening ceremony attended by the Emperor and all the members of the Academy of Sciences. Everyone praised the Prefect. They took turns standing up and speaking eloquently of his resourcefulness, his determination, his devotion to the health of the city, to the cause of science, to His Majesty's desire to make public improvements. The Emperor smiled sleepily through the whole thing. After every speech the crowd—mostly workmen who wouldn't have jobs at all if not for the Aqueduct—applauded with merry incomprehension. Hurrah for Haussmann! they shouted, and in the streets beyond people leaned from the windows and waved flags. Hurrah for Haussmann! There was not a single dissenting voice in the whole crowd. Flags flew; the Prefect turned a symbolic valve and water (so it *was* water!) filled a cistern with a deep, mysterious chugging. The Emperor applauded politely. Hurrah! All the papers, at least all the ones which had not been closed down, reported on the event. Everyone agreed that this was a magnificent time, theirs a magnificent Prefect in service to a magnificent Emperor, who together had given them the most splendid city in the world. Hurrah! The flags snapped in an untroubled April sky.

That evening Haussmann arrived at the apartment like a conquering army. — Come here, Mouse! he said.

But she did not come.

— I'm the good Sister Madeleine, she said. No pleasures of the flesh for me! Would you like me to read aloud from an edifying book?

Haussmann, who got more than enough of that at home, growled and grabbed for her waist.

— La, sir, refrain! You must not profit from the ignorance of a girl who's lived all her life in a cloister, and knows nothing of the world.

— Enough, Madeleine. I've only got an hour.

— Only an hour, gallant knight? But true love knows no hours, nor no minutes, isn't that so? I haven't read that Galahad carried a pocket watch. Not even one as fine as yours.

— Ha, said Haussmann, touching the watch involuntarily.

— What business takes you so soon from your paramour?

— Paramour? Well, that's more like it. Give your swain a kiss.

— Not until you answer.

— Dinner with the Emperor. Madeleine, do you know what he said today? He said that he was considering making me the Count of Champagne, and do you know what I told him? I told him that Count wasn't good enough for me! What do you want, then, he asked me, a duchy? I said that a duchy wasn't good enough either. The Emperor said, well, my infernal Prefect, what do you want then? I said, Sire, if you are going to give me a title, you must make me an Aqueduke! An Aqueduke! Can you imagine? He laughed out loud, I don't think he'd ever heard anything so funny. An Aqueduke, nothing less... Well, Haussmann said apologetically, we've got to pass our hour together somehow.

In a kinder voice he added: — What's the matter, my love?

— Nothing's the matter.

She peered out the window as though on the lookout for an arriving ship. No ship seemed to be on the way, though, and a moment later she asked, — Why don't you take me anywhere?

— What?

— Are you ashamed of me?

— I took you to the theater last week, and didn't we go for a ride in the Bois afterwards?

— In the middle of the night.

— The night air's refreshing. Isn't it?

Madeleine said nothing.

— Besides, I took you to dinner at the Café Anglais, or is that not what you call somewhere? It's good enough for everyone else, anyway.

— Yes, you took me. At midnight, and you didn't introduce me to anyone!

— But, my dear, one doesn't introduce one's mistress.

Madeleine was crushed by the self-evidence of that. It had been clear to her all along that she was his mistress—what else could she be? She had even used the word "mistress." It had in her interior discussions of the subject a deliciously public intimacy. It was a secret relation between two people which must be talked about everywhere. She had never considered that, from within, one might see the affair only in its private aspect, that, in other words, in consenting to be Haussmann's mistress she had stepped from one seclusion into another.

— Come here, Haussmann said. Sit beside me.

— What is it?

— Sit.

Haussmann kissed her hair. — The earth doesn't hold another treasure like you, he whispered. No one will ever dig another up. He kissed her neck. — Now tell me, Sister (he cupped her breast), did the convent educate you in this?

Which of course it had, but Madeleine couldn't think of a way to tell him so.

She received a large box the next day with a note from the Baron. Dearest Madeleine, it read. Where would you like to go? With much love, your brilliant and inventive M. Anonyme. The signature was done with flair, Madeleine had to give him that: all lighthearted and looping, as a lover's signature ought to be. Below the note, folded in tissue paper, a dress.

13

THE MAGNIFICENT SMUTS

VIOLLET-LE-DUC, in his *Reasoned Dictionary of Architecture*, wrote that "as always happens when a system, adopted long ago, is pushed to its limits, one ends up losing all trace of the principles on which it was based." He was referring to the arches and buttresses of the Gothic cathedral, to its ribbed vaults, its gables, to the decoration of every piece of stone which might, without risk of structural infirmity, be carved with reliefs, crockets, and foils, so that, in the end, the cathedral became like one of those historical paintings commissioned by this or that rich burgher, in which absolutely every detail of an important event (including many that could not possibly have been visible to anyone at the time) must be depicted in lucid and full-fleshed detail, until nothing whatsoever can be clearly distinguished—forgetting altogether its (the Gothic cathedral's, that is) original purpose, to be a magic lantern for the divinity to bring to life, its colored legends turning in infinite space according to the motion of the sun; but Viollet-le-Duc might, in the same words, have described the ladies' fashions of the Second Empire. The crinoline dress, symbol, in fashion, of the Empire's artful if unwieldy excesses, gave its wearer the silhouette of a handbell, and much of that instrument's charm. Its upper part adhered more or less closely to the lady's form, or at least to some idealized version thereof, sculpted by hidden whalebone stays; the skirt, on the other hand, ballooned away from the legs in a great hemisphere of fabric, supported within by a set of concentric metal hoops. Often the skirt was so wide that it could not pass through doorways; as for getting in and out of carriages, well, it took an accomplished wearer. What the original purpose of this dress might have been, it was impossible to guess. Was it to keep the rain off? To flatter the form? Was it a sort of fortification, this steel-belted skirt which you would need a ladder to besiege? Or was it a diving bell, in which ladies might travel underwater? But its weight militated against that: a full crinoline, with its hoops and ribs, its folds and ribbons and knots, weighed eighty pounds or more. Whatever its intent, the gown's form recalled the cathedrals of old: its sides supported by wide-arching ribs, its bustle buttressed, its surface ornamented everywhere ornament might be affixed.

Such was the dress Haussmann sent her. It didn't fit. Madeleine wondered, as she stood looking at herself in the mirror, why he had sent it. A crinoline had to be fitted to the wearer; each one was as singular as a face, similar to the others only in the number and general arrangement of its features. She turned, turned back, tried to alter herself to fit the dress. What was brilliant and inventive about someone else's dress? Perhaps she could get the Baron to borrow de Fonce's pants, and they'd do some play-acting together. Then, at the bottom of the box, she saw a square of pasteboard, one of the small photographs called *cartes-de-visite*. It showed Haussmann seated in a chair, reading a book, evidently pleased with himself. And no wonder: behind him stood a beauty, tall and fair-haired, resting her hand on his shoulder. The dress she wore in the photograph was the one Madeleine held in her hands. Worse and worse!

Haussmann had sent along one of his old mistress's dresses, and although Madeleine couldn't imagine what the point of that was she knew it was bad. Brilliant and inventive indeed! She imagined cutting the dress into patches and sending it back to him, to show him what sort of invention she was capable of. Then she turned the photograph over. On the reverse was written, "M. HAUSSMANN and his daughter Fanny-Valentine, February 1864. Studio of M. RAYEUX, photographer to His Highness Napoleon III of the French." Valentine. Haussmann had spoken of her before. She was his younger daughter, and he said that he loved her very much. Where would you like to go? Dressed as Valentine... Madeleine trembled. Dressed as Valentine she could go anywhere, but it was ridiculous to think that anyone would mistake her for Haussmann's daughter. She was dark and Valentine fair, she was short and Valentine tall, and in any case it was ridiculous. She called for a maid to help her off with the dress. When it was folded in its tissue paper again she turned back to the mirror and was surprised to see her own body there, cool and naked as any other.

At dinner Madeleine told de Fonce and the Widow Couvre-feu about Haussmann's gift. She tried to make it clear that she had no intention of impersonating the Prefect's daughter, but the Widow, detecting, perhaps, more uncertainty in her voice than she was herself aware of, said, — You needn't worry about the real Valentine getting in your way. Apparently she does whatever Haussmann tells her. The poor creature!

— Why poor?

The Widow reported what she had heard from the younger M. de Goncourt, who knew everything: how Haussmann had forced his daughter to break off her engagement with a young member of the National Assembly whose politics were more republican than Haussmann would have liked. — And that's not all, the Widow said. Madame de la Vallée says that Valentine used to be the Emperor's mistress. With her father's consent, of course...

— Stop it! You're just saying that because you hate him.

— Am I? All sorts of men are loaning their daughters out these days... De Fonce raised an eyebrow, and the Widow concluded awkwardly: — And in any case people will gossip about anything.

— I wonder what she's like.

—Valentine? I hear she's clever, and quick with words, but, my dear, that shouldn't concern you in the least, because if anyone came close enough to hear you, you'd be sunk. What a stupid scheme! I suppose it's what you'd expect from our magnificent Prefect.

De Fonce said only, — If you don't think you can pull it off, my dear, then by all means don't try.

In the spring of 1865, Haussmann and Valentine went to the Opéra; afterward they dined together in a private dining room. Haussmann and Valentine went to the Bois on Sunday and passed the Emperor, who wished them well. Haussmann and Valentine attended the unveiling of an equestrian statue of Napoleon the First. Haussmann and Valentine visited the Samaritaine department store and bought all sorts of things and tipped the clerks handsomely, and if some of the items they bought were not, strictly speaking, the sort of things a father and daughter ordinarily buy together, the clerks weighed their coins and kept their mouths shut. No one else remarked on it, either. Why should they? The public eye looked as far as the dress and stopped there, because what would be the point of having such a singular dress if more than one person could wear it? If the interior of Chartres were gutted and some philistine set up shop within selling hats, would those passing by say,

— Oh, there's the hat shop! No. They'd call it a cathedral and walk on. So Haussmann and his daughter went everywhere together, and everyone walked on.

Besides, there were more important things to think about. Cholera had broken out in Naples, and the citizens of Marseilles were turning away Italian ships from their port; merchants were angry, prices high, and profits low, and if you spent too much time looking at ladies' dresses someone might pick your pocket, figuratively or in fact. There was news in Paris, too, electrifying news: the Magnificent Smuts was coming to town. Handbills found their way to lampposts and the sides of public urinals, to the Morris columns and to the windows of dry goods stores; the advertisement ran in the papers of the left and right and center, in journals Catholic and atheistical, in the sporting press and the ladies' circulars, next to the patterns for a new kind of stay: Hypnotist Extraordinaire. Acclaimed on Four Continents, Advisor to Emperors and Kings of All Principalities, Counselor to the Grand Turk, J. Smuts will Unravel the Secrets of the Human Mind for your delectation. Smuts Sees All. Ladies Cautioned. Exclusive Engagement at the Théâtre de l'Ambigu, June... Set above these phrases was a picture of the Magnificent Smuts, a pop-eyed gentleman with the posture of a garden snake, and below the text the magician's sigil, a pyramid bisected neatly from apex to base and split open as though it were a bonbon full of sweet liqueur. Word made its way from the heights of the city to its depths: Smuts was coming. Smuts, who had foreseen the death of the Great Bey; Smuts, whose eyes had cured the Cardinal Ottonase of pleurisy and soothed the fevered brain of the Tsarevitch; Smuts, who, it was said, stood closer to the Divine Powers than anyone had since Swedenborg retired from the flesh to the peaceful and airy Beyond. Smuts would perform!

The crowds who watched the great man's carriage roll from

train station to hotel put to shame the turnout for the Universal Exhibition. There wasn't room for another eye in the street,
and not a dry eye among them. Those who'd seen the carriage
pass felt a frisson, as though the curtained brougham contained
a powerful magnet tuned to the frequency of the heart. The
spectators returned to their homes more solemn than when
they'd left, and when the dishes had been cleared they reflected
as one on the mysteries of the soul and the difficulty of obtain-
ing tickets to Smuts's performance.

Naturally Haussmann couldn't resist. As soon as the show
was announced, one of his aides reserved a box for it; he told
Madame Haussmann that night that she might learn something
of his interest in the human spirit, if only she'd pay close
enough attention. But she never saw it. Madame Haussmann
was unwell; she had been unwell for several days, and her un-
wellness had spread outward from her aging body to the heavy
drapery of her bedroom; when the disease had spread so far
there was no cure but a change of scenery. So she planned a
trip to Bordeaux, to her father's house, to listen in all tranquil-
lity to the small gossip of wine merchants and stud farmers, a
world of men dwarfed by the weather.

— You'll miss Smuts, Georges-Eugène cautioned her.

— I'm sure, Octavie sighed, that you'll tell me all about it.
But really I'm not well enough for such a carnival...

— Carnival! My dear, he's a scholar. A cartographer of the
brain. A magnetic genius! Haussmann looked at the rug. — And
he might make you well.

— Is *that* it? Octavie asked. You'd make me stand up in a
theater and tell half Paris of the terrible pain in my womb...

Haussmann winced. — My dear, you mustn't say "my womb,"
some of the doctors say one thing and some of them say another.

— And point to where it hurts! And pull up my skirts like a

fishwife... The conversation ended badly. In such moments, when Octavie's aches pull her face tight, Haussmann wants only to contain her, to put her voice in a box and bury the box deep underground. — If you'd only come with me to Bordeaux, she said.

The Baron turned his back to the room and stared into the glass over the mantel. His boxy, handsome face was still calm; it was a face he could present without shame to the Emperor or to any dignitary who happened by. Behind him Octavie had rung for the maid, and was explaining to her which of her things to pack. He reached up to stroke his beard, then absently his cheek, his eyes focused on a plane beyond that of the mirror or of the reflection. He left without saying another word to Octavie, and only nodded when the servant came to his private office to inform him that she had gone.

When the prefectoral coach arrived outside the Théâtre de l'Ambigu and a footman scrambled down to open the door for the personages within, it was Madeleine whom Haussmann assisted to the ground. Madeleine, splendid in Valentine's dress and diamond earrings she'd borrowed from the Widow, drifted on Haussmann's arm as though she were a domestic sprite, brought by the Prefect as empirical proof of the spirit world.

— Thank you, father, she said as he handed her down.
— Of course. Valentine.

Did he blush? The yellow light of the theater stole the color from everything, and Madeleine could not tell.

Of course Haussmann was not ashamed. All day his head had been aching, probably because of the extraordinary difficulty of being Prefect, and also, perhaps, in illicit sympathy with his wife's complaints. Tonight, when he'd come back to the

apartment after Octavie left, he found the real Valentine sitting
in his armchair, her hands folded in her lap.

— Mother says she's leaving for good, she said. What have
you done this time?

— Nothing. I invited her to see Smuts.

Valentine laughed. — But Father, she's devout! She probably
thinks Smuts is the devil.

— I thought it would be good for her to learn something
about the magnetic operation of the, of the...

— You didn't want to go alone, admit it. Well, I'm ready to
offer myself up as a sacrifice. I've already seen the Devil and he
hasn't done me a great deal of harm.

— You've seen him? Haussmann asked, thinking guiltily of
de Fonce. Where?

— Why, at the Samaritaine. He was buying a butterfly net.
He said that the souls of men were too cheap these days, and
he'd resolved henceforth to collect only the souls of bugs...
What time are we going?

But Haussmann had already written to Madeleine, asking if
she would like to go. — I won't drag you along, he said. In fact
I'm not feeling well myself, probably I'll stay at home.

— As you wish, Valentine said, but if you meet the Devil, be
careful you don't offer him anything that's not yours.

She kissed his cheek and left him to reflect, as he did every
time he spoke with her, that he had no idea whether she was
joking or not. He wished that Valentine was with him now. His
headache had come back, and laughter was the only thing that
seemed to make it go away; and Madeleine, delightful as she
was in other ways, did not know how to make him laugh.

The Théâtre de l'Ambigu was packed to the gills with trades-
men who'd waited in line all night, wrapped in greasy over-

coats, coughing against the wind; small merchants and civil servants with their overstuffed wives dolled up like a child's play-
room attempt at majesty. Spiritual old women cracked their
knuckles in the shadows of the pit, and behind them a gaggle of
hangdog students from the Faculty of Medicine laughed and
plucked motes from their threadbare vests. All Paris looked
down on them: the imperial box half full of relations by marriage and their fathers confessor, who sat stupefied as though
they'd just eaten well; the Count de Morny was of course in attendance, though drunk; he supported his head with difficulty
on the shoulder of the young Marquise de Viandhachée, whose
wine-red lips hovered by the ear of the fat Chevalier Gastofouard, a bachelor like de Morny but not, like de Morny, by in-
clination; it was said that he'd lost something besides a company
of dragoons to the Russian artillery in the Crimea. Haussmann
watched them all with distaste, his head throbbing. It's marriage, he thought: marriage disagrees with you. When would
the show begin? People were staring at him from the pit. A pale
young man whom Haussmann remembered from somewhere
looked furtively upward, then down at his shirt front, on
which, Haussmann noted with disgust, he was taking notes.
Perhaps that was Fillier? He would have his spies look into it.

In the meantime he urged Madeleine to sit a little farther
back in the shadows of the box. — That young man is looking
at us.

— I thought he was looking at *me*, Madeleine said.

— All the worse, then...

Before Haussmann could carry the thought any further, the
show began. First there were tumblers, who threw themselves
into the air and sprung up from the ground with abandon as
though to prove that the body as well as the mind is capable of
the most extraordinary contortions. Then came a fire-eater
who sang comic airs even as he inhaled a column of flame; for

a chorus he belched smoke and blue light. A knife thrower from the Amazon jungle came next, and amazed the impatient audience by throwing a stiletto so precisely that it bisected the earlobe of his assistant; but then the crowd would have no more sideshows, and with much stamping demanded that the performance begin. So, with a flourish of trumpets and a rolling of bass drums such as hadn't been heard since Wagner assaulted the ears of Paris with his mountain-heavy *Tannhäuser*, the Magnificent Smuts was ushered onto the stage by a pair of houris in skirts of fine black tulle. The actual, fleshly Smuts was if anything an improvement over the lithographed version that had already charmed half the city. He carried himself with careful grace, as though even the soles of his feet were delicate instruments which had to be kept calibrated; his hands swung to and fro with the ease of metronomes, and his narrow chest rose and fell so evenly that it might have contained a miniature steam engine in place of a heart. He was dressed in a black coat and magnificent purple cape. Smuts walked to the center of the stage, and bowed slightly to the crowd which, at the sight of him, had gone still.

— Ladies and gentlemen! he cried in a French accented a little with the Beyond, and a little more with the East End of London. — Tonight you will learn the darkest secrets of the human soul!

— Watch, Haussmann whispered, here's a man who knows something!

— Are you ready for the most profound revelations? Look for a moment into your hearts, open the chest of your conscience and ask yourself whether you will, on your honor, be able to withstand the weight of so much knowledge! Ladies and gentlemen the human soul is not a garden! It is not a park such as your lovely Bois de Boulogne, in which I have recently had occasion for a meditative walk! Milady, Milord—did Smuts *curtsey*? he might have, but such was his hold on the audience that no one remarked on it—the human soul is a dark and a deep well, into which many things have been thrown which would be best forgotten. Tonight we will cast a bucket down into that well, and pull up what we may. Gentlemen and ladies, esteemed doctors of the court, have we any secrets? Tonight they will become known. Members of the Academy, colleagues, brethren, have we *fears*? Tonight they will walk! Have you any *wishes*? Tonight you will burn with them. Have you any long-ings? You will be consumed by them. Have you any hopes? You will breathe for them, only for them. Ladies, gentlemen, my children, tonight I will lay your hearts bare.

Haussmann sighed from the depths of his uneasy gut.

—You have only to watch, gentlemen, to watch, ladies, and not to hide your faces behind your fans, and you will see, pre-sented for you on the stage, the truth, the unmistakable truth. Watch now!

The houris, who had stepped into the wings, returned with swaths of cloth, swords, boxes, ropes, torches, wands, chains, hoops, and a table bearing three glasses of water.

— Pay close attention, my brothers and sisters, watch me as you have never watched yourselves, watch my hand! Smuts pulled from one cuff a gray mouse, who climbed his sleeve to perch on his shoulder. — Watch my eyes! From the other cuff he produced a flower, held it to his lips, and blew on it, where-upon it burst into flame and, ash now, fell to the floor silently. — Watch! Watch! With a sweep of his arm Smuts gathered three doves from the air where no doves had been before, and dropped them one by one into his hat, which, when he held it up for the audience to see, turned out to be empty.

And so it went, from parlor trick to parlor trick, each more splendid and fiery than the last. The houris jumped into the air and did not come down; the mouse turned into a bat and flew

up to join them; the water turned to blood and the blood to a
fine burgundy, as attested by a distinguished monsieur in the
first row. Haussmann clutched the sides of his chair, his mouth
dry and his stomach heavy. These were the secrets of the human
heart? These parlor tricks? Where was the magnetic fluid which
healed the sick and on occasion had been known to raise the
dead? Where were the miraculous confessions, the lost memories, the second selves? Smuts pulled a chain of handkerchieves
from the trouser leg of an apprentice carpenter.

— So *that's* where you've been keeping them, he cackled,
and a half-dozen eggs fell from the folds of brightly colored
cloth. — You reek of the henhouse, varlet, begone! The audience clapped as though they'd just now learned that apprentices
are notorious thieves.

Why, Haussmann thought, these tricks are nothing at all!
(Ah, a voice called up from his stomach, that's the trick.) Really
he didn't feel well: there was a knot in his right calf, and it was
too hot in the theater. Couldn't someone have done something
to keep the unwashed masses from coming in such great numbers? He wiped his forehead with his handkerchief. He was
going to leave, dragging Madeleine with him if she'd come
(though she seemed to have a fine appreciation for this sort of
chicanery, and clapped when the rest did) and leaving her behind if she wouldn't, when one of the houris rolled the box
onto the stage. It was just the size and shape of a coffin, a pauper's coffin, for the wood was unpainted and unadorned.

— And now, called Smuts, for one of the greatest conjura-
tions which it is my humble privilege to perform. My fellow
acolytes, I learned this wondrous transformation in the country
of the Turk, where it is the custom for wise men to float
above the ground. The man who taught it to me was one of
the greatest alchemists the world has seen, a wise man who can
not only make gold of lead but knows the secret of turning

flesh to glass, so that you can look right through a man's chest and see what secrets are in his heart! Sirs and dames, sires and dams, this man was no Turk, but an immortal Frenchman, the great Flamel, who as some of you may know took refuge in the city of Constantine after his supposed death! Watch carefully, and you'll see the wisdom of a man who cheated the grave.

With this, Smuts climbed into the box, waved for the last time, and allowed one of the houris to replace the lid. While the orchestra played a funereal number, the girl tied the outside of the box with rope, then fastened the rope with a chain, and the chain with a lock, the security of which she invited a member of the audience to test. Then, with the help of the same volunteer, she nailed the lid of the box into place. Wordlessly she gestured to the box, then draped it with a purple cloth. Holding the cloth by its corners, she pulled it up so that only her fingertips were visible; it hung there a second, a curtain between stage and pit. Then the curtain dropped, and it was Smuts who stood atop the box, but a Smuts transformed: he wore the costume of one of his assistants, and with rouged cheeks grinned at the shocked, then roaring audience. He paraded back and forth in front of the box for a minute or two, showing off a pair of rather thin and ungainly legs. At last he consented to pry the nails out of the lid, to unlock the lock and untie the rope, and, when the lid was lifted, struck the side of the box. A dozen frightened pigeons lost themselves in the gloom above the darkened chandelier.

— There you have it, Smuts called, my children, there it is, the great transformation of man to woman and woman to bird! There you have it, one of the secrets of Nature, all can be changed. That's it, gentlemen and ladies, one of the wonders, one of the great wonders. The curtain fell for intermission and the audience, as if delivered from a spell, began to clap, to rock

back and forth, to shift and scratch and rub their tingling
thighs.

Records exist in the letters provincial businessmen sent home
to their wives, and in the papers, which adored Haussmann
then the way a coral shell adores the animal within, in the
Goncourts' *Journal*, and in the memoirs of the Chevalier Gastofouard, which, though never published, achieved a certain no-
toriety, for in them he described the lengths to which society
ladies would go to get a rise out of a eunuch—records exist of
the end of the show: how Haussmann rose from his box, and,
once on his feet, clapped his hands to his face; how he tottered
like an ill-built column, and cried, I'm blind! Valentine, reported
the *Araignée du Matin*, "took the Prefect's hand, and led him
from the box, very much like the dutiful Antigone leading
sightless Oedipus to his final resting place..." which, in this case,
was the carpeted floor of the corridor, where he lay, stretched
out, hands fisted and eyes tight shut. Everyone remarked on the
Prefect's great height, which was much more evident from this
position.

In a moment the crowd was cleared, and the innumerable
bottles of smelling salts, perfume, brandy, and cool water were
pushed aside by a pair of ushers, whose families, by one of the
coincidences which are common in eventful times, had been
expropriated by the Baron not three months before. They bore
him no ill will. If not for the demolition men, the ushers, who
were scarcely more than boys, would still have been living at
home; now, with the money they'd got off the government,
they shared a room in a boardinghouse, where one slept before the theater and the other one afterward. It was a good
life, never dull, and if they complained about anything—
Gastofouard doesn't mention it—they would have remarked on

how heavy Haussmann was, and how difficult it was to get him anywhere against his will. The next morning, the *Illustrated Girls' Gazette* had a picture of it: beside the prostrate Baron a wide-eyed Valentine, copied from a popular portrait of the time. Around the two a circle of smiling pipe smokers, lifted from another engraving in lieu of an audience, on account of the short notice. Everyone knew that something had happened to Haussmann, although among the illiterate Parisians there was a great deal of uncertainty as to what, exactly, it was.

PART III

THE PLAGUE YEAR

(1865)

14

THE FLOWER MARKET

DEATH BEGINS IN the smallest things: a whisper, a wind, a drop of water. A woman draws water from a well, and fills her pail; her thirsty daughter drinks it down, cool cool water. Her daughter is hot, sweat beads her brow; the woman soaks a towel in water from the well, water on water; she gives the girl a cup and takes a drink herself. A kiss with parted lips, a pearl of warm water. Her daughter is burning up; she calls the doctor, who calls for water; the daughter drinks and knocks the bucket over, it spills into the gutter, the gutter flows into the river, water into water. Who can say how far a single drop will spread? The daughter's dead, her mother follows after. There was no way to tell. The sexton pulls the rope that rings the bell, the rain falls on the woman three days dead and sinks into the ground, seeking the level of the water. The water rises in the well. Where will it end? The sexton shakes his head. There is no way to tell.

In Paris, in 1865, everyone drank from the same cup: what touched one, touched all. Of course it started small. Two cases were reported on June 4, eight on the 6th; on the 11th twenty-three, and on the 12th sixty-one; two hundred on the 22nd,

and then it was official: the cholera had returned to Paris. After
a tour in the provinces and abroad, it came back with a fine
color and a number of odd habits, such as bleeding from the
ears, which it had learned in the wilder parts of the world. In
other respects the cholera of 1865 resembled those of 1854 and
1849. Like a painter, its work favored different colors in different periods. In the White Period you got the runs, then vom-
ited a whitish fluid like rice gruel; then your calves ached and
you began to hiccup. Then you went blind. Your face, hands,
and feet grew cold; your skin stiffened and black spots appeared
on your nails. This was the Blue Period. Many patients, weak
canvases for such frosty art, collapsed here and so never saw the
painter's third, or Red Period, when the chill turned to fever,
stiffness to spasms, and spasms to delirium, which might end in
a congestion of the heart, the bowels, or the brain. This was the
general way of it, but the cholera's career was different in each
patient. In some he forwent the White Period and began with
the Blue; in others, fortunate though not particularly comfortable, he got stuck in the White Period and exhausted his talents
there. Sometimes, like a master returning to the influences of
his youth, the cholera might dabble in White, Blue, or Red
months after the disease was presumed to be over; sometimes
this late work achieved the finished quality which the earlier
essays had lacked.

What caused the cholera? On this question opinion was divided. The dominant school held that it was caused by the noxious vapors which rose up from the ground in unhealthy parts
of the world. This was the theory of infection. The opposing
camp held that cholera was contagious, in other words, that you
caught it from other people. This was by far the less popular
opinion, as it had terrible moral consequences. If people made
each other ill, then mothers might abandon their children, and
children their parents; brother would sequester brother and

soon Paris wouldn't have two citizens to rub shoulders with. On the other hand, the thought that the ground exhaled poison wasn't so pleasant, either. How could you fight the breath of the earth? The Parisians, who didn't like to be stumped by any question for long, soon came up with a cure-all foolproof prophylactic remedy against anything the ground or their fellow men might waft their way: flowers. Stern gentlemen who had never bought flowers for a lady walked about with nosegays pressed to their moustaches, which brightened the streets around the Palace of Justice and Hôtel de Ville, and did a little to offset the dullness of so many black dresses, shawls, hats, gloves, and armbands. The Parisians favored persicaria, which in the language of flowers meant "restoration"; they sought white poppies, which meant "my antidote." The Flower Market was so popular that you had to get there by seven in the morning if you wanted to find anything; by half-past eight there was nothing left but pennyroyal ("flee away") and cardamine ("paternal error"). Even these were bought up, along with the shrubs and the nonflowering or nonodoriferous plants people purchased because of a belief, dating back to the alchemists, that anything which was like a flower ought to have something like the same effect. It didn't help. The gentlemen with nosegays died at approximately the same rate as those without; those who'd invested in shrubs died; the flower sellers died rich and were succeeded by prudent relatives who, like anyone with any sense, had already fled to the country to wait out the plague. By August even the Flower Market was deserted.

Haussmann was one of the first victims, a circumstance which would be remarked on much later when the cholera had passed and people tried to make sense of what had happened. He was carried from the theater straight to his prefectoral bed, where he lay groaning so loudly that his servants were afraid to come near him. It was as though a great beast had gotten into the Prefect and was gnawing its way out; they did not want to see what face that beast would wear when it had burst free to walk among men. Even the doctors were inclined to give their patient up to the course of his disease. Only Octavie sat by his bedside; she held his hand without trembling and shamed the doctors into doing their job. The servants whispered that Haussmann was a dead man; they said that his blood steamed when the doctors let it out of him, and when they put a wet cloth to his head the cloth came away brown and crisp like an old piece of paper. But when they saw Octavie offering tea to the doctors, and talking to them quietly about the weather in the provinces, they too were ashamed, and went about their work with eyes cast down.

Every morning Octavie went to the Flower Market and bought a spray of blue flowers. Blue for Empire, between the white of the old Bourbons and the republicans' red; she thought that if any flowers would move the Baron to health it would be these, belladonna, with bells enough for a cathedral and a breath like the breath of night. They shriveled in their vases by midday. At one o'clock Octavie went to the market again, and again paid what was necessary for two dozen blue flowers. By evening their petals drooped, and by first light they were practically gone—and this too the servants took as a sign that the Baron must die soon. When a man's breath withers the petals of four dozen flowers a day, then there must be much death in his frame, even if it be a frame so large and formerly full of life as the Prefect's. Octavie did not relent. Twice a day she went out, dressed in a brown dress and shawled in brown; twice a day she came back with fresh flowers for the Baron, and swept from the floor the remnants of the old. Four dozen flowers a day for the Empire! Soon it would need more than that, for it was ailing, too: Louis Napoleon had bladder stones and they consumed some of his icy, enigmatic will; France lurched, and already the Prussians and the Austrians were shaking their heads and sharpening their swords. No quantity of blue flowers could cure that ill.

For nine days Haussmann roared. On the tenth he grew quiet and slept. The weather had got cooler, too; fall advanced the city a week of breezes and gold light. The flowers kept together, and a good thing it was, for there was no more belladonna to be had for any price at the Flower Market, and Octavie, if her husband's illness had continued, would have had to choose the colors of another allegiance. On the eleventh day the Baron opened his eyes and saw Octavie by his bedside, reading the second volume of a *Life of Menno*.

— What's that smell? he asked.

— Belladonna, said Octavie.

— Ah, said Haussmann, and fell asleep again. When he woke it was another day. — My dear, what time is it?

— Almost nine o'clock.

— In the morning, do you mean, or at night?

— In the morning.

— Do I have any appointments?

— No, they've all been put off.

— Make me one for nine-thirty, Haussmann said weakly.

— Whom would you like to see? Octavie asked. She smiled indulgently as the Prefect struggled to compose himself.

— My secretary, he said.

— I believe he's sick.

— Then his assistant.

— Him, too.

— Well, who's left?

Haussmann took every measure he could to keep the cholera under control. He ordered the sick transported to plague wards and quarantined, transformed barracks to hospitals and omnibuses to ambulances; he paid the doctors double and the gravediggers treble salaries; the railroad brought medication by the carload. Of course cholera was caused by vapors from the ground; but just in case it wasn't, he decreed that the belongings of the deceased be burned in public bonfires, which entertained the survivors for a while. Who would have guessed that mattresses burn yellow, and beds orange? That a cedar chest blazes like a firework and smokes like a forest aflame? Or that papers in sufficient quantity burn blue? Who knew that in the baggage of an ordinary life there lurked this sound-and-light show, this circus, this festival! Everyone who could stand came out to watch the fires, although not all those who watched them approved.

— Only I don't see the point of it! grumbled a thin bourgeois gentleman in the place de la Trinité. Why burn what you could sell?

— Haven't you heard? asked a man in a Republican-era nightcap.

— Heard what?

— It's the Prefect, said the republican. He's the one as gave us the disease.

— The Prefect? Why, whatever for?

— Dullard, are you? To drive the prices down.

— Speak sense, man. What prices?

— The price of a house, citizen. When we're all dead and buried, he'll get our houses for nothing.

— I doubt he wants *your* house, my friend! Eh, Delesse, what do you say?

The thin bourgeois' fat friend quipped, — Not if *he* lives there.

— O, laugh, citizens, laugh. He'll buy them so he can knock them down, wait and see.

— Be reasonable...

— Knock them down and give the land to the Jew Rothschild to build his personal privy on, that's what'll be, citizens.

— I doubt...

— That's your modern Paris! A place for your rich gentleman to shit upon.

— Hear, hear! said a man close by in the crowd.

— Now that's enough! The Prefect serves the Emperor, as we all do, isn't that so?

— The Prefect's a Jew! asserted another spectator. Hasn't he got a German name?

— Is that right? Well, that explains it.

— Explains what? Please, gentlemen, please...

— Hear, hear!

— You're speaking the purest nonsense. I happen to know that Haussmann's as much a Frenchman as you or I, said the fat gentleman.

— That's what they all say, growled the republican.

— Anyway you look a little Italian.

— Italian? Me?

— Ignore him! He's an Italian terrorist.

— In any case, the fat gentleman said, Haussmann couldn't give you cholera if he wanted to. Comes from the ground, don't you know? Poison vapors and all that.

— No, there you're wrong, said an old man. It is written: when the ruler of the city has a black heart, then the city sickens.

— Hear, hear!

— And where's that written, old man? asked the skinny bourgeois.

— There's a judgment's been passed here.

— Listen to him!

— Hear, hear!

— I'll tell you where cholera comes from, too. It's that Aqueduct! I swear his foreign water must have poisoned half

the city by now, and if the other half's still sound it's only because we (he tapped the side of his nose) know better than to
drink it. Down with foreigners, and foreign water! Down with
the Jews!

— Down with Haussmann!

— Hear hear!

Did discontent really spread in such haphazard exchanges,
from mouth to mouth to mouth? Or was it something in the
air? Infection or contagion? Either way the result was the same.
As the hospitals turned to hospices and the graveyards to char-
nel houses, Paris sickened with mistrust. Their Prefect was no
longer Haussmann the Magnificent but Haussmannoff the
First, tyrant of Paris. They called him the Butcher Baron and
accused him of every sort of wrongdoing from embezzlement
to witchcraft. The plotting that once seemed industrious now
struck the citizens as sinister: what was Haussmann up to in
that office of his? Pedestrians who had to pass the Hôtel de
Ville at night crossed to the other side of the square and did not
raise their heads. They feared Haussmann as villagers for centuries have feared their local sorcerers: impotently, from a distance, muttering curses.

In the house opposite the Parc Monceau, everything went on
as before but with slightly fewer people. The cook came down
with something and, fatally, kept working for a day or two; then
all the servants fell sick except the few who fled to the country.
Only de Fonce seemed immune. He called for his carriage at
dawn and sprang into it with such vigor that those who saw
him wondered whether the horses were really pulling the carriage along or whether the demolition man hadn't found some
way, from the inside, to push. He came home after midnight
and went straight to his office; if he slept at all, no one caught

him at it. Business had never been better. From the dead and the dying he bought up a museum's worth of treasures, and filled his house with them from cellar to attic, a stock against the day when death would seem a little more distant, and people would be buying again. Land, too, came de Fonce's way in great swaths; he returned home with his pockets overflowing with deeds, and worked through the night drawing up contracts, bills of sale, the papers that finalized his possession of a fortune in real estate. He did not tire. In fact de Fonce had never seemed as cheerful as he did then: he drank his wine off in great gulps and told Madeleine stories about the curious people he had known on his travels through France before he settled in Paris. He spoke fondly and at length of his life in the Auvergne, before he was apprenticed to the smith: a happy though solitary childhood, marked but not marred by the deformity of his foot. He used to take an interest in animals, insects, birds, and in all kinds of life; with his keen eyes he soon learned to tell the species apart, and might have gone on to be a great naturalist if only he hadn't been shackled, figuratively of course, for so long to his master's anvil.

— Ha! I could have been anything, he exclaimed, but nothing would have made me happier than I am now. He kissed Madeleine and his lips burned where they touched—or was it Madeleine who felt a little warmer than usual? As the guests stopped coming and the servants fled, de Fonce seemed actually to grow larger, as though to replace everything that was missing. His feet sounded louder coming up the stairs; his appetite was larger, even his candle-cast shadow was larger against the walls of the bedroom, when he came in just before dawn to embrace Madeleine. And in bed—well, he seemed larger there, too; Madeleine didn't know whether to be pleased or alarmed. The butler left for the country, and de Fonce buttled with clownish flourishes; the cook went off to die and de Fonce

took his place in the kitchen, where with more determination
than skill he prepared the rustic dishes he'd eaten as a child.
When the last servant left, or almost the last, de Fonce beamed,
— Now it's just the two of us, my child, but you and I are
world enough. Aren't we? At least you are world enough for
me, and, as for myself, I will endeavor to be everything.
Madeleine imagined a planet from which everyone but the
demolition man had disappeared: de Fonce, large as a cathedral,
strode up and down, tending with enormous fingers to all the
things people had left behind.

Despite de Fonce's increased presence it was a lonely time
for Madeleine. First she had no news of Haussmann, except
what was reported in the papers, which gave so many conflict-
ing accounts of the Prefect's collapse that she stopped reading
them altogether. Then, weeks after the Magnificent Smuts had
played his final trick, she got a letter from the Baron saying
only that he was recovering, but very busy with measures of
sanitation, etc., etc. and would visit her in a little while. In the
meanwhile he begged Madeleine to be patient, and offered her
a friend's concern for her health, and a lover's for her heart.

— He's the one who must be *patient*, de Fonce joked when
she showed him the letter.

— But what does he mean, a little while? A week, or a
month?

— Well, no prefect's perfect. De Fonce took Madeleine in
his thick arms. She shivered.

— Don't cry, he said, and Madeleine looked up quite dry-
eyed. — What's wrong, my dear? You're shaking.

— It's nothing. Now let me go.

Madeleine grew colder as the days went by; then she felt
warm and tired and could not sleep, but lay awake on a sofa in
the demolition man's office, watching his pen appropriate the
city in giant plots. Not that she was sick: in fact she felt very
well, thank you, and she would take another bowl of soup to

prove it; then she would go for a walk in the park. But when
the soup would not stay down, and the ground would not
remain still, but tossed her about like a baby in a blanket,
Madeleine had to admit that something was wrong. De Fonce
didn't hold with flowers; he summoned so many doctors that
Madeleine wondered if she'd been transported to a medical
college in the night. She learned what Nasérie had lived with,
and marveled that the marquise had endured it for so long: the
unpleasant taste of medicine, the hands that woke you when
you wanted to sleep, and vanished when, in the middle of the
night, you could not sleep and wanted only to be touched. The
agony of minute fluctuations which came from knowing too
much about your condition, the helplessness to do anything
about it. Madeleine would have liked to sneak off, as Nasérie
had, but really she did not feel well enough. She was queasy
and ravenous by turns; one moment she cried and the next
smiled at the doctors, who scratched their heads. This was not
how victims of the plague were supposed to behave. Where
were the wasting limbs, the blotched and blued skin, the relent-
less chattering teeth and the delirium? Something was amiss.
The doctors questioned Madeleine; then they consulted with
each other. When they returned they were smiling, inappropri-
ately, it seemed to her.

— Well, we have good news. As for the cholera: you never
had it.

— Then what's wrong with me?

— Well... the doctors prevaricated. You could certainly have
chosen a better time.

— For what? Madeleine wanted to know.

We should never try to understand the past. For it is not the
past that we spend in the attempt, but the future; to study the
past is to turn time back upon itself, to bring fruit to a tree

which has already let its last leaf go. Don't deny that your own
end approaches! Or that when it comes you will not want to
know the past, but to spring forward like a lover poised on the
lip of a cliff. You will want to know the future then, and want
the future to know you: such was my name, and such my deeds;
in such particulars you owe your life to me. Leave the past un-
buried in your understanding; leave it on the surface; leave it
not as it was, whole, but as it has become, dry, frail, clean. Its articulation visible.

In July 1865, while the city purged itself of inhabitants, and
Haussmann worked, and de Fonce profited, Madeleine discovered that she was with child.

She refused to leave the shadows of her canopied bed.
Madeleine lay in the dark and thought of her old neighbor
in the cour Carence, Madame Arnaque. Arnaque had been a
sometime midwife; she brought babies into the midnight reek
of her shop's back room in return for drink and what she val-
ued more than drink, news of the House of Bourbon. This was
not her only peculiarity, but it was her most harmless one: she
remained absolutely loyal to the deposed royal family, perhaps
because their name, in the half-deaf garble she made of the
world, meant "good drink," and to good drink she would remain loyal no matter how many revolutions intervened. The
Good-drinkers had been driven across the water in 1830:
Charles X and his family ruled over a small household in a city
which was, in accordance with Mme Arnaque's mood, and her
liver, either London or Prague or an unspecified town in farthest China; in any case it was a household about which Mme
Arnaque considered herself an expert. She knew that Charles's
grandson, the Count of Chambord, was of average height and
distinguished looks. On weekends he dressed in a red coat and,

atop a horse that was itself of noble lineage (its great-grandsire having carried Louis XVI through the park at Versailles), he hunted foxes with a cast of British aristocrats, Czech rabbis, or Chinese sages. Arnaque knew that he was in love with a British (Czech, Chinese) girl, a commoner, whom he had seen washing linen in a stream when the fox hunt cantered by. Whatever her nationality, her name was Charlotte, which pleased Mme Arnaque no end, for it was her own name as well. She had heard reports of various conversations between Charlotte and the Count, which began with declarations of love and ended after more or less dilation with promises of marriage and an eventual queenship. And if none of this was the least bit true, at least Mme Arnaque was a better midwife for it, for she believed that every child was born in kingship's nimbus, heir presumptive to a number of imaginary domains.

Madeleine wished she could see Nasérie, or even her Absence, again. She lay on her side, on her back, on her belly—carefully, though, for fear of jarring its curious contents—and squeezed her eyes shut. Nothing. No whisper nor creak of the door. She stayed awake for a long time waiting, and then fell asleep; when a hand touched her she woke to see de Fonce peering down.

— How do you feel?

— Not very well. Madeleine told him what she had been thinking about Mme Arnaque—at which the demolition man clapped his hands, delighted.*

He paced back and forth before Madeleine, and in the candlelight his shadow seemed to fill the room; his head brushed the ceiling and his broad shoulders braced the walls. — Madame Arnaque indeed! Don't worry, my dear, we'll find you a better

*Arnaque means, roughly, "swindle," which gives you some idea what the demolition man was thinking of.

midwife than that. You'll live, of course you'll live, and in com-
fort too. Haussmann will take care of you! He's certain to feel
his obligation to the child. Think of it, Madeleine: he has no
sons. If it's a boy... Do you know what it is to a man of fifty-
eight, almost sixty years to have a son? A son, an heir. Do you
think that he loves his wife?

— Octavie? Madeleine was taken aback. — No, I don't
think he loves her too well.

— You're certain? Has he told you about her?

— Just a few things. How she... how she reads a great deal.
And I don't think she likes Paris very much. And she's often
unwell.

— Ha! De Fonce threw himself into his chair, then sprang
out of it again. He could not be still: even as he walked up and
down he would stop now and then to straighten the bottles on
her vanity. — Would you like to be his wife?

— You're joking. It's unthinkable. No.

— And yet, my dear, he *is* a Protestant, which means he can
divorce... De Fonce cackled. — Ha! Married to Haussmann!
Oh, Madeleine... He seemed for a moment quite diabolical, his
red glasses flashing in the unsteady light. Then he wiped his
eyes with the corner of a handkerchief and was again a benevolent spirit, a genie, uncorked and ready to give her the world.
— No, you're right, my dear, we must not think of marriage.
No... although a comfortable settlement for the child... that we
can think of. Hm? Wonderful things await you, Madeleine.
Wonderful things.

15

THE GREAT CROSS

HAUSSMANN RECEIVED A LETTER the next morning. Sir, it read,

You have been called the busiest Prefect in the history of our city, and the most *prolific*. For years I have been an admirer of your works, and of your ideas as well, as you have reason to know. You have an eye for the future, sir, to which the future will be indebted; generations of Parisians will call themselves your spiritual *heirs*. I have been told that I have a sense for what will last; without meaning to flatter myself, I tell you frankly that I am of the opinion that your *family* name will be remembered long after other names, which may loom larger now, or be adorned with gaudier titles, have been forgotten by all excepting those who pass by their graves. Indeed, sir, if I may be so bold as to remark on one quality in particular of your legacy, it is that Paris will hereafter be more hospitable to *children*, who are less likely to lose themselves in wide streets than in narrow ones; children who will grow sturdy on clean water and the light of the sun; children who in short are likely to prosper, and to thank you in their nightly prayers. If only you will pay me a visit this evening or the next, I will congratulate you, sir, in person, as the *father* of our modern city. Yours, etc., etc.,

DE FONCE

Haussmann did not have to puzzle out the meaning of this letter, because another arrived in the same post, shorter and considerably more to the point:

I bear your child and I must see you.

MADELEINE

When Haussmann went to see de Fonce that evening, the thought foremost in his mind was that no one must know about the child. He had even considered how much he'd pay to buy Madeleine's silence: enough to subsidize the confinement and the birth, and a generous sum besides to cover the cost of never again speaking of it. He had decided that thirty thousand francs would be enough, or fifty if de Fonce seemed really angry. But when he got to the house on the boulevard de Courcelles he found that de Fonce wasn't angry at all; in fact the demolition man seemed quite pleased with himself.

—You got my letter?

—And I know what you're getting at.

—Really? Then de Morny's talked to you?

—De Morny?

— I had dinner with him last night. He told me that the Emperor is thinking of awarding you the Great Cross of the Legion of Honor. To recognize your services to the city.

—I...

—Congratulations, Baron, congratulations!

De Fonce insisted that he drink something to celebrate. —To the future!

— To the future, Haussmann said. He didn't know how to
mention the child, let alone any hypothetical settlement which
would buy Madeleine's silence. They were still talking about
the medal—what an honor!—when Madeleine herself came
downstairs, her face luminous as though a spark had been
struck and some invisible, combustible stuff in her heart was
now steadily aflame.

— My darling! She took the steps two at a time, and
ran into Haussmann's arms, which closed without hesitation
around her.

— I'll leave you two alone, de Fonce said.

Haussmann had never embraced her as happily as he did in
that moment, when she asked in tears whether things could
ever be the same between them? And he reassured her that
even if everything changed he would see to it that the change
was for the better. Didn't he know how to make improvements?

— Of course. Madeleine rubbed her eyes. But I was so
frightened...

— My poor mouse. Haussmann stroked her hair. There's
nothing to be frightened of. If he could have paid fifty thousand francs to be made into a god at that moment, what would
he have changed about the world? Nothing; and that was a
change which cost nothing at all to make.

The child was their revolution, their glorious revelation. It
made them comrades, if not exactly brother and sister, and in a
moment had Madeleine announcing that if the child was a boy
she would call him Georges, while Georges said that if it was a
girl they must call her Eve-Marie-Caroline, after his mother.
Seated one beside the other on a divan, hands clasped, he looking down and she up, as intently as ever lovers read the future in one another's faces, they sketched out the constitution
for a new regime, a government of governesses and nurse-
maids, a benevolent dictatorship with their baby at its head,

and themselves installed as viceroys. (Meanwhile, in the secret court of the Baron's mind, a revolutionary tribunal convened and found his earlier weakness treasonous. Buy Madeleine's silence, indeed! The idea was culpable, and it would be punished; he ordered it guillotined without ceremony and never spoken of again.)

Those who can't understand any action except in terms of self-preservation and self-advancement may choose to see de Fonce's hand in the Baron's change of heart. This would be a mistake. For love is not less genuine when swayed by circumstance; and it is always swayed by circumstance. Witness the innumerable lovers who declare themselves in the presence of a vast sunset, an alp, or a roaring waterfall. The Great Cross of the Legion of Honor played just that role in Haussmann's mind: it was the little parcel of the sublime which reduced him to such insignificance that it was no work at all for him, in his mind, to join his nothingness to someone else's. Therefore be still, cynics, and keep your mouths shut even as Haussmann suggests that Madeleine ought to leave Paris for the duration of her pregnancy. Discretion has nothing to do with it; he worries only about her health. On account of the cholera. If he were to lose her and the infant both...

Frightened by a description of what he has seen in the plague wards, Madeleine agrees. She wants to live, and to live, and to live. She holds Haussmann's arm. — I won't be gone long, will I?

— I believe the term is fairly standard.

— And you'll write to me? Often?

— Like clockwork, Haussmann says. He rests his chin atop Madeleine's head, perfectly content, until she says, — That tickles.

• • •

From Hyères, a village on the Mediterranean, full of yesteryear's stylish villas, Madeleine wrote to Haussmann:

My darling!

I miss you terribly, terribly, terribly. I wish you were here to take me away, or, at least, to take me to dinner—there's a restaurant in Toulon where the Widow promises we'll go when I'm fit to be seen in public. All here is boats, boats on one side, and goats, goats on the other, & it's awfully dull! I long to be in Paris again, to see you, to hear your voice & to embrace you. Although carefully! I should not like to be back here next summer; in fact, if I am never here again, I will have been here too often. Of course you're far away, but I hope you think of me. & even if you were here, we couldn't go to dinner, as I look as though I've eaten too much already! The doctor says that I will get my figure back in a matter of months. Though I wonder what he knows of it—his own (figure) is like an &, round on top and round on the bottom, with scarcely a straight line to hold him up. I know you are busy, busy, plotting all sorts of improvements, but I hope when I come back you will want to see me! I'm sure you'll know me even if I am a little changed. The days here go by slowly! I think if I didn't know their number, I would not stand it. & here the Widow is wagging her finger at me. It is time (she says) for our boating expedition. I am tired of the sea! It's you I long to see. But time and tide wait for no man, & I suppose no girl either, & so I must go. Kisses, and all my love & longing,

your,
M.

Haussmann wrote back:

My dearest Madeleine,

I am glad to hear that you are keeping your spirits up. As to your figure, I don't think you ought to worry. I have heard of other young ladies your age to whom something similar has occurred, and I hear that their recovery was complete in its physical, cosmetic, and moral dimensions. Therefore I expect you with the greatest pleasure in January, and I hope to offer you a dinner to rival anything you may find in Toulon. Did I tell you that I was once Prefect there? That is, I was Prefect of the Var, and Toulon is, as you know, the capital of that department. It was only for a few months, and I cannot say that I was sorry to leave. What a miserable people the Toulonnais are! All the time I was there, they clamored for a road to be built around the periphery of the city, to speed transport from one district to another, wholly overlooking the fact that no quarter of Toulon holds any attraction whatsoever, and there is, accordingly, no point in moving about the city at all. At last their demands became so tiring that I saw fit to write a letter to the Minister of the Interior (at the time, M. Louche). I'll only excerpt a short part of it here, in the hope that it may entertain you for a moment or two. "The chief need of the Toulonnais (I wrote) appears to be useful occupation, and their chief deficiency an (understandable) lack of civic pride. Therefore, I propose the following project, which will have the threefold advantage of improving the city, satisfying the population, and costing practically nothing at all. In order to edify the people of Toulon with the spectacle of battle at sea, and so that they may have some immediate satisfaction in their city's being a naval port, I propose the construction, on the place de la Liberté, and occupying the entirety of that place, of a giant Naumachia, that is, a great pit filled with water, in which naval battles may be staged in miniature. The digging of the pit (which, according to my calculations, ought to be no less than a hundred meters long by thirty broad, and three meters deep) will occupy all the idle persons of Toulon for (again, according to my calculations) a period of ten months, and will engage them in labor so arduous and wearying that they will have little, if any, time to complain about anything else. As the pit does not, properly, fall under any of the purposes for which the funds of the Republic may be sought (this was in 1850, remember), I recommend that the work of digging be undertaken entirely at the expense of the Toulonnais, who will reap ample reward in the form of increased visits from strangers, to say nothing of the satisfaction of having carried out an important work on a grand scale."

Of course, my dear, I am joking. But you see that I have tasted the bitter fruit of exile, and found a little something to sweeten it.

Then, in a different hand, as though Haussmann had put the letter down and not come back to it for several days:

Madeleine! I long to touch the column of your neck, and the breastwork of your breasts, your legs as smooth as obelisks, and the scrollwork of your hair! I pine for you, my dear, and I hope you'll indulge the follies of an old, affectionate man. I remain, in outward form,

        your humble servant,

          and, in my heart, your eternal admirer,

            M. ANONYME

To which Madeleine replied:

> Darling,
>
> Thank you for your kind letter. I long for you, too. I
> may not sit up for long, as the doctor wants me in bed all
> the time now—I hadn't realized how confining a con-
> finement was! But I suppose there's a good deal of truth
> in words, and if there is, then I hope this letter will tell
> you, as surely as I could if I were there, that I love you.
> Think of me now, and see me soon.
>
> Your
>
> MADELEINE

In the middle of October the north wind, the mistral, blew
down the Mediterranean coast, singing a song of monotony
and discontent. It scrubbed the sky and polished the leaden sea,
making everything bright and dull, clear and hard to look at.
The wind scratched in the trees and hissed in the sand; it set
signs creaking, rooftops rattling, and men complaining. Inside it
was as bad as out; the wind found every crack under every
door, every gap in every window, and moaned through them,
day and night, like a motherless child that nothing in the world
can put to sleep. Madeleine stuffed her doorsill with rags and
pulled her shutters to, but it was no use; the wind found its way
in all the same and kept her up all night, mumbling words that
she could almost make out, *house*, maybe, or *cow* or *vow* or *owe*.
Her head hurt and she could not sleep. The Widow was if anything worse off; her temper became so foul that the local servants would not come to the house, and only Constance,
her Parisian maid, remained to sweep away the sand that the
wind blew in, and listen to her complain. — The bitter fruit of
exile! she hissed one night, insomniac, at Madeleine, insomniac
also. — I'd like to see him sweeten this fruit, and eat it, too.

Madeleine murmured that the Baron had survived Toulon without much harm, but Couvrefeu was unimpressed. — He was probably here in the summertime, asleep under a tree. Really, if I stay much longer I'll commit homicide, she said, eyeing Constance, whom she'd awakened out of spite.

Madeleine soothed the Widow as best she could, but when two weeks had passed and the mistral gave no sign of letting up, she wondered whether any of them would survive. Her child kicked incessantly; in the still moments between gusts she thought she could hear it moaning. After three weeks of wind she wrote to de Fonce to ask if there was still much cholera in Paris? A little, he replied, but less and less; everyone here agrees that it is passé. She wrote to de Fonce that she was coming home, then; better to take her chances with the plague than to stay here and go mad. With the same post, Madeleine wrote to Haussmann:

> Dearest,
> You will see me sooner than you expect, I think. The Widow and I will be back in Paris in just a week, to taste the sweeter (I hope!) fruit of homecoming.

Whether because the wind jogged Madeleine's writing hand— I picture a dot of ink streaked across the envelope, like rain on a window—or because of a mix-up at the Hyères post office, which was small and poorly organized even in seasons when the weather was less unkind, Madeleine's letter was delayed, and arrived in Paris the morning she left Hyères. That afternoon a messenger arrived at her villa with a telegram which, because she was not there to receive it, was signed for by the groundskeeper, one of the servants whom the Widow had frightened away. In the normal course of things he should have sent a reply, but as the message was from Paris and its recipient

was going to Paris, the groundskeeper assumed that things
would sort themselves out; and besides he couldn't be bothered
to pay out of pocket for the convenience of such unpleasant
people; and besides who could think with that wind blowing?

The telegram read:

SITUATION HERE DIFFICULT STOP REMAIN IN
HYÈRES FOR TIME BEING STOP MISS YOU TERRI-
BLY STOP LOVE FOREVER SIGNED ANONYME.

16

THE BOX

————

AS A CHILD, Georges-Eugène had asked his father—a Protestant child, mind you, asking it of a Protestant father who was a general to boot—what if the dead could feel? What if they could see, and smell, and hear? How terrible then to be in a box and listen to clods of earth falling on the roof, then nothing at all, nothing at all ever again? But how much worse not to have the box. His father had laughed the question away. Ha! That's why they call it dead, boy, and a merciful thing it is, too. Don't you know that the soul, in the moment of death, ascends? It sees things the way birds see, climbs higher, the world is a map for the ascending soul, and in the end it goes all the way up to God and that's the end of the story. Poor Georges-Eugène! Utterly unconvinced by this hot-air account of the afterlife, he lay in bed imagining himself in the box. He didn't sleep for three nights in a row, and when he slept on the fourth it was only for a few hours between midnight and dawn. So he has slept ever since. Fortunately it left him time to accomplish a great deal.

Late one night in the summer of that plague year, he sat by the window of his office, watching the shadows of the rooftops

below and the last few lights in the homes of the sick, the in-
somniacs, and the debauched. There was a great number of
problems to consider, always a great number of problems. For
instance the sewers were likely to run grossly over budget, and
there would be the Municipal Council to deal with; he would
have to bring some doctor to convince them that unless the
city disposed of its shit, and soon, cholera was certain to break
out again (doctor: he made a memorandum of it). And then
there was the Great Cross of the Legion of Honor, which
he had, unaccountably, not received. Probably the Chevalier
Gastofouard, that scrivening lackey, had calumniated him to the
Empress—or perhaps the journalist Fillier was the one to
blame; he had enemies enough. How little it meant, in the end,
this distinction! A few thousand livres in food, wine, and connections; a medal to wear to banquets; a special contingent of
mourners when they put you in a box, in the end. (He made
another memorandum: Gastofouard.) Yes, in the end you ended
up in a box, and what good was a distinction then? Haussmann
knew how quickly such things were forgotten. His own grandfather had been a revolutionary during the Revolution: glory!
Then the poor man stayed a revolutionary through the Empire,
and the Restoration, and the July Monarchy, and so on until his
death, his glory buried under thirty years of enforced silence. To
live was well, for as long as you lived you could speak. As long
as you spoke you might be heard, and remembered, but when
you could speak no more? You wrote, Haussmann supposed.
(He made a memorandum of it: memoirs.) Nothing could
be worse than to die and know that you would be forgotten.
That was why it was necessary to honor the dead: so that
dying would be eased by the prospect of veneration. Thus far
Haussmann's thoughts were as they should be. But veneration,
which on other nights had led him to the difficult problem of
what to do with all the people who had died of cholera, for

whom no accommodation could be found in Paris' graveyards, led him tonight to venery, and thus to Madeleine. He saw the narrow back into whose arc he had fit the sagging contours of his chest; felt the grip of her hands about his wrists, and the tendons in the backs of her thighs. If only she were a public work, Haussmann thought, that he might get from her something of lasting use! That was the problem with venery: expenditure, all expenditure, and in the end nothing to show for it. Nothing but... Someone was knocking at the door to his office.

—Father?

—Valentine.

—Are you busy?

—Not too busy for you, child.

—Am I your Antigone, Father?

—Pardon?

—You shan't have it. "Mlle Haussmann took the Prefect's hand, and led him from the box, very much like the dutiful Antigone leading the sightless Oedipus to his final resting place." It's a good thing I was there to help you. Only I wasn't there. Was I?

—I don't follow you.

—You followed *someone*. Who is she?

—She? Valentine, this really isn't the moment...

—No; I should have asked you weeks ago. But I wanted to wait until you looked a little less deathly.

—How considerate! But I can't, I really can't, right now. We'll talk about this tomorrow.

—Is she your lover?

—Is that what you think?

—I'll think what you tell me.

Haussmann rubbed his temples. —Valentine...

—Yes, Father?

—If I tell you, you'll have to promise not to tell anyone. Not your mother, no one at all. Do you understand?

—Yes.

—Promise me, then.

—I promise.

—She was a friend of the Emperor's. She wanted to see Smuts, and as he was otherwise engaged he asked me to take her. She looks a little like you, and the light wasn't very good... You can imagine that the papers were encouraged to draw the wrong conclusion. I should have told you, of course, but...

—What's her name?

—Her name?

—She has one, doesn't she?

—Madeleine.

—Madeleine what?

—I've told you enough, I think.

Valentine considered what he said. — You've told better lies.

—Lies are often better than the truth.

—Is that the truth?

If you looked at the question in the right light, you could say that Valentine was asking, is a lie really better than the truth? To which Haussmann could answer with perfect honesty, — It is.

Valentine was silent a moment. Then: — Poor Madeleine.

—Oh, I'm sure she got away all right.

—Got away?

—From the theater, I mean.

She looked at him, long-faced.

—Well, I mean, her reputation...

—Is that what's important?

Valentine left the office before Haussmann could answer, which was just as well, for he would have answered: *yes*. Though he wouldn't have meant it in the way Valentine thought. Without reputation you were nothing: it was the armor that protected your designs, the diving bell that allowed you to live in the inhospitable world of men.

In the end he decided that the best thing to do would be to give Valentine a present. He bought her a box with a green enamel lid and a gold interior, a little thing that came, the man who sold it to him said, from Egypt, where they were always making boxes of one sort or another. As he did on important occasions, he had devised a script to accompany the gift: he would ask Valentine to open the box and, when she remarked that it was empty, he would say, That's because it can't contain my love for you. He would kiss her then, and, having made amends for the half-truth he'd told apropos of men and their reputations, he would hope that she asked no more questions. If she did he would say, *The answer is in the box*.

But Valentine was not at home. The maid downstairs said she was resting upstairs; the maid upstairs said that she had gone downstairs to sew. Perplexed, Haussmann went to look for his wife.

Octavie was in her customary chair, reading her customary book. — Lost your watch, my dear?

— My daughter.

— Which one?

— Valentine.

— Isn't she here?

— That's what everyone says. No.

— Then I have no idea where she might have gone, Octavie said, smiling. Which meant: she knew. Valentine was visiting her lover, probably, that rodent of an Assemblyman whom she had promised never to see again. Haussmann ought to have been angry but was, in the instance, relieved. If Valentine had broken her promise, then he had something more for her than a box; he could give her his forgiveness, or, if it came to that, his silence, which was worth more than a dozen boxes.

He set the box on the mantel, sat opposite his wife, and stared at the vase of blue flowers on the table between them. Octavie kept the flowers around even now that her husband was out of danger. She liked the way they smelled, she said, and what was the harm of taking an extra precaution? No harm, Haussmann thought. No harm. He thought, uncustomarily, of the time when he was a subprefect, handsome, young, and unmarried. The mothers of every mademoiselle over the age of fifteen courted him—some of the girls courted him too, but from the mothers he received a barrage of invitations and tender looks, none of which he was inclined to return. His friend Jean de Laharpe invited him to spend a weekend in Bordeaux, and he accepted, happy to get away from the pressure of so much matrimonial expectation. What a surprise, then, to meet Jean's sister, a quiet young woman named Octavie who asked nothing of him at all. She was attached to her parents, to her brother, to Bordeaux; she dreamed of no distinction, no advancement, no going forward, only an endless staying in place in a world where everything had its place. She wasn't much to look at—a gibbous girl, almost entirely filled out though she wasn't more than nineteen years old. But her stillness... Her stillness worked on him like the moon on the ocean: he was moved despite or perhaps because of the distance between them, which he could no more hope to bridge than water can hope to climb up into the sky. Haussmann spent three days in Bordeaux, and saw Octavie twice more; each time she was as quiet and as remote. And yet, and yet, when he was leaving Jean took him aside and said, — I believe she's taken a fancy to you, which Georges-Eugène would not believe until she wrote him

a letter. Mostly news from Bordeaux, but at the end of it she
invited him to return, and he did, and, in hours of solemn conversation, discovered, wonder of wonders, that he had reached
the moon after all, and was walking about on its surface, learning its customs, becoming, as visit followed visit, a familiar and
welcome guest on that other world. Then they were married,
and the moon grew more and more familiar; in no time it became only his world, the ordinary ground on which everyone
walked.

He looked up at the brown-shawled woman in the armchair opposite, dowdy and moon-faced, his wife. — Is it too
cold for you? Too warm? No? Haussmann smiled. — I swear,
he said, that I'll be glad when my work here is done. Let someone else be Prefect, and take the lumps. Where will we go then?
Back to Bordeaux? Octavie, lost in her book, nodded absently.
Her pain, whether it had been in her womb or elsewhere, did
not trouble her so much as it had before—and perhaps that too
was the influence of her blue flowers. So they sat, Haussmann
and housewife, listening to the clock and smiling at each other
from their chairs.

On October 15 Octavie got a letter from her brother Jean
telling her that their mother was dying. That evening she
packed for the trip back to Bordeaux. — I wish you'd come,
she told Haussmann. But whatever loyalty he felt to his memory of Octavie's family, to those nights when he had looked
upon love's satellite, was confined to the past; and if you want
to know how he felt about the past, look at what he did to
Paris. By 1865 whole neighborhoods which had leaned against
one another since the Middle Ages were gone, and the city's
great axes had been drawn north and south and east and
west. The boulevard Saint-Michel was under construction, and

Saint-Germain almost finished; the boulevard de Sebastopol had been open to traffic for three years, long enough that people had already begun to forget what had been there before. Not to mention the church of Saint-Jacques-de-la-Boucherie and its medieval carvings, which were broken up and sold to decorators, to ornament the living rooms of businessmen with feudal sensibilities. All of this is only a long way of saying that Haussmann refused to go. He would revisit Bordeaux in his imagination as many times as you pleased—that was where the past belonged, after all, in the imagination—but in reality it was out of the question. — The city, my dear, leaves me no time, none at all... So Octavie went to Bordeaux alone, again, and Haussmann stayed where he was.

The Prefect's memorandum book has the following entry for November 2, 1865: "Sweden?" Why he wrote that has been lost to us altogether. The entry for the day before, however, reads:

VIOLLET FILLIER
~~REILLIF TELLOIV~~
~~RELIEF TILILOV I~~
~~OLIVE FILTLIER~~
OLLIVIER (!) ~~FILLET~~
~~FILTEL~~ OLLIVIER
~~LLIFTE~~ OLLIVIER
~~FLITEL~~ OLLIVIER
~~ELL~~

The journalist had resurfaced. In an article entitled "Peccadilloes of the Prefect," Fillier insinuated again that Haussmann was more than kind to de Fonce, if less than kin. What was more, the journalist noted that de Fonce had a pretty daughter, and speculated, with what the Baron hoped was entirely fortuitous accuracy, that a "rubble girl" (Fillier's term) would be a fitting consort for the Butcher Baron.

Who was Fillier? Haussmann spoke to the Prefect of Police, and gave him the description of the young man who'd been snooping at the Magnificent Smuts's performance. The Prefect of Police, who didn't like Haussmann very much, promised to keep an eye out for thin young men with moustaches, and in the meanwhile he questioned the editors of the *Lanterne*. They knew nothing. Fillier mailed his articles from the big post office on the rue du Louvre; his manuscripts were written in a copyist's featureless hand. He collected no payment for his work, nor asked for any. He had been seen at no party, no evening meeting, no rally for any cause. The secret police knew nothing about him, nor did the spies, the turncoats, the censors, the stoolpigeons, the mail readers, the agents abroad, or the public librarians. Most likely that was not his real name, though. "Viollet Fillier" was almost an anagram of "Emile Ollivier," and Ollivier was a republican deputy whom Haussmann had thrown in jail years ago for writing a seditious pamphlet, the contents of which both of them had now forgotten. But the anagram was not exact. Unless Ollivier was playing a doubly pseudonymous game, the cipher was no good.

On the same day Haussmann got a letter from Madeleine, to say that she was coming back to Paris. Absolutely not! he wired back. He wanted to see her—venery was as much on his mind as it had ever been—but not while Fillier, by that name or another, remained at large, and he was reduced to fretting anagrammatically.

De Fonce sat in his study, reading a treatise by a German physicist which demonstrated that a perpetual motion machine could never be built. The proof had something to do with the fact that you could turn wood into fire but not vice versa. In the thick of equations which demonstrated irrefutably that the universe was nothing more than a log ablaze in some unimaginably vast hearth, de Fonce's mind wandered: he thought of the fire he'd tended long ago, when he was Fonce the blacksmith's apprentice, and how the gnarled man he was allowed to call only Master had told him, Fire is hungry. Fire's got a big stomach. Like the Nidhogg, Master said: the beast which gnaws perpetually at the roots of the world-tree, Yggdrasil. When the Nidhogg has eaten up the tree, then the world will end, that was how the story went. Then the Jotuns will arise from their home and the gods will descend from theirs and there will be a great battle and when it's done nothing will remain of the universe, save perhaps a pair of humans, a man and a woman, with whom things may start again on a different footing. Perhaps Master wasn't wrong, de Fonce thought drowsily. Equations demonstrate that the world is eaten, consumed, used up. And if that's the way we're going? he thought. Finding the hidden truth in all the old stories, one by one, until even the most outlandish beliefs will be confirmed by Germans with impeccable credentials. Then Haussmann and I will have nothing to disagree about. A great confluence of stories and theorems...

As if summoned, the Baron came in. He didn't look well, even when you took into account that he'd nearly died not all that long ago. Pale, his hair, what there was of it, awry, his eyes wide and mouth fiercely set, and all of him somehow reduced, as though the cholera had been in him all along, taking up space, and had left a sort of cavity behind when it departed.

—My dear Baron, what brings...

—Did you see the *Lanterne*?

—Fillier's article, you mean? I saw it.

—And?

—The writing was a bit flat, if you ask me.

—Flat! Haussmann laughed. — He's as good as figured us out.

—He hasn't got a scrap of proof.

—You're not worried?

De Fonce put down his book. — What can Fillier do? He makes noise, but at the end of the day he's a scrivener and you're the Prefect.

—Hm. Yes. But I need to be sure of your discretion. In the matter of the... you know what I mean.

—The child? But my dear Baron, I'm as much at risk as you are.

—Still, promise me.

—You're working long hours, aren't you? Sit down, drink something.

—Promise.

—You needn't worry, de Fonce said.

Haussmann sighed and sank into a chair. He rubbed his temples, closed his eyes, and, when he opened them again, smiled faintly. — How am I ever going to repay you?

The door opened. — Darling?

Madeleine stood in the doorway. Her hair was down, and her dressing gown hung open above her swollen belly, a little farther than the painted Modesty on the ceiling would have approved.

—You're here! she said to Haussmann.

—*You're* here, he said weakly.

—You're surprised? Oh, *this*. She touched her stomach. — Amazing, isn't it? But apparently it returns to its original shape afterward. You don't know how I've suffered! We had the most terrible wind, it blew and blew and, and... what's wrong?

—Didn't you get my telegram?

—Did you send one? You don't look well, you know. Have you been working too much?

—Won't you sit down? De Fonce tapped his pipe against his shoe. We've just been talking about turning fire into wood.

—You can't turn fire into wood. Everyone knows that.

—My point exactly, said de Fonce. Why don't you join us, my dear? You can help us to agree.

—If you need my help, Madeleine said, you're lost.

—Does anyone know that you're here? Haussmann asked.

—What a question! No one knows, but you, now. Should I have put an announcement in the paper?

—No!

—Really, you're looking at me as if I were a ghost. Madeleine kissed Haussmann's cheek. Aren't you glad I'm back?

—Of course I am.

—Then don't look so sad! You can stop pining for me now; I'm home.

Madeleine pulled her robe closed and perched on the edge of the sofa. Haussmann sank back in his chair and steepled his fingers. My family, de Fonce thought. They *were* his family, the one he'd forged for himself. Forget their titles, their names, forget what anyone else, seeing them together, might think, or wonder. They were his and that was enough. He relit his pipe and chided them, —Why so quiet? The three best minds in Paris ought to have something to say to each other.

—Four, soon, said Madeleine.

—True: four. What do you say? Daughter? And you, Baron, that makes you my son-in-law. Or out of law, I ought to say.

Madeleine giggled.

—I don't think you ought to say that, said Haussmann.

—Just a joke.

Haussmann looked at Madeleine. — Do you think it's funny?

—Not at all.

—I don't think it's funny either.

—I stand corrected. Baron.

Was he really upset? What a fool, if he was. What was the use of not laughing? It changed nothing, in the end, anyway. The universe is burning down, and when all the fuel is spent... De Fonce sank into his chair. His eyes on the ceiling, he imagined the ultimate end, the day when the cosmos would be a cloud of smoke through which the bodies of stars sped like spent coals, black as blacksmiths and cold as corpses. But there, Haussmann's feathers were all ruffled. After a moment he excused himself, pleading that he did not, really he did not, feel quite well.

When he was gone, Madeleine asked, — Does he know?

—I don't think so.

—He could have guessed, though.

—He could have. But I don't think he did.

—He's blind, in a way, isn't he?

—In a way.

—Are you coming to bed?

—I'll finish my pipe first.

—While I wait for you, you mean? You're all blind, Madeleine said. Men.

—Yes, I think we are, de Fonce said after a moment; but Madeleine had already gone upstairs to wait for him.

17

BORDEAUX

BORDEAUX WAS THE LAST THING on Haussmann's mind, so it was with a little surprise that he found himself traveling there the next morning. But here he was on a train, watching brown and uniform fields hurry northward under a November drizzle. He was not running away. He had woken up just after dawn, as he did every morning, and got his coffee and a précis of the day's papers. He felt calm, better in fact than he had in weeks. His stomach was settled, his mind awake. Everything he wanted was possible, and everything possible was within his power. He smiled at his reflection in the coffeepot. The odd thing was that he wanted nothing at all. When the servant came in to take breakfast away, he said, — Pack my bags. An hour later he leaned back happily into his cushion as Paris dissolved behind him in puffs of steam. But he was not running away. The doctors had advised him to get rest and fresh air, unless he wanted the cholera to hang a retrospective in his weakened body; they warned him he wouldn't survive that great exhibition. Therefore: he was resting. Certainly he wasn't running away from Madeleine. De Fonce's joke about fathers in and out of law was in poor taste, but de Fonce was an old friend and he

could excuse the occasional lapse of taste. And Fillier... but he
would think about that when he got back to Paris. And
Madeleine pregnant, and the child. He could see no end to the
fear that someone would find him out, and what was he going
to do? He turned to the window. His breath made flowers on
the glass, and then his fear seemed no more substantial than
that, an exhalation, a mist, a hot circle which faded and then
you could see out again. He settled into the cushions with a little of the stubbornness of a child pretending to sleep in the
hope of stealing, somehow, an extra dream.

He arrived after dark and went unannounced to the Laharpe house, where a number of carriages were gathered. He
had not telegraphed that he was coming and no one expected
him. The house was quiet the way woods are quiet after a snow.
He stirred the fire in the parlor and brought it back to sputter-
ing life, then went upstairs to Mme Laharpe's bedroom. Everyone was there: Octavie and her brother Jean, whom he hadn't
seen in years, a half-dozen family friends, and a minister who
sat by the bedside mumbling something about the permanence
of the idea of life. Mme Laharpe lay on her deathbed with her
eyes closed. There was a stir when Haussmann came in: the
others had been waiting so long for her to die that, when the
door opened, they turned to look at him as though he were
Death itself; then they saw that it was only the Baron—only the
Baron! Jean smiled and Octavie came forward in silence and
took his hand. — You're just in time, she said. — But why
didn't you let me know you were coming?
    —I didn't know myself.
    Octavie looked at him again. — Are you well?
    —Tired. The train...
    —You're pale.
    —I'll say hello to your mother.
    Haussmann stood by the bed and looked down at old Mme

Laharpe. In life—she was not in life, now, although the covers
still rose and fell over her thin chest—she had been a kind
woman, if childish and overly willing to be waited upon by her
children. A woman who had trouble letting go, a difficulty
which she evidently still had, as, according to Octavie, she'd said
her last words three days ago and still she breathed.

—Hello, mother, he said. It's Georges. Your son out of law.

The minister looked up, surprised. Haussmann winked at
him. — A little joke.

—Come downstairs, Octavie said. I'll get you supper.

—Go in peace, the minister said.

He followed Octavie downstairs.

In the parlor she wanted to know, was something the matter? Because really he looked not well. Haussmann denied that
anything was the matter. If anything was the matter it was that
he hadn't come sooner. He would have come sooner if he'd
known... what? If he'd known how badly off she was, he said,
then regretted saying it. — Not that she's so badly off, I mean.

—She's dying, Octavie said.

—Poor woman.

Octavie corrected him: — Not poor. Old. Then she said: — I'm
glad you came. In the end.

—Of course I came. How could I not come?

—Well, but your work...

—Can wait! He kissed Octavie. — You are a lovely woman.

She shook her head and went into the kitchen to find
something for him to eat.

The next morning he went hunting with Jean. The last of autumn's flags snapped and twisted in a strong easterly wind.
Everywhere Haussmann looked there were blotches of color, as
though the pieces of an enormous jigsaw puzzle had been

hung up to dry in the trees. The land rose and fell with abandon; the pines and holm oaks grew of their own accord to be as
tall as they liked, and the sky began right above them, and rose,
unobstructed by clouds or buildings, what seemed forever. The
air smelled of leaves and leaf skeletons and things burning far
away, and of cold, a sharp nonsmell which made the Baron's
head ring like the silence after a concert. The smell of winter
approaching. Patches of frost covered the fallen leaves; their
horses left practically no tracks in the road's half-frozen dirt. On
either side of the road the trees grew so thick that you couldn't
tell whether they belonged to a forest or a copse, whether on
the other side of their black boles the land might open up again
in farmers' fields, where, according to the season, the last crops
ought just now to be coming down. Five hundred kilometers
to the north the first Parisians were getting out of bed, yawn-
ing, scratching under their nightshirts, stirring the fire, setting
pots to boil, drinking coffee, opening their doors to the cold
morning's first carriages, blue in the light of the not yet risen
sun, slow, like blood returning to a sleeping limb, the business
of the city getting under way. Ahead of him and on either side
the sound of gunfire. How good it was to be out of Paris! Here,
atop a chestnut mare with the grace of the ocean in her step,
Haussmann was sure he wasn't running away. Surely he was
running toward this, and surely, now that he was here in the
middle of it, there wasn't any reason to ask why? He spurred his
horse ahead and looked back to see if Jean was following.

— Don't look so sad! he called to Jean.

Jean smiled at him, puzzled.

— After all, everyone has to die.

— What?

— Everyone has to die!

Jean said something he couldn't make out.

—The parents die and the children live on. That's natural!

—Wait up! Jean called, but Haussmann would not. He
wanted to ride fast into the trees, to see what was ahead.

Jean was soon out of sight, but never mind. The air was good,
and the light had resolved itself into a high hazy glow, and the
mare's gait lulled Haussmann into a kind of still wakefulness.
The forest rustled with the movement of living things. Now
that he was out of Paris, he could see how ridiculously he had
been behaving there. All that worry about reputation, and
posterity! As if the dead mattered, as if they mattered. This
was what mattered: the uneven ground, and the regular breathing of his mount, the clouds of her breath like the woolly,
globular winds inked in the corners of some maps. There is
no such thing as the dead, Haussmann told himself. There is
only what we see before us. And all of it is living: look at
those birds! When he was younger he knew what kind of
birds they were, but long absence from the forest had stripped
that knowledge away. Everything that matters is before you,
and everything else exists only as long as you think about it.
What a relief! He laughed aloud — but softly, as befit a man
in possession of himself. Haussmann rode into unfamiliar
hills and valleys broken by streams where water whispered
around black wood. The consciousness that he had left behind
a situation, between himself and de Fonce and Madeleine,
which was dangerous to say the least, remained dully present at the center of his mind, like a spot of skin gone numb with
too much rubbing. But even this thought faded as he fathomed the forest, his rifle forgotten along with any thought of
hunting or even of what, if he were hunting, he would be
hunting for.
    Haussmann came back late to the Laharpe household. He
was singing a tune that had been in his head all afternoon, with

words of his own devising—a hidden talent, he thought, but he would not keep it hidden forever; he was Haussmann and sooner or later the world would know the full import of that. *All in all*, he sang, *I wanted to know gaily,*

> *That pleasure's not enough for man, but daily,*
> *He must have at least the semblance of*
> *Undying love.*

He stopped short when he saw Octavie on the threshold, her face as improbably still as if the moon itself had announced that it would no longer turn. — My dear, he said, what's wrong?

—Madeleine?

—Yes, my love?

De Fonce sat on the edge of her bed. — When did you see the Baron last?

—You know when.

—Do you think he's angry at you?

—He's gone away somewhere.

—You'll see him soon, though?

—Tomorrow night, he says.

—Good.

—Is something wrong?

—I don't think so. But treat him gently, will you?

—You make him sound like a broken vase held together with glue.

—Not far from the truth, I think. Does he look well to you? The last time he was here, I could swear I saw cracks in his glaze.

Madeleine laughed. — I won't drop him, if that's what you mean.

—That's just what I mean. De Fonce kissed her cheek. — I wonder if you aren't too good for him.

—Oh, he'll do.

He kissed her neck. — Far too good.

—Not too good for you, though.

—Oh yes. Too good for me also.

—Well, don't let that stop you.

—Don't worry. If I let that sort of thing stop me I'd still be selling scissors in the Auvergne.

—Mm.

—Perhaps you'd like that better, though? Very romantic, scissors selling.

—Of course I'd like it better.

—We can begin tomorrow, if you want. I'll tell the servants to close up the house and give the money away.

—Do. In the meanwhile, will you—ow!—get off my arm and go blow out the light?

A great transformation had taken place in the apartment on Headless Woman Street while Madeleine was away. The griffon-footed armoire was gone, and the old table, and the candelabra, and indeed practically everything which had belonged to the Old Regime of their affair, as she referred to it now. She had replaced all of it with furniture of her own choosing, paid for by Georges. Even the wallpaper in the nursery was her design: it had a pattern of flowering vines interwoven with trees and waves and tongues of flame, horses and birds and fish in blue and gold, which she had copied from Nasérie's robe. Madeleine wondered whether she would tell Georges that story, and thought she might, in time. Where was he? Everything else was ready. The room had chairs, there were two of them, large enough and pleasant to sit in. Madeleine sat in each of them in turn and found they hadn't changed since morning. The rug was soft under her feet; it was a good rug, which would stand the oppression of shoes and bare feet equally. If different pieces of furniture have different characters then rugs are the saints of the inanimate. They bear what must be borne and hide what must be hid; and though they are lowly, their faces are turned always upward to the ceiling. The rug, bless it, came on time, but not the Baron. She expected him at eight, which meant that in the ordinary course of things he would arrive at nine, or at the latest nine-thirty, and here it was almost ten, and Madeleine was going to wear the rug out on its first day with her walking back and forth.

She settled in a chair—still good, still good, where was he?—and picked up a history of the Middle Ages, which she'd brought from de Fonce's. "With the loss of the alphabet a spiritual darkness fell upon the land," it told her, but the words meant nothing. What was a spiritual darkness? Was that when the spirit couldn't see? and, if so, what did it see ordinarily, when there was spiritual light? As the author of the history was not present to explain, Madeleine put the book away—out of sight, so that Georges wouldn't think she was interested in anything so old—and picked up the Turkish bird. She wound its spring and the bird hopped and sang. It brought the apartment to something like life, and that was good, because life has gravity, Madeleine thought; it attracts other life, and if things get lively enough then Georges will be here soon. If only he were here, she thought, then she would not feel, as she did, waiting for him, dissatisfied and a bit insubstantial, as though what she had arranged in the apartment was the decor not for her life but for a play. Why was it that everything seemed less real when she lived it than when she imagined it beforehand? If only Georges could be on time for her as he was for everything else, she thought wearily, she would have no need to ask such questions.

The bird hopped to the edge of the table, then hopped off, attempting its first flight. Whether because its wings weren't made for that sort of work or because the mechanism of its voice overloaded its little body, the bird tumbled, landed on one of its wings, and lay still. Madeleine picked it up. The wing was bent out of shape, and the beak, which opened and closed as the bird trilled, hung askew. She wound it again and let it loose, but the mechanism of its legs must have jammed, for it walked unevenly a step or two, lifted its wing, and froze. Its voice did not come out at all. After a moment the bird shuddered and fell over on its damaged side.

Just then footsteps came up the stairs; the bell outside rang (why did he use the bell? Madeleine wondered), and she opened to a grin atop a dripping armful of red and blue flowers. — Mamzelle de Fonce? said the delivery boy (a man, really, thin-faced, with the uneasy eyes of a burglar).

—Yes?

—For you. Where do you want 'em?

The messenger set the flowers in the kitchen. There were a great many of them—they covered the counter, threatened to tumble into the washbasin. — Don't know what you'll do with 'em there, but it's not my business. Oh: before I forget:

He took a sealed envelope from his wallet.

— Will that be all? It's cold out tonight. Only November, but it feels like February! Why, walking around as I do, a man gets a chill... thank you, thank you, you're very kind. And I'm off! A good night to you, Mademoiselle!

Was that a wink? The messenger was gone, his boots clattering down the stairs. Outside, he rejoined a fat, cloaked friend, and the two of them ambled off, the messenger jingling Madeleine's coins in his hand.

The note read:

Madeleine,

Business has kept me here longer than I expected—
but I hope you'll take these flowers as a promise of my
prompt appearance, and as some slight consolation for its
(unavoidable) delay.

Did that mean that he would be along soon? Madeleine
thought so. She settled into the sofa again, holding one of the
flowers—she'd left the rest in the kitchen, for they had no vases.
She twirled the flower in her palms, sniffed it—what were these
blue things called? and set it down beside the broken bird. She
watched the street, watched the curtains rustling in the wind,
which had, indeed, got a little cold; she closed the windows and
waited in the apartment, silent now, for Haussmann.

But he did not come.

Madeleine to Haussmann (delivered by hand the next day):

Where are you?

Haussmann to Madeleine (by post, the day after, and addressed to Mlle Madeleine de Fonce):

Dear Mademoiselle,

I received your note of the 6th inst. Unfortunately I
am unable to see you now, indeed, I do not know when
I will be able to see you again. However great my power
may appear to you, yet it is fragile as the glass bell under
which some specimen of the natural world might be
preserved: one tap from the hammer of Public Opinion
and it shatters, and all the beauty encased within soon
crumbles in the noxious outward air. This glass must be

preserved no matter what the cost, as I'm sure you understand, for you have a reputation of your own to protect. Therefore I hope you will be understanding and
above all patient. In the meantime I beg you to accept,
Mademoiselle, the expression of my most sincere admiration, and my most vivid regret.

G–E HAUSSMANN

—What am I supposed to do? she asked de Fonce, and de
Fonce replied, — Wait.

Madeleine finished the history of the Middle Ages, which
ended badly; then she read about the steam engine and the *Ro-
mance of the Rose*, mechanics and minotaurs, until everything
became a blur; the staff Yseult planted in the ground became a
coal mine run according to the most modern principles and
then became dragon's teeth in a blast furnace of flame; Cadmus
sowed the teeth in the bosom of the earth and got cadmium, a
bluish white metal obtained from furnace deposits, and made
from it swords and shovels to do the dragon in. All history,
Madeleine thought, was more or less the same story: people
tearing things from the ground and making them sharp, people
doing violence to one another and sticking each other in the
ground again. She suspected that Haussmann had found another mistress: some slender girl with a better voice and no
child on the way, or a child with no voice, or a girl with a
childish voice and hips which promised nothing. She told de
Fonce her idea about the mute; he laughed and told her to be
patient.

She picked up Passerelle's *History of Natural Fortifications.*
"Vauban once remarked that Nature is the greatest engineer of
all. Accordingly the highest degree of the engineer's art consists
in building nothing, but in choosing those places where Nature
herself keeps one's enemies at bay." The book described cliffs

and other heights, Natural Moats and Shifting Sands, Brush and
Mud; there was a chapter devoted to Thickets and another to
Streams. Passerelle noted that the seasons each have their defen-
sive value: Spring and Fall are suited to campaigns on forested
land, while Summer and Winter lend themselves more to open
ground, to rolling hills and running battles. Despite herself
Madeleine was caught up in the history of a Persian general
whose only fortification was a weather witch, who foretold the
periodic rains that turned the Persian plains to mud: "for the
genius of Natural Fortifications is not in stillness but in movement, which accords itself with the endless variety of natural
hindrances." Madeleine fancied herself the general, circling on a
sodden field. She loosed volleys of arrows at her mired foes and
retreated, the better to charge and to emerge victorious, just as
she'd done among the river reeds in the days when she gov-
erned an empire of mud. How dare Haussmann keep her waiting? Madeleine felt something strange and hot animate her; it
pulled her from her chair and sent her pacing across the room.
How dare he put her off? This new emotion clenched her
hands and opened her eyes; it made the book, the chair, the
window, everything around her seem more worthy of attention
than it had previously. Each object wore a halo of importance,
of reality, like the ring around a street lamp when you look at it
through tears. Where this feeling had come from, and why it
had come now, Madeleine could not say, but she could give
it a name: it was fury. She had waited enough. While de Fonce
was out buying and selling parcels of whatever he sold now,
Madeleine got dressed, called for a carriage, and told the driver
to take her to the Hôtel de Ville.

18

DESPOIR'S ROOM

AFTER HE SENT his last letter to Madeleine, Haussmann wondered whether it had been the right thing to do. Of course if *he* received such a letter he would understand; but then he was fifty-seven years old, and he had learned a thing or two in the course of those years which had made their one-way trip past him like aristocrats on the way to Madame Guillotine. Madeleine was not so old, nor so wise; she was at the uncomfortable age when people change, deftly and irreversibly, into what they are going to be for the rest of their lives. Would she understand?

Haussmann remembered how he had been at twenty-two, when he was already secretary-general of the Vienne, in Poitiers. It was his first administrative post, his first year away from Paris and his family. What a lonely time that had been! Haussmann remembered the old Prefect he'd served, Boullé, whose father had been a prefect before him, and who seemed in his slow way to be making civil service into something dynastic; and his assistant, Sproul, quiet as a shadow and as hard to pin down. Sproul had played a trick on him, hadn't he? Yes, he had tried to cheat him out of his official lodgings, and sent him to

live in a boardinghouse, a dingy, unpleasant place where he had
spent a few months before he figured out what was what.

Haussmann rubbed his temples: amazing how long ago that
year seemed, yet how much of it remained visible in memory.
He saw himself arriving in Poitiers after three days' journey
on rough roads, and there was Sproul, a thin old man who
appeared beside him the way shadows appear, imperceptibly,
in silence, and with a composure that spoke of immutable
habit. Sproul was apologizing. He had not expected the new
secretary-general so soon, he said, stroking the tines of his gray
moustache, and there were no accommodations at all in the
center of town just now and so he had taken the liberty of
sending Haussmann's bags on to the Two Hearts. — The Two
Hearts? Sproul took the young man's arm and led him, still
dazed from the journey and ignorant of his prerogatives, across
the river, to a gray ramshackle building at the city's edge.

The place got its name, said Madame Prosequi, the landlady,
from the travelers' superstition that your heart did not leave a
place where you had fallen in love until you saw the church
spires of another town. As the Two Hearts sat atop a low rise
from which you could see the spires of the cathedral of Poitiers
like a pair of ivory needles over the next hill, the lovesick trav-
eler who stopped there might be said to have two hearts, one
still enthralled elsewhere, and the other, barely palpable, his
own. Poitiers had grown since the inn was named, producing
squares and streets, lumber yards and depots and apartment
houses and shops without any heart at all, to judge from the
murk of their interior and the blank aspect of their outsides.
The travelers who once flowed through the Two Hearts in accordance with the systole and diastole of the mail coaches
slowed to a sluggish trickle, and at last stopped flowing altogether, leaving the stable empty (it was torn down soon after)
and the rooms full of a sort of human sediment. When Hauss-

mann moved in, the other boarders included Charpentier the singing teacher, who gave a recital every Christmas in the Hô-tel de Ville; Boussole, a celebrated bootmaker's representative for all of western France; Aragonax the advocate, who claimed to be descended from a great Gaulish chief; and half a dozen others, not one of whom seemed to want more from the world than he presently had. Haussmann felt badly for them, and for himself when he was in their presence. He kept away from the communal dinners served by Madame Prosequi in a dining room that smelled of injured marine life, though those fish that entered it generally left again unharmed.

Haussmann's room was on the top floor, but it was large and light, with a soft bed and a pair of windows from which the cathedral spires were clearly visible. There was another room across the landing, which was occupied, Madame Prosequi said, by a medical student, but for a long time Haussmann did not meet his neighbor. He left the Two Hearts early in the morning for the prefecture, at first because he thought he was needed there, and then, when it became clear that his job consisted only of signing official documents and storing notarized copies in the appropriate file, in the hope that he could somehow make himself needed.

He filled the shelves of his office—at least he had an of-fice—with volumes of law and local history; he went on expeditions through the region and met with farmers and busi-nessmen, aristocrats and curates, and lepers in the Vienne's last leprosarium, a former monastery on the heights outside Chatellerault. Like a doctor mapping with deft fingers the inte-rior geography of a patient, Haussmann listened and studied and in that way acquired a sense of the secret pulses that ani-mated the region. He made frequent appointments with Boullé to tell him that the townspeople at Champigny-le-Sec needed water or that the schoolmaster at Chauvigny was less patriotic than one would like. Boullé heard him out good-naturedly, then told him that if the matter was important it would already have come to the Prefect's attention. Occasionally Haussmann had the satisfaction of hearing him call for Sproul and ask, in a hushed voice, whether the schoolmaster...? Haussmann did not hear how Sproul answered these questions, but he suspected that whatever action the prefecture took was advantageous most of all to Sproul.

In the evening Haussmann went to Boullé's house to play billiards or whist. Sproul was always there, although he did not play, because, he said, he objected on principle to games of chance. Also present was the Prefect's cousin Adèle Bellebecq, a bony, brown-haired girl who was visiting from Saint-Brieuc. As soon as the new secretary-general appeared, she stopped speaking of going home; she looked at Haussmann with unmistakable interest, and he understood that, if he played his cards right—which, in this case, meant losing systematically to the Prefect—he might one day enter the Boullé dynasty. In the absence of any better prospect, he chatted with Adèle, who was, it turned out, intelligent and not unkind; and he played to lose. Haussmann went home late, and, as he walked through the empty streets of Poitiers, wondered whether this was what people outside Paris called *a life*, and, if so, how they put up with it.

One night as he went into the Two Hearts, he passed a young man on his way out. He wore a wide-brimmed hat and a cloak, but what Haussmann could see of him was not bad-looking: a squarish face and blond hair that hung down almost to his eyes. His shoulders were broad and his columnar legs looked able to bear loads much greater than his own not inconsiderable weight. His boots were heavy and scuffed, but there was something almost dashing about him, going out on a mysterious errand at an hour when the rest of the city was asleep. Haussmann would not have been surprised to find a sword under his cloak, or a letter from the Queen.

He greeted Madame Prosequi in the parlor and asked,
— Who was that?

— That's your neighbor, she said. He's called Despoir.

In Paris Haussmann would have forgotten about him in a
day or two, his face obliterated in memory by a dozen more interesting faces, his mysterious errand replaced by a dozen less
penetrable mysteries. It was doubtless only because Poitiers offered so little else to think about that Haussmann remained curious about Despoir. He interrogated his landlady, who could
tell him only that Despoir was from Normandy, that his parents
were farmers, and that he was the oldest of many children. He
often went out late at night, she said, and did not come home
until early in the morning; then he did not go out during the
day. Whether this comprised a part of his medical studies, or
was in addition to them, or had replaced them altogether, she
did not know. When Haussmann heard Despoir's boots on the
landing he tried to guess where the medical student was going,
but the heavy footfalls going up or down the stairs told him
nothing. Once, returning from Boullé's, he found Despoir
standing on the bridge, looking upstream. He asked the medical
student some inane question about his health, or whether he
enjoyed the night air. Despoir answered curtly. He had to be
going, he said; when he left it was in the direction of the Two
Hearts, as though some pressing business awaited him there.
The fellow is a brute after all, Haussmann thought, and left him
to his sleepy, useless existence. He was glad only that Despoir
kept quiet, for the wall between them was thin.

How surprised he was, then, to see, one morning in the
middle of a vile and interminable February rain, a young woman
standing outside Despoir's room, murmuring through the door
to the occupant. And what a woman! Her hair was the color of
burnt wood; and her face, though no larger than your hand,
concentrated within those dimensions all the innocent perfec-

tion that you find in girls at a country dance, when the leaping firelight covers up in shadows the traces of pox and the work of dancing brings out marvelous colors beneath the pallor of a winter spent indoors. She wore a long dress of no particular color, and over it a webby shawl of gray wool, like an old woman's, but there was no hiding a beauty like that; even if she had been shrouded like a Turk's bride her eyes would have given her away; they were gray, but shone like shells on a beach at the end of a summer rain. And her lips! They were the palest red, like a field of poppies, if you saw it through a gauze veil... Haussmann could not say exactly what they were like, but he could say that she was beautiful. Despoir's answer was not the one she wanted; she blushed more deeply and murmured something else, then turned, paused a half-step from the door, and ran down the stairs so quickly that Haussmann hardly had time to take off his hat. A moment later Despoir came out of his room, one hand in his matted hair and the other raised in some imprecation—but as soon as he saw that he wasn't alone on the landing, he spun on his heel and disappeared into his room again. The door closed behind him and it didn't open again for days afterward.

Haussmann could think of nothing else. Who was the beauty who'd come to see Despoir, this miserable medico, this lump? And why, good Lord, why would he turn her away? In the course of his visits in the town, Haussmann stopped at the Faculty of Medicine. He happened to mention to its Director that he was staying at the Two Hearts, a fine place, he said, in fact he lived next door to a medical student, a fellow named Despoir, and had the Director heard of him? The Director had not. Well, that was no surprise; there were hundreds of medical students in Poitiers and one could not be expected to keep track of them all. A handsome fellow, though... By the way, what was the situation with cadavers? Did they have enough?

Haussmann drew the Director out on this and other pleasant
subjects, and left the medical school informed, if not satisfied.
He went to the cafés near the university and asked the students
about Despoir, but none of them seemed to know him, except
one or two who thought that he had already graduated and
gone on to practice somewhere. The booksellers had sold him
no books; the postman had delivered no letters for him; the
pawnbroker had pawned nothing that belonged to Despoir. He
seemed to have passed through Poitiers without leaving a mark.
Whether he had loved or been loved, no one could tell; and
Despoir kept to himself.

A month later Poitiers gave itself over to a winter ball: one of
the heated events that make the season in a provincial town,
which is remembered long afterward by everyone associated
with it in any way, from the baker who prepared the braids of
white and yellow bread to the chandler whose shop is nearly
emptied out by all the orders for candles of various sorts, to the
wineseller, the carter, and the Parisian glovemaker whose window has nothing left in it but bare ivory hands. Even those who
pass near a provincial ball speak fondly of it; they remember
how they stood outside staring at the orange-and-gold light in
the ground-floor windows, and how long was the line of carriages waiting at the front door; and in this way they forget all
sorts of unpleasant things: how the melting snow trickled from
the hems of their coats into their boots, and how they coughed
raggedly, and how a little farther down the road their cart got
stuck in a patch of mud and it was nearly morning by the time
they got it home. — Well, asks the wife then, and where were
you? — They're having a ball up the road, you sigh, and fall
dead tired into bed; that night your dreams are better lit than
they are at any other time.

Haussmann understood from certain half-sentences uttered by M. Boullé, phrases about the pleasure of dancing and the importance of seeing one's youth happily employed, that he was supposed to look after Adèle Bellebecq. This he did, in dance after dance, and in the stuffy rooms where refreshments were served, so well that if, at midnight, he had proposed that Adèle begin a new life with him aboard a pirate ship, she would certainly have accepted. He had however no intention of asking her for anything—until he saw the woman who had visited Despoir. In simple clothes she was lovely, but in a ball gown, with flowers on her wrist, jewels at her throat, and jewels in her hair, her beauty was such that in comparison to it the ladies of Poitiers looked like so many overstuffed owls. Even so, if it hadn't been for Despoir he would have done nothing. He felt his duty to Adèle—and to Boullé, who had been winking at him all night; personal interest would not have moved him to abandon that. But if he acted on Despoir's behalf... It was a pity, really, that such a beautiful woman should be rebuffed. A face like that was meant for happiness, just as Despoir's strong, rough features were meant for adventure. If he were to step in, to see, for Despoir, what the situation was, he would be doing something akin to a public service—the closest he would come in Poitiers to civic improvement, he thought a little sullenly. With a serenity felt more often by the narrators of stories than by those who play in them, he asked Adèle if she would excuse him for a moment and went to ask Despoir's lover to dance.

Her name was Hermione de Néuville; she was the daughter of the Baron Néuville, a stern old gentleman whose estate contained some of the finest orchards in all the province. She said that she would be delighted to dance, and asked whether the young men of Poitiers were afraid of her? Because not one of them had spoken to her all evening.

— I wouldn't know, Mademoiselle; I'm from Paris.

— How unusual! Hermione said. And are yellow gloves really in fashion there?

Haussmann blushed. His gloves were indeed yellow; the color was favored by "advanced" circles in Paris, in other words dandies and poets and idlers. In Paris he would never have worn them. The gloves went with a life which was not his own: a flamboyant life that involved, from what he gathered, a great deal of drunkenness and the love of actresses; it involved nights spent singing in the streets at the top of one's lungs, and Haussmann could not sing. If he had worn yellow gloves his friends would have laughed at him. Haussmann a dandy! They would no more believe it than if he told them he was giving civil service up to cross Arabia on camelback. But they were not here—and for the first time their absence seemed as though it might have advantages.

— Some people wear them, he murmured.

They danced endlessly, then caught their breath and spoke of everything. Hermione, Baron Néuville's youngest, had grown up among the ranks of apple and pear trees which shed blossoms each spring in such profusion that the hillsides themselves acquired her complexion, while fruit the color of her lips smiled from among the green branches of the trees. Later, Haussmann would hear that when she turned fifteen the trees were blighted, struck by a burrowing disease that seemed to sap the will of the fruit to ripen; in the same year she had run away from home. A coachman never cursed the way she cursed when they caught her, people said, hiding in a hayrick a dozen miles from her father's house; indeed, she herself admitted to knowing the whole of the language, and not only its nicer parts, for her father, she said, insisted that no part of the world was evil in itself, and thus everything was worth knowing, as long as it was known in the right way. There were other rumors that she had taken lovers in all her father's villages, and bore a stranger's child, and drowned it in the river; but whether these stories were true is highly doubtful, for the stuffed owls of Poitiers were so jealous of the beauty who flowered in their midst that they made up all sorts of gossip, most of it so improbable that it withered at once into a whisper, a gasp, a quaking of China-painted fans. Despite the rattle of stiff paper and bone that followed her wherever she went, Hermione was as though irradiated by the ball; she beamed, and sighed, and admitted that she had thought of little but dancing since the orchard crackled with the season's first night frost. When she was younger the hills and alleys of crooked trees had been all to her, but, as she grew, she found her interest transferred to places farther and farther away, until it dropped below the horizon each night with the sun, and, like the sun, seemed to traverse half the planet while she slept.

They spoke of everything but Despoir. He tried to say his neighbor's name more than once, but each time when he hesitated, Hermione asked him a question about life in Paris, or told some old farmer's joke (her sense of humor, like her tongue, was rough and even a little cruel). He laughed, and hesitated, and they danced again. Soon it was after midnight. The dancers had slowed in their rounds; as they came out of the ballroom they stared a little, wondering perhaps whether Haussmann was one of the lovers they'd heard of. Oh, stare, he wanted to tell them, stare at us, we are elegant and worth staring at!

But Hermione murmured, — Come outside, and took his hands. In the courtyard it was too cold to speak. They walked arm in arm and admired the stars, which shine brightest at that time of year, when the earth is closest to them. What a curious happiness that was! Enjoying the warmth of Hermione's arm, and thinking that the girl had mistaken him for a suitor, when in fact he was there on behalf of someone else. It made him almost dizzy, knowing that at any moment he would say the word that made him no longer simply himself, but a surrogate for another. It drew Haussmann to her. For a moment, in the dark, he imagined that he was Despoir, or, if not him, then one at least as good, who might take his place without any imposture—wasn't he the one who, at twenty-two, had been named to a post that a man of forty might hold with honor? Wasn't he the Parisian, the one with fine clothes, the one for whom the future held everything, the one who looked ahead and was not afraid? He was Despoir but with courage, and if Hermione de Néuville came to the door of his room he would not send her away. He wanted to say something to this effect, and who knows what sort of nonsense might have left his lips then, if Hermione had not stopped at the farthest point from the lights of the ball, and turned to look him square in the face.

— Mademoiselle, I...

— Ssh! she cautioned, and they held the rest of their conversation in whispers. — Sir, I do not know you...

— I fear you know me very well...

— But I think I may have seen you once before. Don't you live at the Two Hearts?

Haussmann blushed all his answer.

— You live on the top floor? And you have a neighbor? Then, my friend, I must ask something of you, which I would not ask of another, but I can see from looking at you that you are to be trusted, and, if you'll oblige me, you will deserve my greatest confidence... She took a letter from her bosom, and asked him would he deliver it to Despoir?

Haussmann bowed. Almost before he could raise his head she had gone inside, leaving the letter in his hand and a kiss— so light that if her lips hadn't been cold, he would hardly have felt it—on Haussmann's cheek.

Sproul was practically the only person left within. He told Haussmann that M. Boullé had driven Adèle home. — I hope you've enjoyed yourself? he asked, and before Haussmann could answer, he turned away. Haussmann walked home alone through the streets of Poitiers, which seemed to him then the most desolate of provincial towns, and stopped on the bridge. Hermione's letter was still in his pocket. The city was very quiet. He let the letter go there, over the parapet, unopened. It landed on a patch of foam and drifted slowly downstream, white on white. He watched it go. Then he turned and crossed the bridge, toward the Two Hearts.

The rest of the winter passed without event. And yet, as the days brought their gray light to his window earlier each morning, and the square below kept its orange luster later into the afternoon, Haussmann began to entertain the strangest possibilities: he wondered whether the letter had really been addressed to Despoir, as he assumed at first, or whether it might not have been meant for him. How Hermione would have heard of him before the ball, he had no idea, unless his reputation as secretary-general had somehow reached her. It occurred to him that she might have been holding the letter for the first brave suitor who came along, that it might have contained a plea for help of some sort—perhaps her father was a cruel man, and kept her locked away against her will; or perhaps she'd gotten into trouble, debt, an unwanted engagement, in short she needed to be rescued from something. Haussmann regretted the impulse that had caused him to throw the letter away unread, but it was gone and without it he knew nothing. He dared not write to Hermione, for then he would have to admit what he had done, nor could he ask Despoir about her. He could do nothing but wait; so he waited.

Cousin Adèle had gone home to Saint-Brieuc the day after the ball, and without her there weren't enough people for whist; it was a good thing, Boullé observed dryly, that his secretary-general knew how to entertain himself. Haussmann had not enjoyed the evenings at the Prefect's very much, but without them he had nothing to distract himself from his thoughts of Hermione. She had once visited the Two Hearts at sundown, and often as not Haussmann managed to be seated in Madame Prosequi's parlor at that hour. At first his landlady took this as a touching offer of companionship for a lonely woman, but when she saw that her boarder was too distracted to make conversation, and answered every question with — Hm! It's very well! she guessed what Haussmann himself did not yet know, namely, that he had fallen in love. She got the story from him (except the part about the letter), and, when it was told, said frankly, — Go and see her, then. — But I hardly know her, Haussmann protested, while to himself he said: *she loves Despoir.*

Afraid that Madame Prosequi would discover this objection, too, Haussmann went up to his room. Whereas before he had avoided the Two Hearts as much as possible, now the evening often found him lying on his bed, his chin propped on his hand, staring at a book. His work did not benefit from this diligence. Half his attention waited for Hermione's footfall on the stairs, and the other half waited for Despoir to leave his room. *Does she love Despoir? Then he will go to her,* Haussmann thought. He waited only for the proof, or, what would be better, proof to the contrary: if Despoir never went to see her, then it must mean that they did not love each other, which meant in turn that her heart was free... And Despoir continued lazy as ever. He went downstairs at night for his customary walk; sometimes Haussmann, in a fit of restlessness, decided to stretch his own legs as well, but by the time he'd put his boots on and gone downstairs, Despoir had vanished.

Haussmann no longer spent very much time in the prefecture. What was the good of it, when Boullé would not even give him a quarter-hour to discuss improvements to the roads, or a new method which Haussmann himself had devised to stimulate the growth of the paper industry? If they wanted nothing from him, then he would give them nothing. He went to work at ten, at eleven o'clock, and left at three or four. When Sproul saw him, he raised an eyebrow and said, — The young secretary! What are *you* doing here? To which Haussmann could think of nothing clever to say; he raised his hat and mumbled, — I was just leaving.

He wrote less and less often to his friends in Paris, and their letters to him were more and more perplexed, as though he had offered to loan them money and urged them to take it from his empty hand. To his mother he wrote that the provincials lived by a different rhythm than the Parisians, and that news could not be expected to accumulate as quickly here as it did at home. He was well, he said; he did not lack anything; he would write again when there was something worth saying.

He walked through Poitiers but saw nothing; in his head he composed a confession to Hermione de Néuville. My dear Hermione, he would say, I never delivered your letter to Despoir, but you must forgive me, because I love you, and isn't the fact that I am a poor messenger proof that I may be a better lover? When he got back to the Two Hearts and took out a piece of paper the words seemed ridiculous. He was a civil servant, not a lover! With fresh determination he opened a treatise on accounting, and copied a phrase, "debts must be recorded twice, once at the time the obligation is incurred, and again at the time of the disbursement of funds..." into his notebook. He studied the drafting of contracts, the burial of the dead, and the prevention of fires, but it did him no good. What use were books? The Prefect did not rely on books, but on quiet, evil men like Sproul. Lovers had no use for books; what they needed were letters, or meetings, yes, encounters... He lay back on his bed, studied the ceiling, and waited for Despoir to stir.

One morning when he went to the prefecture, he found Sproul in his office, signing papers.

— Just a few contracts that need to go out today, Sproul said. The Prefect didn't know if you'd be in, so he asked me to sign...

Haussmann picked one of the papers up. Sproul hadn't even bothered to spell his name correctly: he had left off the last *n*. He pointed this out.

— It's good to see you so concerned about your work! But don't worry. No one reads the signature.

— *I* read it. And if I saw a forgery like this, I'd throw the document out.

— Would you? Well, fortunately not everyone is as careful as you are. Anyway, it's better than if they weren't signed at all.

— I can't believe that M. Boullé...

— Ask him, then, ask him. Sproul waved him to the Prefect's office.

M. Boullé received him coolly. — The signatures? My dear boy, isn't it too late to worry about them now? Unless you want to copy all the contracts over? No? Then we'll let them go. You can sign too, if you want. Put Sproul's name under your own. Will that make you feel better?

— No, I...

— Really, you don't look well. What's the matter? A late night?

— No, not at all.

— You're pale; you ought to get some rest. Even a small city can wear you down... Sproul! Call a carriage. M. Haussmann isn't feeling well; we're sending him home at our expense.

A letter was waiting for him at the Two Hearts. His mother

had written to tell him that his father had heard from a friend at the Interior Ministry that he, Haussmann, had received his first official evaluation, and that it had been largely, alarmingly, unfavorable. "I know people must be jealous because you've accomplished so much so young," she said. "Please write soon, and reassure me that there's nothing to this rumor but their malice." Haussmann put the letter on his table and lay down. He was very tired. It seemed to him that he had been running a race all his life, a race whose course was unmarked, with no flags at its finish line, so that, for all he knew, he might be in the middle of it, or at the end, or already past the finish and running for no reason at all. Where had it got him? Haussmann looked out the window at the spires of the cathedral, chalk-white in the afternoon light; then he closed his eyes.

For three days he did not leave his room.

What he thought of in all those long hours is difficult to say. Often he wondered what Despoir was doing in the next room; occasionally he pressed his ear to the wall and tried to make out the sound of some activity, but could hear nothing except the pigeons scratching about on the tiles of the roof. He thought sometimes about how his life had been when he was a child, when his parents had sent him to stay with his grandmother and grandfather at Versailles. He had been happy then, he thought, a country child, building snares to catch frogs and lying at night on a hill, watching the roof of the world turn on its lazy axis. His grandfather was a general, and he had a box of ribbons that came from many wars. He let Haussmann hold the ribbons and told him that he would grow up to be brave, but Haussmann, back then, anyway, didn't care about bravery; what he loved were the colors of the cloth, which reminded him of the ribbons in his mother's hair... He remembered when his mother had taken him to see his grandmother before she died, and what sort of cakes he'd had, and how the birds had gath-

ered just outside the window, turning their heads to one side
and the other, waiting for crumbs. He had been afraid that they
would eat him up, but had fed them all the same, from his shaking hand.

The red light climbed the wall of his room as the sun set,
and he could see all sorts of pits and brownish stains in the paper, which, he thought, he must take care of, and while he was
at it he might give the floor a good scrubbing, and polish the
windowpanes—but by the time he thought of these things it
was too late to begin. He put on his yellow gloves instead and
looked at himself in the mirror. He smoothed his hair, straight-
ened his collar. He imagined that the mirror was a window into
Despoir's room, and that he was looking at Despoir, which was
to say himself. He thought of what he would say to Hermione,
and what she would say in return, and how she would take his
hand and tell him that she understood who he was, he was
Haussmann the dandy! Then Hermione laughed at him and the
scene dissolved; he saw only himself in the mirror, or less than
himself, he saw the image of someone pretending to be him in
ridiculous gloves. He took them off, put them back in their
box, and began a letter, *Dear M. Boullé, You will not be surprised to
receive my resignation from the post of secretary-general...* which he
would never finish. He did not think of Hermione again, or
when he thought of her it was only as a sort of footbridge to
thinking about Despoir. He listened at the wall and wondered
what might be happening in the next room, or looked out the
window and thought that it must soon be time for Despoir to
take his walk; or he lay on his bed and thought about nothing
at all.

Haussmann might have become anything then, or he might
have become nothing, if it had not been for a change which,
though it had nothing to do with him, returned him almost at
once to himself. One morning—it was just after midsummer,

and Haussmann, who'd gone to bed long past midnight, woke up to find it nearly noon—there was a clattering on the stairs, a scraping and thumping as of heavy objects being dragged about. Haussmann opened his door and found a gray man and his bonneted wife, who, though not wealthy, nonetheless gave the appearance of being extremely respectable, watching as a servant carried a trunk downstairs. They wished Haussmann a good morning and fell silent again. Despoir was not in his room. The trunk must have been very heavy: the servant, who looked to be even older than his master and was sweating heavily under his checked shirt and greasy leather vest, had managed to drag it as far as the top of the stairs, but could not find a way to get it down. First he tried preceding the trunk, but it pressed so heavily on him that he almost fell down the stairs; then he tried pushing the trunk before him, but again its weight was such that the servant was nearly dragged down after it. Haussmann couldn't help but offer him a hand. It was indeed extremely heavy, and Haussmann wondered what was in it: medical textbooks, probably, half of them unread and the other half not understood. Despoir's shabby clothes, a journal perhaps in which he'd drafted letters to Hermione. And between the pages of the textbooks were pressed, perhaps, the flowers which had fallen on the day Despoir and Hermione met, and somewhere perhaps there was an invitation to the ball where Haussmann had seen Hermione—there was an entire love affair in that trunk and it was only then, staggering down the stairs under its weight, that Haussmann realized how little he knew about it and how little he would ever know.

No one thanked Haussmann for his assistance. He helped the servant to lift the trunk into a farmer's cart, and the old couple took their places opposite the trunk, facing backward. Haussmann felt sorry for them. He saw, as if he had been in their place, what must have happened: the letters from their son

which were nothing but one excuse and the next, attestations
of illness at exam time and the vindictiveness of certain profes-
sors, the experiments that failed in their sixth month. How
long had they believed the letters, and for how long after they
had stopped believing them did they continue to send whatever small sum they had sent—it could not have been much, or
else Despoir would never have taken such a room—hoping,
somehow, that things would sort themselves out? And what had
decided them at last that things would not be sorted out?
Haussmann could have cried with pity for them, for the terrible deception that Despoir had wrought. For Despoir himself
he felt nothing at all, or only contempt, mixed with relief that
he would never see the so-called medical student again. All the
same, when the poor farmer's cart had driven off, away from
Poitiers, and was gone from the horizon, Haussmann went into
the room that had formerly been Despoir's. Only dust and a
broken bottle on the floor suggested that it had once been furnished; a pale spot on the wall indicated the place where a portrait had hung. Now that it was empty, Haussmann thought, the
room looked nothing at all like his own.

He went to his office at seven-thirty the next morning. When
Sproul came in at half past ten and told him that he ought not
to be working in his condition, he held up a procurement order, by which the Ministry of the Interior proposed to buy certain furnishings from Sproul's business partners at a price that
was more than fair. There was nothing improper about that—
except that Sproul had signed it, "Secretary-General of the Vienne, J. SPROUL."

— A slight irregularity, Haussmann said. I was just going to
forward it to the Minister for review...

— There's no need for that! I'm sure we can find an explanation, you and I? But what a mess your desk is! Let me clear some of these papers off, now that you're back among the living.

That summer Haussmann explored the countryside around Poitiers, and found it beautiful. He climbed all the neighboring hills and went off on long fishing excursions, from which he returned with net sacks of twitching silver catch; these he presented to Madame Prosequi, who prepared them in a number of delicious ways, and, as they sat together in the parlor after dinner, sighed to herself. As if to say—Haussmann thought— *well, so we've found that there's more than one fish in the ocean!* He walked everywhere; he avoided only the estate of the Baron de Néuville, which in any case was far away and not in the most pleasant part of the countryside. By the fall, he and Sproul had come to an understanding: he would overlook Sproul's questionable transactions, and, in return, Sproul would see that Boullé gave him credit for the civic improvements he thought of with increasing frequency. Water came to Champigny-le-Sec, and the schoolmaster at Chauvigny was replaced, and the lepers at Chatellerault donated, by unanimous accord, their cadavers to the medical school. His mother wrote to tell him that the Interior Minister himself had asked, in a not unapproving voice, who this young Haussmann was.

In time everyone dismissed the previous winter's episode as a strange illness which must have had its origin in the river water, and indeed other cases of it were found to have occurred in the same year: there was a poor girl who'd somehow convinced herself that she could ride an unbroken horse, and snapped her neck in a nighttime fall; and at the lycée two students had, for several weeks, refused to speak in anything but Italian, although between them they knew no more than fifty words of the language. A pharmacist had drowned himself in the Clain and was found in an eddy, with a bundle of waterlogged prescriptions in his pocket, an illegible symptom of the uneasy times. But those times were over now; even Haussmann resigned himself to a sort of benevolent incomprehension of the affair. He was leaving the Two Hearts, having wrested his official lodgings back from Sproul.

A few nights before he moved into the new place, he went out to stretch his legs and found himself, as always, walking in the direction of the river. On the bridge he passed a young man who was dressed well, though not neatly, as though he'd just been in a scuffle. It was Despoir. He greeted Haussmann politely, though with a little embarrassment, and Haussmann replied in just the same way. Neither one seemed to want to spend much time in the other's company, so, after they'd asked after each other's health, they turned away—but Haussmann, without knowing why exactly, reached for Despoir's hand, which he withdrew, rudely, Haussmann thought. Still he was moved to ask: —You knew Hermione de Néuville, didn't you?

Despoir cursed most vilely; for a moment Haussmann was afraid that the other might throw him in the river. But Despoir only laughed. — Why, that whore! If it wasn't for her I might have made something of myself. Good night! With that Despoir hurried across the bridge; in the darkness nothing more was visible of him but the ribbon of his hat and the white dash of his smile. Haussmann could not tell, for the life of him, whether Despoir was lying, or what he meant about *making something of himself.*

The next day, to celebrate his coming up in the world, he bought himself a golden watch chain. He looked at himself every which way in the jeweler's window, and found himself quite dashing, a young man with prospects in life. You're quite a catch, Haussmann, he told himself as he made his way back to the Two Hearts. Even Madame Prosequi seemed to think a little more of him: she opened the door wide-eyed, as though a second life had settled on him, firmer, clearer, and altogether more admirable than his own. He was in a talkative mood that night and so couldn't help but tell Madame Prosequi how he'd seen Despoir. At which the old woman looked at him askance and told him that it was better not to joke about such things, Despoir having hanged himself a year ago, almost to the day.

There his memory was probably tricking him, though: he must have met Despoir earlier, or else he had seen someone else on the bridge. It was strange how memory changed things! Apart from that one detail the story was as clear as if it had happened days ago, but Haussmann could no longer understand why the medical student had fascinated him. Despoir was a lost soul, one of those people who sets out well enough in life but gets tangled up in something on the way. That hardly made him unique: most people got tangled up in something, sooner or later. How fortunate I am, Haussmann told himself, to have kept track of where I'm going! He thought as much when he was promoted from secretary-general to subprefect, and when he was made prefect he thought exactly the same thing. He thought it again when he met Octavie and asked for her hand in marriage, and again when, by a stroke of something he could not characterize as anything but luck, he happened to be in Paris on the very night of Louis Napoleon's coup d'état. Haussmann remembered that morning well: he had seen Louis Napoleon the night before, and the President (soon to be Emperor) had advised him to go to the Interior Ministry early the next morning to get his orders. Haussmann was there at seven o'clock sharp and demanded to see the Minister, whereupon the servant looked confused and asked him which minister he wanted to see?

— Well, I haven't come here to see the Minister of Agriculture, Haussmann said, annoyed.

— I mean, does Monsieur desire to see Monsieur the Count de Thorigny or Monsieur the Count de Morny?

De Morny a minister? At once Haussmann understood what had happened, that things would no longer be the same, that they might never again be the same. He sent his card up to de Morny and was the first visitor to call on the first minister of the Second Empire. And all because he knew what was what! If Haussmann had hesitated at the door he might have made the wrong choice and if he had made the wrong choice then he would certainly not be the Prefect of Paris today. Every action had its moment: the law, though cruel, was inflexible.

Haussmann understood that Madeleine wanted to see him, that she needed or thought she needed to see him: but it was the wrong moment. When the time came he would explain it to her and she would understand. Why, she might even benefit from the lesson: it would help her to live not according to her feelings, or at least not always, but according to something larger: principles, immutable as the stars. So the Baron reasoned, and reassured himself. His intentions were the best throughout, and if he seems to have remembered a long story to no purpose you must excuse him. He was tired from overwork and all sorts of stories came into his head while he stared at his plans for Paris, so many stories that if I told you half of them we would never come to the real cause of his last regret. And if I have chosen this story to tell you among all the others, I have chosen it because it is the story of what might have been and was not, which is Haussmann's story, which is the story of everyone who lives with what he has done.

19

MANY CIVIL SERVANTS ARE DEPORTED

THE GUARDS OUTSIDE the Hôtel de Ville had orders to admit no one. Too many journalists had been skulking by, waving their pens of malignant affliction and asking to interview
clerks, however petty, to squeeze from them the truth of the
Prefect's plans. Was Haussmann going to tear down Notre-
Dame? Would he expropriate the Deity, and, if so, how was
payment to be arranged? — Keep them all out, the Baron said,
until I tell you otherwise.

They knew their orders, and the penalty for disobeying
them—reassignment to the dimmest and farthest corners of the
civil service, of which it had many—but how were they to resist entry to a poor girl, visibly pregnant and dressed in black,
carrying a basket of white flowers and protesting that it was her
father, she had to see her father, for her mother had only just
passed away?

— What's your father's name, child? the guards asked, but
the girl sobbed so much that they did not insist.

— I'll take you to him, offered a handsome young guardsman for whom the prospect of reassignment held few terrors.
The girl was, after all, quite pretty; she had the sort of beauty

which only gets better with mourning. Her pale skin caught the shadow attractively in its furrows; her lips even without makeup were a deep blood-red where she had bitten them in her grief.

She shook her head, and held up the flowers entreatingly. — May I go in?

— Sure you may, waved the handsome young guardsman (who, if you're curious, spent five unpleasant years watching convicts in the Cayenne penal colony, until the Second Empire ended and it was safe for him to return to Paris).

Madeleine, for of course it was she, now murmured to this clerk and now to that: — Pray where is the Prefect? I've come on urgent business... Her interlocutor saw her face, her big-bellied figure, her flowers and mourning costume in that order. Well, each clerk thought in turn, if she's come this far it must be really important, and showed her on to the next-highest clerk, who, of course, thought just the same thing. O the manifold relocations that followed in her wake! Madeleine could not have done a better job of scattering the civil servants if she'd fired on them with grapeshot. One ended his days on Mauritius, another on tiny Réunion; several went to Algiers and met the range of fates which awaited French colonists in those times; still others were packed off to Lorraine until the Germans took it and called it Löthringen; then they were transferred to Lille, to Brest, to every dreary corner of the Third Republic, and it had many. The fact that they had once been disgraced led others to disgrace them further, and so Haussmann's displeasure survived his term as Prefect, and hounded them like a curse from an antique play.

In no time Madeleine stood outside the Prefect's office. She tapped lightly on the door. — Yes? — It's me. Madeleine... She was pulled into the office before the clerks, who had all gathered to see how the interview went, heard her so much as gasp.

A quarter of an hour later she came out again. Evidently the interview had not gone well. The girl was in tears, and the Prefect in a state one dares not observe in one's superiors. His face was red and his hair awry; his hands were fists and veins danced in his neck to the harsh suck of his breath. The clerks ran like geese before a gale, but not before they overheard Haussmann hiss, — Tell him I'm not so easily bought! Then the door slammed, and the girl hurried out as quickly as she had come. The guards watched her go, little suspecting that she was practically the last Parisienne they'd see, and certainly the most beautiful. She ascended the steps of her carriage and was gone in a chorus of wheels and equine agitation.

Fortunately we're not clerks. We can peek into Haussmann's office without fear of transportation, and hear, a few minutes earlier, Madeleine's imperious question, — Why have you avoided me?

Haussmann, conciliatory when cornered, hedges: — Why my dear, didn't you get my letter? I've been working...

— Your letter didn't say anything. "A terrible struggle." I don't know what you mean by that. Aren't you always struggling terribly?

— Does it seem so? I am afraid I do often... work...

— Are you ashamed of me?

— Ah, Madeleine, Haussmann sighed, you're so young! And you don't understand so many things. I'm not ashamed of you: on the contrary. But you must think of me as two people, my dear: Georges-Eugène your lover, and Haussmann the Prefect of Paris. If only we could go our separate ways! Georges-Eugène would be with you every night, while Haussmann labored to bring the fruits of progress to an undeserving city. But alas, we have only one body between us, and that body must remain here, where it can be seen, leading on this... this lot. By the way, how did you get in?

— Surely your body's been seen here enough that you can spare it for a night or two?

— Georges-Eugène regrets that Haussmann cannot tell you more. In a month, two months, you understand, he may be free, but now...

— Well! Please tell Georges-Eugène that if he wants to see me, he will do so tonight, or never again.

Haussmann shrugged sadly. — If he had a choice in the matter, I'm sure he would go.

— A choice! You're free to do as you like. Your servants don't have any choice, but you...

— I am less free even than they, for I answer to my work. It does not forgive and its memory is long.

— Hmph! said Madeleine. And do you think I'll forget how you treated me? Do you think I'll forgive you?

— When you see all that I've accomplished, perhaps...

— If you don't come to me tonight, then you'll accomplish nothing. Baron.

It was as though she'd struck him with her fist. Haussmann recoiled; he raised his hand, to strike back, she thought, and shouted, — De Fonce is behind all this! Isn't he? He put you up to it, confess! He's trying to blackmail me, to twist my arm. The conniving cripple! Tell him... tell him that it won't work. Tell him that it will be his own ruin he engineers, and his alone. Or his and yours, and that of your child. But you'll have nothing from me. Tell him you'll have nothing. Go.

— I don't believe you've understood, Madeleine said. My father has nothing to do with it. But I see that he was right: all you value is your reputation. You don't care whether what you do is right or wrong, as long as you're remembered for it! Well, you'll be remembered, I promise you: you will be remembered.

— Go! Haussmann gargled, and, except for the Baron's final exclamation noted above, the interview ended.

· · ·

Of Saint-Grimace not even rubble remained. The inn or convent that had survived atheism, revolution, superstitious nuns,
and profiteering geologists had vanished altogether; the front
half, where the convent proper had stood, was now a deep
ditch; the rear, the former garden, was being dug up, along with
the rest of the rue de la Licorne, which had been stripped of its
paving stones. Clods of earth flew into the ditch as though in
preparation for a score of funerals. Beyond the old convent lay
other streets similarly naked, and between them an unrecogniz-
able jumble of stonework: some buildings had been pulled
down to their foundations; others stood half-demolished, bar-
ing their smoke-spotted insides for the first time to the light
and the rain. Like Prometheus chained to the rock they were
ravaged by nesting pigeons, who rose from the hulks in clouds
each time a mattock struck home nearby. Only by staring
fixedly at a building for the moment left intact, a flophouse on
the rue de la Vieille Draperie, did Madeleine recognize something of the district: these were the walls she had seen from the
convent windows, these the facades, gone now, all their busy
order turned to mud, confusion, and the clang of metal on
stone.

How had so much managed to pass unnoticed? Madeleine
would have liked to stop the coach, to descend and inspect the
site. But a procession's worth of carriages waited behind hers;
she waved and let herself be carried on toward the opposite
bank. She looked back indignantly at the muddy future road.
Why had no one protested the demolition? The nuns might
have objected; theirs was after all a holy place (in her anger she
forgot the years that separated her from religious fervor), and
full of precious antiquities besides! Not every Parisian might
have known of the convent, for there were others, and greater

ones, in profusion; still, its disappearance would leave the city somehow less fit for its purpose, the way a dictionary loses value if words are cut from it, even—or perhaps especially—if they are words no one knows. And what, she wondered, had become of Saint-Grimace's clientele?

(In fact the demolition had been protested by a single petitioner. Jacob, who watched its windows long after his daughter had fled, and continued to watch them even when they no longer turned yellow at vespers. With Madeleine gone, the windows were his only connection to the world which, he thought, had opened to him when he fished the girl from the river: a romantic world of bastards, intrigue, aristocrats, devotion, and—who knew?—perhaps a great fire in the end, to kill off the villains. So he waited. Haussmann replaced the city's oil lamps with gas lamps, and many lamplighters were laid off; Jacob was among them. He no longer made the rounds on the Île de la Cité; his walks now took him only from one bar's counter to another, less and less far every night. No longer a lamplighter nor a voyeur, he told his fellow drinkers how his daughter was a noblewoman, how she had been educated in a convent, how she consorted with the greatest names in Paris, with de Morny and Rothschild and with Haussmann himself! I'll bet she does, said Jacob's fellow drunks, winking. One night as he staggered homeward he passed the place where Saint-Grimace had stood. The convent was half-demolished, and, for the first time, he saw what was inside: only rubble and rooms, which, in the white gaslight, looked like any other rooms anywhere. — Abomination! he roared. Catastrophe! He ran up and down the street, shouting to anyone who would listen, — They've ruined everything! First the lamps and now this! Monstrosity! O cruel, cruel, cruelty! To which the few passersby replied, — You're drunk, old man. Go home. Jacob got blind drunk that night and nearly fell into the Seine; he left the city the next morning and went to work in a mill town where voyeurs were unheard of, for the inhabitants snuffed their lamps and went to bed a half hour after nightfall. So we respond to the moralists who criticize the excesses of the Second Empire and the demolition of so many beautiful old buildings: even destruction may, when seen in the right way, have an edifying effect.)

Madeleine let the coach carry her back to the boulevard de Courcelles. She sank into the cushions with a sigh almost of relief; still, as she rested her hands on her belly, she wondered against herself what had become of Saint Grimace's stone hand.

PART IV

ANTIGONE

(1869)

20

THE ASPARAGUS FIELD

STUMBLING OVER THE HORIZON, arm in arm, here come Hennezel and Delesse, the Baron's spies. They are covered in mud. And they are singing,

O where the green tree grows, where it grows, where it grows,
My love said her vows, said her vows, said her vows,
There began all my woes, all my woes, all my woes,
For she's gone from my house, from my house, from my house,
Where she's gone no one knows, no one knows, no one knows.

Their voices are as rough and out of key as lockpicks. If they were burglars then Hennezel would be a second-story man: he's tall and thin as a sapling, with a spring in his legs which sends his thin hair flying up at every step. Dense and dark Delesse, with his wheezing soft voice, the flickering of his intelligence which revels in combinations, would be a safecracker. On a country road twenty kilometers north of Paris's roofs and safes, the pair still seem unfocusedly criminal, as though they were casing the earth and plotting how best to crack it. The mud which mars the cut of their coats and extinguishes the fine stuff of their cravats only makes them shadier; they look as though they belong to the legendary race of soldiers who sprang from the ground when Cadmus sowed the dragon's teeth, or like living proof of the funerary adage that, as men are born from dirt, so they return to it sooner or later.

They have not always been thus. Ten years ago Delesse was the finest assistant police inspector in Paris, and Hennezel the keenest police inspector's assistant. They cut their teeth on the Poirier ring, and played a part in the breakup of the Stampfli plot; it was Delesse who, disguised as a Milanese furrier, thwarted the attempt to blow up the Pont Neuf as the Emperor's carriage passed over it; thanks to Hennezel, his junior in rank but by no means his inferior in intellect, he escaped from Strozzi's cellar and lived to describe the strange ritual practiced there. They had already made names for themselves when the Villefranche affair came to a head and they were commended once again—not so much for the perspicacity of their investigation, this time, as for the discretion with which they kept its results to themselves. Promotions were in order, and who knew to what heights they might have risen, if Haussmann hadn't needed a couple of intelligent men who could keep their mouths shut. He requested Hennezel and Delesse's services as his personal spies, a job which, though less glamorous than police work, paid considerably better, and brought them, they thought, closer to the heart of things. For ten years Hennezel and Delesse have been wherever the Baron required them: at the Exhibition Ball they played aproned waiters, pouring champagne and listening for seditious talk. When Haussmann went to see de Fonce they waited outside, regardless of the weather, smoking their pipes, keeping an eye on the traffic. Later on, when Haussmann and Madeleine met on Headless Woman Street, you can bet Hennezel and Delesse were there first, disguised as building inspectors, snooping up and down the stairs, peering through keyholes, putting banknotes in the concierge's palm. It was Hennezel who delivered Haussmann's letter to Madeleine; and Delesse, if you want to know, who stole into Valentine's wardrobe and took from it a single dress. If we have not noticed the two of them until now, it is a testimony to their tact and their ability to keep out of sight.

When suddenly, Haussmann stopped going to the apartment on the rue Le Regrattier, Hennezel and Delesse were relieved: surveillance was dull work, and winter was the worst season for it. Since then, though, the Prefect's orders have become stranger and stranger. First he had his spies set up a medical office and impersonate doctors, a business that ended badly when they were called upon by an anxious crowd to care for a man who'd been run over in the street. For months Hennezel and Delesse watched de Fonce's residence, noting everyone who went in and out; then Haussmann sent them to buy, of all things, a rocking horse; then he ordered them to destroy the horse and to drown its remains in the Seine. He kept them waiting day and night to deliver an urgent message, but the message was not ready; it must not have been that urgent, either, for he let them go at the end of a week and did not call them back for a month afterward. They thought something might be afoot when he dispatched Delesse to spy on the offices of the *Lanterne*, but nothing came of it, and with heavy hearts Hennezel and Delesse received the order to take up their station outside de Fonce's residence again. Now, four years later, the days when they watched over the Baron's affair seem like a comfortable, happy time, a Golden Age of skulduggery, gone now and never to return.

Delesse hasn't always been as portly as he is now, nor Hennezel so taciturn; both took better care of their clothes when they knew whom they were supposed to impress, or deceive. Both drink more than they used to. They talk from time to time of quitting the Baron's service, of quitting the police force altogether and going into some other line of work—Hennezel thinks that he would be a tailor, and Delesse an accountant. But the money comes in as it always has, more than they would make doing anything else. Hennezel, when he is sober, admits that his fingers are no longer nimble; Delesse, hung over, allows that he doesn't have a head for figures. Sober or drunk, neither of them will admit the truth: that four years of mysterious orders, whose import they only occasionally comprehend, have made Hennezel and Delesse like the acolytes of a religion of which Haussmann is the only priest, worshiping a God even more unknowable than the one revered by ordinary Parisians. They are united by the faith that however little they know, they know more than anyone else. Has the Prefect lost his mind? Is the demolition man plotting to give the Prince a booby-trapped hobbyhorse? Are they getting closer to the truth? The truth is that they are getting closer to one another. When they stop for a drink, the barkeep will often as not ask them if they are brothers? Or cousins? Fat Delesse and skinny Hennezel chuckle, thinking of their secret orders. A kind of small utopia is happening here, practically unremarked upon by the two whose fortune it is, good or otherwise, to constitute it. Hennezel and Delesse walk from one end of Paris to the other, handing back and forth a heel of bread, some cheese, a lewd remark, a thoughtless companionship which, at bottom, is more mysterious than anything written in the Prefect's sealed letters.

As they pass through an orchard, Hennezel jumps up and picks an apple, which he chews with an absolute and enviable lack of reflection. Delesse's mouth works, too, but on nothing, or on words. A track of spittle explores the crevices of his chin, leaving a white streak. — I say, Hennezel, he manages.

— Hm.

— Hennezel!

—You don't have to shout.

— We've been humiliated.

Hennezel arches an eyebrow. — Really?

— How can you be so cool about it? Look at you: you're as black as the shithouse in a coal mine.

Hennezel takes note of Delesse's coloration, which is similar, and spits an apple seed.

—You shouldn't have got drunk, Delesse says.

— It was you who drank.

— Me? Only a sip. And you, you asked for more.

— I did no such thing.

— Most excellent, you said.

— I had a sip. Just like you.

—You shouldn't have been drinking at all.

—You were twice as drunk as I was.

— Me?

Hennezel considers a reply, evidently thinks the better of it, shrugs, and spits an apple seed. — The question is, what are we going to tell the Baron?

Their orders were clear enough: *Purchase the farm called the Garenne du Maubuisson, in the Commune of Méry-sur-Oise. Pay whatever price you must, but under no circumstances reveal that you are buying it for me.*

— So we're speculators now, eh, my dear Hennezel?

— My dear Delesse, how we've come up in the world!

They took a mail coach north to Méry, and stopped, dumbfounded, by the edge of the road.

— What, my dear Hennezel, do you suppose our sainted master wants with this?

— I don't have the faintest idea, my dear Delesse.

They stood at the edge of a vast asparagus field. Purplish

tufts wiggled skyward all the way to the low hedgerow that
marked the horizon. Hennezel and Delesse, accustomed to the
varied stalls of Les Halles, had never seen so much of a single
vegetable in one place before. There was enough asparagus here
for all Paris to dine on *asperges à l'hollandaise* (though the quantity of butter which would be required to prepare the sauce
staggers the imagination), and enough left over for a *velouté
d'asperges* the next night.

—An Asparagus Bank, to safeguard against shortages?

—Perhaps, Delesse, perhaps.

—To corner the market and drive up the price?

—Possibly.

—Or has he finally cracked? *He* being Haussmann, of
course.

—It could be.

—What do we do?

—We buy it, my dear Delesse.

—You're right, my dear Hennezel, as always.

The farmhouse called the Garenne du Maubuisson sat
among a clutter of sickly bushes at the edge of the Oise, a green
trickle of a river that had forgotten its source, and, unable to
imagine reaching its mouth, wound unenthusiastically through
the landscape. The Garenne was not out of place in this setting,
nor was the plump, kerchiefed woman who answered the door:
house and woman had long ago renounced the idea of destination; they had been inert for so long that they regarded anything which seemed to be on its way to or from any other
place with mistrust.

—What is it? the woman asked.

—Is your husband in, Madame?

—Who are you?

—My name is Professor Delafosse, and this is my colleague,
Professor Halevy.

Hennezel bowed.

—Are you surveyors?

—Surveyors? No, goodness, no. Delesse waved the thought away with an ivory-gloved finger. We are scientists.

—Scientists? The woman watched Delesse's finger as though it were a divining rod of as yet unproven merit.

—Is your husband in?

—Scientists. Then Haussmann didn't send you?

—The Prefect, you mean? Oh, no, we're from the Imperial Astronomical Society. We'd like a word with your husband.

—What about?

Delesse lowered his voice. — About the advancement of human knowledge, Madame.

—I don't see what Duclos has to do with *that*, she said, but all the same she led them through the kitchen, where a cauldron of what was unmistakably asparagus stock simmered over an open fire, into the parlor. — Duclos! she shouted. Wake up!

An old man slumbered in an armchair by the window. He was as immobile as the brass clock over the fireplace, the footstool covered with a cloth to keep the dust off, the massive endtable on which a vase of dried flowers had been erected, solid as a fortress on a mountaintop.

—Eh, Duclos, visitors!

At this word the old man opened his eyes and stood up, his hand outstretched in greeting. He gave the impression of being less an independent, animate creature than a sort of ornament who could be brought out on special occasions to make a good impression on those guests important enough to be allowed into the parlor. — How do you do? he said.

—Are you the gentleman of the house? Delesse asked.

—Gentleman! Madame Duclos laughed. He's my husband.

—I am Professor Delafosse, and this is Professor Halevy.

— Please, gentlemen, sit down.

— Ask them if they want something to drink, Madame Duclos said.

— Would you like a drop? I take one myself in the afternoon.

— Well...

— A drop, please, said Hennezel.

Madame Duclos visited the kitchen and came back with three glasses and a bottle of something brownish-green, like pond water.

— This, Duclos said, is a specialty of the house. He poured them each a fingerful. — To your health, gentlemen!

— God! Delesse spluttered. What is it?

— Asparagus brandy, sir. I make it myself. Is it too strong for you?

— No, Hennezel said, it's just right.

— I like to make it strong.

— Delightful, said Delesse. Now sir...

— The gentlemen are from Paris, said Madame Duclos. She had left the room only nominally; through the door to the kitchen her bulk could still be seen. — From Paris, she repeated.

— We've had a number of visitors from Paris, said Duclos.

— Is that so? That's very interesting.

— Surveyors, Madame Duclos said.

— There are a lot of them about, Hennezel remarked.

— People of inferior quality, mostly, said Delesse.

— Measuring everything, as though we were livestock to be sold!

— They lack education, Madame; they lack manners.

— Surely, Duclos sighed, you didn't come all this way to tell me that.

— No, sir, absolutely not. We've come to talk about Science.

— About what?

— Well, sir, Madame, let us explain our business. Professor Halevy and I are members of the Imperial Academy of Astronomy. Really, that brandy is most excellent. Might I have another drop, Madame? Thank you. Now, as I was saying...

Delesse explained that conditions in Paris, with the arrival of universal gas lighting and rumors that electrical light wasn't far off, not to speak of the pollution and the noxious fogs, had deteriorated to the point that, three nights out of four, not a single star was visible anywhere in the city. Not even a planet, or a meteor, or a comet... In time Delesse came to the point: that, given the elevation of the land, and the hills that prevented the eastward motion of cloud, given the near-total absence of ambient light and the proximity of the farm to Paris, given, in short, given everything, the Academy was keenly interested in establishing a new observatory here, in the precise location where the farm called the Garenne du Maubuisson stood. — With our modern apparatus and your, ah, your perfect darkness, sir, who knows what we will discover? Planets as yet unseen by man, and, ah...

— Comets, said Hennezel.

— And comets that foretell the rise and fall of great powers, and, well, sir, you see that this is a matter of great importance not only to the Academy, but, sir, if I dare to say it, to all of mankind.

— You're out of brandy, Madame Duclos said. I'll fetch another bottle.

When the bottle had arrived, and been relieved of a little of its greenish contents, Duclos said, — You want to build an observatory? Here?

— Exactly.

— But what would I do?

— Oh, I don't doubt that you would be able to make a

contribution of some sort to the, ah, the scientific effort, said Delesse.

— If you want to, that is, Hennezel said. If not you can do whatever you like.

— I can see, sir, that you are a man who respects Science, Delesse continued. You grasp, sir, you grasp visibly the principle of distillation... But let me assure you that we don't expect you to give up your land for the love of Science alone. The Society is prepared to make you an offer, a generous offer, for your house and land, indeed, sir, you have only to name a price.

— What?

— They want to buy the land, Madame Duclos said.

— The house and the land. Lock, stalk, and barrel.

— The house and the land, Duclos repeated.

— Stalk. That's a joke. Stalk and barrel?

— I don't understand, said Duclos. Why not just the house?

— It's on account of the light.

— There isn't any light.

— None *now*, said Delesse. But once the observatory is built here, you can imagine that other establishments will follow. We'll need to protect our darkness.

— Well spoken, Professor Halevy.

— Thank you.

— But... Duclos spread his hands, then closed them on the neck of the bottle. But, sirs, it is impossible. This land has belonged to a Duclos for two hundred years, you see, and I, I am a Duclos...

— And you aren't, said Madame Duclos.

— I understand your objection, said Delesse. Indeed, sir, I anticipated it. Pride in the family land! Of course, of course you feel that. No sum of money—not even fifty thousand francs—would induce you to detach your name from this as... from this farm. That's—your health, sir!—that's why I have been specially authorized by the Academy to inform you that if you consent to our proposition, we will call this place now and forever after the Duclos Observatory. We will write the name in brass, in letters, what do you think, Hennezel?

— Halevy.

— Professor Halevy, yes.

— I think two meters high would be right.

— In brass letters two meters high. In the Roman style, you understand. How does that sound?

— It sounds...

— Ask him where he's from, Duclos, said his wife.

—Yes, my dear. Where are you from, sir?

— From the Imperial Academy, that is, Society, the Imperial Academical Society of Astronomy. Madame.

— Let's drink, Hennezel said. To the Duclos Observatory!

When they had finished their glasses, Duclos stood up. — I think I'll have a breath of air.

Hennezel and Delesse followed him outside. Beyond the reach of the yellow window light there was nothing to see but the sky, stretched over the land like the pavillion of an enormous exposition.

— It's just perfect, Delesse said. Absolutely the right thing.

A trio of hens clucked quietly from their corner of the courtyard. How unbelievably silent the world is, Delesse thought. He put his hands on the small of his back and craned his neck backward to look up at the stars. And how unbelievably vast. Amazing, he thought, how the stars make you feel as though you are at the very center of everything, and how everything seems to turn gently around you in particular. — Hey, Hennezel, take a look at this!

— Stargazing?

Duclos stood beside him, head tilted back also.

Delesse composed himself. — I have a professional interest.

— One thing I've always wondered, Duclos said. Where's Cassiopeia?

— Cassiopeia?

— I can't ever seem to find it.

— Isn't that, er, a constellation? We don't do constellations. We're astronomers, not astrologers.

— You don't know where it is?

— Of course I know. But it's, er, difficult to explain. Hen... Halesse? The gentleman wants to know where Cassipopia is.

— Cassiopeia.

— Quite. Point it out to him, will you?

— Can't you do it?

— My glasses are dusty.

Hennezel gave him a dark look. To Duclos he said: — Do you see that bright star, right, um, right over there?

Behind Delesse something said, — Click. He turned. Madame Duclos, backlit by the doorway, held a blunderbuss of antique manufacture, the caliber of its barrel—which, as it was aimed directly at him, Delesse was in a good position to judge—more suitable for shooting elephants or architecture than human beings.

— Go back to your Baron, Madame Duclos said, and tell him it's no use.

— Hennezel?

— Now look down and to your, ah, right.

— Hennezel?

— What?

— Run!

They had reached the edge of the courtyard when the rifle went off—in the air, as it turned out, when they climbed out of the muddy trough into which they'd jumped and saw Duclos and his wife laughing at them, pointing skyward and laughing.

— What's that smell? Hennezel asked on the way to the Paris road.

— Smell?

— Asparagus. You must have pissed yourself.

— I did no such thing. It was you, you're smelling yourself.

— Me?

They reached Paris at dusk, or rather, the city crept up on them through a thickening undergrowth of ramshackle towns, the shanties of itinerant workers, laundries, tanneries, and churches where they celebrate Mass in Polish and German and ungodly languages. The road gathered pavement, sidewalks, trees, and, finally, lights, odors, and the clatter of women busy in the kitchen; when the noises ceased to be individual sounds, became an enjambed and incessant murmur, they were at the city wall. Half an hour and the omnibus set them down outside the Hôtel de Ville. Hennezel and Delesse stood in the great echoing square, looking at each other with the wariness of exiles who have sneaked back into their native land.

— You go in first, Hennezel. I'll tidy up a moment out here.

— No, I'll follow you in, my dear Delesse. You're the one who ought to give the report.

— You know as much as I do, my dear Hennezel.

— I won't go in until you do.

— I'm not going in first.

It was the gathering autumn cold that drove them in at last, their teeth chattering, trying to usher each other through the blazing doors of the prefecture. They were still saying — After you, my dear Hennezel, — No, I insist, my dear Delesse, when the building swallowed them up.

They found Haussmann in his private office. — Back so soon? He took no notice, apparently, of the mud which they had been equally unable to brush from their clothes and from their persons. — Have you got the deeds?

— Well, sir, the truth is...

— We told him we were astronomers...

— We were disarmed by force...

— After a struggle...

— It was his three big farmhands...

— And he drugged us. The coward!

— Stop! Haussmann cried. Gentlemen, please stop. Now, one of you, tell me what happened.

— Tell him, Hennezel.

— No, you, Delesse.

— Inspector Delesse?

When the Assistant Inspector had finished, the Baron tapped a pen to his lips. — Ha.

— Something funny, sir?

— Be quiet, Assistant.

— Ah, that's, ah, Inspector, sir. My colleague Hennezel is the assistant.

— Is that so? Haussmann took a sheet of paper and wrote furiously. He blotted the page and passed it to Hennezel. — Read that, Monsieur.

— "Paris, nineteen September, 1869. To Monsieur the Prefect of Police. Esteemed Sir: By this patent..." Well, the gist of it is, I'm to be promoted to assistant inspector, and you, Delesse, are demoted to an inspector's assistant.

— What?

— Ssh! Haussmann was writing again. He folded this letter into a plain envelope, scrawled a name across its face, and gave it to Hennezel. — Now, Inspector, I trust you'll carry out your first commission swiftly?

Outside the Prefect's office, Delesse spluttered. — The nerve! The nerve of him! And now he's sending us on another wild goose chase, I'll bet. Well, I'm not going. Not until I've had a hot bath and changed my clothes.

— Shut up, Assistant.

Hennezel turned the letter over in his hands, and wondered what the Baron could have to say so urgently to de Fonce after so many years, and whether this meant that things were going to make sense again at last.

Haussmann unfolds a map and studies its lines. Green stripes surround a white box with a question mark in its center. A dotted line leads south; here and there black squares like structures are scattered within the green lines. Where's the legend? Here, here is one: the green is the forest of Sylviacum, ancient, mighty oaks which have not stood in this spot for two thousand years. Druids gathered leaves in that forest, and danced around the foot of the trees, which were gods to them; they burned their enemies alive in oak-bark cages, and rubbed their bodies with the ash, so that their enemies' gods might not see them and take revenge. The druids were great believers in revenge. If one of their number was slain, they might wait years, or decades, to catch the offender or one of his offspring, and set them on merry fire. If necessary they would wait generations.

When the land was civilized, two thousand years ago, the Roman Prefect at Lutetium sent his troops to drive the Sylvanectes, as they were called, out of the woods. The soldiers marched north from Paris into the green lines, and did not return. The Prefect sent a second party, larger than the first, armed with torches and burning arrows; they, too, went into the forest and did not come out again. At last the Prefect himself, at the head of an army, marched to Sylviacum. He forded the Oise at dawn. On the far side, where the forest ought to have been, there was only an ash-white field; of his soldiers, of the druids, of the oak trees, no trace remained, unless it was the smell of combustion which hung in the air like a question mark. Not all prefects are good at solving riddles; this one, once he had surveyed the land, shrugged and considered that magic had done his work for him. Only, as he crossed the Oise again, he surprised a few men washing themselves, their faces dark with ash. He called to them, but they turned away and vanished into the river mist. The Prefect ordered a stone erected at Méry to commemorate his victory; then he followed his dotted road back to Paris, and did not think of Sylviacum again. Where the ash-faced men went, the map does not say.

Of course there's another legend; there is always another legend. This one is written in the fine capitals they teach in the School of Cartography: GREAT PARISIAN CEMETERY OF THE NORTH. In this story, the dashed line is the boundary of a graveyard that does not exist yet. The dotted track is the proposed railway which will service it; the green stripes mark off the land already purchased by the City of Paris, and the white square is the land that the city does not own. The Garenne du Maubuisson, the asparagus field. But what is this about? Why, you've overlooked the large letters. Written across the map like the name of a country, so large you can hardly read it, is the problem of Paris's dead. By 1869 (the year is in the lower right-hand corner, next to the cartographer's name) the city's grave-yards were full to bursting with crosses. The number of dead people had grown and grown, while the cemeteries stayed the same size; unless something was done about it, the graveyards would soon overflow, and the little crosses spill out into the streets beyond. Already there was no room to bury the poor properly. No graves for the penniless; they were dumped heel to toe into long ditches and covered with a layer of earth so thin that a heavy rain would do grave robber's work. If the population kept growing at its present rate, soon there would be no room for anyone at all to be buried anywhere. Where would their bodies go, then? Corpses would literally litter the boulevards, until, in the end, no one would be able to say whether Paris was a city for the living or for the dead.

The Great Cemetery of the North was Haussmann's answer
to these problems. Half again as large as all the graveyards in
Paris put together, its boulevards would house the dead for centuries to come. Here, study the map; admire the length of the
avenue which leads from the front gate to the columbarium!
There's the central plaza, and these are streets radiating outward; these are statues of the famous dead to give the view
from the center some gravity. Forget Paris. This is an ideal city,
the ideal city, perhaps: clean, bright, and regular, above all, regular. Not one of its inhabitants will have cause to complain.

Now look at the map again, as Haussmann does, scowling,
his chin propped on the palms of his hands. See that patch of
white at the center? Without the asparagus field, the cemetery
will not come to pass—it would be a poor beast indeed, broken
in two, not a Great Cemetery but two Semi-Teries, neither one
equal to the job at hand. But the asparagus field does not belong to Haussmann. On this point the legend is unequivocal.
What drama there is in these signs! If you study the question
mark penned over the Garenne du Maubuisson closely enough,
the minute jags of its curved neck will whisper to you how the
Baron's own notary, M. Delapalme, was deputized to purchase
the asparagus field, and how Duclos sent him packing. The
Mayor of Méry-sur-Oise, M. Belier, went to reason with Duclos, but fared no better; with an emphatic downstroke of his
head, the farmer rejected all offers, present and future, to buy
his land. To this stern resistance, which has lasted for months,
Hennezel and Delesse's recent mishaps are only an appendix,
the dot at the bottom that makes the figure complete. So the
land languishes and nothing is built. Our second legend is just
as unreal as the druids who danced through the fog among the
trees.

21

THE WORLD WITHIN THE WORLD

HER EYES WERE GRAY, though the doctors had promised
for years that they would turn brown. They never did: like pho-
tographic plates which would not take the image shown to
them in their little box, they refused all the colors of the world.
At four, Elise looked out of her eyes with as much amazement
and as little comprehension as she had at two, at one. If you
showed her a flame, she might follow it for a moment, and for
a moment twin candles would dance like daguerreotypes in the
depths of her eyes. Then she'd look away, for those gray plates
could hold no image for long. She did not speak. If you said
Mirror she'd pick up a looking glass; if you said *Water* she'd pick
up a water glass, and that was all. If you said *Elise!* she'd turn her
head, and for a moment you were in the picture, framed in
gray, faintly, distortedly visible. Then you, too, were gone, as
though the eyes were dissatisfied with you, as though they were
waiting for some other, more impressive object which had so
far not come along. She didn't cry, which upset the nurses most
of all. — How do we know when she's hungry? they grumbled, and: — It's like feeding a doll. — Be patient, Madeleine
said, and be kind to her. How can you expect her to speak if

you're not kind? Be patient, and she'll turn out all right: so
Madeleine had advised them, and herself, for four years. The
queenly baby who spoke so clearly in gurgles when Madeleine
nursed her, regal Elise, had frozen. No one could say when it
had happened, least of all Madeleine herself. In the winter of
1866, two months after she saw Haussmann for the last time,
Madeleine gave birth to a daughter, whom she named Elise after Nasérie Élise de Saint-Trouille, although she told no one
about Nasérie. De Fonce told her that the child was beautiful;
the Widow told her the child was well; but Madeleine could
not stand to see it. She stayed in her bed, where she closed the
curtains on a world which had, for a spell, gone as gray as Elise's
eyes. When she could leave her bed and went to see what had
become of everything, she found that the Widow had taken
Elise in, and, because the child had to be explained, was passing
herself off as the girl's mother. (No one was surprised; they at-
tributed the child to Couvrefeu's new lover, a major with a red
moustache, and so virile, rumor said, that he could father babies
on any noun of the feminine gender. The birth of a daughter to
the fifty-year-old Widow was just another of the difficult facts
which the nineteenth-century Parisians had to make room for,
along with natural selection, the saxophone, and the superiority
of rifled or spinning bullets to those which did not spin.) And
Elise... Her eyes were still gray, as though a splinter of a world
without color had lodged itself in them and could not be re-
moved. Six months later, Madeleine remarked that the baby was
awfully quiet.

At first she blamed her disappointment on her own impatience to have someone to talk to. When a year had gone by
and Elise was silent as ever, she blamed the Widow, the nurses,
the utterly beside-the-point governess: what was the good of
having all those people around, if not one of them could hold
the child's attention for a minute at a time? When a second year

had passed and Elise was no more inclined to speak than to fly, Madeleine blamed de Fonce, Haussmann, everyone who had participated in the plot by which she was, first of all, deprived of her daughter, then made to sit by while her daughter was deprived of words, of cries, even of tears. A third year went by, and a fourth, and Madeleine grew tired of blaming anyone at all. Elise was as she was: a silent sailor, pushing a wooden boat around a room she had never, again and again, seen before. Was there not, in the end, something wonderful in those eyes? Madeleine thought there must be something, a resistant property, an ability to refuse, which might, in the end, prove more astonishing than anything ordinary children might do, or even extraordinary ones.

One afternoon in the autumn of 1869 Madeleine came home from the Widow's, from Elise, wondering again at the child's capacity to take the world in and keep it out at once. She found an old man seated on the parlor sofa, hat in his hands, grinning.

— M. Duclos, de Fonce said. A jewel in the crown of Paris's suburbs.

He seemed an unlikely jewel of anything except perhaps a museum of natural history. His brown, scored face bore the marks of violent washing; his suit, which was either green faded to gray or the opposite, would have been antiquated before the Revolution. The clothes, along with his sunken eyes, yellow fingernails, and sparse, curiously lifelike hair, gave him an air of authentic membership in a bygone era, like the bodies scientists occasionally dig out of bogs and dress in period costume for public show.

— A humble farmer, ma'am, said Duclos.

— Not for long, my friend, de Fonce said.

— That's true! I'm in town to hear a will.

— Oh? Madeleine hadn't heard of will reading as a touristi-
cal activity, but Paris was increasingly full of attractions which
she did not bother to understand.

— It's my cousin who's passed away, said Duclos, and
touched his eye in a pantomime of grief.

— You may be surprised, my dear, to hear that I'm the ex-
ecutor of the estate.

— And your father's invited me to dine with him to...

— To soothe the pain, de Fonce said.

— Well, I hope you'll be able to forget your sorrow a little
while, Madeleine said. For what scheme, she wondered, had de
Fonce dug this poor creature up?

— Come over here, my dear, where we can see you. My
daughter Madeleine is the very portrait of a Parisienne, don't
you think?

— She's better than a portrait! She's the real thing! Duclos
spluttered, then swayed from side to side for a moment, stunned
by his own wit.

De Fonce smiled paternally. — Now, how shall you spend
your day in Paris?

Duclos pursed his lips. — Well, the wife has given me a few
commissions. I'm to buy muslin. And satin. And... and pins, I almost forgot. And pins.

— Come, sir, you're not a mercer! If you'll trust me, I'll send
someone out for all that. Of course it's no imposition. My
household is at your service, as I am myself.

Duclos turned to Madeleine.

— Don't look at me! she said. I'm quite worn out. And I'm
sure my father has wonders planned.

— Only dinner. You'll find it modest, though it's the best we
can do. Then perhaps something Parisian? A cabaret? Well, if
you like. Though you'll find no one but tourists there, these
days. I'm afraid Paris is so diluted that one sees it best at home!

Now, if you ask me, the way to spend an evening is in a private
club, with a cigar and a game of cards...

— Good day! Madeleine kissed de Fonce and left the
farmer, who followed her with the dull eyes of an oft-charmed
serpent.

What Duclos saw, when Madeleine came in, was so far re-
moved from anything his eyes chanced upon in the ordinary
course of his years that, in order to make any sense of it at all,
he had to refer to that rarest (for him) of events, attendance at
the little church of Méry-sur-Oise, where a sulky priest read
aloud in a language which neither he nor any of his compatri-
ots had the slightest hope of understanding. In that church,
along the right side of the nave, hung a tapestry, faded and
smoke-darkened by the years, but not entirely illegible. It
showed a great battle, with rampant horses and swords argent,
quartered corpses and sable smoke rising from among the trees.
Duclos, when the Madame brought him to hear that polysyl-
labic nonsense, once or twice a year, preferred to lose himself in
the tapestry. For a moment he forgot that he was a farmer; by a
sort of imaginative and entirely heretical communion he became a linen soldier shouting across the confines of a flaxen
plain that the Saracen was dead, the English slain, the Spaniard
spitted, and the German gored. The battle was won before you
could say *ita, missa est*; and Duclos had to look elsewhere for his
entertainment. Fortunately the maker of tapestries, whoever he
had been, wherever he had lived, understood what it was to be
bored by a language you cannot understand; he provided, in
addition to the bloodshed in the foreground, a second rank of
stories hidden among the trees, half-lost in the columns of
knights and smoke. Here was a highwayman holding his dagger
to a merchant's throat; and here a ship, its sails half-full; in the

high left obscurity of the weaving rose a castle in flames, and, in the opposite corner, a mountain range. Any number of stories began in those mountains, and where they ended, Duclos could not say, for the trick with the bread and wine was soon done, and he had to stumble into the light wishing the mass could have gone on twice as long.

One story in particular drew him in: if you wandered in the upper right-hand mountains, you were bound, sooner or later, to come to a tower, with no door and only a single window. You craned your head back (Duclos! Are you nodding off?) to see in the window, and a lady appeared, fair as nothing in the old cloth was fair, fine as no needle could be fine. From the length of her hair and the sad set of her eyes, you knew she'd been there a long time; from her smile, and the impossibility of getting in the tower, you knew that she was good. You wanted to climb up to her; you braided a rope, bent your saber into a grapnel—but before you could reach that window and touch the hand which flickered at the very limit of your ability to perceive detail, long-fingered and warm, your wife pinched your cheek—and you opened your eyes (how will you get to Heaven if you sleep through everything?) to the coarser, brighter, too attainable world.

When Duclos saw Madeleine, he thought of the woman in the tower. Wasn't her hair long? And weren't her eyes sad? Her costume was a tapestry in itself, woven, for all he knew, from unicorn's fur (did they have fur?), from dreams. In truth, the whole of his impression of her was no more that this: she was beautiful, incomprehensible, and unhappy. But we're weavers all, trying, from the threads at our disposal, to knot together some picture in which to lose ourselves. So Duclos, finding the Madeleine thread not entirely different in color from the tower-woman thread, wove the two together, so that, in the old and tyrannical part of his understanding which weaves without words, Madeleine became the woman in the tower, calling down to be set free. The linen soldier knew what to do: battle was all over the foreground of this scene. Without the slightest understanding of the fact that he spoke as a character in a tapestry, or of the unhappy ends which wait for those who try to solve story puzzles in life (and not, as is proper, vice versa), Duclos, ferocious and noble, reared up on the sofa and gruffly announced the call to attack: — Cards? Well, why not. Have you got anything to drink?

Madeleine, fortunately, did not hear him, nor see his story-expression. A servant had come up to tell her that she had a visitor; she kissed de Fonce and retreated, very much like the tower woman, out of the farmer's ken to where her guest was waiting.

— Who is it? Madeleine asked the servant.

— Monsieur Echs.

Madeleine groaned. Echs was the latest in a succession of young men who had, of late, made ever more frequent appearances in de Fonce's home. First there had been Auguste Eue, whose father owned a department store in Marseilles; then Philippe du Tournevis, a banker with an almost helical nose; then Guillaume d'Abelue, a scholar with a good chance of being elected to the French Academy, if only he could refrain from writing anything too interesting in the next twenty or thirty years. With each man the same events had happened in a succession which took anywhere from a day (Eue: ugh!) to (in d'Abelue's case) two and a half months: an introduction at some party, a dinner invitation, an afternoon or afternoons of chit-chat, then a walk in the park, a declaration of love from the young man, sometimes with overt reference to de Fonce's fortune, more often without. Thus far Madeleine had sent them all packing, though Eue was rich, Tournevis noble, and d'Abelue passing intelligent. She told de Fonce it was too soon; she had barely got over Haussmann, and couldn't possibly begin to love another, yet. De Fonce pointed out that she hadn't seen the Baron in four years. — Well, said Madeleine, but I haven't seen anyone like him, either.

Where was she with Echs? They'd had dinner together the week before, which meant this was an afternoon chitchat. She smiled wearily and settled herself opposite him.

Echs was a government minister's son, who had already, at thirty-one or thirty-two, won a seat in the National Assembly, representing some blighted part of the country where they raised goats. To tell the truth he looked like a good representative for them: more than a little goatish himself, with a protruding chin and a low, narrow forehead, yellow teeth, a flat nose and a bleating laugh.

— How's your flock? Madeleine asked.

— Oh, they wear me, they wear me down, Mademoiselle! I think it is a contest to find out whose head is harder, mine or theirs?

— Yours, I'm sure.

— Do you think so?

— I'd say you were quite determined.

— Thank you. Echs bowed from the waist. He was blushing.

— Mademoiselle, since you speak of my determination...

Oh good, Madeleine thought, we can skip the walk in the garden. — Yes?

— I wanted to speak to you of a most personal matter, to ask your advice.

— Of course.

— You know my father is the Minister of Roads and Bridges.

— You've mentioned it.

— And I've told you that he wants me to follow him into public service...

— Which you've done most dutifully, Madeleine said. *Baa*, she thought. If I asked him to eat some string, would he do it?

— What if I tell you, Mademoiselle, that nothing is farther from my heart?

— Oh?

— I must ask you a geographical question now. How much do you know about the North Pole?

What Echs confessed was not love, exactly, or at least not as it was usually conceived. He wanted to travel, at the head of a scientific expedition, toward the Northern Lights, he said, until he reached the marvelous world the lights signal, and protect. Did Madeleine know that the earth was hollow? Yes, it had been proved past a doubt by three members of the Academy of Sciences, working only with pendulums, pencils, and the laws of mathematics. There is a world within the world, Echs said, and its entrance must be somewhere in the vicinity of the North Pole. His face flushed, he described the indescribable joy that would belong to the first human to set foot down that grand staircase which led to a place he called Inner Earth, and see things men had never imagined.

Madeleine hadn't heard about it, but she was sure that such things would be worth seeing.

— Worth seeing! They would be worth dying for, Echs said. Then, recalling himself a little, he said, — What do you think?

— About what?

— It will mean leaving politics. My father will be disappointed, maybe he'll disown me, I don't know. But if I stay behind and someone else reaches the pole first I'll certainly die... I don't know. What should I do?

— Will you bring any women on the expedition?

Echs frowned. — Women? No-o, we hadn't planned on it.

The hardship... and the close quarters... I don't think it would be the place, really, for a woman to go.

— Then you should go.

— But what will I tell my father? How will I convince him?

— Your enthusiasm speaks volumes. But in case it doesn't... wait here, let me get something for you.

She went upstairs to the library. Madeleine had read so many books since the Haussmann Era ended, that was how she put it to herself, that she no longer remembered which one was which, or even, sometimes, which memories came from books and which from other sources. She was sure, however, that she had read something about Echs's Inner Earth not long ago, and she was determined to find it for him. She would happily give him a dozen books, if she had to, in order to be sure that he went away and did not return. A story about a sailor, yes, there was a sailor in it; in fact she had read part of it aloud to Elise, but Elise didn't care for it any more than she cared for anything else and so Madeleine had loaned it to de Fonce. It must be in his study. Certain that Echs would wait (*baa, baa!*) as long as she cared to keep him waiting, she went to find it among the heaps of paper that were her father's business now.

Like the philosopher who traded the love of one boy for the love of two, the love of two for the love of all, and the love of all boys for love itself, de Fonce had abstracted himself from the world of objects. First he dealt in land, then in deeds to land, then in deeds to deeds, in bonds backed by deeds, in obligations and futures and papers more mysterious still, which might, for all Madeleine knew, give him title to the color ochre, the idea of purpose, the months October and November. He was vastly richer now than he had been before. Why else would Eue and Tournevis, d'Abelue and Echs come to visit, or the older men, Rothschild himself and Isaac Pereire, who was rich as Midas, and jaundiced as though he had accidentally turned himself to gold. All Madeleine wished, at the moment, was that they would leave her alone. She would, of course, eventually marry—perhaps she'd pick one of the suitors at random, or organize a contest for her hand, the way they did in stories—but what was the hurry? She was twenty-nine, which was not too old. Even de Fonce agreed that she was if anything lovelier than she'd been at nineteen. She still had practically the entirety of her future to look forward to, he said, even if the prospect wasn't as delightful as it had been before. Madeleine closed her eyes. When she left Saint-Grimace, the time ahead of her had been a labyrinth. When she fell in love with Haussmann, it became a boulevard, broad and bright, with something suitably rich at the far end to guarantee the agreeability of the perspective. Now the future was like one of those drawing studies where two walls seem to converge in the distance, so that, although where you stand there's plenty of room, you can't imagine how you will pass between them when you're farther on. Every step she'd taken had, when she took it, seemed to lead toward greater freedom; only now, when she looked back, it seemed as though she'd always been moving in the same direction, toward the distant point where the walls meet.

She pulled a volume from a heap of the demolition man's correspondence, a few sheets of which fell to the floor. *The Adventures of Arthur Pym*, by Poe, in Baudelaire's translation. It wasn't a strong argument for polar expedition, but perhaps Echs wouldn't understand that it was fiction, and that it didn't end happily. She stooped to collect the fallen papers and stopped. There, at the bottom of a letter, was a familiar scribble: "To you, G.-E. HAUSSMANN." Weak-legged, Madeleine picked it up. "My dear de Fonce," the letter read, "I anticipate your surprise at receiving such an unusual request, and I hope I will not compound it when I tell you that, among all those who make their business buying and selling real estate, you are the only one whom, by virtue of our common bond, I am certain that I may trust..." The letter went on to say something about buying a plot of land, about discretion, about (Madeleine stood up) "the Asparagus farmer *Duclos*, who is as tough-willed as his stalky vegetables." At the end, "Certain that you will consider this matter, whether favorably or unfavorably, with absolute discretion—and with the caution that, should the matter become known, it will be as much to your disadvantage as to mine, I entrust myself," and there it was again, "To you," and the Baron's signature. Well, she thought, but really she didn't know what to think, and Echs was waiting. Madeleine folded the letter and slipped it into the sleeve of her dress, and hurried downstairs to give him the book.

— Bring it back when you return from your expedition, she said.

— Thank you. My friend.

Echs kissed her cheek, a brief unpleasantness, and was gone, off, presumably, to tell his father about the hole in the world.

It was long after midnight when de Fonce came into the parlor, blowing on his hands and stamping his feet. — It gets colder out there every fall, he observed. No one dares to admit it, but I'm convinced that it's true. Did you see young Echs?

— Saw the last of him, I think. Madeleine told de Fonce what the minister's son had said.

— Well! De Fonce laughed. What an idiot! His timing couldn't be better, though. I've got a letter from Cornelius Waille, who owns practically half of Brussels. Says he'll be here next week, and where was it, hm, he's heard of my illustrious family and wants to pay his regards to its younger members, which means you, I think.

— Wonderful. How was your game of cards?

— Oh, magnificent, magnificent. There's nothing like lega-
cies to make men lose their heads. De Fonce tapped the side of
his glasses as though adjusting their focus. — I have something
for you, too.

He gave her an envelope.

— What is it?

— See for yourself.

It was... the proliferation of legal words made it hard to say
exactly what, but the gist of it was that de Fonce had made over
to Madeleine a great deal of money, to be kept for her in a sort
of trust and paid out at intervals over the remainder of her life,
and to Elise after that. The sums—were they sums?—anyway,
chains of numbers, were hard to decipher, but Madeleine
thought that if she had read them right, they would be enough
to make arithmetic forever after unnecessary.

All she could think to ask was, — Why?

— You ought to have money of your own.

— Because I'm not married, you mean.

— What?

— Because I'm not married, because I have no one but
you, that's what you mean, isn't it?

— Not at all. I only want you to feel free, Madeleine. It's
time you were free of me. I'm afraid I... I don't want you to feel
as though I'm keeping you here against your will.

— I don't.

— In any case you've earned it.

— Earned it?

— You've made me so happy, I should give you ten times as
much. He closed his eyes and, after a moment, chuckled.

— What?

— Your explorer. What if he's right? His father will take
credit for the whole thing and we'll have to take up a subscrip-

tion to build a road to the North Pole, a bridge to the inside of the world! O, we're going toward madness, all of us. The nights get colder quicker and we're all going mad.

— Go to bed, Madeleine advised.

De Fonce took her hand, but she said: — By yourself.

When he was gone, she looked over the deed of trust again. Of late Madeleine hadn't thought much about freedom. She had presumed it missing in the wreck of her affair with Haussmann, sunk in the same ocean which had swallowed Elise's words. But perhaps that was not the case. Perhaps freedom had only been waiting for her to find it again, hidden but not entirely lost, like Echs's world within the world. With her own money she could go anywhere. Wouldn't that be good enough? Wasn't that what it meant, to be free? Perhaps what she wanted wasn't freedom, though, Madeleine thought. She went upstairs to her room, Haussmann's letter still hidden in the sleeve of her dress.

22

THE RAILROAD OF THE DEAD

WHY DID HAUSSMANN CHOOSE de Fonce, out of all the buyers and sellers, the peculators and speculators who might have got the land at Méry-sur-Oise? Two reasons. The first was the one the Baron admitted to himself: he knew de Fonce, and thought, correctly, that the demolition man might be able to win out where no one else had. Even if it had been a long time since they'd last seen each other, he thought, on the strength of their old bond—hadn't they stayed up half the night once talking about the difference between ghosts and telegraph machines?—that he could still trust de Fonce, especially as the demolition man stood to make money on the deal. The second reason whispered itself to Haussmann late at night, when he should have been thinking of something else. If he wrote to de Fonce, de Fonce might write back, and the two of them might meet, and he might go to de Fonce's house, and it might happen, as it had already once, that, in that damned allegorical parlor of his, Madeleine would be waiting...

Haussmann puts down his pen and rubs his eyes. Here is what might happen now: he thinks woefully about how long it has been since he last slept. He wonders what will happen if he does no more work tonight, though it's only ten o'clock, and, after a struggle, concludes that the Great Cemetery can live without him until morning.

At ten-fifteen, the light in his office window goes dark.

Those who watch Haussmann—there aren't many of them any more; the eyes of the public are turned eastward, to where the Prussians and the Austrians squabble over territory—conclude, variously, that the Prefect is ill again or that he is recovering, that he is relenting in his desire to make Paris over in his own image, or that he has retreated to another, more secret office to make plans so terrible that even the light by which they are written must be concealed. But Haussmann is asleep, too exhausted even to roll from side to side, his entire body for once immobile. He does not dream, or, if he dreams, it is in a language that cannot be translated into letters, a language of touch which, if we could speak it while awake, would make love the simplest thing in the world, though other forms of human activity might suffer thereby.

He wakes at his accustomed hour and goes to his office. The plans for the Great Cemetery are unrolled on his desk. By daylight they look like collections of lines; for a moment he cannot remember what they are for, let alone why he worried about them so much. Then the lines assume their familiar character: there is the ceremonial gate and there the pond, the rotunda, and so on. Somewhere underneath the plans is the letter he got back from de Fonce. "My dear Baron," it says, "I am happy to oblige you in this as in all things. But what gives me even more pleasure is that you should think of me again. I don't pretend to know your mind, but if you should want to write back, I hope you will consider that I have given you the opportunity. For fear of saying too much in this vein I will say no more at all, and only add that, although you may not expect to hear it, I remain, Your friend, DE FONCE." Haussmann considers this letter

again. Was he wrong to break with de Fonce? You don't know
how many times he has asked himself this question. Haussmann
doesn't know how many times he has asked it and his talent for
accounting is legendary. What he knows: each time he asks the
question, the answer that comes back, sooner or later, from the
part of him that he regards as most essentially Haussmann, not
the lover nor the bureaucrat who needs to sleep now and then,
but the servant of that great pen which writes its strokes on the
world in a way that time will not easily erase, you know, *that*
Haussmann, answers, *You were right*. He asks the question again.
For a long time all of him is silent. He would like breakfast. He
notes that the sun is out, that the day will be warm. He wonders what has happened to that stern, essential Haussmann?
Perhaps it is still asleep. Half the morning passes and he has
done no work, nor has he answered his own question. At
eleven-seventeen ante meridianis (he notes the time on his
English watch) he tells his secretary to tell his majordomo to
tell the coachman to tell the groom that he will need his carriage.

Paris has been washed by something in the night. It shines as
it does not usually; even the accumulated refuse in the gutters
looks clean enough that one might allow it to stay there a
while. Here is the route Haussmann follows: from the Hôtel de
Ville he takes the rue de Rivoli all the way past the Louvre and
the Tuileries—they don't look bad this morning, either—and
at the place de la Concorde he has the driver turn right onto
the rue Royale, which ends, inevitably, in the place de la
Madeleine. There she is, like something out of Greek antiquity,
making only the slightest pretense of being Catholic, or French,
or modern. Why was she built? Haussmann cannot think of the
reason for her just now, but he tells the driver to bear left, to the
boulevard Malesherbes, a strong, straight boulevard of which he
is justifiably proud. He watches the place Saint-Augustin go by,

then he has reached the rue Monceau, the Parc Monceau, and he tells the driver, — Wait here, please. I won't be long.

Haussmann has never had such a vivid sense of what it is like to hold the edge of a hat. He holds his now, rubbing the brushed silk brim between gloved fingers, in preparation for the moment when the door will open and he will raise his hat and say, — The Prefect of Paris to see Monsieur de Fonce. What a strange fact, that humans should attach such rigid objects to their heads! As if heads were not hard enough. He thinks of the inflexibility of his own character, and how strange it is, in general, that one thing follows another. — The Prefect of Paris to see Monsieur de Fonce, he will say, and if Monsieur de Fonce is not in he will leave his card, on which he will write, *I have taken the opportunity*. Haussmann fingers again the brim of his hat, and the door opens and

But Haussmann did not do everything he set out to do. Some of his plans foundered for lack of money, others for want of time, others still because no one would have them. They ought to be collected some day, these plans, the *Unbuilt Works of M. Haussmann*. It will be a handsome book, a volume for collectors, printed on paper guaranteed to last forever, bound in leather that looks as though it's already been around since the beginning of time. Perhaps many people will care to read about what Haussmann did not do, perhaps only a few; all I know is that, when the book is written, this scene will be included in it somewhere.

Haussmann put down his pen and rubbed his eyes. He was disgusted with himself for letting so much time slip past: nearly an hour if the English watch was to be trusted. He'd noticed an irregularity in it, like a heart with an extra beat, which caused the hands to lurch forward faster than they ought at times, and at others to lag behind. In the end the two evened out, he thought, but there was no way to be sure. All at once Haussmann grew still. He closed his eyes; a tremor rose through his legs and departed from the top of his head in an invisible puff of what his recklessly scientific contemporaries might have called spiritual fluid. *Joy has seized me*, he thought, while maintaining a certain indifference to his own thinking. *How calm I am*, Haussmann told himself. In fact he held himself at a fearful distance from his emotion, like a child who has spotted an enormous rabbit on the path before him, and holds his breath in order not to scare the beast away. For some reason he remembered a snatch of Isola's song in *La Perdue*. Is this the legendary night / when the stars turn all to milk? Haussmann sighed. There was no holding to such moments; one could only try to get from them what one could, some piece of oneself that would otherwise have been lost, forever perhaps, to silence. He touched the watch, tick-a-tock, tick-a-tock. Time to work.

Though he was in a hurry to bring the new graveyard to a vote, Haussmann neglected no stratagem which might give him an advantage when it came time to face his enemies in the Municipal Council. A month before the vote he invited the press to examine the plans for the new cemetery. Representatives from the *Presse* and the *Figaro*, from the *Petit Journal* and even the *Lanterne* were there; papers loyal and loyally opposed (the disloyal ones had all been closed down) sent their best men to see the plans for the Great Cemetery of the North. The map hung on the wall of a salon at the Hôtel de Ville, the same room in which, years before, Haussmann had danced with the Queen of England. Few of the assembled journalists remem-

bered what an elegant figure the Baron had cut then, and how
they had applauded when he made his speech about whatever
he had spoken about. If they remembered the Haussmann
whom they had called Magnificent at all, it was with a certain
disappointment: fourteen years ago he had promised them that
the future would all be dancing, and now that it was the future
he had nothing to promise them except this, a roomy place to
die. Here was the Grand Gate, the mausoleum, the central avenue, the railway station where passengers would arrive and,
some of them, depart again; the tail of the rail line. Over here,
on the opposite wall, sketches of how it would all look when it
was real: the tombs of limestone and the view from the gate,
the tables of the Café Anubis, the statue of a vague equestrian
figure meant to suggest that life gallops on no matter how the
mourners feel about it.

— You can ask questions now, Baron Haussmann said.

— Sir! shouted a man from the *Presse*. — This, ah, this
graveyard is awfully large, isn't it?

— Well, yes, it is large, but as you'll see from this chart,
Parisians are dying at a really extraordinary rate...

— Why is it so far away?

— Hydrological analysis, gentlemen, tells us that the soil is
healthy there, and that the cemetery won't infect the municipal
water supply. And I believe health is something we can all appreciate these days.

— Speaking of water, a man called from the back of the
crowd, is it true that your Aqueduct caused the cholera?

Haussmann tried to make out the impertinent journalist's
face, but the shadows made this impossible. Fortunately Hennezel and Delesse were in the crowd.

— Absolutely not. The Academy of Sciences...

— Sir! Is it true you're going to dig up the parish graveyard
of Saint-Jacques?

— It's on the list of sites to be transferred, if that's what you mean...

— List?

—Yes, we're going to move several of the little churchyards. As you can see, gentlemen, we have plenty of room...

— Several?

— A list? Where's the list?

—Which ones?

— How much are you paying them, sir? In compensation for their trouble and all.

— Are you going to dig up the Catacombs, sir?

— How about moving Père-Lachaise?

— Sir! Who's going to take the tickets from the departed?

— Sir! Sir!

Like gnats they were, these buzzing people, Haussmann thought, and himself the unfortunate wanderer in the woods, a delicacy for their narrow palates. Let them prick, let them prick, however. The Great Cemetery would be built and they would see that he was right to build it. He answered their questions with an even temper: — No, we're only moving the small graveyards. — Fourteen miles from the city. — Transportation? By railway, of course. Why, you must have eyes, gentlemen, can't you see it on the plans?

The next morning the *Lanterne* trumpeted THE MONSTROS-ITY OF MÉRY-SUR-OISE, a Necropolis as large as all Ver-sailles and twice as remote. "Those Jeremiahs who foresaw that our era would end in catastrophe may point, for their proof, to the plans on display at the Hôtel de Ville," wrote the *Siècle*, and in the *Temps* they said M. HAUSSMANN WILL EXPROPRIATE THE DEAD. Cartoons in the illustrated papers showed Hauss-mann as a corpulent gravedigger with a shovel in one hand and in the other a bunch of asparagus, over the caption "How M. the Prefect Gets Fat." They showed him as the Angel of Judgment condemning the souls of the poor to the distant, dismal suburbs, while a few rich men were admitted into the gates of Paris. "All that nonsense about camels and needles!" read the caption under that one, "Why, the afterlife is just like the opera!" The papers reserved their strongest criticism, however, for the train that would carry the dead from Paris to the former asparagus field, fourteen miles from the city's edge.

It was to leave hourly from all the major terminals: Montparnasse, Montmartre, Père-Lachaise. Duration of the journey: twenty minutes. Cost: five francs for an individual, twelve for a family. O monstrous unbuilt monument! A special station would have been prepared at the back of each cemetery: with ticket windows of white marble and a quay of jet, where trains would have arrived on crepe-muffled wheels to carry all the coffins of Paris to the end of the line. There would have been a car on this train for city officials (first class) and a car for priests (second); in the third-class coach the families of the deceased would ride, mourning dress to mourning coat on cold benches, while the funerary engineer consoled them with a requiem on the steam whistle. No dining car and no couchettes; at the end of the train passengers would watch the coal-black corpse coach lurch along the winding track, rattling loud enough to wake the freight. On Sundays there would be special trains, and on the Day of the Dead half the city's rolling stock would be pressed into service; doubtless there would be collisions, and the coffins flung into cow pastures would lie open for mourners who would never use the return portion of their tickets. Excursion fare for the quick, and one-way for the dead: the railroad companies would grow rich as Charon on the inevitable custom of every Parisian whose body survived his demise.

The affairs of the dead touch here and there on the affairs of the living; when they do, the contact is usually felt most strongly in the imagination. So it was with the railroad. The papers could not express enough outrage at the idea; they called it the Iron Horse Express to the Grave, the Route of Death, haunted by the ghosts of all its passengers. To move living paupers about was one thing; to move dead ones another. Fournel, a fiery critic, anticipated "the deportation of corpses, centralized in a necropolis which will be the Botany Bay of deceased Parisians... A few years more and you will see a worthy completion of the system with the invention of steam engines for burying people..." He had an eye for the large problems, Fournel. "Woe to the frivolous generation which turns away from the tomb, where, as it has been so rightly said, are the sources of life!" Yes, this is it, the beginning of the end; this is the point where we hide the corpses in the name of sanitation—freeing us up, as we know, to produce corpses in industrial quantities with our steam engines and gas motors... The infernal modern world, Fournel, begins with fourteen miles of hypothetical track, the greatest and most inevitable blunder in Georges-Eugène Haussmann's career.

The criticism, evidently, caught Haussmann by surprise. Was not the Railroad, in its own way, as pious and proper as hecatombs and the sacrifice of oxen, as stained-glass windows and votive candles and all the other outmoded ways of respecting the Power greater than the powers of man? Wasn't the railroad station to be done up like a mausoleum? And wouldn't the carriages be draped in black? What sign of respect had he overlooked? Anxiously the Baron reviewed his plans. He had overlooked nothing. The plans looked just as they had a day before: wholly and immutably correct. Impatiently the Prefect ordered

them to be taken out of their display cases, and had the journalists thrown out on their ears. Profit! That was all those hacks
were after, to sell their sensational misapprehensions to a city all
too ready to believe the worst. They were as bad as the speculators, or worse: they bought up the truth and resold it as lies. If
you assembled all the city's journalists in a public square you
might fire a cannon into the crowd without hitting an honest
man. What a barrage that would be! Haussmann smiled. It had
been a mistake to show his hand; well, he would not make it
again. There were other ways to win out and of those ways he
was the master: hadn't he built the Aqueduct? and the sewers?
and more streets than anyone before him, even kings? There
were other ways to win out, secret ways, and Haussmann would
walk them. Meetings in private and considerations and contracts and the thousand paper instruments of his power. He
would begin by teaching the journalists a lesson. And among
the journalists, why not begin with Fillier? It had been years
since he was any sort of threat, but Haussmann still remembered him with irritation. Make an example of him. Something
strong, Haussmann thought. Make the rest think carefully before they japed at his work again. He called for Hennezel and
Delesse, and instructed them to find out who Fillier was. I don't
care how you find him, and I don't care what you do with him
when you do, he told them, but don't bother trying to be discreet.

And Haussmann's honesty? Well, perhaps there's more than one
kind of honesty, in which case, Haussmann thought, the one
he honored was certainly the more important. It was the honesty of principle, immutable, almost inhuman principle. Haussmann's honesty rose above corruption, above the speculators
and bureaucrats and their endless parade of exceptions. It was a

towering eternal honesty which cities might be founded on, a brilliant honesty which would serve as an example to the world. And in fact—so great was the Baron's penchant for synthesis in his moments of inspiration—all his thinking about Madeleine, far from distracting him from his work, had in fact led him to this solution.

Antigone, the newspaper had called her (by mistake, admittedly) after the Smuts episode. Let Antigone lead him, then. Haussmann remembered the rest of the story: how Oedipus's daughter buried her brother outside the city walls and was put to death for it by Creon, the heartless administrator. He remembered Creon's punishment, how he lost his wife and his only son, but did not die himself, and had to go about until the end of his days the captain of a desolate city, the empty monument of his folly. It all came, Haussmann supposed, from irreverence. The divine law commanded you to bury the dead; only the laws of man balked at it. Creon, given the choice, had trusted the latter. If he had done otherwise things might have gone better: the brothers buried, Antigone wed, everyone alive in the end. Haussmann was not such a fool that he could not see the similarity between that situation and his own. Some things must be honored above the law, and among them the dead. Haussmann the Magnificent, he told himself, live as fits your desire. Otherwise you are nothing, and no trace of you will remain on this earth when you are gone from it. When had he thought that before?

23

THE ENEMIES

THE LIBRARY OF THE CITY of Paris stands not fifteen minutes from the Hôtel de Ville, but in purpose as in prestige the
two buildings are entirely opposite. No one ever thought of
throwing a party in the Library: its reading room invites soli-
tude, and even the long tables seem designed to keep people
apart. Individuals inhabit the Library, not crowds; in fact it
might be said that each reader inhabits a different Library,
which consists of a book or series of books, framed by high,
cloudy windows, a wooden table, and the pervasive smell of
dust. And what books! They say that every story ever written
about Paris has found its way to that place, the true histories
and the false ones alike, written in all the languages men write
stories in. In the cellars, the city's official records are kept like
tuns of wine waiting to be bottled: the tax rolls and censuses,
the edicts and bulletins, the maps and plans. Everything that is
officially known about Paris is known there. Fortunately no
one knows all of it at once, for the Library is very large, and
even if you, my reader, sat down in your childhood to read
everything that is gathered there you would be an old man before you had read half of it. And it is well, it is well, for if we

knew too much we would lose our pleasure in stories, which are after all the imperfect complement of our knowledge, smaller than what we do not know, but made of the same stuff.

Into this dim hall came an unusual procession: five men in cloaks with scarves pulled up almost to their noses and hats pulled down to screen their eyes. They whispered to the clerk whose job it was to guard the collection, a timid Cerberus with only one head, albeit four-eyed, and filed through a door reserved for the Library's staff. Down a steep staircase and at the bottom of it another, they descended to a defunct storeroom where, until recently, ladies' periodicals had been kept. These were Haussmann's enemies. The stairs were so narrow that they must walk single file, and so pass before us in review. At the head of the column was Émile Ollivier, a delegate to the National Assembly, with the rumpled look of a professor awakened from a nap. Ollivier, a republican firebrand, had the misfortune to cross paths with Haussmann in Marseilles; as a result of that encounter his fire smoldered awhile in a Marseilles jail.

After Ollivier came Jules Ferry, for whom at least one street in every French city must be named: Ferry the lawyer-cum-pamphleteer who can't keep his pen out of trouble, or his sideburns groomed; he looked as awkward as if turkey legs had been grafted to his cheeks, and as sad. He was the author of *The Fantastical Accounts of Baron Haussmann*, the companion piece to the *Fantastical Tales of Hoffmann*, published in French a few years earlier. Hoffmann, if you don't know him, wrote of hunchbacked devils and wind-up girls, poison letters and lettered poisoners, and all the tricks of the romantic trade. Ferry's pamphlet was no less chilling. He told a tale of dummies and revenants, of financial instruments as complex and subterranean as the sewers. Until Haussmann, the city spent what it had; after him, it borrowed against what it might have ten years hence if it spent the money now—it borrowed, in other words, against its own debt, like a gambler playing double or nothing who has lost too many times in a row to stop, and waits for the lucky toss of the dice when the whole debt will be cleared. Then there were the delegation bonds and the finishing bonds, diabolical instruments by which Haussmann paid his contractors for their finished work before the work was begun, only to have them give the money back to the city as a guarantee they would finish the work. Fantastic accounts, indeed. Ferry's pamphlet exposed the Baron's every trick; but Haussmann kept the magic show going, oblivious to the Parisians who mumbled that they knew how it was done.

After Ferry came Léon Say, who, because he has largely been forgotten by historians, must have been nondescript. Imagine him as a thin, short man with an Adam's apple the size of his protruding nose. Say was of the curious opinion that the public should have some say in how its money was spent; curiouser still was the trouble he got whenever he spoke his mind. Then a slim figure in a blue cape; then a dark-haired older gentleman, also holding a lantern. This latter, when he reached the relative safety of the cellar, pulled off false eyebrows and beard, revealing real beard and eyebrows, and—*voilà!* Victor Hugo, returned in secret from Guernsey, where Louis Napoleon invited him to spend the rest of his life contemplating cows. Hugo hated Haussmann as he hated the Empire, for its tyranny and the idle flamboyance with which it ground democratic sentiment into rubble.

— I swear that clerk saw through my disguise, Hugo grumbled as they filed into the room. — We ought to have come in through the sewers.

— You and your sewers, said Ollivier. Can't you think of something else?

— Haussmann built the sewers, said Say.

— I think of everything, Hugo said majestically.

— I said, Haussmann...

— Be quiet, Léon, said Ollivier. To Hugo: — Well, I hope you'll know what to think of *this*.

In the cellar, everything had been prepared for the party of Haussmann's enemies: copies of the municipal budget and of Haussmann's various laws and speeches and official letters; records of what was sold to whom when and for what consideration. Every official document pertaining to Haussmann's rule was collected there: a monumental heap of books and papers which filled half the room. If Haussmann's misdeeds had left a trace the conspirators should have been able to find it. Ollivier had an eye for corruption, and Say a head for numbers; Hugo of course knew how to keep an eye on the big picture. And then there was Ferry, whose style had already made him Haussmann's most famous detractor, to write it all down. Coffee steamed in two silver urns beside a joint of meat, sundry cheeses, bread, smoked fish, cigars, enough provisions to sustain the lot of them for a week if need be. With a minimum of conversation the conspirators got to work.

Impossible, in the absence of day or night, to say how much time passed before they closed the books again and looked up in wonder:

— The man, said Ferry, is a sort of devil.

— Or at least a devil's familiar, Hugo growled.

— A careful devil, though, said Say.

— I don't understand, said the personage in the blue cloak.
— Has he broken the law or hasn't he?

— Of course he has, said Ollivier. All we need is proof.

Proof! They had been looking for proof for hours, days; they were all exhausted except Victor Hugo—well, but he was used to monumental labors. And still no proof. Fantastical accounts indeed. The municipal budget balanced as approximately as an elephant rides a child's bicycle: even if the balance is true, the weight of the burden is such that balancer and balanced seem perpetually about to collapse. Haussmann spent Paris's surplus revenue and borrowed against future surpluses; he shifted expenses so that the whole budget seemed to be a surplus, and borrowed against that. Like a child who asks for all its future birthday presents this year, Haussmann exhausted Paris's income for generations to come. As the provisions dwindled and their heads nodded to the table, the conspirators' distaste gave way to grudging wonder. What a piece of work the Prefect had wrought, corrupt or no! How admirably he borrowed and carried, promised what had already been delivered and took away what was not yet there, so that misery seemed abundance, and loss profit!

It was Hugo who summed up the way they all felt, and nicely, too. The others couldn't help but imagine themselves players in some fine drama of the sort where good men hide in catacombs and justice is done in the end. — Numerous wonders, terrible wonders walk the earth, but none is the match for this man. His craft is clever beyond all dreams. He wears away the oldest of the gods, the Earth, with steel plows and steam engines, miners' picks and macadam. Haussmann the master, ingenious past all measure, past all dreams the skills within his grasp! He forges on now to destruction, now to greatness. But cursed is the man who weds himself to inhumanity. Never share my hearth, never think my thoughts, he who does such things!

— Ah, ah, the conspirators sighed half-admiring sighs as they read Haussmann's accounts.

It was the one in the blue cloak who broke their fiscal reverie. — I told you this wouldn't work. Duelling's the way to bring a man down, gentlemen, but if you won't have bloodshed—not when it might be your own—then scandal's second best. No need to find your magic numbers, either; scandal's easy enough to invent.

The others looked at their companion with distaste. Hugo

would not speak to her at all, and Say was cowed by her assurance. Ferry was still lost in the account books, so it fell to Ollivier to ask, — Well, Mademoiselle, what do you propose?

She smiled. — What do you know about a demolition man named Fonce?

— Go in and see her, said the Widow. I think you'll be pleased.

— Why? asked Madeleine.

— Just go in.

Madeleine followed Constance back through the apartment, furnished with the finest of the Empire's creations: chairs as massive and confusing of line as those trees which seem to grow in some special relation to gravity, so that their boles are all gnarl and corkscrew; gold clocks on marble pediments, and marble figurines rising from gilt socles; more detail than the eye could take in, and still, somehow, nothing to hold the mind. In the nursery, Elise was sitting on the floor, looking at herself in her little glass. — Mirror sailor, she said.

— Yes you are, Madeleine said. You're a little sailor in a mirror.

She turned to Constance. — How long has she been talking like this?

— Just today, Madame.

— What else has she said? Have you been listening? Madeleine turned the glass so that a sawdust-stuffed harlequin was reflected in it. — What do you see now, my love?

— Mirror sailor.

— Can she say anything else, or only that?

— Only that.

— Oh.

Madeleine turned the glass so that Elise could see herself again. — Elise, she said. You're Elise, aren't you?

The child touched the glass; a mirror finger met her finger.

— Aren't you Elise? Aren't you?

— You can't expect her to learn everything at once.

— Yes, yes you are.

When Constance had left, Madeleine sat on the floor beside Elise. — Mirror sailor? Sailor mirror? Mirror mirror? It was like being one of those thieves who had to say the magic word to get their treasure back, she thought, then wondered if that was how the story went. — Sailor? Mirror? Madeleine wondered whether it would be possible to have a language consisting of only two words: "sailor" would mean yes and "mirror" no, and for everything else you'd use them in combination. What a slow language that would be! And no wonder, under those circumstances, that you wouldn't bother to speak. — Of course everything is hard for you, she said aloud. To say a single sentence, you'd have to write a book! Isn't that right, Elise? What's "mother" in your language? Sailor... oh, never mind.

Madeleine held up the looking glass again. — Mirror.

Elise glanced at it and said: — Yes.

— How is your Echs? the Widow asked.

— Who? Oh. He's confessed his true passion: to be a polar explorer.

— North or south?

— As far as I'm concerned, he can go to whichever one's farther away.

— Isn't he in the government?

— He says he wasn't made to govern men, but to lead them.

— That's inane.

— Yes, but he made it up himself. He's very proud of it.

— Fools, my dear, all of them.

— How's the Major?

— I've been promoted to a colonel, thank you.

— Is he handsome?

— Like a statue. He's bottom-heavy, so the proportions will look right when they set him up on a column.

They spoke for a while of the detestability of men in general, and in particular of all the ones the Widow knew. It was a subject she had studied for years, in a great variety of circumstances, and one for which, once her words were warmed by a glass of brandy, she had a great deal of evidence both anecdotal and conjectural. As the years passed, and Tournevis succeeded Eue, and gave up his place to d'Abelue who lost it to Echs who ceded it to the impending Belgian Waille, Madeleine was more and more inclined to agree with her.

— And yet you'll have to marry some day.

— Some day I will.

— Make it soon, for Charles's sake. (She meant de Fonce.)

— Why for his sake? I don't think he should have anything to say about it.

— Oh! Do what you want, Madeleine. I only know that he's been pestering me to find you a husband.

— Oh?

— It doesn't matter if he's rich or not, he tells me, as though there were any other quality to recommend a man. But find me someone before it's too late!

— He tells you that?

— Constantly. I tell him not to worry. If I can be a mother at *my* age, then certainly you could be a bride for years and years yet. Really, Madeleine, what is it?

— Nothing. Madeleine was thinking of two things. First of all, if de Fonce's assertion that she didn't age had been only a bluff, then the opposite must be true: she must be, or at least look, horribly old. Second, although she hadn't understood the subtlety of his reasoning, she'd been right to guess that de Fonce was giving her money because no husband, so far, had. This conclusion, though based on nothing more than fact, was like an insult; it gave her status as an unmarriable woman an official character.

— Anyway, I told him that he'd have to find someone himself, so you ought to prepare for a fresh onslaught. But you look heartbroken, my heart. What is it?

— Nothing, Madeleine sighed. Only I ought to go home.

This didn't displease the Widow, who was in any case expecting her Colonel soon. As she arranged Madeleine's shawl, however, she said, — But I hope you won't stay away for long. We ought to see more of each other, don't you think? Come back, come back any time you like. Part of this effusion was real sympathy, and part pity for the girl, or really woman, now, who left her house with bowed head and melancholy eyes.

Madeleine didn't want to go back to de Fonce's right away. She wasn't ready to accept his kindness, or even his forgiveness, which, though it came without condescension, had its own sort of weight. Without any particular destination in mind she let herself be moved by her dislike of the Widow's furniture, and told de Fonce's driver to take her somewhere old.

— Sorry, miss?

— Anywhere old will do. But go quickly, please.

The carriage rolled away from the fashionable Chaussée d'Antin and the great boulevards, past the pit where the new Opéra, half-built, stood wrapped in scaffolds like a ruin in progress. There was the dark bulk of the Louvre—but Louis Napoleon had ordered its galleries extended to make room for the Ministry of Finance; scaffolds and heaps of stone littered its courtyards. They took the Pont au Change (which was old

enough, but not convenient to stop on) across the river, but
even on the Île de la Cité, in the oldest heart of the city, everything was construction. Saint-Grimace, of course, was gone;
they were putting up a hospital where it had been, the Hôtel-
Dieu it was going to be called as though God had decided to
open his doors to the tourists who visited Paris for a week or
two during the summer, or on the occasion of an exposition.
Headless Woman Street wasn't far away but Madeleine did not
want to go there. On the other side of the river it was the same:
the Petit Pont gave way to a square as distended as a snake that
had swallowed a dog; the bulge was called the place Saint-
Michel, and the rest of the snake a boulevard also named for
Michael, but whether Michael, that famous enemy of snakes,
would have had anything to do with the receding rows of over-
wrought stone which were going up on either side of his
boulevard, Madeleine doubted very much.

— I'm sorry, miss. Which way should I go?

— I don't know. Left?

That way ran the streets Madeleine remembered from her
childhood. Some of them ought still to be there, she thought.
But the boulevard Saint-Germain took them to the new rue
Monge, which took a crescent bite from the hill where Saint
Geneviève had her church; and the first turn from the rue
Monge took them past a Roman arena, recently dug up, which
caused Madeleine to reflect that sometimes when you tried to
make things new you made them very old indeed; but it was
not what she was looking for. Where was her empire of mud
and streets? Where were the alleys she had walked with Jacob
nights and nights ago, the hills where buildings lay atop one another like a giant's leftover building blocks, where were the
shadows and the courtyards and the cats, where was the light
that found marvels in small things, the uneven surface of paving
stones and the mottled faces of old, old buildings, and where

was Jacob? Where was the cour Carence, where everything had been together and all of it had been hers, where was Hector, where was Madame Arnaque and where was Fauteuil, where were the fountain and the clothes hanging in the sky and where, and where was Jacob?

— Take me to the Bièvre, she said.

— The rue de Bièvre, miss?

— No; to the river.

— But... I'm sorry, I don't know where it is.

— Well, there aren't ten thousand rivers here.

— I'm very sorry, miss, but here there aren't any rivers at all.

No more were there. Sometime while Madeleine was away—while she was in Saint-Grimace, or learning from de Fonce how to walk lightly and to give her suitors hope—the Bièvre was covered over; it became a part of Haussmann's comprehensive system of sewers. Where the river once ran, now there was a street, or really several streets—and none of them, by the way, the rue de Bièvre, which was named for a canal dug alongside the river centuries ago. But Madeleine, who had heard nothing of the river's disappearance, knew equally little about the street. It might, she thought, be a sort of memorial to the vanished Bièvre; and—as they rounded another too angular corner and found themselves again on the boulevard Saint-Germain, caught in a flock of eastward-creeping carriages—it might be the closest she would come to seeing anything of the city into which she'd been born.

— All right, the rue de Bièvre, then.

When they disentangled themselves from the opposing traffic, Madeleine found that they'd stopped in a nondescript and narrow street. She couldn't remember having seen it before, but the shadows were deep even at midday; the far end of the street hid itself from sight with a curve as artless as the unfolding of a magician's hand. It belonged to the past. In its mouth, just a lit-

tle way from the boulevard, a café sent an advance party of tables into the street.

— Wait for me here, Madeleine said.

She found a seat inside, behind the window, and read the
name lettered backward on the glass: the ANTIQUE CAFÉ. The
place had the charm of a child too young and too otherwise
occupied to notice that all its buttons are misbuttoned, and that
it has put its trousers on backward. Mismatched tables crowded
one another without, and within old engravings of Napoleon's
campaigns, the grounds at Versailles, and the first hot-air balloon
flight jostled advertisements for Impermashave, the waterproof
shaving cream, and Pétromane, the lamp oil that never quits. At
three o'clock in the afternoon the Antique Café was nearly
empty: a pair of hollow-eyed scholars in the corner of the room
inside; outside, a gentleman with a beard almost up to his eyes
stroked the head of his woolly dog. He looked up when
Madeleine sat, then, finding her perhaps insufficiently hirsute to
merit further contemplation, looked away. It was just as well.
Madeleine closed her eyes, and wondered how so much, and so
much that was important, had been allowed to disappear.

Now a word about ghosts. O. Why pretend? We don't know
anything about them. They don't come to us anymore, or when
they do, we call them something else. What's a ghost, really?
What haunts us. What's lost but not gone, gone but not forgotten. Ghosts are like books, like photographs; they are memory
continued by other means. For there's no reason to believe that
all ghosts were once people; in Japan they tell stories of animal
spirits with cold blue fox eyes; and many's the stable where
long-dead horses kick their traces on windy nights. Ghost ships
sail before ghost winds; ghost trains wail across the plains, terri-
fying mortal engineers; and there must be houses which appear only when the moon is right, and the fog has settled all

around—why, anything might become a ghost, provided that it dies too soon, provided that it has unfinished business with the world.

What, for instance, was that, gurgling below a circular grille at Madeleine's feet? Running water, Madeleine thought; she leaned toward the manhole to hear a little better. Water coursing underground. Madeleine thought she could see it through the interstices of the grille: a faint, dancing light. Probably it was her imagination. A ghost river, Madeleine thought. The Bièvre, not lost at all.

Madeleine wept. The thought that something so intimately connected to her could survive her absence for so long, could display such fidelity as to return precisely now, when she had no idea in what direction to proceed, was a kind of consolation she hadn't felt since the earliest days of her childhood, when Jacob, home from his rounds, would lift her up with sooty hands and tell her that, as long as he was living, she would not have to fear the dark. The consolation had nothing to do with his words, though, or not much. The words existed only as an outward token, addressed to an invisible audience, of what was essential: his presence in the room, his hands, the fact, demonstrated by his speaking, that he was still alive and able to speak. And Madeleine, who had spent her life refusing to be touched by anything old, was touched now. The ghost Bièvre held her imagination in its ghost hands; it whispered to her, though she didn't need to hear the words, *It goes on. It goes on.*

Underground, a second light joined the first.

Madeleine was not surprised when the whisper of the water became a man's voice, uttering most ghostlike words: — Left here, and hurry! It must be almost dawn.

— Are you sure? a second voice asked.

— Of course I'm sure, said the first, testily. Do you know how much research I've done?

— You said you were sure last time, said a third voice.

— Oh, shut up, Say, said the other two.

— Do we have much farther to go? a woman asked.

— Not far, Mademoiselle Fillier. We're practically out.

— You said that an hour ago, said the third voice.

— Shut up, Say, the others said, and the lights moved on.

— Fillier? the Widow said. You mean the journalist?

— That's right, said Madeleine. A woman, as it turns out.

— Well, that's odd. I've just... oh, here, listen. The Widow
took a letter from her writing table and read: — "And by the
way, my dear, a friend of mine has been plaguing me to introduce you to her. Apparently—here's a little scandal for you
—the Viollet Fillier who writes those nasty articles for the
Lanterne isn't a he but a she—" Thank you, Colonel! We've figured that out. "—and a pretty and good-natured she besides.
Not that you should think of being jealous!" As if I'd care.
"She's heard all about you, and is quite in awe of you, or at
least, of your reputation. She yearns to meet you. I told her we
might arrange something for next week, at the Expropriated—
but be careful what you tell her! I wouldn't like to see my
name in her column. In any case..." and the rest of the letter is
sentimental idiocy. So, you see, this Fillier and I must be fated to
cross paths. I'll have to write back to the Colonel. And she was
underground?

— I don't know how to explain it.

— With three men, you said? It sounds scandalous.

— I wonder how they got down there.

— I'm sure it was easy enough. You can go anywhere in
Paris with the right connections. Well! I was going to miss the
Expropriated this year, but perhaps I'll go. One doesn't refuse
an opportunity to learn something new about vice.

— Where will you go?

— The Ball of the Expropriated.

— I've never heard of it.

— Of course not. It's all artists and drunks. Not your world at all. Fillier must be quite something, though. Do you think she's intrigued by my looks? Madeleine?

— I'd like to go, too.

— To the ball? You wouldn't enjoy it.

— It can't be worse than a Belgian industrialist.

— But it's all ruffians, dear. Charles would never forgive me.

— Tell him you're doing as he asks.

— Oh, is that what you're thinking? But you won't meet anyone to marry at the Expropriated.

— I don't care.

— Then why do you want to go?

— Just for a change, Madeleine said. Now tell me: what does one wear for artists and drunks?

The Widow arched an eyebrow. — A disguise.

Two men are pissing in a public urinal on the boulevard de Sébastopol, which has been open to all sorts of traffic now for nearly seven years. They cannot see each other but each can hear what the other is up to and approves. It doesn't matter what they do for a living, really, but we'll call one of them (a bony fellow who hoards a small supply of hair at the back of his head) a dry goods merchant who makes his living in the vicinity of Les Halles, and the other a retired policeman who fishes for eels off the quais and is not above a little afternoon drinking. He's filled himself for this occasion like an old wineskin which drains in chugs and spurts into the green wrought-iron trough at his feet. Never mind that over his head there's a two-color advertisement for G. PAS silk handkerchieves, or that at his feet his own tired plumbing is coupled for a moment with a system of plumbing which, even drunk, he cannot imagine. It takes what he and his neighbor and everyone else in Paris have

got and sublates it downstream to Achères. Our men don't
know anything about it, nor do they want to know; they're
honest and God-fearing Parisians for whom everything that
disappears into the ground is lost until the Last Judge comes
with his angelic shovel to dig it all up. These are honest citizens,
Monsieur, even their piss rattles honestly against the lip of the
trough. They are the sort of men whose ignorance has the
power to make every wonder ordinary. Whether they piss on
Achères or on the gates of Hell is all the same to them, so long
as no one requires them to think about it. Call one of them
Calcaire and the other Argile. They have known each other for
seven years and it is a mark of their honest simplicity that, in
that time, they have never thought to ask each other's names.
Nevertheless M. Argile recognizes the footfalls of M. Calcaire,
and withholds his micturation until he hears the micturation
of M. Calcaire begin, and M. Calcaire in like wise waits for
M. Argile to finish before he buttons his threadbare pants and
cinches his belt around his sagging waist. What passes between
them while they stand mutually unseeing in the urinal's cruci-
form is not friendship, nor is it—don't get ideas—love (the urinal is ringed by a little fence to keep out curious eyes, but it
isn't by any means private). It is enough for them to talk about
the weather.

— Ah, we've had one hell of a rain today, says Argile.

— The fall's coming early this year, which means the winter
will be warm, Calcaire replies.

Now and then one of them ventures a remark about politics.

— Have you heard what Poléon told the Prussians?

— He told them where to get off, all right. Go up against
the French Army! I'd like to see them try. It'd be like going up
against Napoleon himself, the First I mean, Argile says and
shakes himself dry.

It isn't much of a friendship, but it is enough for these two—who, for all they know, might be more than two; who's to say that the same M. Calcaire always enters the stall next to M. Argile, or that when M. Calcaire does show up the same M. Argile is always waiting there? Except that Calcaire, a civil servant of the old school, always goes home at the same time, and Argile, a man of conservative habit, invariably has to piss when he's closed up shop, and so it is always the same two, like a pair of clocks which, wound by different hands, still strike the same time.

In the fall of 1869 two men, MM. Argile and Calcaire, are pissing on the underworld, when the cover of a hole in the street not two paces behind them rises and rolls aside. A whiskered head appears level with the pavement, blinks, coughs, curses. A demon from the Pit, Calcaire thinks; he doesn't know whether to cross himself or button his pants. — Eh, he mutters to Argile, look at that.

Meanwhile the head grows into a bust, and the bust into the torso of a well-dressed if bedraggled gentleman, who raises himself out of the ground like a modern-day Orpheus, followed not by Eurydice but by a florid, jowled gentleman in a black silk cravat, who rubs his pate and spits in the gutter. The second apparition is followed by a third and the third by a fourth and so on until five gentlemen (one of them quite small and slender) stand shoulder to shoulder, straightening their frock coats, popping their cuffs and brushing dust from their hats. By now Calcaire has decided in favor of his fly. In his stall Argile does the same.

— Dammit, sir, I thought we were coming out at night, one of the gentlemen says.

— I thought it *was* night, says a second.

— It must have been the rain.

— Well, it's done now. Let's go.

They file off toward the rue de Rivoli.

— Well, says Argile, men coming out of the ground.

— Well, Monsieur, do you want them to fall from the sky? says Calcaire.

— All the same it's not normal for them to come out of the ground like that. In broad daylight, even.

— Ah! you know gentlemen, Monsieur, they do whatever they like and to hell with the rest of us.

Having given the definitive opinion on the subject, Calcaire left. After a decent interval Argile, too, went home.

24

THE DEMIMONDE

THE WIDOW COUVREFEU WAS BORN to an old Norman family which called itself noble, though its patents had been lost along with the trunk and roots of its family tree in a church fire two generations before. She came from a line of stern men. Her grandfather was said to have been so inflexible in his habits that he walked the same way through the woods even after the woods were cleared and replaced with tilled land; turning before each former tree he traced an uneven path across the furrows and made a nuisance of himself spring and fall alike. The Widow's father lived to outdo his father in everything: he walked farther, held his back straighter, tied his boots tighter, and ate his soup faster than old Father Couvrefeu had; in the discipline of his daughter, too, he tried to show as much backbone as his old father had and then some. The metaphorical backbone produced, as if by sympathetic magic, dozens of other bones besides: the ribs of a whalebone corset, which pinched, and the ridges of an ivory cane, which stung; even the bone-black of her drawing charcoal seemed another version of her father's great spine, and so for a long time the young Widow (who called herself Marie and was not yet a widow at all) drew straight lines. She took pride in her posture, but pride, as we know, goeth before a slump if not actually a fall; and at last Marie had cause to hang her head. She'd met a boy named Gilles and in the uneven darkness of the stable had done the thing which wrecked her rectitude, and made everything that had been straight about her curve wildly.

Marie, as yet unmarried, disgraced, fled straight to Paris, where she was reassured by the preponderance of crooked streets, crooked backs, and crooks. Only in Paris did she discover how slight her claim to nobility really was: no records, no registers, no seals, nothing but a straight back and not even a very straight one at that. From that moment on she was classed a commoner, but, by virtue of her upbringing, she rose into that most Parisian of purgatories, the demimonde, the half-world. She found it not unlike the underworld in the heroic tales of old: all right if you were a hero and were assured safe passage onward; rather less pleasant if you had to stay there. When she married the wool merchant Marie thought she might leave its twilight fields; then she buried the merchant and returned to her old haunts with a little more money and the proud title of Widow, which, forever after, was her title, her station in life, and everything else that needed to be said about her. She was the Widow.

The life of a demimondaine wasn't particularly hard in 1869: if it was purgatory then it was the innermost circle, where nothing very terrible happens to you so long as you do not try to move up. There were balls and dinners enough, and interesting people in profusion. Some had descended from above, and others came up from below; a handful, like the Widow, arrived laterally from the provinces. What a gay crowd that was! Gay because they had nothing to lose, or nothing to gain; their social mobility was like the hands of the clock, taking the aristocrats and commoners again and again over the same ground, but bringing them together only infrequently and never for long. The Bal Mabille, where the English tourists changed pounds sterling for the currency of love, was only the periphery of the half-world; the closer you came to its heart, the stranger, and often (though not always) the more lewd were its customs. There were seats in the practice rooms at the old Opéra where gentlemen paid a fee to watch the dancers rehearse, and bickered about who would go home with whom; there were mistresses and madams and *fêtes galantes* where the same dancers made their encores half-naked, in costumes which were meant to suggest naiads but came off more as succubi. At the crepuscular heart of the half-world lay the Ball of the Expropriated. It began honest to its name: a dozen-odd merrymakers who'd profited from the demolition of their homes saw fit to spend their gains on a great party. Over the years, however, the party grew even faster than the ranks of the expropriated, and so gradually, as such things always did, it became the province of rich, well-housed young men with and without artistic professions, dancers and odalisques, and the Princess Pauline Metternich, cousin to the Austrian Ambassador, who wore a domino to indicate that she was attending the party in an unofficial capacity.

Only one thing was constant throughout: at midnight the guests drank a toast to that fabled place, Paris As It Was. This was a new city that came into being sometime around 1865. As the novelty of Haussmann's construction wore off, and people became accustomed to the conveniences it brought them, they began to take stock of what they'd lost. All of a sudden it seemed to them that a great many buildings had been torn down which ought to have been left standing, and that the streets which no longer existed had been the most picturesque, the richest in heritage, the quietest, and the least deserving of destruction. The boulevards are too wide; it was much better when they were al-

leyways! And the water does not taste as good as it once did.
Where are the local markets, the camaraderie, the Gothic architecture, and the mixed smells of cooking and tanneries? Give us
back Paris As It Was! Because this city was perfectly irrecupera-
ble they felt free to mourn it as much as they liked. Some drank
more and others less to Paris As It Was; some did not drink at
all but folded their arms and scowled; these latter, however,
were marked by the crowd as police informers and were shown
the pavement ear first. Not all the guests at the Ball of the Expropriated were hypocrites. Some genuinely regretted the loss
of so much beautiful architecture and would gladly have traded
running water for medieval dignity. For the rest, the ball was a
way of expressing something deep and intractable which passed
itself off as fashionable discontent. The Chevalier Gastofouard,
whose instincts were in this matter as in all others infallible,
summed it up. "We Parisians," he wrote, "suffer from a *manie du
dernier cri*. We must always have the latest thing even when we do
not want it. If an inventor were to announce tomorrow that he
had made a device to abolish the sun, the day after tomorrow
our tailors would be overrun with demands for evening
clothes." Or, as he says elsewhere, "How can we have peace
when the train for Lyons leaves every night and we may go anywhere?" This is the insatiety at the heart of the heart, and it requires that we change, change quickly, or else we will come to
know ourselves.

Some heroes won their way into the underworld by cutting a
golden bough from the Tree of Knowledge, and others sailed
past the western edge of the ocean; some sang their way in, and
others were swallowed willy-nilly by the earth. Madeleine had
only to call for de Fonce's carriage, and to give the driver the
Widow's address. Couvrefeu was waiting; she got in beside

Madeleine. She wore the costume of a great lady of the Ancien Régime: a blue taffeta dress with ruffled cuffs, bows all down the front, and a choker of imitation roses made of silk, but scented like the real thing. She'd powdered her red hair rose-pink, and rouged her cheeks to the same color, so that, on the whole, she looked like a middle-aged version of the goddess of the dawn, out for some entertainment before her daily chore began again.

— And who are you supposed to be? she asked.

— Can't you guess? It's Valentine's dress.

The Widow paled. — What are you trying to do, Made-leine?

— Well, you said to wear a disguise.

— But not that! The rue Mouffetard, please, she told the driver. — Really, what are you going to say if someone asks who you are?

— The truth.

— I hope you won't be that stupid. Couvrefeu considered the dress. — At least it still fits you.

— Thank you.

— I'm going to say that I'm Madame de Sévigné. A great wit.

— Wasn't she the seventeenth century?

— Was she? Well, no one will know that, where we're going. Who were the wits of the eighteenth century, anyway?

— Voltaire?

The carriage passed the place Maubert, the covered market, where a collection of ragged folk gathered around a red- and gold-trimmed stand on which Madeleine could read only the word BEST.

— Yes, thank you. I'll say I'm Voltaire dressed in ladies' clothes.

— Or Marie-Antoinette?

— Everyone is Marie-Antoinette. Besides, I don't think she was much of a wit.

— Madame de La Fayette, then?

— What, and babble about America? You're no help. But here we are; I'll have to improvise.

The carriage stopped outside an arch of light. Hundreds of people were going in, so many that the arch, though wide, couldn't take more than a fraction of them at once; the rest lined up on the sidewalk, in the street, practically to the corner. The Widow, however, was expected: as soon as the carriage stopped, hands opened the door and offered themselves to La Couvrefeu; they helped her to squeeze the wide skirt of her dress through the door and tugged her down into the street. She motioned for Madeleine to follow. As she, descending, leaned backward, and Madeleine, advancing, leaned forward, their heads came close together. Couvrefeu whispered, — Anything but the truth, my heart, anything but the truth.

The crowd pulled Madeleine in; impossible to go against that current. Half-costumed and half-drunk, pushing, shouting, singing, speaking a slang which Madeleine had never heard before:

— Tell me old flame, did we watch sheep together?

— A dozen oysters and my heart.

— Eat it yourself and you'll be a dinner for thirteen.

What were they saying? What did it matter; they seemed to like it. They laughed and slapped one another's shoulders, kissed, roared, cursed—but what curses! They swore by a pantheon of gods—the actor Hervé and Brebant's restaurant, Mogador the actress and Rigolboche, whose dances had half the city twitching—of a kind no one had ever invoked before, living deities who kept them supplied with drink, gossip, and entertainment. They moved so quickly in and out of the vestibule that their motion could be comprehended only as a series of disconnected still images, one after another, the connections between them lost if there had ever been connections at all. A bare-shouldered girl, all of fifteen, dressed as a girl, looked into the mirror, held a lipstick to her mouth, and stopped; her reflection was a sphinx. An overcoat burst open, hatching a stoop-shouldered man tricked out as a Venetian sailor lad. A Spanish prince. An Egyptian queen with a bottle of patented tonic. Three old women like the fates—all of them Atropos, evidently. A powdered gentleman with painted fingernails inhaled something from a tiny flask, and sighed, — Morpheus... Were these new gods, or very old ones?

— Then play the girl of the air! someone said.

The Widow called, — Come on! and, taking Madeleine's hand, pulled her through the vestibule toward the rising sound of the orchestra. Here, the ball was... but Madeleine could not say what it was, any more than she could describe the tune, if it was a tune, the musicians were playing. We need new ears to hear that music, new eyes to see the picture.

Whose eyes? Try Manet's; in 1869 they were among the newest around. "In a figure," he said, "you must look at the brightest lights and the darkest shadows; everything else will come of its own accord." We'll take his advice. The brightest lights? The twin chandeliers that hung from the ceiling, splitting the room into two circles of candle-yellow, if you want to be literal about it. And the countless mirror chandeliers reflected in the glasses on the walls: lights to infinity. Is that what Manet meant? But ours is a living tableau, and light's a measure of something more than candlepower. The brightest colors in this picture are reserved for the human luminaries, like the chandeliers two in number, on whom the light of the composer's attention was focused. In the right foreground of the room a circle of pink and yellow, and a vertical stroke of white at its center: a young man in a frock coat addresses a circle of female listeners, whose poses, bent-kneed, hands to their chests, suggest every kind of admiration. The young man is smoking; a wisp of white curls from his mouth like the banners unfurled from the trumpets of angels in old pictures of the Annunciation (for even the newest scene has in it a few pieces of the old). His smoky words are inaudible in the crowd, but a pretty girl in the costume of a dancer likes them very much; she throws back her head to laugh, closes her eyes, and the light catches mostly the whiteness of her throat.

The composition of the left half of the picture is harder to follow. Everyone is dark, and everyone wants to be in the foreground. The short stand on tiptoes, and the tall won't take their place at the back of the room, but elbow forward, their faces here and there illuminated by a cigarette or by the yellow light from above. Where is our eye to rest? Let it wander, let it wander, and at last it finds a white oblong directly under the left-hand chandelier: a woman in a chiton, her hair braided and coiled at the back of her head. Once we find her, there's no question that she's the one we're meant to watch. Worn face, dark eyes, and red, down-turned mouth; her skin has less of rose than of copper-green. She turns away from us, as though she didn't want to be seen. Her hand reaches toward her face. Who modeled for that pose? It could have been a dressmaker's apprentice, lured into the studio for a few sous and the promise of an afternoon in front of a charcoal stove; but it could as easily have been one of the great courtesans, not the classic beauties but the magnetic ones, who build allure from well-placed imperfection the way walking's a matter of well-paced losses of balance. A demimondaine of the first water, so confident of her charm that she agreed to occupy only a small fraction of the canvas, knowing that, like the King who makes the head of the table wherever he sits, the center of the canvas would stand where she stood. Her aversion, her hand: false modesty. She knows we'll look.

And the shadows? In the foreground, so close to us that we almost overlooked him, a black back hovers by the bar. A tall youth in evening dress which, whatever its intent, looks on him like a costume. We've seen him before: the reporter for the *Illustrated Girls' Gazette*. His face, reflected in the mirror behind the bar, betrays a mixture of diffidence and acute anxiety, as though an oracle had told him that he would fall in love tonight, provided only that he make no effort to do so. He looks at us, looks away, looks back again.

Above everything, in the gallery, is gathered an extreme unction of black coats, worn by the grave gentlemen daring enough to attend, but not, for one reason or another, interested in disguising themselves. Among them is a familiar bony face, and beside it a fat form we've seen before. — Look at the one in the bedsheet! Magnificent, isn't she? — A beauty, Del... — De l'Est's the name, friend. — O yes. And I'm? — Rapunzel. Like the... — Never mind that. Keep your eyes open.

— And there's the Colonel, says the Widow. What an idiot he looks in that nose!

The nosepiece indicated by her finger is of gold, or gilt; it's attached to a portly man in the gallery, who waves hello.

— Let's go make the fool suffer, the Widow says, and climbs the stairs.

The smoker waves his hand and the white-frocked girl turns her back; the crowd billows forward and back. With an unmistakable expression, the young man quits his post at the bar. The picture's always changing. The important thing is to capture what you can of it with whatever sort of eyes you have.

• • •

Madeleine let the Widow introduce her to the Colonel de
Saint-Saenf, who kissed her hand and asked whether she was in
costume?

— I...

— Can't you guess, Henri? She's the year 1864.

— Of course! The Colonel smote his forehead. That skirt!
The glory of the Empire. Paris as it was, indeed, indeed, an ex-
cellent disguise. And you, my powdered one, must be Marie-
Antoinette?

— You see? the Widow murmured to Madeleine. To the
Colonel she said, — Tell me who you are first. Cyrano with the
syph?

The Colonel's face was so pocked and veined it looked like
a sort of winy mustard. Madeleine wanted to ask whether it
was a disguise, but, from the flask which he sipped at whenever
he couldn't think of something to say, a state which was, given
the scope of his imagination, practically continual, she guessed
it was his real skin.

— I'm Tycho Brahe, the celebrated astronomer, he said.

— Really? What was he celebrated for?

— Well, for having a golden nose.

— The genius! If Henri were an astronomer, all our stars
would be named for drinks.

— A fine idea, my queen. The planet Port, and the Winy
Way! Hey, Georges, did you know Marie-Antoinette was such
a wit?

Madeleine stood on the outskirts of their conversation for a
little while, then let it move away as the crowd circulated slowly
around the gallery. The people upstairs were, by and large, the
spectators who'd come to gape at the crowd below. Madeleine
soon found herself doing the same. The smoking youth—what
dark eyes he had!—had stepped out of his circle for a tête-à-
tête with another gentleman. The girl in the chiton moved

elliptically toward the back of the room. She looked up for a
moment at the gallery.

I want to leave her there, and Madeleine, looking down,
equally frozen; I want to speak of ghosts and twins and tricks of
the light and generally all the reasons why one sees the dead in
the midst of the living—but these moments of recognition,
which, in stories, are drawn out past all recognition, are, in life,
over so quickly that all one keeps of them, really, is an afterimage, a sense that one has just been touched by a certainty
which is already fading, resuming the appearance of ordinary
things. This is the rhythm of recognition. The face below was
Nasérie's. Was it her face? Almost as soon as she saw it
Madeleine wasn't sure; it looked like her, but all the circumstances which made that impossible, like the clear but less dense
air over a fire which warps the light, changed the face, making
it unknown again.

Madeleine descended from the gallery. The diameter of her
hoop skirts was, on the average, slightly greater than the distance between the individuals who made up the downstairs
crowd; she found herself quickly immobilized while others,
with less encumbering costumes, whirled past. The chiton girl,
Nasérie or another, was nowhere. Madeleine waited in the
hope that she would come by; and indeed, a minute later,
someone behind her murmured, — So that's where you went!

She turned as best she could. It was the gangly boy from the
bar, who, up close, had a charm all the more rare for its complete lack of grace. He held his body awkwardly, bent forward
from the waist like one glancing into a well; his face was green
as pond water, and curiously ornamented with a black moustache and imperial goatee. Ordinary glasses sat crookedly on his
nose. He smiled too broadly, then, remembering perhaps a
friend's offhand remark that his face, smiling, was not at its best,
returned his lips to their neutral position, which, taken together

with his downturning moustache, made him appear to be
frowning.

— I've been looking for you since I saw you come in, he
said.

— Oh?

— You're very... He stopped what was evidently going to be
a compliment before reaching its substance, and, with a furtive
shrug, as though to say that anyone might pay a compliment,
but it was more original to leave such things unsaid, continued,
— What brings you here this evening?

As he couldn't possibly expect an honest answer, Madeleine
gave him one: — Revenge on an old lover.

— Oh, that's the best kind.

— Of revenge you mean, or of lover?

— Why, both, I suppose. After all we're here to celebrate old
things.

— What old thing are you here for, then?

The boy blushed and didn't answer.

— Or did you come to see the costumes?

— No! The youth took a step closer, as though afraid that
he'd be misunderstood on account of the distance from which
he spoke. — I don't believe in sight. He waved defensively, as
though warding off an invisible dog. — But I'm very rude.
Here we are speaking, and I haven't asked if you'd like something to drink.

— No, thank you.

— Then a cigarette? He held out a red box on which PARIS
HAND ROLLED BEST was stamped in gold.

The cigarettes sold as Paris Hand Rolled Best were no ordinary
Turkish or Virginian blend. They were secondhand cigarettes,
assembled from the butts and pipe scrapings discarded in the

streets. An army of beggars scoured the city every day for tobacco and brought it to the place Maubert, where what was
perhaps the city's strangest commerce took place. In the Market
of Butts, three stands at the back of the square, used tobacco
was bought for a pittance—a franc and a half for two pounds of
cigarette leavings; two francs for the equivalent amount of half-
smoked pipe blend. What a crowd gathered there! Paris's worst
they were, grimy as though they had been rolled by hand or by
other means the length of a gutter or two. Jacob worked there
briefly, at the end of his stay in Paris... but that's another story.
The tobacco bought by the butt merchants was stripped of its
burnt paper and its most charred parts by a horde of specially
trained urchins. Other children twisted the cleaned substance
into cylinders and rolled it in cigarettes, which were packed in
handsome red cases—the operation's only real expense—and
still others sold them as Paris Hand Rolled Best.

The curious thing is that although the cigarettes tasted foul
and left the throat as if scoured by steel brushes, there was,
toward the end of the Second Empire, a sort of vogue for them.
It began with the English and German tourists. On account of
the handsome cases and the humble origins of the vendors,
they thought the Paris Hand Rolled Best ("the Best" for short)
"authentically Parisian," and so, in some hard-to-articulate way,
worth having. The mind conditions the body even in its tiniest
sensation; so belief in the cigarettes' Parisianness eventually
convinced the Britons and Teutons who smoked them that
their taste, though difficult to appreciate at first, could be savored, even enjoyed. One began to hear of travelers who, returned to their native countries, spoke longingly of the Best's
complex aroma; and of other travelers, richer or more fore-
sightful, who brought packages of the Best home with them by
the dozen, or went to Paris specifically for the purpose of buying those red-and-gold cartons from children overjoyed, if a lit-

tle surprised, to sell them in such great quantities. One began to smell the Best in London's most retiring clubs, in the drinking haunts of Heidelberg's most ferocious *Studentenbunden*, in New York salons and the pagodas of the East.

Parisians resident abroad received so many compliments on their native cigarettes that they, in turn, began to wonder whether the tobacco which, as they knew full well, was scavenged from fag ends, might not possess some virtue which they'd been unable to appreciate while at home. Expatriate Frenchmen bought packages of the Best on their visits home. The force of a taste multiplies in proportion to the square of the number of people who share it; before long, the taste for the Best had spread even to those Parisians who lived in Paris. The artists adopted it first, then the rakes, then the rich young men who were their friends; then their mistresses, then society girls, and, if the Best never became entirely respectable (Louis Napoleon never smoked one; nor did the Chevalier Gastofouard, though he knew some people who had), at least they're a good example of the strange things to which people are driven by taste. An example, too, of how old things can be made new without demolition artists and municipal bonds: in order to make newness, all you need is a little ingenuity, colorful boxes, and an army of cheap talent at your disposal.

— I believe that the things we don't see are the most beautiful. Imagine... well, here's an example. You go to... to somewhere far away. To Constantinople, if you like. You go because you've heard that there's a beautiful church there, well, really it's more than a church but because it's not quite Catholic you'd hesitate to call it a cathedral... I'm not boring you? Well, all right, so you've heard that this place, it's called the Holy Wisdom, is so beautiful that you've traveled all the way to Constantinople to see it. You stop in a hotel... it doesn't matter which one, let's say it's the Elephant, just on the eastern bank of the Bosphorus...

— You must travel a good deal, said Madeleine.

— Me? Oh, no, I've never left Paris, said the youth, whose name, given in the interstices of his ill-joined sentences, was, improbably, Paul Poissel.

— But I was saying: You leave your bags at the hotel... you see, you can't wait to see the church. You call for a taxi, and you drive practically to the place where you can first see its spires rising over the tops of the houses, but then, you see, you see... well, ordinarily when I tell the story it's a beautiful woman, but perhaps for you a man would be better?

— Go on.

— Anyway a lovely someone. She—or he—is walking away, and the church, you reason, is staying still, so you tell the cab to follow the girl, or lad, and, in the story at least, well, the long and short of it is, that you fall in love, and she lives far away, and because you're in love you want to be near her as much as you can. Some time later, though, you fall out of love, or she leaves you, and you can't stay another minute in the city. You don't even go back to your hotel, which, to tell the truth, you haven't visited in days; you have the porter send your bags to the train station, and you collect them there, and it's only as the train pulls away that you remember that you never saw the Holy Wisdom—but what a beautiful cathedral it is now, in your imagination! For it's got all the force of your lost love in its buttresses, and, painted in the gilt of the dome, your lover's face. Do you see what I mean?

— I think so, said Madeleine.

— You do?

— You mean that we can't see everything, and that's the only reason we see anything at all.

Poissel scowled, inadvertently, perhaps—he seemed not to

be unhappy, and, though he didn't look at Madeleine, nor
speak, she had the impression that this was his habitual manner
of thinking. Then he turned to her again, and, putting on his
too-broad smile, without regard for what anyone might or
might not have said about it, he began to speak; only just then
a familiar voice accosted them.

— Brahe, the Colonel said, was invited to dine with the
King of Denmark, who was, if you know your history, a stick-
ler for decorum.

— Why, my dreadful girl, have you found yourself a pauper
already? But you must come with us. It's almost time for the
toast. Yes, I'm stealing her from you, the Widow said to
Poissel, but with a face like yours, you'll find that life's often
unkind.

— Please excuse us, said Madeleine.

Poissel bowed.

— Are those cigarettes? asked the Widow.

— Would you like one?

— If I close my eyes, I might almost imagine that you're a
gentleman. No, don't light it; I'll smoke it in other company.
Thank you, thank you! And we're off.

— I hope I'll see you again? Madeleine said to Poissel, but
already the crowd had closed between them, and she wasn't
sure that he'd heard.

The Widow took Madeleine's arm and pulled her along.
— I've spoken with Miss Fillier. Do you know? She wanted to
sound me out about Charles and the Baron. About you, too, my
dear.

— What did you tell her?

— Oh, I know better than that. You don't tell stories to a
journalist unless you want to read them in the paper.

— About the Baron, you said?

— Yes, she's quite rabid.

—Where is she?

—Somewhere over there, I think, the Widow said, waving with her cigarette at the extreme end of the room. — Tycho, will you give me a light?

— Certainly, my queen. But you haven't let me finish my story. Brahe died of drinking with the King...

— Never mind about that now.

— What does she look like?

— Who? Oh, Fillier, you mean? Mannish.

— I'd like to meet her.

— Well, I certainly won't introduce you. I made you out to be a chaste and modest thing, who never leaves her father's side.

— Really?

— She was disappointed, I think. She'd figured you for a siren. Who was that odd-looking boy?

— A writer, I think.

— Oh, how terrible. If you've got to have someone poor, find a painter, my dear, please. At least you can get portraits from a painter; from a writer you get nothing at all.

Pleased with her bon mot, the Widow took a drag on her cigarette; then, paling visibly, asked, — What is this thing?

— What is it, my dear?

— Writers! I've been poisoned. Henri, will you help me outside?

— If we were at the King of Denmark's, I'd have to refuse.

— Damn your king! Just, just help me get out. I need some air. Madeleine...

But Madeleine was gone, moving awkwardly in the direction the Widow had indicated with her fan.

Mannish, unfortunately, described half of the ball's population, and not the half you'd expect. Still encumbered by her crino-

line, Madeleine navigated awkwardly through the crowd a little
way, but, as she couldn't find anyone who looked like a journalist—she imagined a stern-faced lady with a little notebook
ready in her hand—she prepared to retrace her path, to look for
Poissel again. Here, under the brighter of the two chandeliers,
she recognized the blue-coated gentleman who'd been the center of attention earlier on. At this distance, Madeleine could see
that the gentleman was no gentleman, was no man, but a
woman of about her own age, her hair tied back and her body
confined in a stiffly embroidered jacket and vest. Nothing
strange about that—she wasn't the only woman who'd appro-
priated men's clothes at the Expropriation Ball; so numerous
were the girlish gamins and buxom boys that the attendant
pederasts left early, disgusted by the unreliability of their objects. No, the odd thing was that the woman, catching sight of
Madeleine, turned as if she'd been struck, and asked, in a voice
barely under control, — From where do you have that dress?

— It was a present, why?

— Oh! But this is too much of a coincidence. Do you
know Fanny-Valentine Haussmann?

— I know who she is. But who are you?

— Oh, excuse me, yes. Viollet Fillier. Really, it's astonishing:
Valentine had a dress just like yours. Did you see her somewhere, and have it copied?

— No, Miss Fillier. It was her father who gave it to me.

— Her father? The Prefect, you mean.

— That's right. It was a gift from the Prefect.

— Well, how charitable.

— I was his lover, but in public he passed me off as his
daughter.

Fillier gawked. — Do you know who I am?

— You're a journalist. You write against Haussmann.

— Be careful what you tell me, then.

— If I wanted to be careful, Miss Fillier, I wouldn't talk to you at all.

— How courageous. What's your name? Or is this to be an anonymous confession?

Madeleine told her.

— Why don't we sit somewhere quiet and talk? said Fillier. She led Madeleine to the darkest part of the room, where (so Manet was right!) she got the picture.

At the end of the interview, Fillier gave her a card with an address written on the back, and told her words to murmur at the door. — Ask the clerk for the Crocodile, and he'll direct you.

— The Crocodile?

— You'll see. And you'll bring the letters?

— I will.

— All right. Now don't keep your beau waiting any longer. Go on!

As she stood, Madeleine remembered what she'd wanted to ask. — Are you a friend of Valentine's, then?

— A friend.

— Does she know about, well, about me?

Fillier looked at Madeleine so sadly that Madeleine, in that instant, guessed just how well Valentine knew. How well she must now know.

She hurried outside to see how the Widow fared.

Viollet Fillier, or Fanny-Valentine if you prefer, turned away. (How close Haussmann was to guessing! If only he'd thought that names have more than one way of holding back the truth, he might have got from anagrams to monograms, and thence to what he found out far, far too late.)

●　●　●

Outside, Madeleine found the Widow and told her what she'd done. The Widow looked as though she would be sick again. — Madeleine, she coughed, are you mad?

Fillier left not long after, and went to look for a cab. Two drunks followed her out. — Colder than a wicked tit out here, de l'Est, said one, and the other: — That's a witch's tit, my dear Rapunzel. Rapunzel? To Fillier he didn't look like much of a maiden. But then it was the Ball of the Expropriated; and people had the right to go by whatever names they chose.

Girls dressed in gargoyle masks and little else cavorted through the crowd, spilling champagne into the revelers' eager cups. It was time for the toast. The room grew quiet for a moment as the ball's sponsors, cherubic gentlemen with small, pointed beards, climbed atop a table and made a speech no one could understand. They raised their glasses and called out, — To Paris As It Was! To Paris As It Was! The toast echoed from a thousand dry throats, then fell off as the throats were wetted. The orchestra began again, and the gargoyles or gar-girls danced with the first men at hand.

At the bar, the youth who called himself Poissel called for wine and closed his eyes.

— Why so sad, brave boy?

The woman in the chiton stood beside him. Poissel hadn't seen her before; she must have come in while he wasn't watching the door, which was odd, as he'd watched it practically all evening; or else she'd arrived before he did, which was odd, too, because he'd been at the ball almost since the beginning. Still, she looked at him gently enough, and without disdain. A little amused light flickered at the back of her eyes.

— I've seen a beauty, Poissel said, and now she's gone.

The woman, who was herself something of a beauty, might reasonably have taken offense at this; instead her face took on the semblance of unlimited patience which we adopt when we first hear that a friend is seriously ill.

— Tell me about her.

Poissel did. — If only I hadn't seen her! he concluded. If I had imagined her, I could forget her, or at least imagine someone else. But it's too late for that. How can I imagine someone else now? How can I imagine anything at all?

— She sounds extraordinary, it's true. What was her name?

— I don't know, and that's the worst of it.

— How is that possible? You talked to her, didn't you?

— Oh, yes, but...

— You forgot to ask her name?

— I gave her mine. I wanted to ask, I was going to ask, but that damned redhead came and swept her off.

— But she has your card, isn't that right? She can find you if she likes.

— No, not even that. I told her... but the card... we were talking, and there were so many other things to say.

— Poor thing! Then you can't find her again, is that it?

— That's just it. Oh, I'm cursed, cursed. Idiot Poissel! You can do anything inside your head and nothing outside of it. You'll spend the rest of your life in there! He grabbed the head in question and pressed it between his palms.

— Poor boy.

— But I'm sorry to bore you, said Poissel, remembering himself a little. You haven't come to the ball to hear me prattle. Cigarette?

— No, thank you.

— Well, a drink, then? What's your name?

— She's called Madeleine de Fonce. You'll find her in the Parc Monceau, often, in the morning.

— Sorry?

— Walk by the observatory. You'll see.

— What, do you know her?

— You'll get along very well, I think. But treat her well! Or you'll have me to answer to.

— But how do you know her?

— Oh, from long ago.

Poissel and the woman spoke about Mlle de Fonce, and about the future. He found that her opinions on this latter subject were like Flaubert's on writing, like an ex-convict's on prison reform: sadly given, relentlessly concrete, and wholly irrefutable.

25

HISTORY

MIDAFTERNOON IN THE LIBRARY of the City of Paris. The clerk on duty takes liberties with the present as only clerks in museums and libraries may: he reads the newspaper as though the stories of the day were already fifty years old, and one could laugh as easily at the grand tragedies as at the *faits divers*. What a curious time we lived in! he thinks, when a man would kill for a nothing and sell his soul for a building because it was going to be torn down! A girl drowned herself in the Seine because her lover would not hold her hand—why, what a sensitive time it was, as though we'd all been up all night and anything would set us off. What a preposterous time! Only a nation too tired to sleep would waste its money on such expensive parties when everyone would have been better off in bed. Thinking such thoughts, the clerk finds himself closer and closer to sleep; only the rattle of the door wakes him. A female party well dressed in the rather stuffy way that great personages have of dressing nowadays. During the Revolution it was all so much simpler! You could make anything of yourself with a tricolor cockade and a clean shirt. That was a good time, the clerk reflects, although bad for libraries. But maybe that was good as well.

Maybe what was needed was fewer libraries, fewer books, archives, memoirs, collected and selected letters, old journals, newspapers, filling boxes upon boxes until you could, really, not take any pleasure in today, knowing that ten thousand days like it had been recorded with as much pomp and that when it was gone another ten thousand would receive the same treatment. The female party has asked to be admitted to the cellar. Well, since she seems to know just who is down there already the clerk has no objection; after all there's no keeping a secret from one who already knows it! And she's pretty, and perhaps it will do the basement skulkers good to see a pretty girl. Perhaps then they'll leave off their skulking and come up for some sunlight! It's a beautiful day, the clerk thinks, and when he has shown the female party to the basement he returns to his desk, puts his feet up, and dreams of war.

Madeleine walked slowly down the stairs. The anger that had filled her when she'd decided to revenge herself on Haussmann was largely gone. In truth it had left her at the ball, when she met Fillier (who was really Fanny-Valentine, could it be true?). It was the way Fillier had looked at her: as though her decision to betray Haussmann were just another turning of the same viciousness which had led her to become his mistress in the first place. His mistress... How she disliked the word! She remembered how sad she'd been when she heard it from Georges-Eugène. And what the results of that sadness had been. She had become Haussmann's daughter in the pretend world of their affair; but in the sober world without she remained his mistress. That was what Fillier's look reminded her of. When she chose to pursue the Baron she had become his mistress again, even though this time her pursuit wasn't amorous but vengeful. She'd stepped back into the old role. How else could Fillier regard her? She was an old, angry lover; the Baron—Fillier had said so herself—had more than one of those. All that distinguished her from the others (who were they? the daughters of his other friends? Singers or actresses?) was that she, Madeleine, had the power to ruin him.

She fingered the documents in her bag: the note Haussmann had sent her with the dress, the letters he'd written her in Hyères. She'd read them over before she left de Fonce's. She expected them, in retrospect, to contain subtle warnings that Haussmann was tired of her, that he would give her up. There were no warnings. The letters, even from this perspective, spoke only of love, or at least of great affection, and a slightly strained imagination, like a parent almost out of bedtime stories, trying to put a restless child to sleep. She had stuffed the letters into her bag, and then had carefully tucked into the front of her dress Haussmann's letter to de Fonce. That letter was not hers; she'd stolen it from a man who meant her nothing but good. If the letter meant what she thought it meant—scandal—then the scandal would ruin de Fonce, too. Was that virtue?

Everything which had been clear to Madeleine when she set out was so no longer. It seemed to her that she was descending into increasing obscurity—an entirely metaphorical obscurity, we ought to say, in defense of the Library's caretakers: the light in the basement was bright throughout—and that her path, as it shortened, became harder and harder to find, so that she might get lost only steps from her destination. Should she turn back? De Fonce would be out all day; she could return the letter to his desk and the story would be over. Fillier and the rest... they'd wait for her a while, then go back to their scheming. They might even feel a flicker of wonder that the girl—the woman—who'd planned to betray Haussmann had, at the last moment, been moved by some other moral impulse. The Baron would never know what he had escaped. And Madeleine would go back to de Fonce, and she would marry Waille, why not; then half of Brussels would be hers and although that was a tremendous disappointment in comparison to all of Paris, it was better, probably, than no city at all. She would be rich and there the story would end. Yet Madeleine continued on her forward, downward course. She couldn't let Haussmann go like that. She could not let him go. Even as she wondered whether the best thing to do might not be simply to forget him, to let him go his own way and meet with such justice or injustice as others saw fit to give him, to forget Haussmann altogether and to resume a life which, for all its discomfort, was, at least, not a part in anyone else's drama—even as she thought these things, Madeleine descended the last stairs and reached the door at which she'd been told to knock.

— *Gall, amant de la Reine, alla (tour magnanime!)*, said a man within.

Madeleine gave the other half of the password, supplied also by Fillier: — *Gallament de l'arène, à la Tour Magne, à Nîmes.*

The couplet was from Hugo.

— Ah, Mademoiselle de Fonce.

But who were these two men? One fat and the other skinny, dressed in suits of cheap black cloth, with spots on their cravats and hats in their hands?

— I'm afraid there's a mistake, Madeleine said. I must have the wrong room.

— No mistake, my dear! We've been waiting for you all day.

— For me? But where is Mademoiselle Fillier?

— She was here earlier, but when we came in she became, ah... indisposed. Isn't that right, Hennezel? Indisposed?

— Right as rain, Delesse.

— Apropos, what's it like out? the one called Delesse asked Madeleine.

— Outside? It's cold, but...

— We'd better call a cab, then, don't you think, Hennezel?

— Whatever you say, my dear Delesse.

— Where are you going?

— Are we going, you mean. You're coming with us.

— Sorry? I can't, I have an appointment...

— With the Fillier woman, yes, yes, we know all about that.
We talked to Mademoiselle Fillier this morning, didn't we,
Hennezel? She told us all about you. For instance I didn't know
that you could sing?

Hennezel closed the door, turned the key, and put it in his
pocket.

— She says you have a lovely voice, said Delesse. Isn't that
how you charmed the Prefect?

— Who are you?

— Sing us something, Mademoiselle. Don't you want her to
sing, Hennezel?

— I wouldn't miss it for the world, my dear Delesse.

— And then we'll go.

— Where are we going?

— Oh, someplace where we can talk. We want to ask you a
few questions about your father. By the way, what's in the bag?
Don't want to tell? Well, we'll come back to that in a moment.
No, we won't keep you long. Just a question or two. Is something wrong?

— Well, Mademoiselle de Fonce? I believe it's your moment.

The female party came out of the cellar arm in arm with the two
gentlemen. So she had drawn them out after all! It was well, it
was well. The three looked as though they could use some sun.
They left the Library and hailed a carriage; then they were gone.
The clerk went back to his reading and the sun, most fickle of
bibliophiles, crossed the room slowly, picking out a gilt title here
and there and letting it slip into obscurity again unread.

26

DRAWING STRAWS

DE FONCE HAD FEARED for his sight ever since the morning when he sat on the steps of Notre-Dame-de-l'Annonciation, waiting for the sun to rise; and it had risen; and turned the cathedral, the street, the town, to a forge a hundred times brighter than the one he'd left. (There had been no hammer blow to free him from the shackles of apprenticeship; that was only a midwife's tale, like the intimation that he had fathered sons on his own daughter. Nine years had been the term of his indenture, and, though he had become as a son to the smith, on the first day of the tenth year de Fonce—then only Fonce—had thrown all his work into the fire and melted it down together with his tools, for he understood what his master did not, that it is as little in the spirit of a contract to honor it beyond its terms as it is to break the contract altogether.)

The streets burned, and his eyes burned with them; there was a terrible sound like bones snapping in the crypt of the cathedral, and his head began to ring and pound as though his master had struck it a final blow. The journeyman smith squeezed his eyes tight shut and stumbled into morning Mass, where a kind curate, fearing that the service had made the halt blind, wrapped his head in a cool towel and left him in the sacristy until a doctor could be found to take him into secular care. The doctor was a heavy-footed man whose hands smelled of hair oil and his breath of venison. — Well, my boy, I hope you've seen a few ladies! Because I doubt you'll see any more of 'em. But don't worry! Women are like stars, they shine brightest in the dark... The doctor covered his head in cataplasms of lemon and warm sand. Fonce was glad: no one could see that he was weeping, and he wept for three days for all that he hadn't seen.

When the same doctor, or another equally rank, returned to fit him with a pair of blind man's glasses, however, he found that the world had not become invisible, only slightly dimmer than before. Fonce accepted sight the way a child takes gifts from a capricious parent, mistrustful that yesterday's present will not be exchanged for tomorrow's drubbing. He resolved to see as much, and as quickly, as he could, certain that it was only a matter of months—of days, perhaps—until the rose-madder world faded to a dusk without women, faces, stars. To be blind, to be led by the hand... His eyes had held out longer than he expected. In fact he thought there might have been a slight improvement in their condition; just the other day his glasses had slipped from the bridge of his nose and, before he could replace them, he'd caught sight of the golden-green elms on the boulevard de Courcelles, their leaves veined with sunlight. He felt nothing at all, no pain. The incident left him more frightened than if the boulevard had gone black. Sightless, he could always make a living: he'd set himself up as a sort of Tiresias, judging fixtures by their weight and furniture by its smell. If the Parisians thought melancholy could be cured by strapping magnets to one's feet then they would welcome a purblind seer into their salons. But if his eyes mended? Then, de Fonce won-

dered, who would give him two sous for his taste? For the
Parisians trusted him, he knew, only as long as his gift seemed
magical. If ever they were to guess that he was possessed only of
ordinary vision, as they all had; if they suspected that his uncanny knowledge of furnishings and antiques was culled from
the crannies of the bookstores on the rue Bonaparte, made
malleable during night upon endless night of candle-lit study,
and finally hammered to its present edge by a no more than ordinary will—why, if he gave antiquities half the effort your
lordship spends preparing his toilet, he'd know twice as much
as he does now—they would call him a fraud, a charlatan who
made junk pass for relics.

Such is taste, de Fonce reflected: like the water from the
blessed founts of Montmartre, it goes down smoothly as long as
you don't know where it comes from. Drinking water! The
thought was proof that he'd become careless; else how could
one of the Prefect's dismal obsessions have entered his
thoughts? In general Haussmann was far from his mind. De
Fonce's concern with the future was always practical, and with
the city changing so rapidly he had a great deal of work to
do—almost as much as the Prefect himself, though de Fonce
made less of a show of being busy. The Baron had once imagined that he had established a perfect rapport with the demolition man; in fact the opposite was true. De Fonce had
fathomed Haussmann, and understood his weakness. Though
de Fonce might play several roles in the course of an afternoon,
Haussmann would always be Haussmann. Fearful, priggish, self-
important, plodding Haussmann: the man, de Fonce thought,
was as immutable as if he had been his own monument. He
winced as a twinge of his old pain returned, an ember shot
from the furnace of the past. De Fonce would rather go blind
than see too well, he thought, if it came to that; though, admiring the exquisitely simple agony of the stone head he'd rescued

years ago from the chisel of some cretinous mason, he allowed that he would prefer to see for some time yet.

Madeleine did not as a rule enter de Fonce's office while he was working, but she came in that afternoon and sat down in the chair normally reserved for clients.

— I would like to buy something from you, she said.

— Don't be ridiculous, my dear, said de Fonce without looking up from the leases he'd been studying. — Everything here is yours for the asking.

— Nonetheless I want to buy, Madeleine said, and took a purse from the bag at her feet. — How much money is this? She emptied the coins onto de Fonce's desk.

The demolition man waited until the coins had stopped rattling and then looked up, not at the coins but at the girl who sat, too nervous even to blush, on the seat where his customers waited for him to read their hearts. — Enough, Madeleine. What do you want?

— Something old and small. That, for example. She pointed to a flintlock pistol which de Fonce had set aside for a young major with a keen sense of honor and a weakness for vingt-et-un. The rusted-out barrel might be good for one shot or it might not. Either way the major would be cured of gambling.

De Fonce shrugged. — It's already been sold, he said. What do you want?

— I want to remember, said Madeleine. To remember you and... She turned her hands palms up. — Don't laugh, please don't. I've been laughed at already today.

— Oh?

— I want to leave Paris.

De Fonce smiled. — Done.

— What?

— We've been invited to Compiègne. To see the Emperor and the Empress. You'll like her, she began her life very young just as you did.

— The Empress...

— We'll stay for three or four days. Although I'm sure you can stay longer if you like. You're bound to be a favorite. With your voice! Ah, my dear, and there will be theatricals.

— But I...

— You can't refuse. It's impossible. Refuse the Emperor! De Fonce shrugged. — I've already accepted for you.

— But I mean go away really. Forever.

— Ah. The demolition man sighed. — Forever. Why? Has Paris become too dull? Is there no one left to fall in love with?

Madeleine began to cry. Only her lips moved, and they not much. When she was done she took the coins from de Fonce's desk one by one and returned them to the purse they'd come from. From the same purse she took Haussmann's letter about the cemetery, and gave it to de Fonce. — I didn't give it to them, she said.

De Fonce glanced at the letter, recognized it, and left it where it lay.

— I told them everything else, though.

As best she could, Madeleine recounted how Fillier had told her to go to the Library, and what she'd found there, and how Haussmann's men had driven her to a lonely riverbank just outside the city. How they'd threatened to drown her like a cat if she didn't tell them the truth, and produced a big sack to make good their threat. How she'd told them about the affair, and the child, and how she'd given them Haussmann's letters to her (but not his letter to you!). She told them about the apartment on Headless Woman Street and the dress and Smuts and the baby and the Widow... — I didn't tell them about the land or the graveyard. But I would have told Fillier, I wanted to tell

her, even though it would have ruined you I'd have told her, I
would, and you shouldn't forgive me nor will I ask you to.

— Madeleine...

— I would have betrayed you. Send me away, please, or let
me go on my own. For I...

De Fonce stopped her, laughing. He laughed until he too
seemed to be crying and stopped only when he saw that his
cackles, far from reassuring Madeleine, had made her more
nervous and unhappy than before. He put his arm around her
shoulders and left it there until she consented to be touched;
then he touched her face with his other hand and kissed her.
Ah, de Fonce thought, how much easier it is to be a father than
a lover! One can get away with every sort of tenderness because one means well sincerely. Haussmann, he thought in the
inmost court of his conscience, you are a fool. You and your
thugs! You are a fool, and it is time you paid for being a fool.

— Look! he said. I'll show you a trick that will make you
feel better. Here. De Fonce took three or four quills from his
desk and broke one off just below the feathers. He held them
feathers upmost in his fist and presented the fist to Madeleine
like a bouquet. — Choose, he said. Who gets the short lot has
to smile. Madeleine chose the broken quill and smiled. — Not
good enough, said de Fonce, and shuffled the quills in his hand.
— Choose again. Again she chose the short lot. — Better, but
not good. Again. Again the short lot. — There! de Fonce said,
smiling himself, now you see that I will take care of you.
Madeleine chose twice more and each time the short quill as if
by its own volition found its way to her hand. — That's better.
Now, my dear, isn't Mademoiselle Fillier expecting this? He
pushed the letter back across the table.

— Fillier? She wasn't there. Haussmann's men said they
had... oh no. No. It can't be. Madeleine took the letter. — We
live in an evil world, she said, don't we?

27

COMPIÈGNE

AN ENGLISHMAN QUIPPED that its name, roughly translated, means "with suffering"; for centuries it was the seat of kings. Fifty miles from the gates of Paris, in the middle of a wood famous for its hunting—and rightly so, for it was stocked each season with an empire's worth of game—the château hosted the Second Empire's greatest parties and its greatest intrigues. Every autumn the court retreated for a few weeks to the country, and brought along all its courtiers and pretenders, the Empire's luminaries, those who had distinguished themselves by wit or wealth or cunning in the previous year. What games they played there! Games of skill and chance, games of love and games more subtle still, with men for pawns and millions at stake. Compiègne had only one official rule: the Emperor and Empress demanded that their guests be charming and proper in all things. To meet those demands guests had been known to bankrupt themselves. One merchant of middling means had to sell his factory to buy for his wife all the clothes necessary for a week at Compiègne: three dresses for each day and another for each evening. Even the court at Versailles, the guests joked uneasily, had not known so much decorum, nor so much obligation: to refuse an invitation to Compiègne was unthinkable.

The guests were sorted by *série*: the necessary people came the first week and the bores the second; the third week was reserved for the fashionable ones and the fourth for intellectuals. They made much of this distinction, as they did of every difference between them. From the condition of the ribbons that topped the gentlemen's white silk stockings to the number of medals on the chests of military men, every difference, however small, was an advantage or disadvantage to be exploited ruthlessly or artfully hid. Never had so much been made of such fine distinctions as it was at Compiègne: where you sat and whether you arrived at breakfast early or late (both measured in seconds), the powder on your wig and the fixity of your smile meant strength or they meant weakness; at Compiègne the two were so finely separated that not even a thought could pass between them. At Compiègne, the hunting place of kings, everything was sport and nothing was, and so embarrassment was impardonable. To embarrass yourself was to rend the Empire's celebrated decorum—and through that hole the guests, if they had not been too polite to look, might have seen the great boiling nothing which waited just beyond their every gesture.

Of course the Emperor's guests were not to be entrusted to the ordinary sort of railway carriage; a special train did for the elect what the Railway of the Dead would have done for the defunct. The passengers were lulled to sleep in armchairs by wine and the swaying of the carriage on its tracks; those who could stay awake played cards or talked with amusement and surprise about the Prussian Army, about how brash they'd been of late, and how long would it be before the French had to teach them a lesson? And what would they have for dinner tonight? They'd heard the Emperor's table was good, but how good was it, really? Just as on any train there are travelers sick of traveling and others who have never left Paris before, who make their way to

Marseilles with as much excitement as if it had been the moon, so some in the Emperor's private coach were jaded and others overcome. Haussmann, who this year had been invited to the first and most prestigious *série*, belonged to the former group. Valentine was supposed to accompany him, but, vexingly and incomprehensibly, she'd gone to Bordeaux instead. Surely she wasn't afraid of Louis Napoleon? Her affair with the Emperor, if you could even call it an affair—a single night, and not even a whole night, he'd heard from the chamberlain—was a thing of the past; the Emperor was impotent now, not that he had ever been any great shakes, the pudgy little tyrant. Valentine's note hadn't even mentioned him; she said only that he would henceforth have to make his way in the world alone. "Henceforth": what did she mean? Once again the Baron wondered whether she and Octavie weren't in on some scheme together. (Octavie was in Bordeaux, too.) In the meanwhile she'd left him in the lurch. He'd been looking forward to his daughter's company; now he would have to endure Compiègne, as she said, alone.

As was his habit, Haussmann made the best of what time he had. When the train left the Gare du Nord his considerable height was folded over the text of the speech he would make to the Municipal Council concerning the cemetery, which was a stroke of the municipal pen from being built. It had been a long struggle. After the fiasco in the papers it was all Haussmann could do to keep the Council from rejecting the idea of the graveyard out of hand. But he brought in experts to testify that never in the history of death had there been such a healthy, clean, and altogether proper place to dispose of bodies. He hired painters to render views of the cemetery as it would look when finished, and they produced paintings worthy of a Poussin: avenues of cypresses unrolling into the blue distance, with wreath-hung tombs here and there like the treasures of antiquity. He convened secret meetings, called in favors, owed favors, paid for dinners, doctors, draftsmen, dancing girls (these last out of his own pocket), and in short did everything he could. It was enough. The cemetery lingered in the municipal agenda like a disease that has remitted; then, gradually, it came forward again, all the more splendid for having nearly disappeared. Now all that remained was to call for a vote the outcome of which, by way of the dancing girls, he already knew. It had taken a long time, but *ars longa*, as they said, and *vita brevis*—he had a panel of experts to prove it—*est*.

When the train left the trunk line for the special track which led directly to the Emperor's residence, he was in the same posture; aside from three or four deletions and the insertion of a paragraph on the importance of digging graves to a proper depth he might not have moved at all. He looked up, however, as the train slowed and a familiar voice said, — Yes, my dear, I believe this is the end. Startled, Haussmann looked around; the demolition man seemed to catch sight of him at just the same time, for he came forward saying, — Why Baron! This is a surprise! and holding out a hand the size of a garden spade. — My dear, he said, turning, it's our Prefect.

Madeleine rose from the seat where she'd been reading. She wore a wool traveling cloak and an autumnal brown dress. She had not changed, or seemed not to have changed, since Haussmann saw her last. Her face was as full, her eyes as light...

— Yes, so it is, she said, and held out her hand. It was cool and seemed to have no weight.

— Are you here for the festivities? de Fonce asked.

Haussmann's answer was lost in the hiss of the train's brakes. Around them a country station rolled to a stop, its quays densely populated by imperial servants, porters, and wagons.

— Well, then, I'm sure we'll see you again, said de Fonce. — Come, my dear! Don't forget your books.

That was all they had time for: the doors opened and servants invaded the carriage, hoisting bags and parcels, sweeping
out the remains of the passengers' meals. Haussmann watched
Madeleine and her father descend through that crowd to the
platform, then returned to his seat and gathered the pages of his
nearly completed speech.

The Baron had heard Hennezel and Delesse tell how they'd
caught Fillier at last in the cellar of the Library.
    — She came in without a care in the world...
    — Fillier is a woman?
    — That's right, sir.
    — All that trouble from a woman.
    — Well, she won't bother you any more.
    — Oh?
    — That's right. We took care of her, er...
    — We took care of her in a womanly way, if you follow.
    — Or rather, we in a manly and she in a womanly way, that
is, sir.
    — Oh? Haussmann felt a little distaste at the thought of
that. He'd ordered them to make an example of Fillier, of
course, but if he'd known she was a woman, he would have told
them to be gentle. He couldn't use Fillier as an example now: a
disgraced woman would make him seem villainous. He'd have
to hope that disgrace would keep her silent, too. In any case it
was done, and it didn't do any good to think back on it now.
More distressing, really, was the news that Madeleine had col-
luded with Fillier to bring him down. Like a man learning the
extent of his disease in order to understand its future manifestations, its course, whether its end will be his own, Haussmann
asked them about every particular of the encounter. What had
Madeleine said? How had she discovered the conspirators, how

learned their hiding place? Did her face show anger, or sorrow? Were her pupils overlarge? What was her pulse? His agents shook their heads. They'd been given no orders to examine the subject in that way.

— Yes, but, you see, Haussmann explained, she might have been hypnotized, hysterical, cataleptic, or otherwise prey to the slumbering quarters of her mind. He told them about Sörgel the German foot-chopper, and the errant channels thought might follow in sleep.

— She looked all right to us, sir.

— Did she say why she was there?

— She said... Tell him, Hennezel.

— "To ruin you utterly" is what she said. I believe those were her words.

— Did she go of her own free will, or did someone put her up to it?

— She said you'd ask that. Didn't she say that, Delesse? Why, sir, you must have read her mind, or she must have read yours.

— Answer!

— She said to tell you that her father didn't know a thing about it, and neither did the Couvrefeu personage.

— Were those her words?

— More or less, sir. She called the Couvrefeu personage the Widow.

— How did she propose to ruin me?

— Tell him, Delesse.

— Well, sir, she said, by making the Fillier party party to the fact that you and she had been implicated together.

— Involved together.

— Involved, as you say, Hennezel.

— What?

— She used the word "affair" to describe the situation.

— She said that she would make the Fillier party cognizant
of a certain mutually engendered infant, that is, a child belong-
ing jointly to you and her, that is, Madeleine, not Fillier, if you
see what I mean.

— Had she proof?

— She had some letters for the Fillier party. But sir, we collected those letters and retained them in our possession, and, in
short, here they are. Delesse set a bundle of papers on the
Baron's table.

— So, you see, we've extradited the heart of the plot.

— That is, we've fanged the serpent, sir.

— That is, you've nothing to fear from the Madeleine personage. Isn't that right, Hennezel?

Was it relief which closed Haussmann's eyes, or sorrow? On
the one hand he was safe. Without the letters their affair could
not be proved; still less could Madeleine prove she'd had his
child. If he had stayed with her a little longer, he might have
compromised himself, but as it was... Fillier wouldn't dare print
her accusations after what she'd got. Anyway the Emperor,
who'd fathered a number of bastards on his host of mistresses,
was understandably sensitive about that sort of accusation. Any
paper which dared to print it on the strength of suspicion alone
would be closed down, lest it encourage more such journalistic
speculation. How fortunate Haussmann was to have left Madeleine when he did! Old man, he told himself, your timing's as
good as it ever was.

But that was only half his thought. The other half concerned an image of Madeleine which he'd cherished since their
last interview in the Hôtel de Ville. This image had run from his
office, just as the real Madeleine had; it drove home to de
Fonce's and threw itself on her bed, in tears. It wept; then with
a sort of moral resignation, followed, in the end, by forgiveness,
it understood that things could not have been otherwise. If

Haussmann had been free to choose Madeleine, he would have chosen her; but he was not free. The image rose from its bed. It recognized that the work took precedence. Not because he chose the work, but because it, long ago, had chosen him. One day the work would tire of him; it would let him drop; then he would be free to choose again. The image-Madeleine waited by the window. When, old and limp with lassitude, Haussmann would come back to de Fonce's, it would come downstairs to greet him; it would take his hands in its own and press them to its breast. As Hennezel and Delesse gave their report on the events in the Library's cellar, this image was closed to him. It was as though a wing of his imagination had been inspected, and a flaw discovered in its foundation; the wing, though still standing, was closed to visitors and covered in scaffolding. It waited now only for the demolition men.

Can I say that, when Haussmann saw Madeleine, all his thoughts changed? I think sometimes that I can tell you very little. If I tell you that, seeing her, he was convinced that she could have played no part in the conspiracy against him, at least no witting part, will you believe me? You will ask what caused the change. But events do not cause other events, at least not in ways we can discern. The bulk of any event is hidden from us, like that black part of the moon invisible to the telescopes; we know it not by looking at the sky but by watching the water, and inferring from the rise and fall of waves the mass which must circle overhead. Watch Haussmann's face, then, and see if you can read in it a sign of the hidden gravity of his emotion. His cheeks flushed; his eyes followed de Fonce and Madeleine to their carriage. He put his papers away in the wrong order. What tide is that? What does it mean? I say it means that Haussmann had, in that moment, fallen in love with Madeleine again, but I conjecture so only because I know how the story turns out in the end; as to the exact nature of any of its moments, why, I'm just as much in the dark as you, or almost as much so. I see the waves.

I fear sometimes that there's little I can tell you; yet we must go on. You'll excuse me if I don't do justice to the splendor of Compiègne: to the dinners (well, but the Emperor didn't do them justice either: bored by the pleasures of the table, he led his guests on a forced march through ten or twelve courses in the course of an hour); nor to the evenings spent in wanton pleasure (two couples danced to the mechanical piano, while the others, exhausted by a day of decorum, played cards and yawned behind their hands or fans. A tired servant carried around trays of liqueurs which no one drank. Sodom and Gomorrah! the Chevalier Gastofouard cackles in his memoirs). I'll skip the educational visit to the château at Pierrefonds, which Viollet-le-Duc was busily restoring, though, if we went, we'd learn much about Gothic architecture, and how not everything built at that time was new: the Second Empire had, in addition to its passion for the new, an equal, and not entirely opposite, interest in the old—why, one might say that the old was born in the 1860s, just as the new was. I won't tell you about the Emperor's visit, in the company of a select group of amateurs, to the archeological dig at Vaulepic, and you'll thank me for the omission: the select group of amateurs, their knees muddied and their minds thoroughly baffled by a collection of indifferent rocks, only wish that the Emperor had been as considerate. We'll go directly to the chase, that is, to the hunt.

The hunt at Compiègne served the Empire in lieu of war (at least, for the time being: the Empire would have war enough only a year hence, when the Germans decided to visit Paris). It began before dawn, when huntsmen released the stags into the forest and stood guard to make sure they didn't get too far away. Then came a long pause in which everyone got dressed. By noon or one the guests were ready to kill; someone blew a horn and they rode en masse into the wild, armed with enough guns and powder to slaughter an army of harts. The party dispersed through the forest; some followed the quarry one way and some another; they crossed and recrossed paths in the elaborately rustic villages where refreshments were served. As the afternoon wore on and the refreshments ran out, the hunt's pace quickened. Anything which resembled a stag was fired upon; the villagers were advised to wear bright clothes or else keep out of sight.

At just that hour Haussmann found himself alone in the forest. He'd heard, or thought he'd heard, the stag run in one direction; the other hunters thought it had gone in the other. They went their way and the Baron, never one to yield to the opinion of the majority, went his. He came to a clearing where nothing more could be heard, and there stopped, rifle in hand, waiting for a sign. Before long he heard what confirmed his hunch: heavy footfalls approaching. The Baron checked his rifle. Protocol required that the stag be held at bay until the Emperor could be found to dispatch it, but if one were alone, and the stag not disposed to be held at bay, one might suspend protocol for the duration of a single shot. The rifle would fire. The beast came closer, slowly. Was it wounded? Or had it smelled him out? Haussmann shouldered his weapon.

— Ho! Baron! A head appeared over the brush, then the head of a horse; the bodies of each followed. De Fonce, similarly armed. — It's a good thing my eyes haven't gone dull, he said, or I might have mistook you for the quarry.

— I might have done the same, if you hadn't spoken, the Baron remarked.

De Fonce had not put his rifle away. Haussmann, alarmed, kept his ready also.

— I hoped to find you alone, the demolition man said.

— The others can't be far off, said Haussmann.

— Then I'll speak quickly. I wanted to give you some advice: give up the graveyard.

— Oh?

— You're to make a speech next week, to put the cemetery to a vote, am I right? No need for you to answer: listen. Don't make the speech. Or make it, and say that you've decided against the cemetery.

— On what grounds?

— On any grounds you like. Say that it's unhealthy.

— But it's not. I have the surveyors' report...

— Then invent something. I trust your imagination.

— But, I mean, why should I decide against the cemetery?

— Because, my dear Baron, it will never be built. And if you try to build it, you'll be ruined.

— Can you see the future now, with your glasses?

— It's simpler than that. I have information about it.

— From whom?

— I won't say. But if I was ever your friend, trust me, and let the plans go.

— What if I won't?

— Will you? I ask you as a friend.

— No.

De Fonce looked at him as though he could see forward, through time, to something which displeased him. Haussmann's hand clenched the stock of his rifle.

— Then I have nothing more to say to you. The demolition man shouldered his weapon and turned his horse to go.

— Wait, Haussmann said.

— Changed your mind?

— Tell me something. How is your daughter?

— Well, de Fonce said curtly. Why?

— Does she ever speak of me?

De Fonce laughed. — You won't oblige a friend, but you ask me that? Yes, she does.

— What does she say? Does she... would she, I mean, under the right circumstances, would she see me again?

Probably it was a mistake to ask, but Haussmann could not resist. Since he'd seen Madeleine on the train, he could do nothing but think of her: she was as lovely as when he'd seen her first, in the demolition man's parlor, years and years ago. More beautiful, perhaps; he'd heard that motherhood did that to some women, although of course Octavie had not been one of them. He knew that he had left her, but could not understand why. She was the most beautiful thing he had known. Haussmann was giddy with concupiscence, and lay awake, nights, thinking of her small breasts, of the slow movement of her hands. At Compiègne she would not speak to him. Whenever they risked coming near one another, Madeleine turned away; he tried to pursue her into the seclusion of the garden but she lost herself like a sylph among the trees and he was left to walk up and down, bewildered, afraid to call out lest someone else hear him. In crowds, his eyes no longer found her eyes, though he stared at her as long as decorum would allow, and a little longer. Haussmann was terrified: now that he saw her again, he saw, as he hadn't before, that she was lost to him. He would have torn down parks and streets to have her back.

— It's curious that you should ask, de Fonce said. She did mention that she wanted something from you.

— What was it?

— Nothing you'd agree to, I told her.

— What?

— A trifle, but a trifle indecorous for you, I'm afraid, Baron. She wants you to act.

— What?

— Am I speaking too quietly? She's arranged with the Empress to put on a little play, and she mentioned to me that you'd be perfect for one of the parts.

— What play?

— *Antigone*, by Sophocles. No, don't look alarmed! It's an abridged version. Just a tableau vivant, really. But there; you're scowling. I told her you wouldn't do it.

— She wants me to act?

— Play-acting's not in you, Baron, is it? You're far too serious. You see how well I know you? Don't worry: I already told her you'd refuse. But thank you for giving me occasion to ask.

— Do you know me?

— Have you changed?

— I'll do it.

— Will you? Oh, I see you're serious. All right. I'll tell Madeleine. You won't change your mind? Then I'll tell her. Perhaps you have changed, Baron. Perhaps you have. Now hurry! The hunt's left us quite behind.

In the ballroom at Compiègne the guests, freshened perhaps by their sport, drained their glasses. They had drunk their way already through a series of Pictures of Virtue and Fantastic Tales, scenes of convents and abbeys, balls and romantic urban tableaux. Now the Empress came on in the guise of Memory, and the Chevalier Gastofouard as Sleep; their dance had the audience slapping their knees, and wiping tears from their eyes. It was late already, quite late, when the time came for Madeleine's play; Haussmann, as he staggered to the stage, hoped that sleep would win out over memory, and no one would be able to say tomorrow what they'd seen.

He had been tricked. It was the fault of the wine, and de Fonce's absurd idea that they choose their parts by drawing lots.

— Antigone? How can I...

De Fonce laughed. — Play a woman? But we've all agreed on the rules, my dear sir, and in any case it's just a game.

Then Madeleine chose: — I'll play Haemon, she ventured, and follow you to the tomb.

— And I Creon! de Fonce snapped. Here, Baron, give me your medal and I'll begin.

De Fonce took the Baron's gold medallion, the Great Cross of the Legion of Honor, which he had—finally—been given the year before. It was the highest distinction the Baron received, and the only one for which he would be honored at his funeral. Haussmann himself held a trowel in his right hand. The tool must have come fresh from the gardener's shed, for the tip of the blade was still black with earth, and grayish grains of soil fell onto the cuffs of his shirt when he waved his hand. Madeleine stood before him, looking more beautiful in a plain black cloak than the harridan Empress Eugénie and all her friends in their enormous skirts and trains. Haussmann might as well have performed for a gallery of wilted plants as play for these ladies, who leaned against their stake-straight dukes and bank directors, clapping and covering their gap-toothed mouths.

—Mesdames and Messieurs, de Fonce announced, the spectacle you are about to see begins with two brothers, Eteocles and Polynices, each as like to the other as I am to he (de Fonce pointed to Haussmann; the Empress giggled). Each was heir to Thebes, and each would have the city to himself; so they have killed each other. It is incumbent upon us to dispose of the remains. But I, Creon, say that only one will be buried, and the other left to rot in the open air...

They were laughing at him. Such a lot of wind they produced, and so foul! He didn't know why he'd consented to this. In the bedroom it might give a strange and prickling pleasure

to take the woman's part, but before the court! Fortunately
they were all drunk; beyond their heads the windowpanes had
already begun to clear with dawn. By noon the night would
have been forgotten. By then Haussmann would be gone; he
had business in Paris, plans to read and lackeys to flog, by God!
but he was easier there than in Eugénie's idea of an idyll, a jumble of cold pavilions in the woods. They were waiting for him
to speak. — I *will* bury him, Haussmann said, for he was my
brother and I scorn the human laws where they conflict with
the divine.

The wilted flowers cackled.

Haussmann fumbled his speeches; he could not remember
whether he had buried the body, or only planned to bury it. He
waved the trowel as though it were a sword, clearing a space
before him; he needed room to collect his wits. The audience
laughed; Émile Ollivier cupped his hand to Eugénie's ear. He
needed room, and quiet; something had escaped his attention.
Something important: an appointment he had missed, or a
speech to give before the Senate, or a plan to review, it had
been missed, he needed to glance at his memorandum book.
Only glance at it and he would find the time to make
amends... But this ridiculous play would not end! Creon and
Haemon bickered about the nature of a son's duty to his father.
Then—what fatherly love was this?—Creon kissed Haemon on
the lips. Or rather de Fonce kissed Madeleine. And Haussmann,
years too late, understood that in games of cat and mouse the
cat doesn't always win. Madeleine and de Fonce, all along, kissing in their hiding places, laughing at the clumsy cat who
thought he was a mouse, and begged to be let into their holes.
Crimson now, Haussmann turned away.

The Empress yawned; Ollivier returned to the decanter; a
servant arrived to close the curtains against the morning.
— Creon! Haussmann must have said it more loudly than he

intended; everyone turned to him. He held the trowel over his head. — I... I die! He spoke a little in advance of the script, but never mind: he had decided to end the show.

— Wait! Haemon took a step toward him.— I have something to tell you.

De Fonce leered.

— Your daughter, Haemon said. Valentine, and Miss Fillier... Oh, Baron, don't you understand?

— No! Haussmann said, disgusted by the demolition man's red stare. — No, I die alone. He made a motion to plunge the trowel into his chest. — I bury me!

The wilted flowers clapped. Haussmann bowed deeply to them and made for the door, ignoring Madeleine's whisper, — Viollet Fillier and Fanny-Valentine...

— Don't sully her name by speaking it, Haussmann whispered back. He understood, oh he understood very well: Madeleine was against him; now she'd try to tell him that Valentine had betrayed him to Fillier, too. Nonsense! Fillier was out of the picture, and Valentine in Bordeaux, with Octavie. But let her lie, let them all lie. It did not matter. He would remain honest if they did not, if no one else did. In that sense, and let them laugh as they would, he'd chosen the right part. He was Antigone, the one who buried the dead. His only regret as he passed into the dawn-gray corridor was that he hadn't been able to play the part to the end.

28

ELSEWHERE

— ARE YOU READY to go, gentlemen?

— Ready, Hennezel?

— As I'll ever be, my dear Delesse.

— You have your instructions? Keep the fire lit until you reach a thousand meters; then bank the stove and follow the wind.

— And when we land, your spotters will come for us, isn't that so?

— You won't be out of our sight for a moment. We've... let's see, a breeze from the west. Four knots. You ought to come down by Saint-Germain-en-Laye, and be home for dinner. I'm loosing the ropes, all right, gentlemen?

— Loose the ropes!

— You don't need to tell him that, Hennezel. He's done it already.

— So he has. And up we go! Why, look how small everything's got.

— Hold on... Hey!

— What is it, Delesse?

— I can't hear you up there!

— How do we know...

— I said, I can't hear you!

— Is something wrong?

— I say, Hennezel. How do we know when we're at a thousand meters?

So Hennezel and Delesse left the earth. Their job as balloon testers for the Empire's nascent Bureau of Meteorology was the best they could find after Haussmann dismissed them without so much as a thank you or a letter of recommendation. Not that a recommendation from the Prefect, in that season, would have opened many doors. After all the stink about the graveyard, Haussmann's name was, so to speak, mud; in many cases his friends fared worse than those who had fallen from his favor. The papers said that the Prefect had, in the winter of 1869, lost his mind. They produced as evidence the indisputable fact that he'd shaved his beard. Reporters spoke of his mania for cutting everything down... While others, who did not publish their accounts, said that costume had driven Haussmann mad. Inspectors superior in grade to Delesse (before he was sacked, that is) whispered that their boss, the Baron, had gone to Compiègne dressed in ladies' clothes. They said he'd looked quite gay in that getup; it was the return to a civil servant's black habit which did him in, in the end. Others still—but Hennezel and Delesse did not know them—said that the trouble began a few days *after* Compiègne, when Octavie and Fanny-Valentine returned to Paris. Such shouting as you never heard! they whispered. And then silence which was worse than the shouting. It must have been bad, they said, because the Prefect didn't come to work the next day. When he appeared the day after, his face had a decade of lines scratched in it, and his beard was gone.

So much for rumor. The facts, as sorrowfully apprehended by Hennezel and Delesse: not two days after the Baron's return, the papers cried that Haussmann was in league with a demolition man, that the ignominious railroad he wished to inflict on Paris's dead was to be paid for with stolen funds, with monies misappropriated from foundling hospitals, orphanages, and societies which would otherwise have distributed free wine to the poor. The fact that Haussmann appeared beardless before the Municipal Council to defend his graveyard didn't help. The Councilmen heard his arguments for sanitation, for modernity, for reverence toward the dead; but when his speech was done, all they wanted to know was, why had he made his crooked deal with de Fonce? And what had become of his whiskers?

In truth the Assistant Inspector and Inspector's Assistant were fortunate to get jobs in the civil service at all. Haussmann threatened them with transfers to Cayenne, to Saint-Helena; but, dejected, already looking forward to exile in each other's increasingly trying company, they happened to catch sight of an announcement that the Meteorology Bureau was hiring. The pay wasn't bad; in fact, it was quite good, so good that neither Hennezel nor Delesse could understand why there weren't more candidates for the job. But we were speaking of the facts in Haussmann's case. There was, in addition, the fact that, not long after his return from Compiègne, before the trouble with the papers and the Council, the Baron called Hennezel and Delesse into his office. He appeared not to have slept for longer even than was customary for him. The spies preferred not to remember his face: everywhere but the eyes it was raw and old, as though it had been dragged forcibly into its future. The eyes were simply blank. At most they had a trace of expression, the way you can see the outline of a demolished building still on the building next door.

The Baron told them: — Take a half-dozen policemen and go to de Fonce's house. Say that you have a warrant for the arrest of Madeleine de Fonce—write one yourselves, if you think you'll need it—and take her into your custody. Bring her here.

— To your office, sir? Delesse asked.

— No, to... no. Haussmann's hands covered his eyes. — Do
nothing. Wait. Leave me.

They received no further orders, and so carried none out.
They were the only ones who knew this fact, and it rose with
them into the clouds, it rose and rose.

And Madeleine? For weeks after the Ball of the Expropriated,
the youth who called himself Poissel went to the Parc Monceau
each morning. He arrived not long after dawn and waited in
the scant shelter of the observatory's archways until just before
noon. At last his vigil was rewarded: Madeleine, majestic in a
gray morning dress, appeared, holding the hand of a girl of four
or five. They took the path which ran between the stream (formerly the River Lethe) and the ruins of the naumachia. Poissel
followed them in. Madeleine at last! Poissel thought of what
excuse he would give: Mademoiselle, I happened to be taking
the air... Or would it be better to tell the truth? Someone who
seems to know you well told me I'd find you here... Would she
be frightened? Or flattered? If only he looked less ridiculous!
But Poissel was aware, as only one who claims not to be vain
can be aware, that this was impossible. He had been born
ridiculous—his neck, when he died, ought to be exhibited in a
museum of natural curiosities—and life had done little to
change him. To run up to them, Poissel decided, would be
undignified, and perhaps alarming. He would wait for them to
stop; then he would go up and speak. There. They stopped by a
reflecting pool in the center of the park. He would go... no,
he'd wait a moment longer. In order that they not see him before he was ready, Poissel waited on the far side of a tree.

— Elise, are you listening? We're going to take a trip, you
and I.

— Mirror, said the girl.

— Yes, the water's like a mirror. You can see yourself in it, can't you?

— Mirror.

— To Italy, which is a warm place with pretty things to look at. Then on a ship just like the ones you have at home. With sailors.

— Mirror sailors.

What sort of a language was this? Poissel wondered.

— To Athens, which is in Greece. Greece is... well, it's another place. They have Greeks.

— Greeks sailors.

— Who are famous sailors, yes. And then we'll come home again.

— Greeks home.

Why, Poissel thought, this child was amazing! She'd practically told the stories of the *Iliad* and the *Odyssey* in four words. He was taken with the fancy that this was what all language would become, or ought to become: stripped of everything unnecessary, of everything which came with reflection, complication, abstraction, all the paths by which the world was lost. What an interesting thought! He took a small notebook from his breast pocket and tried to think of a succinct way to write it down.

— No, home to Paris. For a while, anyway. I... I don't know, Elise.

— Italy Italy. Greeks Greeks.

Just write down what she says, fool, Poissel told himself. You'll have time to figure it out later. Let's see. Mirror...

— Does that please you? Well, we'll hope it does. Do you see yourself? Come on, my heart. I'll show you the waterfall.

Poissel scrawled a few words more. It was important to get these things down while they were fresh in your mind;

otherwise you might lose them forever, and that would be a pity. Besides, he felt that this was the beginning of something important. A new language, in which one could say, perhaps, things that had never before been said—or, to be precise, in which one could write things that had never before been written. Amazing, wasn't it, how the world kept making itself new! He would write an article chiding those sad scribblers who said that history had exhausted itself, that there was no going on. There was always going on. As soon as he'd finished writing that thought down—how quickly the words came!—he'd follow Madeleine and the girl, and approach when they stopped again. Although perhaps it would be better if he talked to her tomorrow? Tomorrow his mind would be clear again. And perhaps Madeleine would be alone, which would make her easier to approach... Today has served its purpose, Poissel told himself: I have my idea. Let tomorrow serve another. He put the notebook back in its pocket and left the park the way he had come in.

De Fonce profited, of course, from Haussmann's disgrace, as he did from everything: when the Municipal Council voted not to take possession of M. Duclos's asparagus farm, it was the demolition man who got the land. It lay fallow through the Empire's fall, the autumnal year when Louis Napoleon's bladder and Prussia's nerve shadow-boxed across the Rhine. Then the Prussians invaded and nerve won out, as it tends to do; the asparagus field was trampled under soldiers' boots. When the Prussians left, a year later, the land was not good for growing anything, so de Fonce built on it a country estate in the old style, and planted trees that would make a decent park a century hence. Every year when autumn came he announced his intention of moving there for good and living out his days as a country gen-

tleman; but something invariably came up and his departure
was postponed. For weeks his trunks stood in the hall and then
it was winter; sighing, de Fonce ordered them unpacked and
resigned himself to another year in the city. The truth was that
Paris would not allow de Fonce to leave. He had become one
of the city's vital functions, like sewers, or dreams, the reposi-
tory of everything which the Parisians had forgotten, and
which they paid dearly to recover from oblivion. He died in
Paris, a wealthy old man, his boxes packed for a journey he
would never undertake.

By then Madeleine had come back to Paris. She had been
away longer than she'd planned, and had seen a great deal: not
everything, as Nasérie had predicted, but enough. Elise saw
more. Our century unfolded its dark, grasping miracles around
her, and she lived bravely within them, and spoke of them as
she could. She did not know her father, except by his work,
which outlasted everyone. Nor did she wonder what Haussmann's last wish had been. And they leave us, they leave us and
our stories, and we cannot follow them. Nevertheless I imagine
that somewhere, far off, under different stars, Madeleine found
her marquise again. It is her due.

Haussmann in Constantinople, February 1873. From the balcony everything looks so far away, Haussmann remarks; why,
the muddy white houses below might be models of houses, and
the Bosphorus a glittering construction of paste, dotted here
and there with cunningly wrought replicas of long-necked gal-
leys, their oars lifting and dipping like the legs of a scorpion. A
scorpion like the one he thought he'd seen scuttling about the
floor of the wardrobe before his servant tossed his trunk into
that capacious gloom. They've given Haussmann a flattering
amount of room, considering that his entourage is but a single

manservant, a groom, and an old surveyor who was once employed by the Department of Public Works. The surveyor,
whose name is either Vignon or Fignon, Haussmann can't remember which, was loyal to the last, and defended the Prefect
sternly in the evening journals. — If he is corrupt, Vignon put
the question, then why is he not rich? No, gentlemen, I assure
you, the man is straight as his streets. But it was too late: by then
his enemies already controlled the press. Fignon's article was
one of the few his secretary marked as important, along with a
handful of notices in the British and American papers. How the
secretary had deceived him! — Bring me all the articles which
concern me, Haussmann ordered. How had it come to pass
that, after eleven years, the secretary whose instructions were
nonetheless clear began to tick with his red pen only those rare
columns which mentioned Haussmann the builder, Haussmann
the host of the Empire's most charming parties, Haussmann the
Magnificent? He had asked for no such flattery. Nevertheless it
had happened. It was like... like a servant painting over parts of
a mirror so that a fine lady can admire herself in it; first he
paints a straight nose onto the glass, then perfectly arched eyebrows, then a bosom endowed with the perfect shadows of an
imaginary light. Then come the shoulders, the chin, the hair,
and at last the mirror has become a portrait and not a good
likeness at that. The philosophers apparently wonder whether, if
you replace all the parts of a chair one at a time, it becomes a
different chair, and if so at what point? How much paint must
be applied to a mirror before it ceases to be a mirror?

The river below is smooth now; the galley has passed. No
embankments. Well, there's a place to begin, Haussmann thinks,
and imagines what the Ottomans will say to each other when
they meet on the river promenade after evening prayers. *Salaam
aleikum, salaam salaam*, the only word Haussmann knows of Ottoman, to them he must seem a child, always saying hello, pip

ing and bellowing, hello! in an effort to get all his silent, defiant meaning into the word. Your city will have to go, he tells them, *salaam salaam*, the old quarter will be torn down and you can use the beams for firewood if they're not too rotten, say goodbye to your medina, your donkey-cart streets and hunchbacked hills, but don't worry, here comes the Avenue Ismaïl Pasha and the Galleries Lafayette, *salaam salaam!* To the rats *salaam* and to the beggars *salaam* and to the mice and to the lice and the shacks back of the port and to the wells so foul it's a wonder the whole city hasn't died of cholera by now or of the runs, which the Baron caught on arrival so that half his mind is always on the horrors of the Turkish cabinet, a stinking hole in the stinking ground, and to your turbans, *salaam salaam salaam!*

Where's Fignon? Usually the surveyor, though purblind, respects the time as a draftsman respects a straightedge. Vignon will lead him into the city, today, today they can begin the first measurements. Fignon with his instruments and Haussmann with his fine boots and the velvet waistcoat given him by some gouty ambassador out of gouty recognizance for some gouty diplomatic favor. Fignon, with eye sockets as wrinkled as empty wallets, will carry the tools. The Baron will carry himself erect. Together—Vignon leading and Haussmann behind—they will ply the streets and pull them straight. Constantinople. So small, from the balcony, and so far away. Haussmann shudders, preoccupied suddenly by the fear that the city will not grow when he descends to it, that he will walk model streets dotted with dollhouse-sized houses, he and Vignon, like giants, in a city which will not reveal itself to him except as a model. The fear of never seeing the city, never seeing the real city, rises before Haussmann like a cloak held up by a solicitous attendant: Turn, sir, hold out your arms, there, sir, there. If only Haussmann had relied less on his servants! For they led him into complication, they lead, they always lead into complication. Even friends lead that way; even lovers. If he had never met de Fonce... if he had never met Madeleine... At times the cloak muffles Haussmann's sight; its wool folds stop his breath, and a curious sharp pain begins in the center of his chest, and spreads into his lungs. It's the box, he thinks, not the cloak but the box which covers me now.

Then the sensation fades, and he stands as he stood before, on a balcony, wrinkling his nose at the warm and rancid air, while below him the splendor of Constantinople, which has withstood a thousand years of city planners already, winks at him, the sun caught in a bit of tin on a low rooftop. Ah, he thinks, old city, old bitch, I'll spread your streets like a dancer's legs, and sow Haussmann in all your courtyards, your covered alleys, your dark places, dark no more.

But Haussmann, who had been commissioned to modernize Constantinople by the newly founded Society of Finances and Public Works of the Ottoman Empire, found the Society's coffers as empty of ringing coin as its name was long on pomp. He left the city as he found it, waiting for an architect to put the mark of man once more on the work of time.

In 1889 the Universal Exhibition came to Paris again, and the city was lit not with gas but with electric globes which nested like new-discovered planets in the trees of the Champs-Élysées. Across the river, at the end of the Champ de Mars, rose the tower for which the city has become famous. There is a story that an old gentleman wearing a cross of the Legion of Honor like a gilt crab on his breast demanded to be let in there after visiting hours, "to inspect his own work." The doorkeeper, mistaking him for one of the handymen who'd figured out how to paint the tower's top stories, or perhaps for the engineer in charge of installing the radio mast, unlocked a service entrance and let the old man go up. He came down an hour later, perplexed, like a man who goes into an empty room expecting to see a ghost and instead finds the shifting moon, some dust, and perhaps a broken bottle on the floor.

AFTERWORD

PAUL POISSEL WAS BORN in 1848. He was the twelfth of fourteen children of Charles Poissel, an ironmonger, and Anne Poissel, the daughter of a wine merchant. The family lived in Clermont-Ferrand until 1855, when Charles sold his business and moved to Paris. There Paul won a scholarship to the Petit Séminaire Saint-Roch, in the center of town (about halfway between the real church of the Madeleine and the fictitious convent of Saint-Grimace). Poissel had little use for his religious education. "No god," he wrote in *Mardi* (Tuesday), "could have impressed me less than this one, who showed special favor for old women, rulers, and blackboards." When Poissel turned fourteen his father took him out of school and apprenticed him to the architect Antoine Garnaud. Poissel liked to draw, and remained happily with Garnaud for several years despite his master's fiery temper (a biographer claims that Garnaud once stabbed Poissel with a compass).

In 1868 Charles Poissel died, and although Paul's share of the inheritance was not considerable, he left Garnaud and announced that he was going on a sketching tour of the Near East. No records survive of this trip, and in fact it is doubtful that Poissel traveled farther east than Geneva, where his mother's cousins lived. Nonetheless he returned three months later dressed in the Turkish manner, in wide silk pants and pointed slippers, and announced that he would establish himself as "the finest Turkish architect in Paris"—which, given the scarcity of competitors, may not have been an unachievable goal. Poissel rented an attic on the rue des Blancs-Manteaux, which he furnished as a cross between an architect's study and a seraglio, with drafting tables and cushions on the floor. He was out of money six months later. Few clients, apparently, wanted houses built in the Turkish style; those who did probably mistrusted Poissel's flamboyant clothes and his insistence that he would build nothing "of which the Great Turk himself would not be proud."

To keep himself from starvation, he took a job as a draftsman in the Service of Public Works. This was in 1869, when Haussmann was still Prefect of Paris. The young Poissel—dressed as an ordinary clerk now—may have seen the Baron at work; Haussmann may even have stopped at Poissel's table and looked over his plans and elevations. (If this meeting took place, we can only hope that Poissel did not mention the Great Turk.) What is certain is that Haussmann, or his work, moved Poissel from pictures to words. His first poems (collected after his death and published in 1990 as *Poésie Non Choisie*, by the Éditions Soupir, Paris) are tableaux of street life in the late 1860s. They owe much to Baudelaire's *Spleen de Paris*, but one can hear something of Poissel's own passion for memory, digression, and the odd corners of language in poems like "*À une blanchisseuse*" (To a Washerwoman):

> *Your hands reach into the reflection of the Quai Voltaire,*
> *Where, in a window, a little girl*
> *Reads Sir Walter Scott, and dreams*

Of castles less like the Quai Voltaire
Than like the water into which you reach...

Like his namesake in *Haussmann*, Poissel was a regular visitor to the balls, cafés, and cabarets of the Parisian demimonde. Here, like his namesake, Poissel found love. His journal—which he kept in seven volumes, one for each day of the week—notes that, on a Tuesday in July, Poissel "danced with Y. at the Dépourvu." The same Y. reappears the following Saturday, when she accompanies him on a walk through the Jardin d'Acclimatation. Poissel and Y. visit the Louvre together; they see Sarah Bernhardt in Coppée's *Le Passant* and dine together at Magny's. On September 12 (a Wednesday) Poissel records the following dream:

> I was in a hot-air balloon with Y. We were flying over Paris, and the city looked like an anatomical diagram of a giant starfish. The balloon was losing altitude, because we had not thought to bring sufficient wood (not planned to go on such a long trip), and I wanted to throw some ballast over the side, but each time I reached for one of the bags of sand secured to the outside of our basket, Y. took my hand and put it on her bosom instead, and so we continued to sink, and to sink.

After that Y. appears less often in Poissel's journals. We find her having tea at Hill's on an October Monday; on the first Saturday in November, Y. is mentioned only as a guest at a dinner party that Poissel also attended. Although their affair, if it was an affair, lasted three months at most, there is no question that Poissel had fallen in love. In a letter to his brother Frédéric dated July 30, 1869, Poissel writes, "I have discovered, my dear brother, that the real complexities of love are as far beyond the

comprehension of the heart as the complexities of the stars are
beyond the minds of the astronomers. Happiness is as wrong a
word for my condition, as *ether* is for the invisible ocean in
which our planet swims." He does not, however, tell his brother
who has caused him to feel these things. Discretion probably
sealed his lips: of the various hypotheses advanced about Y.'s
identity, the most likely is that she was Yvonne Dutronc, the
wife of one of Poissel's fellow draftsmen at the Service of Public Works.★ Did she break off relations with Poissel out of consideration for her husband? Did she return his love at all, or did
the real Poissel fare as badly as his fictive counterpart? All speculations are possible. For this, the story of Poissel's great love, we
have little more to go on than an initial, Y., and the record of a
few dances and a dream.

Poissel kept his post at the Service of Public Works until 1899.
After he retired (with a half-pension), he worked as a freelance
writer, contributing articles on fashion and history to the *Journal des Demoiselles*. He also created puzzles for the *Journal*: riddles, tongue twisters, and especially his *impoissibles*, a cross
between a rebus and what we would today call a comic strip. A
simple *impoissible* might show a poor young man saluting a rich
girl's carriage in the street; then the man and the girl before a
marriage altar; then the same man, older, at home, holding his
head as he contemplates a stack of bills; and finally, the man
swimming toward an island on which there is nothing but a
cask of water. Read as a story in pictures, the *impoissible* cau-
tions against marrying above your station; or else, it warns,
you'll have to spend beyond your means, and in the end you'll

★See Marie Thébaud's excellent article, "À la recherche d'Y," in the *Revue
nantaise des études du XIXème siècle*, 54.

Yvonne Dutronc, ca. 1872.
"Love," Poissel wrote, "is the
scaffolding with which we build
ourselves up to the summits of
our being. Even if we are, like
the Tower of Babel, demolished
afterward by angels."
Collection Paul Poissel, Bibliothèque
Nationale

Paul Poissel in 1880.
"What a tragedy if I am
remembered only as I
am," he wrote in his
journal. Poissel was
reluctant to be
photographed, and, not
long before he died,
asked his friends to "think
of someone else as Poissel,
always think of
someone else."
Bibliothèque Nationale

run to the ends of the earth to hide from your creditors. As a rebus, on the other hand, the *impoissible* reads: *fier* (proud), *voeu* (vow), *douleur* (pain), *fût* (cask), *île* (island), or, *fiez-vous de l'heure futile*, "trust the futile hour," one of Poissel's favorite sayings. The *impoissibles* were a great success; indeed, they were the published work for which he was best known during his lifetime.

He must have grown tired of the limits of the genre, however; when his brother Frédéric died in 1904, leaving him a substantial inheritance, he gave up his puzzles and devoted himself entirely to his own work. In the decade that followed, Poissel wrote *Antinomie*, a collection of poems, and *Les faits d'hiver*,★ a series of prose poems inspired by the *faits divers* published in popular newspapers. He also began an *Histoire du Contresens*, which was intended to be "a history of human misunderstanding from the Tower of Babel to the fall of Volapük [an artificial language of the late nineteenth century]," but which was never finished. None of these projects prepared him—or his audience—for *Haussmann, or the Distinction*, his only novel.

Yvonne Dutronc died in 1915. A year later, Poissel wrote to his friend Bartholomeo Facil that he had begun work on "a sort of memorial to our youth, which seems, in retrospect, like the youth of the world." The First World War had by then swept the nineteenth century from the European landscape; the gaudy Paris of the Second Empire must have seemed as distant a memory as the medieval city Haussmann demolished. Yet Poissel's aim was not, I think, to bring either city back to life. The novel is preoccupied not with what was, but with, as Poissel puts it, "what might have been and was not." Although the city

★Translated as *The Facts of Winter* (San Francisco: Paraffin Press, 2001).

Haussmann built and the city he demolished each have an important role in the novel, its emotional center is a city which never existed: the new Paris as imagined hopefully by the old, or the old Paris as remembered with regret by the new. Paris to Come, or Paris As It Was. This city must have had a personal dimension for Poissel. Apart from passionate friendships with his brother Frédéric (until his death) and with Facil, Poissel's life was not rich in human attachments; he lived alone and never married. He must have looked back on the romantic tumult of 1869 with a certain regret, or at least a certain curiosity. It would be overstating the case to say that *Haussmann* is built on a single letter, Y; but, in a life so lightly touched by love, what memory is more likely to stand out than the one of the moment in which happiness seemed possible, and within reach? Certainly, Poissel's Paris is a city informed as much by emotional as by historical fact. He invents characters, changes the look of people and the names of places to suit his design. There are quite a number of facts in *Haussmann*—the Baron had a mistress; he dressed her as his daughter; he tried to build the Railroad of the Dead and failed—but what are told here are the incomplete, circuitous truths of the heart, which no urbanist or novelist has ever been able entirely to set straight.

Paris
November, 2000

ACKNOWLEDGMENTS

This book would not have been possible without the help of many people and institutions. My thanks to those who read *Haussmann* in its numerous versions: Jori Finkel, Anne Greene, Dan Horch, Maureen Howard, Herb Wilson, and Jeff Zacks; and to those who helped me cast my nets for the elusive Poissel: Abie Hadjitarkhani, in whose Paris apartment I first heard of *le poisson qui brille*; Caro Fay and Heather Brady at the Centre Paul Poissel in Aix-en-Provence; Eugene Ostashevsky at the University of Bilkent, Turkey; Christina Gerhardt in Special Library Services at UC Berkeley; Jean-Marie Apostolidès at Stanford University; and Nathanael Greene at Wesleyan University, who shared with me his knowledge of Poissel's era. We have made a fine catch I think. In Paris, Muirgen Gourgues, Leland Deladurantaye, and Céline, Hildegarde, and Gérard Valory were generous with their friendship and hospitality; the librarians at the Bibliothèque Nationale de France helped me immeasurably, both on purpose and by accident. The staff of the Archives Municipales in Toulon should not be forgotten; if a naumachia is ever built in their city I hope they will leave work early to enjoy it. Many, many thanks also to the institutions which offered me time and peace to work on this project: the Camargo Foundation in Cassis, France; Yaddo; and the MacDowell Colony, where I write this note. Finally, heartfelt thanks to Gloria Loomis, my wise and wonderful agent, who saw this book with a writer's eye but without a writer's worries; to John Glusman, my editor at FSG, who understood from the start what *Haussmann* was about; and to Amy Benfer, for what might not have been, and is.